# Look for More Titles by Cassandra Chandler

PARANORMAL ROMANCE NOVELLAS

*Court of the Yuletide Fae*
The Yule Cat
The White Stag
The Krampus

*Court of the Springtime Fae*
Jack Frost
Prince Charming
The Oak King

—

URBAN FANTASY

*The Blades of Janus*
PACK
PROGENITOR
PERIHELION

PARANORMAL - HORROR ROMANCE

*The Summer Park Psychics*
WANDERING SOUL
WHISPERING HEARTS
LINGERING TOUCH

—

COLLECTIONS

*The Department of Homeworld Security*
THE DEPARTMENT OF HOMEWORLD SECURITY OMNIBUS 1
THE DEPARTMENT OF HOMEWORLD SECURITY OMNIBUS 2

# Pack

The Blades of Janus
Book One
(Second Edition)

*Cassandra Chandler*

# Copyright Page

Pack
The Blades of Janus, Book One
Copyright © 2016, 2025 by Cassandra Chandler
Print ISBN (Second Edition): 978-1-945702-83-9
Digital ISBN (Second Edition): 978-1-945702-82-2

First eBook edition: September 2016
Second eBook edition: April 2025
First print edition: October 2016
Second print edition: April 2025
10 9 8 7 6 5 4 3 2

cassandra-chandler.com
P.O. Box 91
Mission, Kansas 66201

# Dedication

*For Kayla and her love of books.*

*Don't miss out on any of the dark alien action. Subscribe to Cassandra Chandler's newsletter at https://sendfox.com/CassandraChandler now!*

# Chapter One

"I don't like the interface. It's too distracting." Marcus blinked repeatedly, trying to adjust to the bright blue gridlines and scrolling data his glasses were projecting onto his field of vision.

The sidewalks and edges of the buildings were mapped out like he was in some sort of 3-D video game. Worse, every person who walked by was briefly covered in a red gridline that changed to green when they were identified as human. Vital statistics flickered around their bodies, disappearing before he could read them. At least there weren't many people walking around given the late hour.

"It took you a while to get used to the earpiece, but now you never go anywhere without it." Vaughn sounded as if she was standing right next to Marcus instead of being miles away—and deep underground—monitoring the night's patrol.

"That was different," Marcus said. "I was already used to you talking all the time."

"Are you saying I'm a chatterbox, sir?"

Marcus snorted. "I'm saying these glasses are giving me much more data to process than your voice in my ear.

Everything is so bright. It's overwhelming my natural senses."

"Your *natural* senses?"

Marcus didn't bother to suppress a low growl.

Vaughn only laughed. "Hang on, let me change some settings."

Marcus heard the unique thumping sound of Vaughn typing on the keyboard that was embedded in her desk back at the ranch. It sounded like someone tapping their fingers on a table, except much faster and with purpose.

The gridlines dimmed to a tolerable level.

"Better?"

Marcus let out a breath. "Much."

"The readouts were fine at the ranch," Vaughn said. "I bet it's because the lights are brighter here. The display matched that level of intensity. I'll put in a lux detector to match the ambient light and be sure to update the instructions when these are distributed to the other bases."

"After the bosses clear them for use."

"Which they will—along with the earpieces. Everyone's already using my dweller database. They're even making mini-versions of my operations room in the other headquarters." Vaughn let out a contented sigh. "How did the Blades of Janus ever manage to help dwellers and humans peacefully coexist without me?"

"Your humility is inspiring," Marcus said.

Vaughn continued her routine, obviously trying to keep

the mood light. "I get how you dealt with the ones who were dangerous. But keeping everything under wraps without my tech helping you had to be difficult."

"We managed."

Having her around did make the job easier—especially keeping their altercations off the radar of local law enforcement. Marcus had his own reasons for valuing Vaughn, though. Ones that had a lot more to do with her ability to keep Marcus calm with jokes and banter.

A trio of laughing women walked by, slowing a bit as they passed and casting appreciative stares his way. Their scents changed—a hint of over-sweet honey cloying in his nose… and making his mouth water. It reminded him of the ham his dad used to make every year around the holidays.

Marcus walked a little faster.

"You need to practice subvocalizing," Vaughn said. "The new earpiece can pick up incredibly small vibrations. And larger ones. I'm waggling my eyebrows, in case you wondered."

Marcus snorted. He wasn't sure how he felt about the subvocalization function of the earpiece. It was hard enough to control himself when he was on patrol. If he had to watch out for letting the tiniest thing slip—like monitoring his penchant for growling—it would be another distraction.

"Seriously, if people see you talking to yourself, it

won't matter how hot you look in those hipster glasses," she said.

"I don't care what people think. I'm only interested in keeping them safe."

"All work and no play…"

"Reduces the body count in Providence."

Vaughn laughed. "Point—Marcus."

A flashing sentence repeated often enough that Marcus could actually read it. Coordinates and a brief warning that lightning was about to strike overhead. There was even a countdown. The heavy clouds above lit up for a moment, thunder rumbling in approval a few seconds later.

"Your tech really is amazing," he said.

"Well, it isn't *my* tech exactly. I consider what I create adaptations on a masterwork theme. Speaking of which, I think I've discovered the main communications relay."

"You *think* it's the communications relay?"

"I'm cannibalizing parts from an alien spaceship. There's a little guesswork involved."

Marcus flinched at Vaughn's choice of words, still working through his reaction to the women who'd just passed. He tried to gloss over it and keep the focus on the alien spaceship—which wasn't difficult at all.

"That's unsettling," Marcus said. "What if it's the weapons system? Or some kind of self-destruct?"

As good as Vaughn was with technology, the Blades had no idea what the ship was capable of.

Okay, they had *some* idea. The glasses were a product of the alien tech Vaughn was studying. As were several of their weapons, vehicles, holding cells… Any number of systems the Blades depended on. At least, in the Providence branch.

With everything that Marcus had seen and experienced, the ship was still the hardest thing to wrap his head around —even after exploring it a few times.

"I discovered those systems months ago," Vaughn said. "If my dad hadn't been such a control freak, he could have shown me around the place before…"

Her voice trailed off.

Marcus waited a moment before saying, "You'll figure it out."

Vaughn's dad had been a world-class asshole from what Marcus had gathered. He doubted that made it any easier for her to deal with the man's death. If anything, it probably made things harder. She had confided in Marcus once that she had changed the name of her dad's company to Vaughn Industries the moment her lawyers finished signing everything over to her, using her mother's last name and legally changing her own to match. Marcus didn't even know what Vaughn's first name was. She said only her mother ever used it and to use her last name instead.

"It would've been so much more helpful if he'd told me about the ship while he was still alive." Vaughn's fingers struck her keyboard harder.

The ship was buried on land that had been in Vaughn's family for generations. When they discovered it a century ago, they hadn't really been able to do anything except keep it secret.

Vaughn's dad had been the one to finally explore it and start bringing parts to the surface. He'd hired experts to analyze, dissect, and replicate the technology—if on a much lower level—never giving away the source of what they were studying. He'd made a fortune and founded a tech company known for innovations.

Vaughn, though, *was* a tech expert. Probably the best on the planet. She'd been putting the alien technology to good use since the Blades recruited her, pooling their resources to come up with amazing inventions.

"I thought you were supposed to be looking for anything that could have been used as a med bay," Marcus said.

"I'm more interested in preventing injuries than treating them. If I can get the communications system back online, I can easily link up all of the satellites orbiting Earth instead of just hacking into them whenever we need to." Vaughn sounded as excited as ever when talking about the alien tech. "Imagine a system of satellites linked to the Blades' dweller database and constantly scanning for malicious activity."

"I have seriously mixed feelings about that."

"I'll make sure your entry is flagged as 'friendly'." There was a brief pause, then she said, "You're glaring at me, aren't you."

"These glasses really *are* amazing."

"Please leave the jokes to the professional," she said.

"Okay, I'll keep it serious. You're talking about linking the satellites that help sustain life as we know it on Earth through an alien spacecraft that you say crashed here millennia ago."

"Excuse me, the geological context of the site says it crashed here millennia ago."

Marcus kept on, ignoring her quip. "A ship whose origins we still have no idea about."

But they did know what originated *from* it.

The hair on the back of his neck rose. For the thousandth time since the Blades had formed a base in Providence and brought Vaughn on board, Marcus asked, "Are you sure it's safe to be messing around with this stuff when you're not entirely sure what it does?"

"It's not just safe, it's incredibly lucrative. You should see the new chip my company will be putting out when the timing is feasible. I'll make enough to fund the Blades for the next century at least."

Marcus took a deep breath to let out another sigh, but froze with the air still in his lungs. Something about it was off. He slowly exhaled through his mouth, tasting it. A faint hint of death clung to his tongue. He turned and took another breath, hunting for the scent, zeroing in on it.

Oblivious, Vaughn kept talking about her technology.

"And I'm careful when I explore the ship. Dexter or Porter always comes with me. Besides, the implications for this are too beneficial to ignore—not just for the Blades, but for humanity. Which, I suppose is repetitive, since we do what we do in order to help humanity. *And* dwellers, I guess. Anyway, when I'm done building the new communications network, we'll be able to link our earpieces to every other Blade in the world. Our *earpieces.*"

"Again, mixed feelings." Marcus started walking toward the scent.

Rotting meat. Human.

"Don't worry," Vaughn said. "I've adjusted the power levels and shielding to make sure nobody gets cancer from their earpiece or has their head explode."

Marcus slowed briefly, their conversation distracting him from his hunt. "That… actually wasn't what I was thinking of." Although now that Vaughn had said it, Marcus was having trouble *not* thinking about it.

Not much could kill Marcus. He was pretty sure having his head explode was on the shortlist.

"Oh." Vaughn was uncharacteristically quiet for a few moments.

"We talk about things on patrol," Marcus said. "Things I don't want the other Blades to know about."

"Right." She drew out the word, undoubtedly filling in the blanks with remembered conversations. "Like when I have to talk you down from a change."

He sighed. That was exactly the kind of thing he didn't want any of the other Blades to overhear.

"Relax," Vaughn said. "It's just you and me now. Besides, when I have everything set up, you'll still have to activate the communication system to talk to Blades in other cities."

"That's *a little* reassuring."

"I always make sure no one listens in on our private conversations. You know I want you all to myself." Vaughn was really laying it on thick tonight.

Marcus snorted. "I think I can hear you waggling your eyebrows this time."

"Really?"

"No, not really." He shook his head.

"How was I supposed to know? I have my super-tech, you have your super-senses."

"Which isn't always a good thing."

The smell was suddenly stronger. Marcus stopped and moved his head around, tasting the air. Two scents crossing paths, which meant whatever he was hunting was mobile—and there might be more than one.

"We have a dweller," Marcus said. "Some kind of animated corpse."

Vaughn groaned. "Ugh, I hate those. I'll put fresh

lemons in the infuser unit in your shower to clear the scent from your system when you get back. Make sure you keep your clothes separate from the normal laundry. Just strip in the garage and go through the decon shower. I don't want you tracking anything into the ranch."

"We won't have to worry about that if I can't figure out where these scents are coming from."

"Wait, 'these' scents? As in plural?" Vaughn was typing again.

"There are two scents that passed this spot recently. Could be the same thing re-crossing its path."

"Or it could be more than one of them," she said. "And in a heavily populated area. That means they can pass for human."

Which meant they were more of a threat.

Marcus felt a low growl build in his chest. The feeling shifted lower. He closed his eyes and took a few deep breaths.

When Vaughn spoke again, there was no trace of playfulness in her tone. "You still with me, Marcus?"

"Yeah." Marcus opened his eyes, scanning the people across the street. Literally, with the new glasses. "Are you getting the readings you need for the database?"

"The sensor webbing built into the frames is feeding me all kinds of data."

Most of the people Marcus was staring at flickered to green. Two didn't. The red gridlines flashed several times, then sentences and words started scrolling through his field of view faster than he could read. Circles appeared around various parts of the two men's bodies, blinking and rotating as different measurements were taken.

His view switched to an artificial infrared that wasn't nearly as nuanced as what he perceived while in his other form. Still, the glasses made it clear that the two subjects' heat signatures were nothing like the people passing them.

More words and numbers flashed in his view. He didn't know how Vaughn managed so many data streams at once.

"It would be helpful if you slowed down the readouts to the point where I could actually read them," Marcus said.

"That's too fast for you? With how often you hang out in the library, I figured you for a speed-reader."

Marcus snorted. "Nobody's that fast."

"Dexter and Porter are. Dexter's helmet has a similar display. I kept yours minimal, knowing you already have enhanced senses and that it would bug you out in the field."

"Thanks for that."

A steady growl filled his mind. Of course *Dexter* could track that much data.

"And in case you have any doubts about me, I can track that fast as well." Vaughn's statement brought Marcus's focus back from… a very dark place.

"Seriously?"

"Yeah," she said. "But then, I *am* a genius."

Marcus might have laughed, but the two men they were studying turned around to face him.

"Fuck." He curled his hands into fists and reminded himself that he needed to stay calm.

"Definitely dwellers," Vaughn said. "Not a type we've seen in Providence before."

"Yeah, they're new to town. But not to me."

Marcus had traveled with Dexter and Porter for years and encountered many different dwellers before they decided to settle in Providence and make a Blades base there. Recruiting Vaughn to the cause had been a big factor in the decision—as had the buried ship. It wasn't like they could move the thing.

Marcus still had trouble believing all of it was real. No matter how many times he walked the eerily quiet corridors of the ship, no matter how many dwellers he encountered. Somehow, it was easier to believe in monsters than aliens. Especially knowing that he was among the earthlings who'd been 'colonized.'

"Don't tell me what they are," Vaughn said. "I want to see if I can figure it out from the data I'm getting."

Marcus already knew. They were Redcaps.

Fairytales often described them as little creatures who roamed battlefields in the aftermath of conflict, dipping their hats in the blood of the fallen to stain them red. The reality was much, much worse. This pair looked like roughed-up humans who hadn't seen fresh clothes or a bath in years. Both had long, shaggy beards that grew halfway down their chests and obscured most of their faces. Their beards didn't just grow down but also out, though the coarse strands were shorter on the sides of their heads. It was still weird to see someone with a circle of hair sticking straight out around their face.

Most humans wouldn't stop to look too closely at either of them. Marcus supposed that was on purpose. The part of their features that wasn't covered with hair was blocked by huge wraparound sunglasses—an odd wardrobe choice hours after sunset.

One was dressed in torn up khakis with a polo shirt and business jacket. The other was wearing a dingy suit with a long-sleeved, button down shirt. The jacket on the first man was from the second man's suit. Their clothes seemed too big on their frames and were stained and... soiled.

There were all sorts of explanations for their appearance. Mundane, logical explanations. Marcus didn't live in a mundane world.

A third man joined them, then a fourth and fifth. They were all almost identical—not just from the neck up and with their choices in personal hygiene. How they moved, how they stood, how they all turned as one to stare in Marcus's direction, ignoring the people passing them on the sidewalk.

They wore bandanas that had probably started out as various colors, but were now mostly saturated with a dark red substance. The thin fabric clung to the tops of their heads, as if something wet and sticky was holding them in place.

Definitely Redcaps.

"The sensors are showing that their body temperatures are way below normal," Vaughn said. "Only slightly above the ambient temperature of the area. Energy signatures flaring in the head and neck, fading into the torso and limbs."

"Vaughn, use your eyes. Take off the gridlines and just look at them."

There was a brief pause.

"Oh. Redcaps." She started typing again, a hail of sound coming over the earpiece. "I will always find it bizarre that some dwellers can be identified most easily based on their wardrobe and personal hygiene. I mean, what is it with these guys? Where do they get the bandanas and sunglasses?"

She sighed, then said, "Logging it in the database. These readings are great. Pretty soon, you'll be just another Guard among the Blades. Safely ensconced in obscurity."

"What?"

"Oh. Did I say that out loud?"

"Vaughn…"

There was an unusual pause before she spoke again. "You're too effective in the field for a Guard working solo."

"I'm not solo. I have you, Porter, and Dexter."

"You have an IT gal, a doctor, and... a super-freaky assassin. And granted Dexter does account for some of our high numbers, but he's not designated as a Guard. He's the boss. And I guess Porter is, too, since, you know... 'twinsies.' My point is, every Blades of Janus base has a doctor and a boss. But most also have half a dozen Guards at least. We have one—you."

"What's the big deal?"

"The big deal is that our outpost is actually more effective at managing dwellers than most. With *one* Guard. Anyone who bothers to run the numbers is going to notice the pattern."

"No one notices patterns like you do."

"Well, thank you. But in this case, it's an obvious one. If I can give other Blades tools that make it look like you're just benefiting from my technical expertise, they're less likely to figure out what's really going on."

Less likely to figure out that Marcus wasn't human.

The skin between his shoulder blades began to prickle. He felt his chest vibrate with a rumbling growl. The damned earpiece probably caught it.

His voice came out much lower than usual and had a gravely edge to it that he couldn't mask. "I don't need you to protect me."

There was a brief pause. Vaughn spoke carefully when

she responded, obviously trying to keep from setting Marcus off.

"I know that. But you and I, we look out for each other. We're not just colleagues. We're friends, remember?"

More skin on Marcus's back started to tingle. He closed his eyes and took several deep breaths.

Yes, he and Vaughn were friends. Partners in their mission to keep the peace between dwellers and humans. Protecting members of either species when it was warranted. Exacting justice when it wasn't.

Above all, though, Marcus protected Vaughn.

A voice that seemed to echo from the back of Marcus's mind rumbled, *"She is your beta. You protect her."*

"Shut. Up." Marcus said the words out loud, wanting to give them more impact.

Vaughn didn't miss a beat. "I'm guessing that wasn't directed at me."

Vaughn was the only person Marcus had told about the voice that sometimes popped up in his head. Having that extra bit of support didn't just preserve their friendship—it helped preserve Marcus's sanity. And it protected Marcus from Dexter finding out. Marcus was pretty sure it was some sort of manifestation of his dweller. Based on the things it told him to do, he sure as hell hoped so.

"Are you still not recording this?" Marcus said.

"You know, we've been having the worst time with our feed tonight. I haven't been able to get a good enough connection to record any audio since you left the ranch. Wish I had those satellites hooked up."

Marcus took a deep breath and let it out slowly. Vaughn wasn't kidding about having Marcus's back. She'd been protecting him in her own ways ever since they became partners. And that was a good thing.

The voice—his dweller—was silent. For the moment.

"Thanks," Marcus said.

"I guess it's hard to find good IT support these days." Vaughn paused briefly. "Seriously though, are you okay?"

"Yeah. I just need to vent some steam. I have a feeling an opportunity is about to present itself."

Redcaps had a standing kill order. There was no reasoning with them. No way to even communicate. And they were carnivorous—with very large appetites. Worse, once Redcaps infested a town, it stayed infested.

The Providence base might need to put in a request for more Guards, which meant bringing more Blades in on Marcus's 'personal issue.' If he could root the Redcaps out right away, maybe they wouldn't be able to get a foothold.

"Let me find you a cozy spot to get to know these guys better," Vaughn said.

"I'll try to figure out a way to convince them to follow me."

"You seem to have already secured their interest."

"They probably think I'm hunting and are wondering if there's going to be any kind of territorial issue."

"I take it you're using the word *think* loosely." She paused for a moment. "Hold on. Who's that?"

A few people walked along the sidewalks, probably heading home after some happy-hour drinks. There would be even more once the bars closed. One woman in particular looked like she'd had an early start.

Marcus logged details about her quickly. Jeans, knee-high boots, tank top, leather jacket, red hair in long curls trailing down her back. She was stumbling along the street —alone—and heading straight for the Redcaps.

*"Easy prey."*

This time, Marcus responded to his dweller internally. Sometimes, its thoughts were too disturbing to share with Vaughn, and he didn't want to explain this one.

*"Not for them."* To make sure he was abundantly clear, he added, *"Not for us."*

His dweller had been particularly active lately, though Marcus was doing his best to hide it from his team. Vaughn's new earpiece was going to make that more difficult.

He shook his head, bringing his thoughts into focus— his *own* thoughts. This woman wasn't prey. No human was prey. Not for him, anyway. The Redcaps were another matter. Four of them turned in unison to watch her as she walked past. The fifth kept his focus on Marcus. The woman stumbled past them, walking backwards for a few steps and laughing.

"Sorry, boys," she said. "You're a bit hairy for my tastes."

"I guess you're out of the running, too," Vaughn said. "Sorry. That was—"

"Find me that private spot," Marcus cut in. "I want to take these things out as quickly as possible."

Vaughn was typing as she spoke again. "You really need to start carrying a sword like Dexter does. He doesn't come home smelling rank. I wish we knew why the smell stays even when their bodies disintegrate. I mean, all of their bodily fluids vanish along with the rest of them when they die—or a few minutes after anything is removed from their main body. Why does the smell linger?"

"I have no idea."

Marcus started across the street as the last Redcap turned toward the woman. All five of them followed her in their awkward gait. She was stumbling almost as badly.

"I guess it helps you track them at least," Vaughn said.

"That's a mixed blessing."

On this side of the road, the Redcaps' scent was much stronger. Marcus gave Vaughn's *subvocalization* a try—not because he was supposed to be learning it, but because he didn't want to let the foul stench into his mouth. Bad enough it was sticking in his nose.

"Definitely Redcaps," Marcus said.

"I feel so bad for you right now."

"Forget washing these clothes. Just burn them."

Vaughn laughed right up until the woman turned and disappeared from sight down a dark alley. "What is she... Oh, are you kidding me? She just walked down a dead-end alley."

Marcus noticed. The Redcaps stopped at the mouth of the alley in a tight cluster. He'd seen groups do this a few times while tracking them. Porter theorized that they were communicating somehow. Apparently, these didn't have much to say. After a few seconds, they headed down the alley after the woman.

Vaughn let out a heavy sigh. "Sometimes I wonder if humanity deserves saving. It's past midnight and she just walked into a dimly lit alley. What was she doing drinking alone downtown anyway?"

"Not everyone has someone to drink with."

The thought made his hackles rise further. No one should be alone. Whoever this woman was, she should have family and friends to drink with.

*"You could make sure she always has someone. Turning her would be a kindness, if you bring her into your—"*

"No." Marcus pushed against the voice of his dweller even harder.

His dweller hadn't just been more active lately, it had been more demanding—with very specific demands. It wanted him to make others like him. To infect them with the same dweller that had changed his body.

The only people Marcus could stand to be around were

Porter, Dexter, and Vaughn. For some reason, the thought of changing them never entered Marcus's mind. Maybe because Dexter could easily kill him, Porter was just so… weird, and Vaughn was… Well, Vaughn was Vaughn.

Marcus felt the skin on his back prickle again. He wasn't sure what had set it off. He wasn't angry, wasn't gearing up to fight—yet. Something about the woman was unsettling.

"A better question is why the hell did she just walk down that alley?" Marcus said.

As if she was answering, he heard the sound of retching.

Vaughn groaned. "You had to ask."

Marcus headed into the alley. A light bulb in a wire cage fought to push back the dark. He could relate. The woman was bent over, half-hidden by a huge metal garbage bin. She was still coughing and retching. The Redcaps had formed a semi-circle near her, blocking the alley's exit. They also stood between Marcus and their prey.

"Gross," she said. She staggered back, nearly bumping into one of the Redcaps. "Oh, sorry about that."

The Redcap opened its mouth, letting out a high-pitched whistle. Its 'beard' twitched to life with erratic movements that were somehow much more graceful than those of its gangly human limbs.

Shiny, stick-like black legs—each equipped with razor-sharp pincers—spread out from the gaping hole in its face. They made clicking sounds as they snapped together over and over. The smell of carrion joined the damp stench of the alley. Marcus shook his head and snorted as he adjusted to the scent.

The fight played out in his mind. As soon as she screamed, the Redcaps would attack. Marcus would grab the two closest to him and hurl them back toward the entrance of the alley. He'd be in range to kick the one on his far right, while also backhanding the one on the far left. One at a time, he'd tear off their heads—the most satisfying way to kill his own prey—and their bodies would vaporize.

Except she didn't scream.

"Ew, what did you eat?" The woman shook her head. "If you had the shellfish, you should have sent it back."

Vaughn laughed. Marcus might have joined her, but that nagging feeling of danger was back. Danger centering around the woman, not the dwellers circling her.

"Wow, she must be completely wasted to not be freaking out right now," Vaughn said.

The woman put her hands in the pockets of her jacket and smiled, apparently not at all concerned that the guy's beard had come to life and was reaching for her. She cocked her head to the side, staring at the Redcaps surrounding her.

No one could be that drunk.

"Why is she wearing a jacket?" Marcus spoke lower than any human could hear. Vaughn's earpiece picked up his words fine, though. Then it started emitting a high-pitched thrumming sound. Marcus resisted the urge to pull the thing out and stomp on it.

The Redcap drew its arms back into its face and stood up straighter. They all did—arms clamped at their sides and spines stiff as lightning rods. That was new behavior.

"An innocent civilian is about to be eaten by a bunch of Redcaps, and you're critiquing her fashion sense?" Vaughn said.

"It's been in the eighties all week."

"And it's only May. The weather ain't what it used to be," Vaughn drawled.

"She's wearing a leather jacket and boots," Marcus said.

If the woman was really that drunk, she would have taken off her jacket to be more comfortable. Even though she was swaying on her feet, her head cocked to the side as she looked at all the Redcaps in front of her, she had left it on.

She must be roasting. His own ankle-length duster was trapping enough of his body heat to make a normal human uncomfortable. He only wore it to hide his scars and to hold the stingray he carried for stunning dwellers when necessary. And for those times when he transformed faster than he could strip.

"She's wearing a jacket, you're wearing a duster," Vaughn said. "Which doesn't go very well with those particular glasses, but I can fix that. I need to design a pair of frames that can hold the sensors and still look stylish."

"Vaughn, think about the tech later. And when you do, can you fix my earpiece to get rid of this horrible whine?"

"What horrible whine?"

"The one that's been rattling in my skull for the last minute. It's distracting."

"I'm not picking anything up. The earpiece is working fine."

"Wait a minute." Marcus turned his head, zeroing in on the true source of the sound—the woman.

He sighed. "She's a hunter."

"Shit."

Marcus could hear Vaughn's office chair rolling across the operations room floor. The sound of furious typing pummeled his ears.

"How do you know?" Vaughn asked.

"Instinct." He could explain the rest later. Right now, he needed his full attention on the situation at hand. "Go silent."

Finished with assessing the frozen Redcaps, the woman's gaze finally fixed on Marcus.

"Oh, hey. You didn't see that, did you?" she said.

Marcus spoke up so Vaughn wouldn't be the only one who could hear him. "See what?"

She smiled as she approached. His heartbeat picked up when she angled herself to slide between a pair of the stationary Redcaps. She was within inches of two deadly creatures and showed no sign of fear.

*"Mmm…"* His guts flooded with warmth as his dweller let out a low rumble. *"I like her."*

Marcus fought against letting out a growl. He liked her, too.

She kept her gaze locked with his. Only Dexter ever stared Marcus down, and that was about dominance. This was more a playful invitation. The warmth intensified, blood pooling low.

It didn't matter how hot it was that she was fearless and challenging without threatening violence—yet. Marcus needed to focus on something other than her curves and her smile and her dark gray eyes, the same color as the stormy sky that had been hovering over Providence for the last week.

Her eyes…

His heart hammered in his chest. Vaughn had said the glasses had a special reflective coating that would obscure the gold color to Marcus's eyes. If they didn't, the evening was about to become even more dangerous. This hunter had incapacitated five Redcaps without lifting a finger. She must have some sort of weapon or device hidden on her body the likes of which Marcus had never seen. And he was certain it wasn't the only one.

He should search her body. Thoroughly.

His hands were curling again, but not in fists. He couldn't keep himself from imagining what it would be like to touch her, to taste her. Marcus took another deep breath of the alley, trying to sort through the scents. Death, rot, and... cut grass. That was unexpected for the middle of downtown. Even stranger, he couldn't catch her scent at all.

He shifted closer, bending toward her slightly. He wanted her scent. Needed it. For some reason, she didn't feel like prey. Marcus had to know why.

On some level, all humans felt like prey to him. They had ever since the attack that killed his family and left him changed. Marcus even had to be careful around Vaughn sometimes. The only exceptions were Dexter and Porter, and that was probably because Dexter was the one who had rescued Marcus—killing *all* of the deadly dwellers involved.

Dexter was definitely not prey. Nor was his identical brother.

The woman brought Marcus back to the moment, reaching out to put her palm on his chest. Her hand was colder than he expected, an odd energy to it.

"You okay there?" she said. "You seem to be listing."

Marcus wasn't sure. He reached out and grabbed her shoulders, pretending he needed her help to stay upright, but really only wanting to get closer. She seemed human, but something about her was setting him off in multiple ways.

She smirked up at him and stepped a little closer, letting her hands slide inside his duster and along his ribcage. Marcus sucked in a breath as his nerves lit up brighter than when he was about to change. Her grip was firm, her arms stronger than he would have expected at first.

They were in an alley with five Redcaps. Five weirdly immobile Redcaps, but still... And that sultry smile of hers was all he could think about. He had the strongest urge to lean down and kiss her, but he didn't think he'd be able to stop there. Scenarios were playing in his head that had nothing to do with patrol or training or anything he'd known for the twenty-some years of his brutal life.

She was a few inches shorter than him. Her hips were round and full—a perfect fit for his hands. The fabric of his cargo pants chafed against him as he hardened for her.

Would it be so bad to let go? He wasn't thinking about hurting her. If she kept her jacket on, it would protect her skin from the brick walls while he did things he should definitely not be thinking about while on an active patrol.

*"Just this once. Just this one."*

What the hell? His dweller asked Marcus to kill people all the time. It had never asked him to fuck someone before.

*"You're just trying to get me to turn her."*

His dweller laughed. *"You have other hungers."*

Marcus shook his head, then stood straight again. If he didn't control himself when he was this worked up, things could go very, very wrong. But he didn't want her blood. He wanted her body.

Not prey. Not for feeding, anyway.

A new hunger was rising within him. One he hadn't dealt with before. One he had no idea how to fight against. But he'd be damned if he would let it win.

# Chapter Two

Tall, dark, and derpy was staring at her again. Tessa felt like she was in one of those movies where the main characters kept gazing meaningfully into each other's eyes.

In another world, she would have been absolutely down with that. Barring his strange fashion sense, this guy was just the type to get her motor revving. But this was the world she was stuck in. She couldn't afford to get sidetracked by... cosplaying hipster hotties? She hadn't quite figured him out, with his nerdy glasses, long black duster, and muscled physique.

"You have any drinks tonight?" she said.

"No."

She shook her head. "That's too bad. The first time you see something you can't explain, it really pisses off your brain. I was hoping you could rationalize it away with alcohol."

"I don't need to rationalize anything."

"Okay. The denial route is a popular choice."

Plenty of people refused to believe their senses when they saw their first dweller. After a while, they could come up with explanations for what they had 'really seen.' It used to be that people would tell stories about demons and monsters. Nowadays, it was usually just stress or weirdoes running around on the streets.

*If only they knew the truth...*

This guy was taking what he'd seen a little too calmly. He might be bottling things up, only to freak out later. Sometimes people developed a nervous tic or habit. Sometimes they lashed out at others. If that was the case, Tessa wouldn't be around long enough to do damage control. She did what she could in the moment.

"I think you might be in shock," she said.

"I'm not in shock."

"Everybody thinks that when they see a monster for the first time. But trust me, you are. Do you have someone you can call?"

"Yes."

"Good."

She didn't have to feign her smile. She was glad to be reminded that people were still helping each other out. Not everyone was alone. Part of why she was a hunter was to help preserve that life for others.

Sir Hipster Derpalot needed a plausible lie for a completely implausible situation. She looked him up and down again, and came up with just the thing.

"You can regale them with your story of getting caught up in somebody else's cosplay that was so realistic it freaked you out a little. If you repeat it often enough, you'll even start to believe it."

She pulled away from him—more reluctantly than she cared to admit—then cupped his elbow, hoping to gently lead him to the entrance of the alley. He wouldn't budge.

"Look, things are about to get *really* weird here," she said. "Denial can only go so far and the human psyche is more fragile than you think. I need you elsewhere."

"I'm not leaving you alone with…"

He glanced over her shoulder at the five paralyzed Redcaps. The five *temporarily* paralyzed Redcaps. She wasn't sure how long the battery would last on the device that was keeping them immobilized, and she had a lot of work ahead of her.

"It's okay," she said, even though it wasn't. "And who says I'm going to be alone?"

She craned her arm up behind her so she could reach one of the weapons she kept hidden beneath her jacket and pulled out a shortened baseball bat made of ash wood. She had sharpened the handle to a point and added electrical tape to improve the grip. It made a pretty good stake for vampires or she could go all cavewoman on things that needed squishing.

In the end, Redcaps were just giant bugs. Giant *space* bugs.

That was the punchline to the joke that was her life. Humans told stories about scary monsters as if they had evolved in parallel with them. They had no idea the monsters under the bed or lurking in the closet were aliens.

She spun the weapon like a baton, ending with the bludgeoning side at the ready. If Derpy saw that she could handle herself, maybe he'd go away.

"Not many people would keep it together as well as you're doing," she said. "I appreciate you wanting to help." When he didn't say anything, she asked, "What's your name?"

"Marcus."

"I'm Tessa."

She switched her bat to her off hand and reached out to him in greeting. He stared at her hand for a moment before grasping it. His skin was warm and much smoother than she'd expected. He stepped closer again.

The light was glinting off of his glasses, making it hard to see his eyes. She could tell his lashes were as dark and thick as his hair. The color of his eyes was hard to make out. A pale amber. Almost… gold.

Her skin prickled as adrenaline flowed through her system, priming her body for action. She pulled her hand back, but didn't step away.

Maybe he was wearing contacts. Maybe he was deep into playing dress-up superhero. If his mind was rationalizing what he'd seen by telling him this was all part of some game, that would explain why he was refusing to leave. After seeing a Redcap open its mouth, anybody would have trouble figuring out what was real. He still should be freaking out a little. She didn't get how he could seem so calm.

Unless he'd encountered a monster before. Maybe something worse than Redcaps.

If Marcus had… she wasn't sure if he'd made it out human. Gold eyes—if his eyes *were* gold—only belonged to a few types of dwellers. Including one of the most dangerous.

Werewolves.

They were the result of yet another microscopic parasite that spread through the human body after it was bitten while the alien DNA was fully activated. Or, in layman's terms, when the werewolf was in its hybrid form. The parasite would infect human cells at an incredible rate, transforming their DNA into something… else.

Tessa wasn't sure if the parasites knew what they were creating or it was just random chance that they made human-alien hybrids that resembled wolves. Maybe they came from a planet of wolf-people? It didn't matter. What concerned her was the fact that the end results were utterly deadly. Werewolves were violent killing machines whose primary prey was humans.

Marcus had said he had someone he could call. If he was a werewolf, he wouldn't need a phone. All of his packmates would be able to communicate telepathically. But he couldn't be a werewolf. If he was, she'd be dead already. And then he'd be in for a *real* surprise.

Her right wrist began to itch. Squirming, wriggling, just beneath her skin. She could feel the disgusting things that infested her arm poking against the elastic of the wristband she always wore to keep them trapped.

Not all alien parasites were microscopic.

Her mouth went dry, heart pounding against her rib cage. She wanted to pull off her jacket and check her arm, to make sure nothing had escaped her makeshift containment system. But before she could do that, he *needed* to leave.

"Make that call, Marcus." She summoned her most commanding tone, let the threat of violence seep into her words. "Somewhere else. Now."

His shoulders hunched and his lips twitched away from his teeth as he bit out each word. "Don't challenge me."

Shit, *could* he be a werewolf? Why would he be hunting alone? And in that ridiculous outfit.

A werewolf wouldn't need glasses. Or a duster. Their dweller nature would keep them comfortable in a huge range of temperatures and would have fixed any issues their human host had with their eyesight right after they were infected.

She had a silver-infused knife in her left boot. Whatever planet werewolves were originally from, their parasites couldn't handle any amount of exposure to silver. If Marcus was a werewolf, she'd only need to nick him to take him out. It sounded easy on paper but was much more difficult to manage in reality. There was no way she'd reach the knife in time if Marcus went for her. But he was holding himself perfectly still. He seemed rooted in place.

She'd given him an order. There was no way a werewolf would have accepted that sort of challenge without doing something about it. Human, then. But messed up.

*We should start a club.*

She couldn't cut him loose. He seemed more and more the type to go ballistic after being shaken up, and she wouldn't have that on her conscience. The whole point of what she did was to protect people. It didn't matter if the threat came from dwellers or a fellow human. She still counted herself as one of them. For the moment.

They were standing close enough that she could easily reach out and touch him again. She tapped the pocket she had sewn into her jacket's cuff to make a tracker fall into her hand. After activating it with a squeeze, she tacked it onto his arm as she grasped his bicep. His muscles were bigger than she expected. She could feel their tone and strength through his sleeve.

*Focus, Tessa.*

"I'm not trying to challenge you," she said. "I'm trying to keep you safe."

He sucked in a breath through his nose. His lips were pressed together so tight, they were bloodless. She could feel him trembling beneath her hand and she upped her assessment to 'severely messed up.'

"You don't need to protect me." He managed the whole sentence through teeth that never once parted. A muscle on his cheek twitched. But he had given her the opening she needed.

"Okay. I get that. You're a... really big guy." She looked him over again. Damn—it was true. If he wasn't some kind of basket case, she'd enjoy their proximity.

"You want to help me?" she asked.

His head bobbed in a brisk nod.

"Okay," she said. "Then stand outside the alley and don't let anyone in. Can you do that?"

"Yes."

She didn't dare allow herself to show her relief. If he thought she was manipulating him, she'd have five Redcaps plus an unhinged human to deal with. *And* the things living in her arm. She couldn't think about that right now. She gave Marcus another order instead.

"No peeking. I need some privacy to take care of these things. We'll talk after, okay?"

He nodded again, then stalked down the alley. As soon as he turned the corner and disappeared, she dropped her bat and tore off her jacket so she could look at her arm. The skin was smooth. She couldn't feel the bastards wriggling under her skin anymore either. Whatever had set them off, they seemed to be calm now. Dormant.

She took a deep, shaky breath, and let it out slowly. Her heart kept pounding. There was too much going on for her to calm herself down more. She didn't know how long the battery would last on her sonic bug repeller, and she still had a Redcap nest to clear.

"Get it together, Tessa."

She pulled her jacket back on and picked up her bat. Her hands were shaking. She took another deep breath and blew it out.

This part she knew. This was her life. Tracking down dwellers and ending them before they could end others— or worse. Leave them with shattered lives like her own.

Infect them.

The familiar hate rose up in her. She used it. Fed on it. Her hands steadied. She checked her grip on the bat and took a few warm-up swings, humming the song her dad had taught her during family outings to baseball games. Hauling back the bat, she swung hard at the face of the nearest Redcap. The wood connected with a satisfying crunch.

Its face caved in as the creature that was basically sitting on the corpse's neck and driving it around was crushed under the blow. Tendrils that had connected to long-dead nerves and moved the body like a puppet streamed behind the thing as it fell to the ground. She stepped clear as the human body it had been using glowed with a pretty blue light. Like paper being consumed by a flame, it vanished, clothes and all.

Not everything about dwellers made sense.

Tessa waited, staring at the quivering thing left behind on the ground. Its sunglasses and bandana had been knocked off, revealing what was nothing like a human head.

Two black globes protruded from its arachnid body. The feelers and limbs hidden in the hair of its 'beard twitched in its death throes. Its back was wrinkled and covered in a viscous red slime that made it look like a bloody brain.

"Fucking Redcaps."

It was taking too long to die, so Tessa helped it along. Two more swings, and it stopped moving. The same blue light flowed over its body, leaving nothing behind.

The best part about these things was their self-cleaning systems. Humans didn't usually find out about dwellers because they self-destructed when they were killed. Even the ichor on her bat glowed and then vanished as she swung it around a few more times.

The worst part about them was their existence.

Memories threatened to flood Tessa's mind, bile rising in the back of her throat when she thought of all the times she'd been too late. Cleaning up human remains was a hell of a lot messier—and not just physically.

She swung at the next Redcap. She had to take her mind in a different direction, had to stay focused on the current moment. This town was still infested, and until she killed the queen, more Redcaps would keep showing up. More people would die.

She started humming, timing her swings to match the music as she hit another Redcap with crushing blows. She paused behind the second-to-last Redcap.

"No one comes back to me. Ever."

The sound of her own voice startled her. She hadn't meant to speak aloud, but had been alone so long, she'd started talking to herself. Besides, it was true.

One of the things in her wrist squirmed, undoubtedly getting comfortable. Making itself at home under her skin.

She wasn't getting out of this alive. No one was. All she could do was take as many of these bastards with her as possible. She could spare other humans from a loss so deep it cut like shards of glass filling her insides. If she was very, very lucky, nothing would crawl up into her corpse and ride it around like a fucking marionette.

She wouldn't leave her destiny to luck. When her time came, all she had to do was make it back to her van. It was rigged with so many explosives, there wouldn't be enough of her left for anything to steer, copy, possess, or cohabitate. In her imagination, whatever managed to finally take her down would be blown up with her.

Everybody needed a dream.

Her last swing was strong and true. The Redcap flew from its host, splatting against the already disgusting wall of the alley and slowly trailing down the bricks before vaporizing.

Tessa wished she could crack open the universe and make a sucking hole that would pull every single dweller into it and leave humans to just mess with each other. Wasn't that bad enough? They didn't need fucking aliens or alien-human hybrids ripping up families. Humans could mess up their lives fine on their own.

Point in case, the hot psycho waiting for her outside the alley. The psycho who was almost assuredly not a werewolf.

She slipped another tracker into her hand and activated it. It wasn't nearly as fun planting this one as it had been tagging Marcus. She pressed it onto the back of the fifth Redcap's head, suppressing a shudder.

Now that she had it tagged, it was time to release it back into the wild—and follow it to the nest. She pulled out the monitor that displayed where all of her active trackers were. Two dots blinked on the screen. Two dots right on top of each other.

There should have been some space between them. That is, if Marcus had actually gone around the corner and a few feet away like she'd asked. She fought the urge to look up at the rooftop over her shoulder.

She looked at the ground instead, wondering if Marcus's tracker had fallen off. She'd never lost one before. The things were designed to hold on to whatever she attached them to, after all.

The hair on the back of her neck rose. If he was a werewolf, he might be waiting for his pack to arrive to attack. He could be lingering nearby, watching her. Positioning himself to strike.

But she had challenged him. No werewolf could have handled that insult. Unless he was the pack's omega. They were often used as scouts. Her stomach twisted with fear. She had to get to her van. It wasn't far.

She stuffed her hands in her pockets and headed for the mouth of the alley. She was walking so fast, she almost bumped into Marcus when he stepped into her path. Yeah, he hadn't gone as far away as she'd thought.

"You in a hurry?" he said.

"I... um. I'm all done here."

Marcus glanced down the alley. "You missed one. Unless you're leaving it on purpose."

She stammered, not knowing what to say.

"You can't track Redcaps with these." He held up her tracker and smirked. At least, his grimace became a little less pronounced.

"You know about Redcaps?"

"I never said I didn't."

Her brain sifted through everything she'd noticed about him. His muscle and build, his attitude, and the duster that was as out of place in the unseasonably hot weather as her jacket. The jacket she wore to hold and hide her weapons.

"You're a hunter," she said.

He stared at her in response.

Typical. Hunters tended to be paranoid, not sharing their trade secrets until their trust was earned. She was just happy he wasn't a werewolf.

She held out her hand for him to drop the tracker into. Once he did, she deactivated it and tucked it back into the pocket in her sleeve. While she was at it, she turned off her bug repeller.

With them both standing on the street, clearly visible by the few pedestrians still walking about, the Redcap wouldn't attack. She was betting it would hop off the body it had commandeered and skitter through the nearest storm drain to head back to its queen. Blue light in her periphery told her she was right.

Marcus snapped his gaze to the alley. "What did you do to it?"

"Tagged it."

He turned back to her. Now that she knew he was a hunter, his piercing stares didn't bother her. She'd hung out with way too many of their kind. She held up her monitor and let him see the blip that was steadily moving away from them. His raven-wing eyebrows actually hitched up his forehead.

"How did you do that?" he asked.

"We all pick up tricks along the way."

He shook his head. "Whatever you're working on, I

want in."

"That fast? Buy a girl dinner first."

Her stupid stomach growled. She hoped he didn't hear it.

"There's a burger joint down the street," he said.

"I was kidding. Besides, I'm vegan."

"They have salads."

Her pride was starting to sting. She needed to change the subject, even though her wallet was almost as empty as her stomach. Granola bars didn't last long with her metabolism and it had been a while since she'd managed a paying gig. She never stayed anywhere for more than a few days anymore. It was hard to get work on that schedule. Summer was right around the corner, though, and as soon as there was grass to cut, she'd be fine.

"The range on my tracker isn't that far," she said. "Once these things have gone mobile, they can cover ground quickly, going places my van can't reach. I need to leave now to follow this one back to the nest."

It had been a long time since she'd run into another hunter. She was glad to know he wasn't a run-of-the-mill psycho. But being a hunter didn't necessarily make him more stable. It just made him more dangerous.

She was damaged goods. If Marcus found out about the 'guests' inhabiting her arm, he would kill her. Worse, he might not give her a chance to tell him how to do it right.

The thought of having company for a little while was

appealing, though. Maybe he could back her up in taking out the Redcap nest. It would be nice to have someone to talk to openly about dwellers—or rather, 'monsters.' She'd have to watch what she said to make sure he didn't get suspicious about how much she knew. She was fairly confident the word 'dweller' was only used among their own kind.

Marcus was probably intrigued by her trick with the bug repeller and wanted to know how she'd immobilized the Redcaps. The fact that he'd followed them into the alley before he even knew about the ace up her sleeve spoke well of his character. Or told her he was crazy. Even two hunters would have trouble against five Redcaps.

He'd remained remarkably calm. He'd be a great asset killing the Redcap queen, if he could stay as cool under fire—literally.

Tessa started down the street, heading for her van. Marcus didn't join her.

Looking back over her shoulder, she said, "Are you in or what?"

She swore he smiled a little before following her.

# Chapter Three

The moment Marcus said that the damsel in distress he was set on rescuing was actually a hunter, Vaughn had hit the keyboard. An entire screen of the ops center focused on the new mystery lady. Vaughn had frozen a frame with a good shot of the hunter's face and was running it through all the facial recognition databases she had access to—which was all of them.

Thank the Internet Marcus was wearing those glasses. She was used to running blind with her partner, only going off of what the early-model earpiece could communicate. Marcus wasn't the chattiest of people. Few Guards in the Blades of Janus were.

Vaughn ran her fingers through her light brown hair, pulling out the plain black band that was holding it back and redoing her ponytail. She didn't want her hair falling in front of her eyes at the wrong moment. It was getting too long and she needed to see everything. The cameras she had worked into Marcus's duster previously weren't cutting it. The cameras in their motorcycle helmets were pretty good, but it was too conspicuous to walk around town wearing them. The new glasses had real potential, though. Vaughn could see the hunter's features with crystal clarity.

It had helped that Marcus couldn't seem to stop staring at her.

Vaughn's fingers hit the controls worked into her desktop even harder. Marcus had always been clear in how he felt about Vaughn. There was no leading on or jibes. But Marcus had never expressed an interest in anyone. Or any*thing* for that matter—man, woman, or dweller. Vaughn had been holding on to a tiny shred of hope that their friendship might change into something more. She had a feeling that shred was about to be stomped on.

Maybe it was a good thing. On some level, she knew she'd been kidding herself about it. Using her crush to avoid actually trying to find someone—not that the life of a Blade was conducive to building relationships. She refused to give up hope, though. She would find someone someday. Preferably who enjoyed quiet nights at home, basking in the light of a dozen monitors, like the one focused on finding more information about this new hunter.

The search would take a while, even with Vaughn's algorithms on the case. All she could do was listen as the hunter chatted up Marcus.

At least she was still oblivious. Hunters didn't like the Blades. And if she figured out Marcus's darker secret…

Vaughn wished for the thousandth time that she could

work in the field. Even if the bosses didn't think she was too precious to risk, her agoraphobia was usually bad enough to keep her locked up inside. Besides, the field was fucking terrifying.

The thought of Marcus out there alone was almost enough to make her want to tell the bosses to get bent and figure out a way to join her partner among all the ghasts and ghoulies and things that went bump in the night. Her only comfort was that Marcus was one of them.

Instead, Vaughn sat in front of her wall of monitors, watching camera feeds from all over the city, refining her algorithms for predicting dweller activity. Coming up with new jokes to take the edge off when Marcus came home—and new technology to make sure he made it.

The light above the main door to the ops center flickered to amber, then turned green again. Company, but someone with clearance. There were only two other people at the ranch, so it was probably Porter coming to check on the night's patrol. Sure enough, the door slid into the wall with a soft whoosh, and one of the bosses walked in. She still wasn't sure which one it was.

Dexter and Porter took 'identical twins' to a rarified level. They kept their dark hair the exact same length and style—short on the sides and spiky on the top. They always wore the standard Blades uniform. Black cargo pants, black T-shirts, and black combat boots.

Their outfits matched their black eyes perfectly. Vaughn

had never seen anyone with such dark eyes. She would consider them hot, if they weren't so freaking creepy.

It usually took about five minutes of conversation for her to figure out who she was talking to. Dexter tended to want discussions to be quick and efficient. Porter was friendlier. She wished they would put a big 'P' and 'D' on their chests.

"Good evening, Vaughn. How is tonight's patrol going?"

Probably Porter.

"It's an interesting one."

"Interesting good or interesting bad?"

She cocked her head to the side and shrugged. "I'm still figuring that out. The straight-up bad news is that Providence has Redcaps now."

"Redcaps." Porter let out a huff of breath through his nose. "That's a class-C dweller."

"Yup. Humanoid, human-sized, able to mingle with the populace, and once they're in town, you have them forever."

"What's the other news?"

"Marcus ran into a hunter with some interesting tech and some serious issues."

Porter arched an eyebrow. "Interesting tech?"

"Not like *my* tech-interesting, but I've asked Marcus to secure me some samples."

"Exercise caution while investigating it."

"I always do."

Porter smiled his cold, creepy smile. "And what about those issues you mentioned?"

"Every hunter I've observed is pretty messed up, but she's taking it to a new level. She hummed a cheery song as she bludgeoned four Redcaps to death with a baseball bat."

"That sounds like fairly typical behavior for a hunter. She must be good if she could sing while fighting, though."

"There was no fight. It was an execution. She somehow managed to paralyze them. She even tagged one with a tracker."

That caught Porter's interest. He walked up behind Vaughn to get a better look at the screen that displayed Providence's streets illuminated as gridlines. Two gold blips travelled along the roads, following a red blip closely. Vaughn had figured out the frequency of Tessa's trackers and was also tracking Marcus's bike, as usual. Marcus was sticking close to the hunter's van. Another monitor had a view of Tessa's epically crappy vehicle as seen from the camera in Marcus's visor.

"She tagged a Redcap and it worked?" Porter said.

"As near as I can tell. I've piggybacked her signal and am tracking it, too. She only has a proximity tracker with limited range. I'm borrowing bandwidth from one of my favorite satellites to make sure we don't lose it."

Porter nodded, his brow furrowing as he stared at the monitor. "The Redcap is moving under the buildings."

"The hunter said it somehow went into the sewers through a storm drain. If I hadn't already seen her do amazing things, I would think she was nuts."

"How does a Redcap fit through a storm drain?"

"I can have Marcus ask her."

"Please do. And ask how she paralyzed them as well. That would be extremely useful knowledge, now that we have Redcaps in Providence." Porter—and Vaughn was certain it was Porter at this point—smirked again as he started to turn away. "Good work. Keep me posted on—"

Porter's gaze flicked to the screen that was running facial recognition on the hunter and seemed to get stuck there. His eyes widened and his mouth dropped open.

That had never happened. Never once had either of the bosses ever looked surprised. And they had seen some shit.

Porter snapped his mouth shut, put his hand on Vaughn's chair, and leaned in closer. Also new.

"Who is that?"

"That's the hunter," Vaughn said.

"Bring up a clean image on screen two." Porter shifted to stand in front of the monitor he'd indicated, even though each screen was big enough to give a good view from pretty much anywhere in the room.

Vaughn sat up straighter and typed in the command, killing the camera feed of a known hotspot for dweller activity. She brought up a picture of the hunter on the newly-available monitor and removed the gridlines from her face to give Porter a clear view.

"I'm searching databases to try to find out who she is," Vaughn said. "It'll take a while, though. Her plates are bogus, of course. All we have is her face and a first name, which might be fake as well."

"What is it?"

"Tessa."

The door to the ops center whooshed open again and Dexter ran in. *Ran.*

*Holy hell…*

Vaughn wasn't used to seeing the pair together. They stood shoulder-to-shoulder, staring silently at the picture of the hunter. Even with this golden opportunity to compare them, she couldn't find any differences. Not a single hair. It was creepy. It was even creepier when they both looked at her, turning their heads at the exact same time and angle. She wanted to rub her eyes and look again, as if that would rid her of what had to be a trippy case of double vision.

"Transfer the feed to our office," Dexter said. "And compile everything about her we missed up to this point. This takes top priority."

Vaughn shook her head. "Marcus is on active patrol with an unknown hunter heading into a Redcap nest— whatever that is. I can't be distracted. I need to back him up."

"Marcus can take care of himself," Dexter said. "You have your orders. We need a positive ID on this hunter as soon as possible."

Of course Dexter wouldn't put Marcus's safety first. Porter remaining silent was a surprise, though.

"It's going to take time," Vaughn said. "I don't have much to go on."

Porter turned back to the screen and said, "Rhodes. Search for Tessa Rhodes."

Dexter grabbed Porter by the arm, the same wide-eyed look of shock on his face that Porter had when he first saw Tessa. Vaughn had always thought Dexter was the alpha twin, but when Porter turned to glare at Dexter, he dropped his gaze to the ground almost immediately. It was the first time Vaughn had ever seen them look at each other. The few times they'd been in a room together, they paid each other about as much attention as a pair of iguanas. What the hell was going on?

"Rhodes," Vaughn said. "Do you think you know her or something?"

A look of such pain flashed across Porter's face, Vaughn knew she'd never forget it. Before Porter could say anything else, Dexter started pulling him toward the door.

"Send the feed to my office," Dexter said. "Now."

Vaughn waited till the room was empty to speak again.

"'My'?"

That was another weird thing that Vaughn had noticed about the bosses. They always spoke about themselves in plural. '*We* need you to check this out.' 'What are you making *us* for dinner?'

At first, she thought they were speaking on behalf of all the Blades or something. But a pattern had emerged that couldn't be explained away with that. When she had pointed it out to Porter, he'd just smiled and walked away.

Everybody had quirks. Vaughn didn't have much room to talk there. She shook her head as she turned back to her keyboard, connecting to the one world that had always made sense to her—her machines.

# Chapter Four

After ten minutes of silence, Marcus started to worry. Vaughn had never been quiet that long when they were patrolling. Or… ever, really.

Marcus glanced at the section of the display screen of his helmet that would ping Vaughn to get her attention, then said, "You still with me?"

The silence lasted a few more seconds before Vaughn replied. "Yeah."

"What's wrong?"

"Just freaking out a little here." Her voice was tight. "You should know our fearless leaders are seeing everything you're seeing. They ordered me to connect the feed to their office. The video feed. I'm keeping our chats on a private line."

"Thanks," Marcus said. "They've watched the feed from your other cameras before. Why is it freaking you out this time?"

"Mostly because *they're* freaking out. Something about this hunter you've hooked up with has caught their attention."

"She isn't like the other hunters we've encountered.

Even you said you're curious."

"I'm only here for the tech," Vaughn said in a flat voice. "I still want you to nab some for me to study."

Marcus wasn't nabbing anything from Tessa. From what he'd seen, she was barely surviving with what she had. If anything, he wanted to *give* her things. Weapons, support. Food. He'd known she was joking with her crack about buying her dinner, but when her stomach growled…

*"She needs care,"* his dweller grumbled.

Marcus wasn't sure if it was trying to manipulate him— or if he even cared at this point. The urge to protect her was growing.

He'd walked with Tessa to an old weather-beaten camper van that was more rust than metal. Dents and scratches covered every surface, some disturbingly familiar. She must have seen a lot of action in the field already. He couldn't imagine how terrified she must have been with the things that made those marks trying to get to her while she was alone inside.

His skin prickled. If he kept imagining that, he was going to have a problem. Claws got in the way of steering his motorcycle, and his helmet was designed for a human-shaped head. Thinking about what was happening back at the ranch would help distract him.

"Tell me exactly what happened," Marcus said.

"Porter came in to check on things, as usual. He saw Tessa's face and wanted a clearer picture. I'm running facial recognition software to learn more about her."

"Nothing weird there."

"Wait for it. Then Dexter came *running* into the ops room."

"Running?" Marcus said.

"Yeah. I've never seen him move that fast. Outside of the gym or in the field, anyway. He told me to transfer the feed to his office along with a backlog of everything you'd seen and heard. He even dropped their royal 'we' for a minute."

Vaughn had noticed that the twins nearly always used 'we' pronouns and pointed it out to Marcus shortly after joining the Blades. Marcus hadn't noticed it before. He was too busy deferring to Dexter to call him out on grammar.

"Of course, there's no sound in the files," Vaughn said.

"Thanks." Marcus didn't think Dexter and Porter would care about their conversations being left out. Their interest in Tessa was disturbing, though. "If they'll let you get away with it, keep the feed video only."

"Will do. Dexter also told me that figuring out who she is and sending them the file takes priority over everything right now. Even helping you with patrol. I tried to explain how much you need me, but he wouldn't listen."

Marcus laughed. Not because it wasn't true, but because he knew Vaughn was trying to lighten things up. It was how she handled stress. Hell, it was part of how

Marcus could stay so calm out in the field.

"They're our leaders and we need to trust them," Marcus said. "Do as he says."

"You're with an unknown hunter heading for a Redcap nest and we don't even know what that is. I can't leave you alone."

"I'll be with a hunter who just took out four Redcaps by herself and landed the first successful tracker that we've ever seen on another. If Dexter and Porter are that interested in her, there must be a reason." Marcus wasn't sure what it might be.

"Maybe one of them just wants to call dibs."

*"She's* yours.*"* His dweller yelled the words in Marcus's head, then offered some truly gruesome images of what it wanted Marcus to do to Dexter. Marcus shoved the thoughts from his mind.

Adrenaline spiked through his system like a knife stabbing his guts. It spread through his chest, a current of energy that usually preceded becoming hairy and much more difficult to deal with. Taking deep breaths, he pushed back the bizarre surge of possessiveness that threatened to overpower his control.

"Umm… are you okay?" Vaughn asked.

"Yeah. Why?"

"Because you just growled. Like full-on growled."

Shit. That wasn't good. Marcus hadn't even realized he was doing it.

"I was clearing my throat."

"Right," Vaughn said. "I get it. Dibs are yours."

The pressure in Marcus's chest dispersed. Vaughn always knew just what to say, even in a moment as awkward as this.

"Thanks."

"Forget it." The tightness had returned to her voice. "If you need me, you can ping me with the glasses the same way as through your helmet's visor. I'll keep the bosses off your audio feed, but I can't do anything about the video."

"I appreciate it."

"I know. One more thing. I think Porter knows her. He gave me a last name. Rhodes. I'll keep running it down. Be careful out there, okay?"

"I always am."

Vaughn chuckled, then the feed went silent.

The dweller in his head was quiet as well. Marcus could still sense it—an eerie presence—like his thoughts were being watched, along with everything else he was seeing and experiencing. He pushed aside the familiar sensation and focused on the hunter in front of him.

*Tessa Rhodes.*

Red lights shined in his face as she tapped the brakes before turning onto a side street. She parked her van in front of an empty lot. Scraggly grass struggled to grow in the packed earth where a building had probably once stood. Their quest had led them to what Vaughn referred to as the Barrows.

Not many humans came to this part of Providence, especially at night. It was mostly filled with abandoned buildings—warehouses, apartments, and even a derelict factory. Dwellers had crept into this part of town, taking over the waste that humans had left behind.

Marcus slowed to a stop next to the curb and killed his engine. Tessa's door slammed, and he quickly took off his helmet and clipped it to the back of his bike. He barely managed to get his glasses in place before she joined him. There weren't as many street lamps to reflect off the lenses, but hopefully the darkness would make it harder for her to make out the color of his eyes anyway.

"It stopped moving about a hundred yards away." She held up her monitor for him to see. "I had us circle the block to be sure, but sort of figured it out when I saw we were close to a junkyard. It's a perfect place for a Redcap nest."

"Great."

She tilted her head and smiled. "You getting cold feet?"

"No, I just wish I knew more about what we're walking into."

"Don't worry, I'll give you a crash course. But before that…" She looked over at his bike, then back to him. "May I?"

None of the security features of the bike had been activated yet, so he nodded and stepped aside. "Be my guest."

Her expression as she walked around the bike was... hungry. He wondered what it would be like to have her look at him that way. She trailed her fingers over the seat, then along one of the handlebars. His skin prickled, imagining how that touch would feel. If this wasn't her trying to be seductive, he'd be in real trouble if she ever tried to charm him.

"Who do I have to sleep with to get one of these?"

He made a little choking sound, both from the thought of what she was suggesting and how he knew Vaughn would react to the offer.

"That's not exactly how it works," Marcus said.

"Too bad."

She faced him, the hungry smile still in place, and let her gaze travel down his body. He'd already taken a step toward her when he realized what his body was doing, registered the deep purring growl rising up through him from his dweller. Surely from his dweller. He forced himself to an awkward stop inches away from her. She arched an eyebrow, then shrugged and turned back to her van.

"I guess we have work to do anyway," she said. "It'll be dawn soon, and that Redcap nest won't clear itself."

He fell in step beside her, hoping the movement would calm his body down.

"I'm guessing you've only ever dealt with Redcaps on

the street when they're actively hunting," she said.

"I didn't know they did anything else."

"It's time for Redcaps 101, then."

She opened the side door of her van and hopped in. After dropping the tracker monitor on the front bench seat, she squatted down and pulled her hair into a tight bun.

Marcus stood on the sidewalk, staring at her as she bent over the built-in seats opposite the door. She lifted a tattered cushion to reveal a storage compartment. The mellow tone of her voice was like white noise in the background, joining with the rumbling approval of the beast in his belly. It would be so easy to tear off her jeans and—

"Hello?" she said.

"What?" He'd been too caught up in his fantasy to listen. What the hell was wrong with him? He'd been at least half-hard since he'd first followed her into the alley.

"I asked if you had a bludgeoning weapon." She kept digging around in the chests, hips shifting in a mesmerizing pattern.

"No." He'd never needed one.

"I'll hook you up, then. Just give me a second."

Any dwellers Marcus met assumed he wasn't a threat. They didn't attack their own, even if they were of different species. The ones who could reason usually talked to him. It never took much conversation to figure out if the dweller in question needed to be put down for public safety.

Marcus seldom needed a weapon to help him with that.

Every once in a while, they would encounter a new species or a dweller that they thought they could talk down from killing humans. Vaughn had developed a special shock weapon for that. She called it the stingray. If it failed to stun the target—and didn't accidentally kill it— Marcus usually had to take over and finish the job. Dwellers didn't like getting stunned.

What he did wasn't pretty, but it was necessary. He kept humans safe, and even protected dwellers sometimes.

And then there were the hunters.

Marcus had encountered a few in his years with the Blades. As far as he was concerned, they all fell into the 'can't be reasoned with' camp. They thought every human with a dweller—or even dwellers who could survive with non-human hosts—were threats to their kind. They killed indiscriminately. He'd yet to meet a hunter that would sit down and talk with a dweller first. He hoped Tessa would prove an exception.

Then again, hunters didn't know the true origin of dwellers. They thought they were dealing with fairy tale monsters.

*If only.*

"You don't have to wait on the sidewalk. Come on in." She turned and smiled at him. "I promise I won't bite."

Marcus felt his body moving forward, like Tessa had

become his new center of gravity. He clamped down on his muscles, holding himself in place. If he let go of his control for even an instant, he didn't know what would happen.

"I get it." The sultry twist of her lips faded into a gentler smile. "You need your space. That's fine. What we do doesn't exactly build trusting natures. That's one of the reasons hunters usually work solo."

"It doesn't have to be that way."

She let out a little snort. "It's the only way I know how to be."

For a moment, he thought he saw a longing for something else cross her features, but then she smiled and shook her head.

"Damn, that was a maudlin exchange. Do what you need to be comfortable. But if you decide you want to do a little more than throw sexy looks my way, let me know." She waggled her eyebrows briefly and grinned.

Vaughn was going to love her.

Marcus felt himself smile. He noticed because it didn't happen very often, and *never* in the field when he was on his own—unless Vaughn was working really hard to make Marcus laugh. He poked his head through the open side door of the van.

The place reeked of cut grass, gasoline, and gunpowder. The grass smell was centered around a plastic garbage bag on the floor behind the passenger's seat. He was disconcerted by the fact that he couldn't narrow down the source of the other smells. They emanated from spots all over the van.

"What are we looking for?" he asked.

Tessa knelt on the floor next to a pair of cylinders that looked like two old scuba canisters stuck together, complete with straps for wearing it like a backpack. Instead of breathing gear coming out of the top, a hose came out of the bottom. It was attached to a short metal wand.

"Is that a flamethrower?" Marcus said.

"You know it." She fiddled with the wand and straps, checking it over. "Best thing for Redcaps when you're clearing a nest."

"Wouldn't swords be better?"

She cast a pitying look at him. He didn't know how he'd earned it.

"Most things die when you cut off their head," he said. "It's a lot less conspicuous than a flamethrower."

She picked up the ancient device and slid it over the front seat. Was she planning to drive around setting fire to things through the window? With the explosives he could smell all over her van, that seemed ridiculously unsafe.

He looked around the small space more and noticed that the rear window had been reinforced with heavy-duty wire mesh. The metal edges of the back door were fused. It had been welded shut. She put the cover and cushion back in place on the now empty compartment, then gestured for him to sit.

"No thanks," he said.

"What's the matter, Marcus? Can't take the heat?" Some of the playfulness was returning to her smirk.

She stood, hunched over in the small space, and opened the seat closest to the back of the van, gesturing toward its contents. It was filled with canned food, bottled water, and granola bars.

She put the seat cover back in place and said, "You can sit on my pantry if you'd rather."

"Wait. You *live* in here?" Marcus couldn't mask the incredulity of his tone.

"Yeah, I do. So what?"

He struggled to recover from his gaffe. "It's… nice."

"It's a shithole." She smiled at him again. "But it gets me where I need to go and carts around what I can scrape together to kill things."

The Blades of Janus had set up the Providence outpost in Vaughn's family home. It had started off as a good sized cattle ranch, but the livestock were long gone. The main house was set back from the road, giving them plenty of privacy. They were close enough to the city to patrol effectively and had enough space to take care of business.

Marcus and Vaughn had their own master suites, plus an entertainment room with a big screen TV and gaming consoles. They had a library, where Marcus spent most of his solo down time, and a gorgeous kitchen that was always fully stocked.

The sub-basement had a gym, an armory, Porter's labs and exam room, plus Vaughn's workspace and ops center. They even had holding cells that Vaughn had developed for various levels of dweller threats that were under assessment. She'd built them using what she'd learned from the ship that was buried deep below the house.

The cells were accessed by an elevator—which also led down to the ship—and every inch of the place and the surrounding land was protected by a security system that Vaughn had designed. It was all under constant surveillance from the ops center by Vaughn or her algorithms twenty-four hours a day.

Which meant that when Marcus went to his warm, comfortable bed at night, he slept. Peacefully—without fear.

What did Tessa live with?

# Chapter Five

The looks Marcus cast her way seemed to be turning from interest to pity. That did not sit well with Tessa.

Sure, she lived on little. Most hunters did. But she could take care of herself. She didn't need anyone's pity or help. People always let her down. One way or another. They always left.

It would be easy for Marcus to bail, with that sparkly, sleek black motorcycle of his. He must be one of the rare hunters that had money.

There were lines of softly glowing blue lights worked into the body of the bike. The whole thing had to be custom built. It looked like something out of a sci-fi movie. It didn't rumble or even purr when he turned it on. Instead, it just gave a contented sigh.

He was starting to remind her of Kyle. Maybe Marcus was another trust fund poser who had stumbled across dwellers and thought he could play hero with fancy gadgets and limited knowledge. Her teeth clenched at the thought.

She'd been so young when she hooked up with Kyle. He'd promised her a cure. With his degree and resources, she'd thought he could deliver. Instead, he'd ended up infecting himself. If Marcus wasn't careful, the same thing would happen to him.

It wouldn't be *her* that infected him, of course. She would never let that happen. Not again. But sooner or later, Marcus would come up against the wrong thing and he wouldn't walk away. Not human, anyway. He was meddling in a dangerous world. She wasn't sure he realized just how dangerous it was.

"How long have you been hunting monsters?" she asked.

"About ten years."

She wasn't buying it. "You've been on your own that whole time?"

He didn't answer. She doubted he would have survived that long as a hunter relying on cool motorcycles and swords to kill things. Someone had to have trained him.

Hunters only stayed together for extended periods of time when they were teaching each other new tricks or training recruits. Somehow, dwellers always seemed to know when hunters were banding together and they put a stop to it—permanently. Partners could sometimes fly under the radar, but larger groups never lasted long.

The exception was the Blades of Janus. Goody-two-shoes know-it-alls who had set themselves up as the dweller police force a few years back. For some reason, they hadn't been taken out yet. Maybe it was because they didn't just go after dwellers who preyed on humans. Sometimes they took out other hunters, if they thought they had 'crossed a line.' As if *any* dwellers could be trusted to exist.

Who were the Blades to pass judgment? That was probably what kept them from being wiped out by dwellers, though. Plus they had resources and...

*Wait a minute.*

Marcus had resources. He'd said she didn't have to live alone, as if he didn't know the consequences of banding together. And when she'd asked if he had someone he could call back in the alley where this all started, he'd said yes. He had enough confidence to walk into an alley with five Redcaps and an unknown person, so he'd had some training, but the fact that he didn't know he was totally outgunned meant his training wasn't great. Or that he was extremely cocky.

Both characteristics fit what she knew of the Blades. Neither was good for his longevity. And if he was a Blade, being near him could be bad for hers.

She wasn't sure how the Blades decided that a hunter needed to be put down. She might clear the nest and kill the queen only to be executed by the guy who was supposed to have her back. Or he might do something stupid and get them both killed.

Walking into a Redcap nest with another hunter was one thing. She knew they'd be on the same page when it came to dwellers. But going in with a Blade?

She needed to be sure and doubted Marcus would give her a straight answer if she asked—using words, anyway. She had an idea of how to convince him to open up.

"I need some air." She jumped to the ground next to him, paying a lot more attention to every detail she could.

Brand new clothes. Shining boots. No blood stains, not that the black fabric would show any. No tears, rips, or even worn spots. Broad chest. Really broad. Amazing shoulders…

That wasn't what she was supposed to be thinking about. She brought her mind back to task.

"We still have a few minutes," Tessa said. "Want to show me more of that bike of yours?"

"Sure." Marcus only hesitated a moment when she gestured for him to go first. No hunter would casually turn their back to someone that fast.

She let him take two steps so she had room to work, then dropped into a crouch and sprang up at him, rocketing into his ribs with the full strength of her legs. She caught him with her shoulder, spreading the impact over her body and hopefully knocking the wind out of him.

He staggered to the side—toward the dirt and away from the street, as she intended. With him off-balance, she dropped again, this time sweeping the back of his knee with a kick that brought him to the ground. He rolled over, but she was right there.

Her knees dug into the dirt on either side of his head, pinning his face between her thighs. For good measure, she pulled out the knife she kept in her right boot, holding it close enough to his neck to keep him from getting any ideas, but not so close that she was putting him in real danger. She grabbed a fistful of his hair to keep his head steady, just in case.

"You're not a hunter," she said.

His lips twitched away from his teeth in a barely-suppressed snarl. For a brief moment, she wished she had grabbed the silver knife in her other boot. Her heart was hammering in her chest.

Misjudging him as a Blade instead of a hunter would result in an awkward conversation. If he was a werewolf…

*I'd already be dead.*

She shook the thought away and pressed the knife closer, let him feel the coolness of the metal but not the sharpness of its edge. "You're one of the Blades of Janus."

He let out a breath, relaxing a bit beneath her. "I never said I wasn't."

Just like he'd never said he didn't know about Redcaps. Lies of omission—letting her assume what she wanted. He was clever, which was annoying.

She hissed out a frustrated breath. "How many more times are you planning to use that line?"

"At least once."

A laugh escaped her before she could stop it. She

leaned back and slid the knife into its sheath in her boot. "Damn, you're cocky."

"That's only going to get worse the longer you sit on my face."

She laughed again.

For a moment, she wondered how bad it would be to hook up with a Blade. She'd only been with other hunters or civilians before. Guys who understood it wasn't a permanent thing. She had three days in every town she visited. Three days. If she stayed any longer...

Sticking around wasn't an option. The past always had a way of catching up with her—and her past wasn't pretty.

She stood and offered Marcus her hand to help him up. He took it, but she didn't feel any of his weight as he rose. She did notice the raging hard-on that his cargo pants couldn't begin to hide.

Yeah, he had plenty of resources.

"You really know how to tempt a girl."

She managed to force her gaze back to his face, wishing she knew what he was thinking. Those damned glasses made it impossible to make out his eyes clearly. The lenses seemed to have ultra-reflective surfaces for some reason.

"Be quiet," he said.

"Excuse me?"

A muscle was twitching in his jaw. He answered her through clenched teeth. Again.

"Earpiece."

She couldn't believe it. The whole time they'd been together, he already had a partner.

She'd been excited to have someone at her side for a single night. He never had to go it alone, always had backup. No wonder he seemed to space out periodically. He had someone talking in his ear.

"You've got to be kidding me." She let out a disgusted snort and shook her head. "This is the problem with you Blades. You have no idea what it's like to be a real hunter."

"What's that supposed to mean?"

"You come out here to fight bad guys with your fancy bikes and earpieces, then go home to a comfy bed at night. Probably have a hot meal with your pals. We're in the thick of it every minute of every day. You think you get to police hunters and that monsters should have rights. Well, guess what? If a werewolf wants to retain a lawyer, *it eats him*."

She knew she was baiting him, testing him. The nagging doubt in the back of her mind wouldn't go away. It was messing with her head.

"They call themselves dwellers," he said.

"At least you know that much."

She was glad she wouldn't have to be as careful with the words she chose. Most hunters went with the generic term, 'monster.' Her experience went well beyond just killing dwellers, though. If another hunter found out how involved she was in the dweller community, they would definitely try to put her down. She wouldn't even blame them.

"We also know that not all dwellers are evil."

She snorted. "That's news to me."

His lips curled away from his teeth. His reassuringly human-looking teeth.

"If a dweller is capable of reasoning and isn't hurting anyone, it has a right to be left alone."

She laughed again, the sound harsh and brittle to her ears. "I don't care how harmless a dweller might seem. These things want to breed. Eventually, that urge will surface. The Blades have been dealing with dwellers for a few years. Hunters have been doing it for centuries. You're so far removed from reality. You don't have a fucking clue what the world is really like."

"Yeah? And you know everything?"

Tessa stepped right up to him, her body inches from his, *wanting* to get in his face. She wanted... too many things. From this close, his lips looked soft. She could easily wrap her arms around him and put that hard-on to good use.

Dammit, she needed to get it together.

Anger was her constant companion. She called on it to keep herself from doing anything stupid.

"I've been to a dweller dinner party," she said, hoping the memory would help shift her focus away from the heat coming off of him. "And you can bet the steaks they were eating didn't come from a cow. So yeah, I know what I'm talking about."

He did that sort of half-snarl again and grabbed her shoulders, lightning-quick. Instead of throwing her to the ground or striking her, he slammed her against his chest. His lips were on hers before her brain could even process it. Her body, however, didn't need or want her brain's help.

Frissons of pleasure snaked through her, all the way to her toes. The warmth of his chest made her want to melt into him. Her hands curled against his narrow hips, then slid around to cup his ass and press him harder against her.

He let out a low growl as he ground himself against her. If he'd just loosen his grip, she could jump up and wrap her legs around his waist. She squeezed his ass tighter to keep herself from undoing his pants. She opened her mouth as his tongue drove into her, claiming her, demanding a satisfaction that part of her was only too happy to give.

But only part.

The rest of her—the rational her—knew they had a nest to clear and that the sun was rising. Plus a Blade would come with complications she couldn't afford, no matter how soft his lips or firm his ass.

He didn't seem eager to stop, so she'd have to be the one to put on the brakes. She pressed her hands against his stomach and he shifted a little to give her space. He probably thought she was heading for his dick.

*If only.*

Instead, she used the opening to push her arms up against his chest and shove him, hard. He didn't budge. His grip on her shoulders tightened enough that she let out a little grunt.

He let go of her suddenly, as if she was made of lava, and staggered back a pace. He was panting, and she could make out how wide his eyes were even with the glasses. The light was reflecting strangely again, making them almost seem to glow gold.

The butterflies she'd felt in anticipation of... whatever she thought was going to happen, turned to wasps stinging her stomach. Her heart pounded in her chest.

She had *not* just made out with a werewolf. Marcus *couldn't* be one. Werewolves always hunted in packs. Always. They didn't bother with earpieces to communicate and they didn't wear dusters or ride sleek motorcycles.

And—most telling—if he was a werewolf, he would have killed her by now. How many times was she going to have to remind herself of that before she believed it?

She tried to curb her own panting, to bring her body back under control. Even with her bizarre fears, even knowing he was a Blade, she still wanted him. She couldn't remember ever wanting someone so much.

Which was what made him most dangerous.

"Come on, Blade," she said. "You know so much about dwellers, you should know that Redcaps are weakest at dawn. We don't have much time."

# Chapter Six

Several minutes passed before Marcus felt safe following Tessa into her van. He'd lost control a few times since he was colonized, but never like that. He knew he should stay outside, but couldn't stand the thought of being that far from her. He climbed into the van and hunched over next to her, his shoulders brushing the rust-spotted ceiling.

"We're not going to talk about what happened?" he said.

"We have other things to discuss. Important things."

As if what had happened between them wasn't? He barely managed to stifle a growl.

He'd never kissed someone before. Anyone. He'd never been tempted to. But the way she'd been staring at his lips, combined with the scent she was putting off and the way she was challenging him... It was overwhelming.

His dweller whispered to him, almost as if it was hoping Marcus wouldn't notice. But it was kind of hard to miss thoughts floating through his own mind.

*"She's ours."*

*"Fuck you."* Marcus felt the strongest surge of rage

he'd ever felt toward his dweller. *"She's* mine.*"*

His response surprised him. But it felt too potent to dismiss, came too naturally to ignore. She was his.

No. No way. Feelings this strong didn't happen so fast. It had to be his dweller.

*"It's because of what you are."* His dweller laughed. *"It's in our nature. Accept it."*

Marcus shook his head. The only physical activities he'd been interested in since he was colonized were directly related to becoming the most effective Blade he possibly could—and keeping his dweller somewhat satisfied. His work was his life. Keeping people safe was all that mattered to him. People in general. Not just this one.

*"Are you sure?"*

"Tell whoever's talking to you to shut up," Tessa said.

"What?"

"You've been standing there derping at me for the last two minutes. I don't know what they're saying that's pissing you off so bad, but tell them to shut up."

She was right. He needed to get control of his thoughts —of himself. Kissing her was one thing, but if he let himself get too carried away, he could hurt her. And even if he could interact... physically... with her safely, he wouldn't want anything more to happen until she knew that he was a werewolf, which came with its own set of challenges.

The scent she was putting off was amazing, though. It filled the small space, saturating his senses. He could feel her heat, the currents of air she stirred as she moved around the van. He wanted to bend her over the front seat and—

"For fuck's sake." She spun around, then grabbed his head and turned it so she could yell into his ear. "Stop distracting him so I can tell him how to not get us both killed."

He winced as the decibel level of her voice rose to a painful intensity.

"The earpiece is on the other side," he said. "And that isn't what's distracting me."

"What is it, then?"

"I'm having some trouble... adapting to your proximity."

She looked him up and down, her gaze getting stuck on his crotch for a moment. Her breath hitched, but then she tightened her lips in a grimace.

"We don't have time to mess around." Under her breath, she added, "Maybe later."

He chuckled quietly. "Now I have something to live for."

Her mouth dropped open. He probably shouldn't have let her know that he heard her whisper. But then her lips twitched into a brief smirk. She turned back to her storage compartments.

"I'm guessing with your talk of swords, you already know that decapitation kills a lot of things. Fire kills more. But Redcaps ride the dead and eat the living. They're like... spider-headed zombies. You see a body walking around, but the actual monster is sitting on the corpse's neck. That's one of the reasons their bodies can take so much damage before they vaporize."

She opened the middle storage compartment—which was the longest—and started pulling out weapons. Rifles, knives, swords, chains, lengths of pipe, and some things Marcus couldn't even name started piling up on the floor of the van. He had to sit down on her pantry to get out of the way for her personal arsenal.

"What's standard issue for the Blades of Janus?"

"It's pronounced 'yah-noose,'" he said.

She arched an eyebrow at him over her shoulder. "You think decapitating a Redcap kills it, but the real priority is how to correctly pronounce 'Janus?' Is that part of your field training?"

He kept himself from bristling at yet another challenge from her. Barely.

"What are you packing, Blade of Janus?" She mispronounced the name again—deliberately.

He ignored it.

His favorite weapons were his hands. Somehow, he didn't think sharing that would go over well.

"A stingray," he said.

"What the hell is that?"

"It's like a shock gun. It disrupts electrical signals in just about anything, stunning them."

She let out a snort. "I can see where that would be useful for a Blade. But in this fight, you need something good for squishing. Aha!" She lifted a rusty hatchet and flipped it in the air, catching it by the handle. "I'm guessing you're up on your shots. You want this or my bat?"

"I'll take the bat."

"Suit yourself." As she reloaded the storage compartment, she kept talking. "Like I said, Redcaps are these kind of spider-things. They have black eyes on stalks like a crab and they've got the pincers going on."

"I've seen that."

"Good. Most hunters don't take time to notice that kind of thing. What you may not have seen are the tendrils that they burrow into the bodies they ride, connecting to the corpse's nerves so they can steer it. You ever notice how a Redcap's movements don't seem quite natural?"

"Yeah, they're sluggish and kind of clumsy."

"That's because they're controlling a body that isn't their own," she said.

If it wasn't for the amount of damage Redcaps could take, they wouldn't be too dangerous. Well, that and their appetites. They were voracious carnivores. Body counts didn't go up when Redcaps settled in a town—unlike with dwellers who killed for sport. But missing persons reports did. Redcaps were one of the few dweller species that had a kill order out. Destroy on sight.

"Most hunters just lop off their heads and call it a day." She kept rummaging around in her storage compartment as she spoke. "They think the heads self-destruct along with the bodies. But the thing is, the head *is* the Redcap. Decapitate them, and yeah, you've severed a bunch of their tendrils, but those grow back. You have to squish them to kill them, and those bastards are fast when they're not attached to something. They like storm drains for escape routes, especially since their nests are full of tunnels and caves they dig underground."

She pulled out a small box half-full of olive green, egg-shaped...

"Are those grenades?" Marcus stood up so fast, he hit his head on the top of her van. He was lucky he didn't knock a hole in the decrepit thing.

She grinned at him. "Don't worry, I store them separate from the flamethrower." She took three from the padding inside the box, paused briefly, then put one back, mumbling to herself. "Two should do it. I'm running low."

"Grenades seem like overkill."

"For Redcaps, yes. But not for their queen."

He sat back down. "I'm still wrapping my head around Redcaps... just being heads. What the hell is their queen?"

She opened her mouth, then closed it again, a grim

expression settling over her features.

"That bad, huh?" he said.

She sat next to him on the small bench seat. He made an extra effort to concentrate on what she was saying and not her closeness—or the subtle way her scent was shifting from arousal to what he guessed was preparation for violence. He hated to admit it, but he liked both.

"The plan is simple," she said. "We go into the nest, kill any Redcaps that get in our way, fry the queen with my flamethrower till it's nice and crispy, then shove a couple of grenades down its throat and call it a day. Once the queen is dead, its brood die as well."

"That sounds pretty straightforward, except for the part where we're walking into a nest full of Redcaps."

"That's why we have these." She dug in her pocket, then held up a small black disk. "The sound this emits will paralyze Redcaps. Just switch it on, and you're good to go. Unless the battery dies."

"What is it?"

Vaughn would love a chance to examine one. If Marcus could get Tessa back to the ranch, he wouldn't need to 'nab' it. Maybe he could even use it as a reason to get her to go with him. Somehow, he figured if he offered her a hot meal, a shower, and a soft bed, she'd consider it an insult.

Although, the thought of her in a soft bed...

"It's a sonic bug repeller. You can pick them up in any

hardware store."

"You're kidding." The absurdity of it brought him right back to the moment.

She shrugged. "I don't know how it works and I don't really care. I take the win wherever I can get it." She held the disk out to him. "Sun's up in ten minutes. You in?"

Whatever the Redcap queen was like, Marcus didn't want Tessa facing it alone. After seeing how she lived, he didn't want her doing *anything* alone. No one should have to live like this.

He grabbed the disk and said, "I'm in. Absolutely in."

"You seem really keen on killing these Redcaps. I like that."

She rose and walked over to the front bench seat. Bending over it, she started rummaging around for something. Marcus's hands flexed as he thought about grabbing her and—

"You hungry?" she said.

He froze, not sure how to respond. She turned around with two granola bars in her hand.

She tossed one to him. "Eat up. It might be your last meal."

Marcus looked down at the silvery packet in his hand. She had so little, and she was sharing what she had with him openly. Her weapons, her food, her home. Her lips…

She leaned against the front seats as she ate. "It's a nice change to have someone else going into a fight with me."

"I can imagine."

*Too well.*

She smiled and gave the quick lift to her eyebrows that he was pretty sure accompanied her jokes. "If things go south, all I have to do is outrun you."

He didn't laugh.

If things started to go south, he would kill everything in sight—everything that was trying to hurt her.

She tossed her empty wrapper on one of the benches, then wiped her hands on the back of her jeans.

"Sorry." Her voice was quiet. "I didn't mean to trigger you."

"You didn't."

"Denial, again? Even with the glasses, it's pretty easy to tell when you're pissed."

She turned to look out the open side door of the van. "Blades must be good at denial. It's the only way you can think there's a chance for dwellers and humans to live alongside each other peacefully."

The hairs on the back of his neck rose at the multi-leveled insult. He didn't trust himself to respond. If he opened his mouth, he would growl. She had more to say on the matter anyway.

"You swoop in and put down the big bad dwellers and let the ones you think aren't dangerous go. But if you ever have to watch a dweller take its time and play..."

She wrapped her arms around her middle.

"I've seen them play." Marcus's voice came out rough as memories rose up in him.

His parents ripped to pieces. The bloody mouths of the things that had killed them curled up in smiles as they laughed at his attempts to fight them off. Trying to protect his brother and... wishing his brother had died with their parents. An easier death.

And then Dexter had come in, a sword in each hand.

Marcus remembered silver flashing in the room faster than he could track. Limbs and heads flew from the things that had killed his family. The room had been bathed in a blue glow as they vaporized. And then they were gone.

He shook his head violently, rejecting the images that threatened to overwhelm his control. His skin was prickling, all the hairs on his body standing on end. If Tessa said the wrong thing, Marcus would snap her neck or rip her open. In that moment, he might not even care.

When she finally spoke, her voice kept cutting out until she cleared her throat. "People don't become hunters without a damn good reason. I guess Blades are the same." She turned back toward him. "So what happened? Redcaps kill your brother?"

Marcus inhaled deeply through his nose, trying to maintain control. The last thing he needed was for her to figure out that he hadn't exactly made it out intact when his family was killed. Pressing his fists hard on his knees, the skin of his knuckles felt close to bursting.

"It wasn't Redcaps," he said.

She tensed for a moment, not even breathing. Then the air shifted as she approached him, stopping between his knees with her body close enough for him to feel the crackle of energy between them.

He couldn't look up at her. There was too much rage and pain fighting in him, making him want to change. He needed an outlet, and while he was with her, he wasn't going to get one. Not through violence, anyway.

Not through anything.

He shook his head again, fists tight enough that his nails bit into his palms. It didn't matter how much he wanted her—or how much she seemed to want him. Nothing was going to happen between them without her knowing what he was. And then…

Maybe violence would be on the agenda after all.

Dexter could handle her if it came to that. Marcus would cut and run. If this hunter ended up needing to be put down, he wouldn't be the one to do it.

He held on to his humanity, such as it was, and pressed his fists harder against his thighs. Deep breaths. Eyes on the floor so she couldn't see them. They had to be glowing gold.

When she grabbed his hair, at first he thought she'd seen his eyes—figured out what he was hiding. But she turned his head and crushed it to her stomach, wrapping her arms around his neck. Everywhere they touched,

Marcus could feel her trembling. Her scent thickened, all sweetness vanishing. There was no sense of imminent violence, no hint of arousal. Only a heaviness that seemed to fill the small space with grief.

"What was his name?" she whispered.

*His name…*

The question felt like a knife in his guts. Cold and searing.

Dexter had never bothered to ask. No one had. Just like no one had offered Marcus comfort. And that's what she was doing. She was comforting him.

More than a decade had passed since his family had died. Saying his brother's name felt like calling up a ghost, but he did it anyway.

"Daniel. Danny. I called him Danny."

She stroked Marcus's hair. Her voice was dull when she spoke again.

"My brother's name was Brock. It was a family name. I always made fun of him for it. I couldn't say it right as a kid, so we came up with this inside joke where I kept calling him 'Bock-Bock' even when I was older. He called me 'Chicken.' I miss him every day. Every goddammed day."

Not just giving comfort, then. She was seeking it, too. Marcus wrapped his arms around her waist and pressed his face against her stomach. Warmth radiated up from deep in his belly, killing the chill, and seemed to flow into Tessa's body and back into him. She didn't move away, didn't say anything. She just held him and he held her back.

Forget the idea of sex or fighting side-by-side. This closeness—this connection—was the most amazing thing he had ever experienced. The constant nagging feeling that something was missing subsided as she pressed a kiss to the top of his head, then rested her cheek there. He drew his hand in slow circles on her back and she leaned into him more.

"We can't bring them back," she said. "But we can take out these Redcaps and maybe keep other people from losing their families."

She started to pull away, but Marcus kept his arms tight around her waist. He didn't want to let her go, to let go of that moment. He wanted to kiss her, but he wasn't sure what would happen if he did. She tightened her grip, burrowing her fingers through his hair, and kissed the top of his head again.

"I need you to listen to me carefully, Marcus. My life has to stay simple. No complications. I find a problem, fix it, and move on. I can't settle down. Do you understand?"

He turned his face so she could hear him without seeing his eyes, willing himself to calm further. "I understand that's what you believe. But it doesn't have to be that way."

"It does for me. Now come on. The sun is almost up."

She pushed away from him again. This time, he didn't

fight it.

# Chapter Seven

Blades. They had it made and thought they could afford the luxury of mercy. If Tessa had a soft bed every night and partners watching her back, she might feel a little more understanding herself. She'd have to be sure that never happened. She had to stay strong. Cold and aloof, just like her mother had taught her to be. She couldn't let anyone in.

Unfortunately, Marcus was starting to do more than heat her up. He was starting to pluck at her heartstrings— and that was not okay. She glanced in her rearview mirror. He was still a few yards behind her, following her around the block on that amazing bike of his as they headed for the junkyard.

She would cut him loose right after clearing the nest. Hell, she'd probably blow on out of town afterwards. She kind of wished they could have sex before she left, though. He was gorgeous, and *damn* could he kiss. But she already liked him way too much.

"No entanglements," she murmured. "There's enough under my skin already."

Her wrist started to itch. The little bastards were

wriggling around, excited by all the adrenaline in her system. She should just cut her arm off. But she was more useful with two hands. Plus, she wasn't sure she had the guts.

Maybe 'Chicken' was a better nickname than she thought.

Remembering Brock brought tears to her eyes, blurring her vision for a moment. She wiped them away mercilessly.

This was why she couldn't get close to anyone. She didn't want to remember. Didn't want to feel. She needed to focus to stay alive. If she teared up at the wrong time, it could get her killed.

She pulled into the drive that would lead to the junkyard. Sure enough, the blip on her monitor was straight ahead. Tessa stopped her van and leaned out the window, waiting for Marcus to pull up beside her.

"Park here and get in," she said.

A hunter would have balked, but Marcus didn't hesitate. He killed his engine, slid off his bike, and joined her on the bench seat of her van.

Well, that was one good thing about working with a Blade. He knew how to take orders.

Tessa had paired up with other hunters briefly a few times before. There were always ego clashes. Plus she had to be careful not to let on how much she actually knew about dwellers. Hunters were paranoid by nature and she sure as hell wasn't going to explain her sources. At least working with a Blade, she probably didn't have to worry about him killing her immediately if he found out about her little problem.

Probably.

Marcus was helpful and obedient—at least, when she was letting him help her out. She wondered how that would translate into sex. His kiss had honestly rocked her world, but the rest of the time he was sort of spaced out and moody.

Maybe she wasn't as interested in him as she originally thought. Or maybe she could manage to sleep with him without getting too emotionally invested. Hell, if he was as passive in bed as he was going into a fight, having sex would make him *less* appealing.

Her mind was made up. She didn't care if she was rationalizing—she wanted Marcus and he obviously wanted her. It had been too long since she'd let off that kind of steam.

That cheery thought gave her something to look forward to. Clear the nest, jump Marcus, blow out of town. She could manage that. She rolled up her window and started down the drive again.

"Keep the windows up and the doors locked," she said. "I don't want to find any surprises in here if we have to fall back to the van."

"That doesn't sound encouraging."

"We're clearing a nest. Things don't always go according to plan." Reaching over the back of the seat to the floor behind them, she pulled up her garbage bag full of grass clippings. "You have allergies?"

"No."

"Good. Rub this all over your clothes and skin."

Marcus opened the bag and stared into it for a few seconds. "Seriously?"

"I've yet to meet a dweller who isn't thrown off by it. It's the best way to mask your scent."

He dug into the bag and pulled out one of her tank tops. His raven-wing eyebrows rose.

She shrugged. "I don't get to do laundry often. It kills my scent and keeps me smelling summer-fresh."

He gave a little snort of laughter that made her stomach shiver in a good way. What was she, twelve? Ordering herself to get a grip, she focused on the hunt while he rubbed himself with grass.

Summer couldn't arrive fast enough. She could get a fresh supply and make some money mowing people's lawns. Not many homeowners turned her down when she showed up on the front step in a tank top and short-shorts —as long as she did her reconnaissance and made sure guys opened the door. But that would happen someplace other than Providence. Between oversharing with Marcus and encountering the Blades of Janus for the first time, she was feeling exposed. She needed to leave town as soon as possible.

The gate to the junkyard was open. She tried not to imagine how things had played out—and failed.

The Redcaps must have arrived during the day. Otherwise, the gate would be shut. Everyone at work was toast—or rather steak. Any customers would've suffered the same fate. She hoped they didn't have guard dogs. But junkyards always did. Poor things.

Once the nest was established, the Redcaps would prey on whoever had the bad fortune of picking this junkyard for their salvage needs. Anyone who came to check on missing friends would meet the same fate. If police showed up, the Redcaps would fill in the main entrance and any smaller holes leading to their nest and wait things out, maybe digging other exits if they wanted food. They would eat what meat they needed, and select certain corpses to ride around. She had no idea how they chose.

She wasn't sure which fate was worse—being eaten, or being used as a meat puppet.

*Fucking bugs.*

"You okay?"

Tessa jerked away from the sound of Marcus's voice. She'd forgotten for a moment that he was in the van with her. Damn. She wasn't used to working with someone. That could be tricky in the closeness of the nest. Especially with her wielding a flamethrower.

"Yeah," she said. "Just thinking."

"You look like you're ready to kill something."

"I am. You'd better be, too."

She stopped the van in the middle of a cleared area just outside a small building. Floodlights on tall posts lit the whole place. A lovely way to illuminate the Redcaps' trap.

Crushed cars were stacked all around them like enormous metal bricks. The compactor was to their right. Openings in the walls of cars snaked deeper into the junkyard—clear rivers of space that she could drive down if she was a fucking idiot.

The cars had to be full of Redcaps watching them. The ones riding corpses would be on the ground. The thickest populations would be nearest the entrance to the nest.

Tessa clicked the button on her bug repeller. "Turn yours on."

Marcus nodded and did the same. She crawled over the seat into the back of her van and strapped on the flamethrower. She fastened the grenades to a bandolier she'd made herself, which she swung over one arm and across her chest. The rusty hatchet went into a loop on her belt, and so did the tracker monitor. She handed her bat to Marcus and almost felt bad for the guy. Then she remembered his 'stingray.'

Blades were idiots. What did they think would happen when the Redcaps woke up from being stunned? They'd reflect on their ways and become vegan like her?

"What's the maximum setting on that gun of yours?"

she asked.

"Hard-boiled."

"Good. Crank it—as long as it won't make you run out of juice too fast."

"I won't run out."

"I love a man who can keep going and going." She flashed a smile at him, but he didn't return it.

Maybe he was as nervous as she was. Her stomach was so full of butterflies, she was afraid they'd fly out of her mouth—in the form of vomit.

*Keep moving. Keep fighting.*

Tessa recited her mom's favorite battle mantra as she worked up her nerve for the coming hunt. If her repeller battery died unexpectedly...

*It won't.*

She pulled the door open and stepped out onto the packed dirt surrounding her van. Marcus opened the passenger door and joined her. Nothing grabbed their legs to pull them under. Nothing jumped on their heads from the roof.

She had parked as far away from all of the stacks of cars as she could. The closest object was forty feet in any direction. The junkyard owners must have needed the large empty space to operate the huge crane next to the compactor. Its claw hung high over their heads.

Her heart was pounding so hard, her eardrums throbbed with each beat. She opened the side door of the van and picked up her flamethrower, slipping into its harness. Pointing it at the sky, she pulled the trigger for a test burst. Fire belched forth in a radiant orange cloud—death at her fingertips, upon her command.

Very reassuring. Also, very dangerous.

"Leave the duster," she said.

Marcus hesitated. Maybe he thought it looked cool. Okay, it did, but there was no way she was letting him go into the nest wearing it.

"Redcaps can climb up that thing without you being aware," she said. "It's like you're giving them a ladder to get to your neck. Plus, a lot of things are going to be on fire soon. Do you really want a bunch of flammable fabric flapping around you?"

He didn't say anything, but he turned around and set the bat down inside the van.

As he slid the duster from his shoulders, Tessa immediately noticed two things. His shoulders and back were incredible. Broad at the top, tapering down to a narrow waist and trim hips that she couldn't wait to wrap her legs around and squeeze. His arms weren't overly huge, but they were ripped. And they *had* been ripped. Repeatedly.

That was the second thing. Glimmering in the dim light of dawn, row after row of shiny pale scar tissue covered his arms. Some scars were jagged, some straight lines, some grouped in rows like a cornfield planted with pain.

They continued up under his sleeves with no sign of stopping.

"Holy shit," she breathed.

He didn't respond with words. Instead, he dropped the duster in the van, picked up his bat, then slid the side door shut and slammed the passenger's door. When he turned back to her, there was an unmistakable challenge in his expression.

She wasn't going to ask. She didn't need—didn't *want* —to know anything else that would make her sympathize with him more.

"Let's go." She leveled the flamethrower. "Stay behind me, watch your back, and I'll do my best not to set you on fire."

"I'd appreciate it."

She lifted her tracker monitor and started heading toward the blinking dot that represented the Redcap she had tagged when the hunt began. This was not how she had envisioned things turning out. She didn't have any complaints, though. Yet.

They were headed toward the wall of cars near the compactor. That made sense. The Redcaps would need stable ground to dig through. The cars made great spying spots, but the tunnels the Redcaps lived in could collapse if they dug too close to that much weight.

As she suspected, the entrance to the nest was in a stretch of clear ground right behind the compactor. It was wide open—tall enough for them to walk straight down into the earth without having to do more than duck their heads.

"What's wrong?" Marcus came up behind her when she paused.

"I don't know. I've never seen a nest with the door open like this before. I expected there to be a car or something blocking it."

"I thought these things are small."

"Redcaps are small," she said. "Their queens are big."

"How big?"

"About the size of an SUV."

"Seriously?"

Tessa laughed. "And you thought grenades were overkill."

"I will never doubt you again."

She glanced over her shoulder at him, her breath catching at his smile. Damn, she could get used to this.

The floodlights were bright, reflecting off his glasses, but she could still see his eyes glittering strangely. That plus the scars…

No way she was about to walk straight into a Redcap nest with a werewolf watching her back. She suppressed a shiver. Her life was weird, but that would just be crazy.

Marcus was a Blade. That was strange enough.

She gave herself a mental kick, remembering to focus. There had been too many surprises already.

"The queen shouldn't be a problem," she said. "They pretty much just sit at the bottom of the nest spitting out Redcaps. But if our repeller batteries die, its brood will come at us from all sides. Redcaps like to drop down from above most of all. Sometimes, they can fall on you when the sound immobilizes them. If that happens—and I can't stress this enough—do not shoot, hit, or stab me."

"Got it." His cocky smirk returned at last.

She felt herself grinning back at him, even though she tried not to. "Stop it with the sexy smile. It's distracting."

His smile only broadened. "I have to deal with your gorgeous face, rack, and ass. I think you can handle my smile."

Her brain started spinning in happy circles like a dog chasing its tail. He thought she was gorgeous. It shouldn't matter as much as it did. Dammit, she shouldn't care.

"No distractions." She managed to force her smile back to a scowl and spoke more harshly than she intended, but she was mad at herself. If he thought she was yelling at him, so much the better.

She didn't want him to like her. Their situation was already too complicated.

Every nest she cleared, every threat she neutralized, she did while being fine with dying in the process. She was a dead hunter walking. It was part of her edge. But Marcus deserved to keep living his cushy Blade existence. Especially with the badges of honor crisscrossing his arms.

She had to get him out of this alive.

"Into the rabbit hole, then." Tessa pointed her flamethrower at the opening to the nest and did a quick burst to fry anything just inside.

The recent rain had made the ground wet and slick near the opening to the nest. She checked her bug repeller to make sure it was still on. The tiny green light cast a steady and reassuring glow. The flickering ball of orange from the ignition flame at the end of her flamethrower was even better.

She was used to operating in near darkness. The light from the rising sun wouldn't make it far into the nest. She hoped Marcus wasn't depending on some fancy flashlights to keep from tripping.

Redcaps weren't very creative, at least. The trail led straight down at a forty-five degree angle. Eventually, it would widen into the queen's lair. What worried Tessa most were the smaller holes that shot out from the main tunnel—service corridors for the enterprising Redcaps looking after their queen.

She let out another burst from her flamethrower. Only one Redcap fell from above, its tendrils flaming as it shriveled up on itself before that eerie blue light consumed it. So far, so good.

"You okay back there?" she said.

"Yeah."

Marcus sounded a little tense, but who wouldn't be?

She crept forward, clearing the tunnel with a burst of fire, watching a few Redcaps burn, then vaporize. She didn't look back over her shoulder. She didn't feel the need. It was weird to almost-trust someone again.

"This nest is deep," she said. "We should have reached the queen by now."

"Tessa, look."

A few steps further, and the tunnel started to widen. The flamethrower must have been messing with her eyes for him to see it before her.

"Finally." She ran the flamethrower over the ceiling, fire licking every surface as if claiming the territory for its own. "Prepare yourself. These things are butt ugly."

She stepped forward into the lair, sweeping her flamethrower over the space. A dozen Redcaps skittered against the far walls, just out of range of the bug repellers. The fire took care of them, along with the dozen more frozen in place at her feet and that fell from the ceiling and walls.

"This is wrong," she said.

"No kidding. There are so many of them…"

"No. There are barely any here. And where's the queen?"

Tessa's heart dropped through her stomach. In the same instant, her body felt electrified with adrenaline. The ground beneath them started to shake and a rumbling noise echoed down the tunnel behind them.

"Oh shit!" She turned around, hitting Marcus with her arm to keep him away from the flame that was already arcing from her flamethrower.

The fire flew up the tunnel, illuminating the enormous body of the queen galloping toward them on hundreds of dagger-like legs.

It looked like a giant lawn grub, white and pasty, but with sharp spikes sticking out all over its body, raking the sides of the tunnel and causing clods of dirt to rain down around it. Its face was pocked with different sized black eyes in no particular pattern.

Tessa had never seen one this close or this mobile. What the hell was going on?

The queen let out a screech and reared back when the fire reached its face, knocking more soil and rocks into the tunnel as it hit the roof with its head.

"Shit, shit, shit!" Tessa was not going to be buried alive. She was not going to die under the ground.

She let out a more controlled burst of fire, pointing it at the earth in front of the queen. The queen let out another ear-piercing screech. Arms ending in pincers extended from its mouth and clacked at them.

"Back up, bitch!" Tessa took a step forward, keeping the fire going—a low and steady stream that was eating up the fuel way too quickly.

She couldn't think of that right now. She had to focus all her energy on willing this *thing* to back the fuck up.

Slowly, the queen undulated her body backwards. It was still moving its head from side to side, searching for a way to get at them.

"Come on. Come on!" Tessa aimed the flamethrower higher and let the fire hit the queen's face. It screeched once more, then started backing up more quickly. Tessa pressed her advantage.

"Are the repellers still working?" she said.

She didn't dare look. She had to keep her eyes on the queen.

"Yes."

Thank God Marcus was there.

"Take the grenades." She managed to get the bandolier over her head and passed it to him. "When we get to the surface, we're going to need to box it in someplace so we can use those to best effect. If that doesn't work, we need to get the queen to my van. It's rigged to blow and should take out anything within fifty feet when it goes off. There's a controller wired into my wristband. If both of those plans fail, run to your bike and get the hell out of here."

"What about you?"

"We're so far past plan B in these scenarios, I'll already be dead. I'm a hunter. I'm okay with that."

"I'm not."

The queen was still steadily backing up, though it didn't like the situation one bit. Every grudging screech marked another foot closer to fresh air and a chance to go out the way Tessa intended. Preferably alone.

Sunlight seeped into the tunnel around the queen as they reached the surface. The flamethrower's tank was already noticeably lighter from burning through its fuel.

Every time Tessa had encountered them before, Redcap queens were in some kind of trance, spitting out their little spider-demon spawn. Chucking a couple of grenades at a stationary target in an enclosed space would do the trick, especially after a good spray-down with the flamethrower.

Her heart pounded even faster as she glanced around at the level, open area surrounding them. Grenades weren't going to work. She had a clear path to her van. She just had to make sure the queen followed her and was close enough when Tessa set off the explosives.

"Marcus, you need to run. Get to your bike. Now."

Marcus didn't answer. Tessa dared to look over her shoulder.

He was already gone.

A stabbing pain radiated through her chest. Not the familiar physical kind, but one from much longer ago. From when she'd lost her family and been 'taken in' by the thing that killed them.

Edgar.

She'd lost everything she loved, everything she knew of the world, and been thrown into a nightmare—alone.

*This is not the time.*

Marcus was a Blade, and Blades were sheltered

cowards. Maybe when he saw the queen illuminated by the sun, he'd lost his nerve and bolted. She had wanted him to run, anyway. To save himself. But to have him leave like this, so quickly…

*He could have at least left the grenades.*

Fuck it. She didn't need grenades to take this thing out. All she needed was her van. Tessa hit the queen with a brief burst of fire.

The flamethrower sputtered and went out.

Her eyes threatened to fill with tears. She wanted to scream at the injustice of it. There was *nothing* she could count on in the world. Nothing but herself. And she could count on herself to go out on her own terms.

She was going to take this monster—and all the wriggling alien parasites in her arm—along with her. She wouldn't become like the dweller who had killed her family and infected her.

Tessa shrugged out of the harness and dropped the flamethrower. It would only slow her down now. She pulled the knife from her right boot and held it in front of her face.

"Okay, ugly. It's just you and me."

The queen paused for an instant, then reared back and let out a howl that rattled Tessa's teeth. It fell forward, legs gouging furrows in the earth. Tessa tucked her body and rolled to the side, lashing out with her knife as she came up in a crouch next to the thing. Gray ichor rained from its body where her knife landed.

That seemed to make it really mad. The queen turned faster than Tessa would have thought possible. She ducked, choosing to keep her balance over striking it again. She still didn't understand why it was mobile.

She turned toward her van and managed two running steps before something wrapped around her ankle, tripping her. She landed hard, teeth clacking together as her chin hit the packed dirt. The iron-sharp taste of blood filled her mouth.

Rolling to her back, she saw a Redcap on her leg, its tendrils twined around her calf. She kicked at it, crushing it between her boot and the ground. The queen had reared up over her again, ready to crash down and do the same to Tessa. She spun out of the way right as its chalky girth slammed into the earth.

Lying on her stomach, Tessa had a perfect view of the ground erupting in front of her. Dozens of little holes were appearing as Redcaps crawled to the surface to help their queen. She glanced at her bug repeller.

No green light.

No light at all.

# Chapter Eight

*"What are you doing?"*

Marcus had never felt his dweller so worked up, never fought against a change so hard. His guts were cramping, skin itching as it tried to take over. He wanted to be at Tessa's side, fighting that... thing. But if he let himself change and ran back to her, she'd be as good as dead.

The queen was huge. It had scores of those little head-spiders running around protecting it. Two grenades couldn't kill *him*. He doubted they would work on something so massive, and Tessa's flamethrower had started stuttering as it ate through its fuel. If he tried to kill the queen himself, all the Redcaps running around would have time to cut Tessa to pieces. The high whine of their bug repellers had gone silent. They needed another solution.

*"You fool. Stop thinking and change."*

Stop thinking. Stop fighting. Let the beast inside take over. The problem was, if Marcus let go of his control, he didn't know if he would get it back. He didn't know if he'd save Tessa or kill her.

He glanced in the section of his glasses that would let

Vaughn know Marcus needed help, holding his gaze there to get his partner's attention. While he did, he ran toward the junkyard's crane. Its claw hovered thirty feet above the ground, but looked big and heavy enough to crush the Redcap queen.

"Come on, Vaughn. Where are you?"

Knowing Tessa's attention was focused on the queen, Marcus didn't hold back as he ran—or when he leapt the last twenty feet to land on the high door to the cabin that controlled the crane. He dared a glance over his shoulder and saw Tessa squaring off against the queen… with a knife.

The packed soil rippled as Redcaps dug their way to the surface, breaking through to scurry toward Tessa. A Redcap had grabbed her leg and she was on the ground. She kicked it hard enough to crush it, then leapt to her feet.

Marcus growled, felt his fingertips start to split. Dark hair covered the backs of his hands.

"Marcus, what are you doing?"

The voice that barked in his ear wasn't Vaughn. It was Porter. Somehow, Marcus could always sense which twin he was talking to.

"Getting a better weapon," Marcus said.

"*You* are the weapon. You need to protect her."

Dexter would take care of Marcus, if he couldn't bring himself back under control. But they didn't know how far gone he was. They didn't know he was a threat to Tessa, too.

There was no time to explain. Instead, he said, "I can't do damage quickly enough to take out the queen before its brood kills Tessa. If you want her alive, give me Vaughn."

Marcus tore the crane's door off its hinges and tossed it away. It landed on a stack of nearby cars with a crash. He would have thrown it at the queen, but Tessa was engaging it too closely. He sat at the controls, baffled by the array of buttons and levers before him, then glanced out the front window.

Tessa was dancing in and out among the Redcaps and their queen, kicking the smaller opponents away and slashing at the queen. She would be overrun any moment.

His dweller howled.

The only chance she had was for Marcus to control himself. He closed his eyes briefly, took deep breaths, and pushed back against the change as hard as he could. His skin still prickled, but his fingertips stopped burning.

Vaughn finally spoke in Marcus's earpiece, her voice shrill with panic. "What *is* that?"

Marcus ignored Vaughn's question. "How do I control the crane? I need to drop the claw on the queen."

"Queen?"

"The giant lawn grub thing," Marcus roared. "Help me kill it before it kills Tessa."

"Right."

He heard a hail of keystrokes as Vaughn sprang into

action. The engine of the crane rumbled to life.

"How the hell do you do that?" Marcus said.

"A magician never reveals her secrets."

He didn't care how Vaughn did it. Marcus just wanted to kill the things that were after Tessa. Vaughn talked Marcus through the controls, helping him figure out how to position the claw.

His attention snapped back to Tessa. She was on the ground again. The queen lurched up, trying to crush her. Tessa rolled out of the way before the queen threw its weight on the ground, then launched herself to her feet, sprinting past the queen and leaping over the seeking tendrils of the Redcaps. When she reached her van, she vaulted up the side, pulling herself to the roof.

The queen rose, its face brushing the ground as if searching for Tessa's flattened body. It didn't seem like it could see very well, even with all those eyes.

It reared up again, then started that earth-shaking gallop toward the van. Redcaps scurried around it, trying to stay out of the way of its piercing legs and crushing body. The queen plowed right over them.

Tessa unzipped her jacket and let it slide from her arms to land in a heap on the roof of the van. She lifted her right arm, and started fidgeting with her wristband.

"Shit!" Marcus said. "She's luring the queen to the van so she can blow it up."

"The crane's in position," Vaughn said. "Hit the big red

button and it'll drop the claw to the ground."

Marcus slammed his palm on the button, holding his breath. Time seemed to pause as he could only register his heartbeat pounding in his ears.

Then the claw fell.

One of its three prongs impaled the queen through the back. The other two crushed it.

The queen shrieked briefly until a sudden loud pop brought an end to its existence. Gray ichor sprayed in a circle around it as its body burst from the pressure.

The Redcaps that had been scurrying around all let out a keening wail, then flipped over on their backs, legs writhing in the air. In seconds, they started vanishing in little flashes of light.

The queen's body took longer. The blue glow spread over it, devouring its still form. Even the ichor around it vaporized.

Tessa stared at the claw with her mouth hanging open. Her gaze traveled up the crane, then back down to the cabin, until it locked with his. She snapped her mouth shut.

"That is *not* a class-C dweller," Vaughn said.

"That was too close." Porter's tone was admonishing.

Vaughn snorted. "Are you kidding? I've seen Marcus's close calls. This wasn't even in his zip code."

"I'm not talking about him," Porter said.

"Right, because who gives a shit about the only Guard

we have in Providence when there's a hot new hunter in town," Vaughn snapped.

Porter ignored the dig. "Bring her in, Marcus. That's an order."

"Understood." He was already planning on it.

Marcus leapt out of the crane's cabin. He pulled out his earpiece and tossed it in front of him. Porter's voice kept calling his name right up to the moment Marcus stepped on the earpiece and crushed it into the ground.

Marcus reached up to the transmitter in his glasses and pinched the spot until he heard a *crack*. The screen overlaid on the lenses flickered briefly, then vanished. He needed some privacy. He needed Tessa to himself.

Tessa climbed down from her van. She staggered back a few paces as she hit the ground. Was she hurt?

Rage boiled up in him and he wished he could kill the queen all over again. But then Tessa turned to look at him and the anger vanished.

She was smiling. More than smiling, she was laughing. Lips spread wide, eyes crinkled at the edges, and the most musical sound he had ever heard soared out of her chest. She ran toward him and leapt the last few feet between them, hitting him hard and wrapping her arms around his neck and her legs around his waist.

Those legs…

"Did you see that?" Her voice was loud enough to hurt so close to his ear, but he didn't care.

"I had a pretty good view."

"That was incredible."

She laughed again and he felt the strangest lightness in his chest. It wasn't from growling. He was laughing, too. And that was a miracle in itself. His face hurt from his smile.

Until she kissed him.

He should have seen it coming, but didn't. She tightened her grip, pulled his head closer, and planted her lips on his.

Heat flooded through his body—much more pleasurable than a change. He wanted to pull her hair free of its bindings and bury his hands in it, to breathe her scent into his body.

Her tongue slid into his mouth, molten and wet. Marcus pulled her closer. His fingers curled against her back. It would be too easy for him to sprout claws, to dig into her flesh, to bury himself in her in every way he could.

Panting, he pulled his lips from hers. She didn't let him get far, biting his jaw and then sucking on his neck. It felt so good. Too fucking good.

He let out a rumbling growl before he could stop himself, but managed to turn it into words. "This is a bad idea."

"I know," she said. "I don't care."

She tightened her legs, drawing his dick against her hips and making it much harder for him to resist. She ground herself against him, her teeth scraping the skin of his neck. He wanted to do the same, but held back. He pressed her against the door of her van instead, thrusting against her.

Wait, when had he walked them over to the van? He froze, struggling against the urge to tear off her clothes. He could have them both naked in seconds, could be buried deep in her heat.

Dammit, he wouldn't lose control.

Tessa let her legs slide down his thighs, but she didn't stop kissing his neck. He heard something rattle and realized it was her keys. Finally, she shifted away from him, unlocking the side door of her van and opening it. He alternated between flexing and curling his fingers to give them something to do other than grabbing her again.

"Tessa, there's something I have to tell you before—"

She pulled her tank top over her head. The creamy skin of her back caught the sunlight, reflecting it back at him. She pulled her hair from its bun, letting it fall down past her shoulder blades. With that devilish smirk in place, she turned to face him. Her breasts were perfect. Full and round, peaked with pale pink nipples that tightened as he watched. He heard himself grunt.

It was better than growling.

She sat down in the open space on the floor of her van and untied her boots, tossing them over her shoulder. Then she jumped back up and stood next to him. "Were you saying something?"

He was. Something important. He put his hands over his eyes, almost crushing the damn glasses against his face as he tried to block out the sight of her. That did nothing for his ears. He heard the zipper on her jeans, and the soft sigh of the fabric sliding over her legs.

Where the hell was his dweller when he needed it? The irritating voice in his mind would help distract him from the temptation Tessa presented—remind him of why he needed to resist.

But he didn't need a reminder. He *knew* what he had to do.

"Tessa, stop."

"Okay."

He let out a huge breath, relaxing a tiny bit. He would tell her what he was and she'd lose interest immediately. She might not even attack him, since she was probably completely naked.

He groaned at the thought. She was standing right next to him—bare—and she wanted him. But only because she didn't know what he was.

He turned around and sat in the open door to the van, hoping to keep her blocked off from her weapons. The last thing he wanted was to have to fight her.

"We need to talk." His hands were still pressed tight over his eyes, his senses saturated with her. He didn't realize what she was doing until he felt her hands on his ankles, lifting his legs and shoving him back into the van.

Damn, she was stronger than he thought. She hopped in next to him and slid the door shut.

"We can talk later," she said.

Her lips were on his again in a flash, tongue demanding entry to his mouth. He let her in, groaning at the taste of her. Almonds and brown sugar.

His hands shook as he ran them along the smooth skin of her back. She was so soft. His senses sparked to life as she pressed her body against his. Breathing deep, he filled his lungs with her scent. Floral, like night-blooming jasmine.

He tried to memorize every nuance of her. Lean, muscled flesh balanced with softness and warmth. He prayed he would have a chance to feel her this way again. If she would listen to him—give him a chance—she could have a real life, a real home.

Her kisses moved to his neck, teeth gently raking his skin. That was too much. Too tempting.

He wanted to bite her back.

He grabbed her arms and pulled them away, rolling over so he was on top of her and pinning her arms above her head. He kept his head down. His eyes had to be glowing golden. He didn't want her to find out about him that way. He struggled to speak, every breath filling him with her scent, making it harder to resist.

"Okay, if we're going to play this way, we need to set

up some ground rules," she said. "My safe word is 'barbecue.' And you need to be very careful of my right arm. The wristband needs to stay in place."

He hadn't even realized it was still on. It was the one piece of clothing she had spared.

He focused on the mystery of that while he panted, trying to find enough breath to form a longer sentence than, "Why?"

"Because it contains a heart monitor that's tied in to the explosives I have rigged up in my van. If my wristband is removed—or I'm killed—they'll go off."

Marcus froze. Was she serious?

*Shit.*

She'd been ready to die a moment ago. If she was as unhinged as most hunters he'd met and found out what he was, she might decide taking him out would be worth sacrificing herself.

He gripped her wrists more tightly, careful of the wristband. "I'm going to tell you something that you won't like. Please hear me out and really think about what we've been through together before making any judgments about me."

"What we've been through?" She snorted, but then her smile faded. "You're not married, are you? Because that's a dealbreaker."

"No, I'm not married. But I can't do this without you knowing more about me."

She let out a frustrated sigh. "I don't want to know your life story. I want to have a little fun."

"It's more complicated than that."

"It doesn't have to be. Look, I'm not telling you everything about me, either. And there's some seriously fucked-up shit you probably would want to know. But I can swear to you that it's safe to have sex with me—no risk of babies or diseases or… anything like that."

The way she had paused and her body tensed made Marcus wonder what she was keeping from him. For a brief moment, he entertained the absurd notion that she was a dweller, too. But there was no way she could be colonized without him knowing.

"I won't even be in town afterwards," she said, "so you don't have to worry about me getting clingy."

"I *want* you in town."

"We don't always get what we want." There was a bitter cast to her words. She let out a puff of breath and shoved against him. "Like now. Get off me."

A shiver traveled up his spine that had nothing to do with her warmth beneath him. He looked toward the front windshield and took a deep breath through his nose. The windows were sealed and the open bag of cut grass interfered with his sense of smell. But he could feel something. A vibration coming up from the wheels, from the earth.

"Do you feel that?" he said.

"It's a little late to try to rekindle the mood."

"Shh."

Something hit the bottom of the van hard enough that the whole thing was airborne for a moment before crashing back to the ground. Marcus grabbed Tessa, wrapping one arm around her as he used his other limbs to brace himself against the ceiling, floor, and side-door.

Another crashing impact came from below, knocking them into the air. This time, the van toppled onto its side when it fell. The window cracked beneath his foot as he regained his balance.

He held Tessa off the ground for about two seconds before she started struggling, trying to get to the compartment that held her weapons.

"Where's the bat I gave you?" she yelled.

"Outside on the ground. Along with the grenades." He'd dropped them when he was running toward the crane.

She handed him a knife and grabbed one for herself. "We have to go out through the driver's door. The side doors are pinned and the back is welded shut."

She was already headed toward the front of the van when something crashed into the windshield. Glass exploded toward them.

Marcus grabbed her, trying to pull her behind him. He wasn't fast enough. The metallic scent of her blood blossomed in the air. Just a trace—letting him know she wasn't badly wounded. Human blood still tested his control, and he'd already fought off so many changes.

His dweller chose that moment to speak up. *"Fool. She's yours. Fight for her."*

*"Thanks for joining us, fuckhead."*

Marcus looked back over his shoulder at the thing that had crashed partway through the windshield. It was too big to fit into the van and seemed to have its head stuck.

It was shaped roughly like the Redcap queen, but was at least twice its size. Instead of being white, it was a sickly shade of purple. A broad streak of red ran down its back. Its head was bright orange, and covered with eyes just like the queen's had been. The middle of what passed for its face was taken up by a huge mouth filled with thin arms with pincers on the ends, like the mouths of the smaller Redcaps.

"What the fuck!" Tessa's voice was filled with panic.

Marcus glanced over to see her eyes wide and her mouth hanging open. "You don't know what it is?"

"I don't know everything about dwellers," she said. "These things are fucking aliens."

"You know *that?*"

"Yeah." She glanced at him briefly. "Wait, you know that, too?"

Whatever it was, the thing screeched, claws clacking as it tried to reach them. The entire van shook.

"I'm guessing it's a Redcap king," Marcus said.

"I didn't know there was such a thing."

*Shit.*

So much for having her expertise to help them out.

The king banged its head into the ceiling of the van, bending the metal and giving it more space to move—to get closer to them. Marcus swung his knife at the arms reaching from the thing's mouth. Tessa backed away, pulling him with her.

"That's not going to work," she said. "We can't escape."

He dared to look over at her. No smirk. No bravado. She dropped her knife, then grabbed his face and kissed him briefly.

"I'm sorry it has to end like this," she said. "But it'll be quick. I promise."

She reached for her wristband and started to pull it off.

# Chapter Nine

Tessa really wished she had been wrong about Marcus in the sack. She hadn't even managed to get him naked. It would have been nice to go out on a happy endorphin rush. Instead her body was flooded with adrenaline and other fear chemicals. It would make her more delicious, according to the dwellers she had been forced to talk to.

This Redcap fuck wasn't eating anybody.

*Guess it's today after all.*

She started to pull off her wristband, but Marcus grabbed her hand.

"What are you doing?" she asked.

"Stopping you from blowing up the van."

"There's no getting out of this, Blade. You knew the risks you signed up for. At least this way we can take the Redcap king with us."

And all of their bodies would be incinerated. Including the alien parasites wriggling like crazy in her arm.

"I'm not giving up," he said.

Optimistic idiot. Her heaviest gauge shotgun wouldn't slow this thing down, even if she could reach more of her weapons.

The van lurched side to side as the king shook itself. The sound of rending metal blended with its intermittent screeches. Her head was pounding.

*Fuck this.*

Nobody dictated how Tessa went out. Nobody but *her*. And she sure as hell wasn't sticking around to become a meat puppet.

She tried to pull free from Marcus's grip, but he didn't budge. He dropped his knife as he crushed her against his chest, pinning her arms at her sides. Damn, he was strong. He turned away from the Redcap king, picked her up, and... kicked out the back door. Just lifted his foot and kicked it out.

The seams she had painstakingly welded shut popped like cheap plastic, and the heavy metal door went flying at least a dozen feet away. With the van lying on its side, all he had to do was dart through the small opening that created, Tessa tucked snuggly at his side.

The scenery blurred as he ran impossibly fast toward a stack of compacted cars. He ducked behind them and set her on her feet. He wasn't short of breath, hadn't broken a sweat while carrying her as he ran flat-out. She hadn't slowed him down a bit.

Tessa had seen and been through so much. The last few minutes, though... they were testing her sanity. She let out a brief laugh, then turned back to her van. She could see it through the cracks between two of the cars.

The Redcap king could sense that they had moved. From the outside, it was even uglier—and bigger. It lurched back, lifting the van from the ground momentarily.

"Tessa."

She looked back at Marcus, no longer sure where she faced the greatest threat. Until he grabbed her wristband and tore it off.

"No!" Her scream was drowned out in a deafening explosion.

Heat and light blasted through the gaps in the stack of cars in front of them. She barely noticed. The wriggling little maggots waking up in her flesh held her full attention.

She grabbed her arm just above where the wristband had ended, wrapping her fingers all the way around and pinching tight. Marcus was holding her against his chest. He had stepped between her and the blast. As if that would protect her from the real danger.

"Put it back on!" She barely recognized her own voice —a shrill shriek.

"What?"

"The wristband! Put it back!"

She didn't dare let go of her arm for a second. If she did, the parasites would spread and multiply, infesting her, devouring her, *remaking* her in their image. It only took one escaping further into her body.

She wasn't ready to become a Hive Mother. She never

would be. And Marcus had just destroyed her exit strategy.

He glanced at her arm, his eyes widening as he saw the movement beneath her skin, the crescent scar from the Hive Father's bite.

"What the hell is that?" he said.

"Put the fucking wristband back on or they'll spread."

Finally, he seemed to understand the danger she was in. He grabbed the small black band and stretched the elastic, pulling it up over her forearm. It was tight enough that he had to tug it into place. After a few seconds, the maddening wriggling slowed, then stopped.

Her stomach was in knots. She took a few deep breaths before carefully letting go of her arm, watching for movement—for any sign that they had escaped into her body or hand. Her skin remained smooth.

She turned away from Marcus and threw up on the ground.

He had the stones to come up behind her and rub her back. She wanted to punch him, to kick him, to *kill* him. But there was no way.

No way she could take down *a werewolf.*

She lurched away from his touch. It reminded her that she was naked. Naked, homeless, weaponless, and stuck in a junkyard with this... Blade?

Another high-pitched laugh escaped her. "I can't believe I made out with a werewolf."

His brow lowered and his lips twitched away from his

teeth. Shit, this was unbelievable.

"You made out with the guy who helped you clear a Redcap nest and saved you from that queen—*and* king. It shouldn't matter what else I am."

"Seriously? You think that's enough to make up for—"

"For what? Being a dweller? I'm one of the Blades of Janus. A Guard. I use the strength and speed being colonized gives me to help protect people instead of preying on them. Like I helped you."

"Don't paint yourself as some saint. You know damned well you should have told me before we started anything."

"I was trying to tell you, but *you* kept kissing *me*."

"My mistake. I sure as hell wouldn't have if I'd known you're infected."

He actually looked hurt for a moment. Then he narrowed his eyes and growled. "We say 'colonized.' And what the hell are those little pets in your arm?"

"Fuck you."

"I didn't think you were interested."

Yeah, she was going to kill him. She just had to figure out how.

She knew it was safe for her to have sex with people. Ever since Kyle and all of his tests. He'd been highly motivated to make sure they could have sex safely. Too bad he hadn't been so cautious in the lab while extracting one of the dwellers from her arm.

*"Please, Tess. I don't feel any different,"* he'd said. *"It's*

*still me."*

She had no idea how many parasites the Hive Father had injected into her body through his bite. She only knew that the tourniquet she had put on right after it happened had stopped their spread. And that she had one less now— since she had accidentally infected Kyle.

She shook her head, pushing away the memory. Running from it. Always running.

Now she had no weapons, no shelter, and no clothes aside from her wristband. This Blade was going to pay.

"Look, I'm sorry," he said. "I should have stopped you right away and told you. I lost control."

"And how many people have paid the price when you *lost control* in the past?"

His jaw tightened and he shook his head. "It's never happened."

She let out a laugh. "I don't believe you."

There was no way he didn't have a body count.

"Believe what you want," he said. "You're the first person I've even kissed."

She laughed again. Wait, what was he talking about?

"I meant victims you've killed," she said. "I couldn't care less how many notches you have on your bedpost." Even if there weren't... any?

He took a step toward her, shoulders rising and hands curled into fists. It was a posture meant to intimidate her. It should have scared the crap out of her. But for some reason, she wasn't afraid of him.

Maybe because he actually *had* put on the brakes. He could have had sex with her easily. Hell, all he would've had to do was lie back and enjoy himself while she took care of the particulars. But he had stopped her so he could tell her what he was, knowing it would royally piss her off and ruin his chance at them having sex.

Which, apparently, he had never had before.

*What the hell?*

"I only kill when I have to," he said. "Only threats."

"Let me get this straight. You're a virgin Blade who also happens to be a werewolf, but you're able to control your dweller nature enough that you never go on killing sprees."

"I guess so."

She snorted. "Is the tooth fairy real, too? Wait, don't tell me. She's actually in charge of the Blades of Janus."

He didn't respond, so she prodded him more.

"What about your pack? Are all the Blades in this town werewolves?"

That thought did frighten her. Dealing with Marcus on his own… she could almost believe him. A werewolf who used his power to make the world safer seemed like something out of a storybook. But the rest of his pack might not be so restrained.

If Marcus was his pack's Omega, that submissive role could be enabling him to control his urges. Most of them, anyway. Her lips still tingled from kissing him.

She didn't think the night could get any weirder. Then it did.

"I don't have a pack," he said.

She laughed.

"There is no such thing as a werewolf without a pack." Not a sane one, anyway. Maybe it had only just happened. "How old were you when you were *colonized?*"

"Sixteen."

A year younger than she'd been when her 'foster-father' had infected her. Or tried to, anyway.

Marcus should be nuts. Insane or dead. Werewolves couldn't function without a pack. They sure as hell couldn't control themselves as well as Marcus did.

She'd met several werewolves in her life—before she started hunting on her own. Edgar had introduced her to all sorts of dwellers while he was playing house with her.

"If we're going to stand around here talking, could you please at least put my shirt on?" He pulled his shirt over his head and held it out to her.

She couldn't bring herself to take it. She was too busy staring at his chest. At his scars.

The ones on his arms were impressive. The ones on his body…

He had been cut to ribbons.

Mauled, bitten, clawed. Not an inch of his skin was unmarked. It had to have happened when he was first attacked—when he was infected. Any injuries after that would have healed without leaving a mark. But to have so many…

"Shit," she said. "You're an alpha."

"I'm a what?"

Her heart started to pound. Her throat was so tight, she could barely swallow. She glanced at his eyes. They were gleaming gold. The glasses couldn't mask it anymore.

*Don't challenge him.* She dropped her gaze to the ground.

An alpha. That changed things. Killing him would be even harder, on multiple levels.

Werewolves toyed with their kills. The pack would… entertain themselves with it. If their prey fought back hard enough, the human might gain a sort of respect among the pack. Sometimes, they would try to infect their victim instead of killing them.

Most of the time, packs only brought in children. Edgar had explained that adult humans were too set in their ways and often insisted on fighting to the death when their families had already been slain or were threatened.

At sixteen, Marcus would have been considered too old to adapt by most pack's standards. If his scars were any indication of how hard he'd fought, they could have considered him a prize worth the risk.

Knowing that he didn't have a pack… That choice could have blown up in their faces. Maybe he had somehow killed them all.

Damn. She almost didn't want to kill him.

Almost.

She finally took his shirt and put it on, her thoughts spinning. Alphas led their packs. If they were capable of controlling the werewolves under them, why not themselves?

But Marcus didn't have a pack. He had the Blades. Maybe he was their leader?

"This place is remote, but someone had to have heard that explosion," Marcus said. "The cops will be here—"

He jerked his head to the side, then turned around, stepping closer and sort of herding her behind him. If only she had a weapon. She wouldn't get a better chance to kill him.

God, his back was covered in scars, too.

Against her better judgment, she asked, "What is it?"

Instead of answering, he wheeled around and lunged at her. He caught her below the ribs, keeping his forward momentum so that she fell over his back. She kicked at him, trying to get him to put her down.

If the cops found her there, she could talk her way out of the situation. Say she'd been abducted or something. But if he took her to his den—or the Blades of Janus—she had no idea what would happen.

Pounding on him did nothing. She bounced against his bare skin, exhausted from struggling. The ground blurred beneath them as he ran at inhuman speeds. Blurred and…

Holes were appearing all around them as *more Redcaps* tunneled to the surface.

"What the fuck?" She stopped trying to get away and instead clung to his back.

There were dozens of them. Even more than before. If he dropped her, she was dead. She'd be torn to pieces—or worse.

Her brain presented a morbid scenario. What would happen if a Redcap tried to ride her body while it was infested with Edgar's spawn? She had no intention of finding out, and her best bet was to stick with the werewolf.

They had to be nearing his bike. But it wouldn't matter if they reached it. The Redcaps would overrun them the moment they stopped. She felt Marcus's muscles coil beneath her as he crouched, and then the ground fell away as he jumped incredibly high. Thankfully, her stomach was already empty, or she would have lost whatever was in it then.

There was no way she would survive their landing. She closed her eyes tight, knowing the impact of the fall would kill her. Except they didn't fall. She felt him land on… something. He shifted his weight and sat on the 'something' floating in the air, then pulled her down the front of his body. She kept her legs tight around his waist and her arms around his neck.

"I actually do need to breathe," he said. His voice was a little strained.

Tessa loosened her grip on his neck a little and forced her eyes open. The ground was so far below. She leaned into him, holding him tighter.

"Relax," he said. "It's okay."

Her brain was trying to figure out what was going on. Soft blue light illuminated the vehicle they were sitting on. Marcus's motorcycle?

"What the hell is this thing?" She craned her neck to look around at it.

Spinning blue disks flanked each wheel, two in the front and two in the back, all of them parallel to the ground far below. They made a kind of *whomp-whomp* noise. The lines of blue that she had noticed before were shining bright, pulses of light illuminating streaks all over the thing. It was beautiful and impossible.

*Like Marcus.*

She groaned inwardly at the ridiculous thought, even though it was kind of true. He was holding her gently, stroking her back as she calmed herself down.

"Welcome aboard," the bike said, in a light, feminine voice.

"Oh my God." Tessa ratcheted right back up. "Is this some kind of AI robot hoverbike thing?"

Marcus laughed. "No, that's Vaughn—the partner who's been talking in my ear. She's just using the bike's comm system."

"AI robot…" Vaughn said.

Marcus scowled at his bike. "Don't get any ideas."

"Hmph," Vaughn said. "Well, I thought you'd like to know that the cavalry has arrived. I detected the movement beneath the ground, and activated the hover function of your bike remotely to help you out. The police will be on the scene in five minutes, so you don't have long to do any necessary clean up."

Another hoverbike flew past them, on what looked like a direct collision course for the ground. A few feet before impact, the disks folded back onto the bike's wheels and it landed, jerking and bouncing as the rider—pilot?—regained control.

He was clad entirely in black. Jacket, pants, helmet, just like Marcus had been dressed, except this guy's jacket was a more sensible length for riding motorcycles.

It was a good thing, too, because the moment he had a handle on his bike, flames shot out of what looked like its tailpipe. Using one leg as a pivot, he swung the bike in a semi-circle, an inferno springing up around him. The nearest Redcaps let out screeching wails as they caught fire.

"Who is that?"

"My boss," Marcus said.

The second rider turned toward them briefly. Flames crackled behind him. She couldn't see his face through the tinted visor of his helmet. He pointed forcefully at Marcus, then toward the overcast sky. He kept staring in their direction for a moment longer, then turned his bike back to the Redcaps, driving through the fire.

*Holy shit.*

The message was clear. He wanted Marcus to get Tessa out of there. She was all for it.

"Hold on tight." Marcus flew the bike out to the street, then brought it down for a landing. He gunned the engine the moment the wheels hit the asphalt.

# Chapter Ten

Tessa's chest was pressed against him, only his T-shirt separating them. Marcus could feel her heart beating against his. Her warmth, her scent, was all around him as they sped away from the junkyard.

Part of him wanted to keep going. They could drive on past the ranch, find another small town to settle in. Maybe convince Vaughn to join them in secret. To keep them all together.

*"Your pack."*

*"Shut up,"* Marcus thought.

He didn't know how Dexter and Porter would react when they found out about Tessa's dwellers. Marcus wasn't sure he wanted to find out.

No wonder Marcus had never really seen her as prey. He could probably sense the dwellers lurking in her, even if they hadn't taken over her entire system.

He couldn't believe she smelled human—as long as the wristband was in place. When he'd pulled it off, the smell of leaf rot had overpowered his senses for a moment.

She seemed so normal. From what he had seen back in the junkyard, she was anything but.

He was just glad she was safe. That had been way too close. He wouldn't let her get in harm's way again. Not with only beaten up weapons and a piece of shit van to protect her.

"Stop nuzzling me." Her harsh voice snapped him back to the moment. She was still holding on to him with a death grip, but her body had gone stiff against his.

"What?"

"You were nuzzling my hair." She hissed the words into his ear. "We're not having sex on your motorcycle. Or anywhere. That ship has sailed."

He took a deep breath, trying to calm himself down. Her scent was honey-sweet around him.

"You should know I can smell your body's reaction to me. I get that nothing's going to happen, but it's still... really distracting."

She made a noise that almost sounded like a growl.

*"So lovely..."*

A rumbling sensation echoed up through Marcus's body. He wasn't sure if it was from him or his dweller.

"It's not you turning me on," she said. "It's the bike."

Marcus let out a brief laugh.

*Whump, whump, whump.*

He stiffened as he heard the sound of Dexter's motorcycle approaching them. Tessa picked up on his tension.

"What's wrong?" she said.

"Company."

"Friendly or otherwise."

"Depends on whether we're still operating as a team."

He couldn't keep himself from grinning at her. The idea of them working together felt right. Her lips twitched up at the corners before she forced them into a murderous frown.

Dexter pulled up alongside them. He stared at Marcus, yet somehow kept his bike going straight ahead. Marcus could only glance over, then had to look back to the road. He couldn't risk crashing with Tessa. He didn't know how much protection or strength her dwellers granted her—if any.

There were always tradeoffs. Humans gave dwellers host bodies, and the dwellers augmented them. And, yes, sometimes drove the human insane or took them over entirely. But only sometimes. Not always.

Tessa had fought Redcaps. She fought her dwellers' influence—if they even tried to influence her to do harm to others. She had lost a brother, had lost her human-ness, but not her humanity. She protected people. Like him.

"Oh, look," she said. "He has a bike just like yours. What's that doing to my scent?"

Marcus knew she was baiting him, but he still felt his heartbeat spike. The pleasant tingling her touch had brought out of him amped instantly to stinging as his hair thickened. His muscles twitched in preparation for a change.

"Not now. Not now," he chanted under his breath.

If he changed, they would crash. Period. But he could feel his boss's stare, even through the visor of Dexter's helmet. It felt like a challenge—a challenge for Tessa.

No matter what Tessa had said back at the junkyard, Dexter was the true alpha. And he was trying to maintain his dominance. It wasn't going to work where Tessa was concerned, and his attempts might have deadly consequences.

"I know I keep asking this, but is that guy a robot or something?" Her voice pulled Marcus back again—a little. She was staring at Dexter.

"No." Marcus bit out the word through a throat that didn't seem quite as built for human speech as it had been a few moments before. The sound was off enough to get her attention.

"Shit. Are you changing? Is he a threat?"

"No." Not exactly.

"Is he bothering you?"

"Yes."

Tessa pushed herself closer to Marcus, increasing her grip with one arm as she reached toward Dexter with the other. She waved her hand at him and said, "Shoo! Shoo!"

Marcus burst out laughing. He couldn't help it. If only she knew who she was trying to shoo away—what Dexter was capable of.

She managed to get Dexter's attention, breaking his hold on Marcus. That plus the laughter dissipated the tense energy that was building in him. Dexter cast a glance at her, then sped up enough to get in front of Marcus, leading the way back to the ranch.

So much for riding off into the sunrise together.

"That guy is an asshole," Tessa said.

Marcus laughed again. "How do you know?"

"You could have crashed with him distracting you like that."

"Your concern for my well-being is touching."

"I don't give a crap about your well-being. A crash wouldn't even kill you, but it could kill me."

Again, her words were saying one thing, but her body told him another story. When she said she didn't care about him, her heartbeat picked up and her voice changed pitch. She was lying. Which meant she did care.

At least a little.

*"She's perfect,"* his dweller thought at him. *"Make her one of us. Start your pack—for real."*

Marcus growled at his dweller.

"I won't let anything happen to you," Marcus said.

"I'm not afraid to die. I just don't know if he has enough fuel left in his tank to kill me properly."

The thought of Tessa's body being consumed by flame… would absolutely set Marcus off again. He shoved it from his mind.

It helped that she wrapped both arms around his neck to hold on. Her legs were so tight around his waist that he could feel her core pressing against his bare stomach.

He shouldn't be thinking about that, either.

He wanted to hold her, too, but knew she'd kick his ass if he tried. This might be the last opportunity he had to be close to her. The thought brought another low rumble from deep in his throat.

"Enough with the growling, already," she said. "I get it. You're the big bad wolf. But I'm Little Red and the Huntsman all rolled into one. Never forget that."

He threw his head back and laughed, grateful they were on a straight stretch of road. When he dared a glance at her again, she was smiling.

Dexter chose that moment to hit one of the sonic emitters Vaughn had built into their motorcycles. It was out of range for human perception, but Marcus heard it loud and clear. He winced, head throbbing as the noise cut through his brain.

His dweller shouted, *"Rip off his head and—"*

*"Not now."*

Marcus was having enough trouble focusing with Tessa's proximity and the fucking noise Dexter was throwing at him.

"What's wrong now?" Tessa said.

"Sonic emitter. The boss is reminding me of my place."

She probably thought Dexter was some incredible

genius who used his tech to force Marcus to work for the Blades. Vaughn had never intended for that device to be used against Marcus, though.

"I guess I was wrong about him." She briefly turned so she could look ahead of them. "He's an uber-asshole."

She didn't smile. Marcus did.

Dexter switched off the piercing sound as he turned down the drive that led to the ranch. Marcus followed. The gate swung open as they approached, then closed silently behind them. The drive parted—one paved road leading up to the front of the house and another circling to the converted barn out back that served as their garage.

Marcus wanted to take Tessa straight to the house. To give her a chance to eat, rest, shower, and change. There were plenty of clothes in her size in storage that would fit her. Vaughn kept all the outposts well stocked in case anyone needed to switch sites.

Then again, Marcus had plenty of T-shirts Tessa could wear. He loved the thought of providing for her—and knowing that his scent would be all over her now.

The main house came into view as they neared the barn. Tessa snorted when she saw it.

"You Blades have it rough," she said.

"Wait till you see the sublevels."

She leaned back enough to glare at him. "You know I already hate you, right?"

Marcus let out a little laugh and leaned closer. "And

you know I can tell when you're lying?"

Her eyes widened, then her frown returned in full force. She could fight it all she wanted. He knew she was just as drawn to him as he was to her. Even if nothing came of it, knowing how she felt soothed him.

Dexter drove into the barn as the doors opened—again automatically, thanks to Vaughn. Marcus followed, slowing down as they passed the two normal high-end cars that they only used for their rare mundane trips to town.

Tessa couldn't see the sloping ramp that had lowered from the floor, leading into the real garage a level below. She sucked in a breath and leaned closer, wrapping her arms around Marcus's neck as they descended. He tried to stifle the low growl of approval that rumbled up from his chest, but failed. She was too distracted by the place to notice.

Full-spectrum bulbs set into the ceilings illuminated every inch of the sublevels at the ranch. The walls were smooth white, reflecting the light so pristinely that it was easy to spot anything out of place on their surface. The floors and ceilings were the same.

The ramp led into a large garage. Four motorcycles and two vans filled the space. They were all jet black, with no markings—aside from the energy conduits built into their surfaces.

The vans had tinted windows so it was impossible to see inside, even for dwellers with heightened senses.

Something about the alignment of the molecules. No matter how hard he tried, Marcus only understood half of what Vaughn ever said.

Vaughn—who was standing in the garage waiting for Marcus, as usual. But with Porter.

Not so usual.

Vaughn was holding a stack of black clothing and glancing back and forth between Porter and Dexter—who was still sitting on his motorcycle. The whole situation must be making her really nervous. She looked over at Marcus, her vibrant blue eyes wide, as if searching for help, but then noticed Tessa and frowned.

*Great.*

Marcus kicked out the stand for his bike and killed the engine. He stood, lifting Tessa from the bike as he did. The moment she was clear, she shoved against his chest. He humored her and set her down. She took a few steps away from him, keeping her distance from the others as well.

"Nice place—" She froze mid-snark.

When she caught sight of Porter, her expression completely transformed. Even her posture changed—her guarded stance relaxing. She looked stunned. Her eyes widened, then filled with tears. She smiled and took a step toward him.

Even weirder, Porter's *scent* changed. The slight mustiness he put off grew stronger. It seemed like it was coming from everywhere. Maybe Dexter was putting it off, too?

What the hell kind of chemistry did they all have going on?

Marcus didn't dare let himself try to keep her from going to Porter. Not when they were standing so close to Dexter—who was always armed with silver.

Dexter threw his leg over the back of the bike and walked to Porter's side. Tessa didn't seem to even notice him. She was too fixated on Porter.

Her voice was weak and thready when she spoke. "Brock?"

*"Interesting,"* his dweller thought.

*"I would have gone with, 'What the hell?'"*

Dexter took off his helmet. Tessa finally noticed him. Her gaze flicked back and forth between the two identical men.

She looked like she'd been slapped. Her shoulders crumpled forward as she sucked in a stuttering breath. She shook her head, hard, then stepped back again—*toward Marcus*. He took a careful step closer, letting her feel him at her back.

Talking about their brothers, they had both stirred up ghosts. Porter and Dexter must resemble Brock, although that baffled Marcus. She looked nothing like them. Either way, he doubted Brock had been a twin.

"My mistake," she said.

His heart pounded as Marcus felt her pain. If he thought

he'd seen Danny, even for a moment…

Marcus dared to reach out to her, resting his hands on her arms. She didn't pull away.

Yeah. She was hurting.

"Okay…" Vaughn dragged out the word, a bewildered look on her face as she glanced around at the others. She turned to Tessa and forced a smile. "Welcome to an uncomfortably awkward moment. I'm your host. You can call me Vaughn."

Tessa actually let out a little laugh. Marcus would have to thank Vaughn later. Tessa's reaction seemed to thaw Vaughn a little and her smile became more genuine.

"Tonight's interlude features a surprise double-appearance by our fearless leaders—and I do mean that literally. These guys are cooler than a pair of disturbingly symmetrical ice cubes. Putting the 'us' in 'Janus,' it's Porter and Dexter."

She pointed at them with her pile of clothes.

Tessa laughed. Even Marcus let out a chuckle. Porter and Dexter didn't look amused. Vaughn edged away from their matching glares, approaching Tessa with her offering of clothes. Vaughn took off the top item—a pair of cargo pants—and handed them to Tessa. As she slid them on, Vaughn handed a fresh T-shirt to Marcus. Marcus quickly pulled it over his head. He didn't miss how Tessa's gaze lingered on his abs as his shirt settled into place.

"And our returning favorite, Marcus Lowell." Vaughn

held up the last item in her pile—a long-sleeved, button-up shirt.

She knew Marcus didn't normally like his scars to show around strangers. Tessa didn't feel like a stranger, though. Marcus wanted her to see his scars. He wanted her to know how far he'd go to protect the people he claimed.

No, *loved*. The people he loved.

His dweller chuckled. *"There is no difference."*

*"I don't even... We just met."*

*"As if that matters. Some things are inevitable."*

Marcus shook his head, refusing the shirt. Vaughn's smile faltered for a moment.

Draping the shirt over her arm like a waiter might with a towel, Vaughn gave a little curtsey toward Tessa and said, "And with special guest hunter, Tessa Rhodes."

Tessa's smile vanished as she backed away from them all. "How the hell do you know my name?"

Vaughn's mouth opened and closed as she looked from Tessa to Porter and back again. Porter smiled while Dexter maintained his neutral stare.

"We think you'll find the Blades of Janus are very resourceful," Porter said.

Another tremor passed through her and her lips tightened. There was something going on between that pair. Something Marcus didn't like. He stepped toward her, but she backed away. Porter held up a hand to warn Marcus to stand down.

"Forgive us for our lack of manners," Porter said. "We're not used to having guests."

"The word 'guest' implies I'm free to leave," Tessa said.

Porter's smile intensified. "Of course. But you're also free to stay for as long as you'd like."

That caught Marcus by surprise. Why would Porter make that offer? Unless... he was thinking of asking Tessa to become a Blade.

It would be perfect. She would have all the resources she needed. Marcus could keep her safe. They could live together, fight together, sleep together... He didn't let his mind go too far down that road.

Dexter had shifted his stare to Marcus. He chafed under the challenging gaze. His mind flooded with images of ripping off Dexter's head. It would be so easy...

Except his imagination wasn't as strong as his memory. If he closed his eyes, he could still see Dexter seeming to almost fly around the room where Marcus's family had been killed, silver swords cutting through the four werewolves who were responsible.

Marcus shouldn't hate Dexter. He didn't want to. But his dweller had other ideas.

"Come on in," Porter said. "Let us show you around."

Tessa crossed her arms. "Can I check out the armory first? I'm feeling a little light."

Porter reached into one of his pockets and pulled out

the smallest model of stingray they had. It was almost completely hidden in the palm of his hand. He held it out to her.

All she did was lift an eyebrow. "What is that itty bitty thing?"

"If I may?" Vaughn stepped forward and picked it up, then walked over to Tessa. "This 'itty bitty thing' is a stingray. It's capable of disrupting the electrical signals—"

"It stuns dwellers," Tessa said. "Yeah, Marcus mentioned them."

Vaughn frowned. "It can do a hell of a lot more than stun. And it doesn't just work on dwellers, so you might want to be careful with that."

"How do I adjust the settings?" Tessa asked.

Vaughn looked to Porter, who nodded. After fiddling with the weapon for a moment, she handed it to Tessa, then pointed out the controls.

"Slight buzz to fricassee," Vaughn said. "Here's the safety."

Tessa immediately set it on maximum and toggled off the safety. Pointing it at a blank wall, she pulled the trigger. A bolt of energy shot out of the business end of it. What looked like a swirling ball of blue plasma hit the wall, rippling over the surface briefly before stuttering out when she let go of the trigger. The surface of the wall was blackened, the metal melted in the center of the blast all the way through. Even the concrete behind it held a crater.

"I guess it's true when they say that size doesn't matter." Tessa slid the stingray into one of the pockets of her cargo pants.

"Put the safety on first," Vaughn said. "And set it at its lowest level."

"Why?" she said. "Marcus said these things hold their power well."

Vaughn let out an exasperated breath. "It's standard procedure."

Tessa pulled the stingray back out and showed Vaughn that she'd already toggled the safety back on.

"But the intensity—"

Porter cut Vaughn off. "Ms. Rhodes isn't familiar with our safety protocols."

"I'm not a Blade," she said. "I don't follow your protocols. But thanks for the ray gun."

"Stingray," Vaughn said. "And it's common sense as well as protocol. Walking around with it on high is dangerous."

"Only for the things I point it at." She glared at Marcus while she spoke.

*"Another challenge."*

His dweller seemed to like it when she challenged him. That was a change. It still wanted to rip Dexter's head off and gauge out his eyes for the challenging stare Dexter was casting Marcus's way.

"We can go over protocol later," Porter said. "Right

now, we have a rather important debriefing. We hope you won't mind joining us, Ms. Rhodes?"

"Tessa," she snapped. "I can't stand that other name. Call me Tessa."

"Of course." Porter typed in his code and placed his palm on the scanner that controlled the door to the rest of the sublevels. The door *whooshed* open, and he and Vaughn filed through.

Tessa cast a look at Marcus. He couldn't tell if she was being wary of him or making sure he was going to follow along. He nodded briefly. Her lips tightened again, but she turned and followed the others. She was looking to him for reassurance. Feeling lighter, he started toward the door.

Dexter caught Marcus by the arm and swung him around, slamming him into the wall and pressing an elbow against his throat. His dweller let out a howl, scratching at Marcus's insides, pushing him to change and claw out Dexter's heart.

The air thickened with the scent of silver as Dexter drew a knife. Marcus felt it hovering near his stomach, ready to disembowel him.

He could sprout claws and rip out Dexter's guts as well. The thought was tempting, but that would leave Tessa alone. Marcus wouldn't do that to her.

"Whatever you think is going to happen with this hunter," Dexter said, "it isn't. Do you understand?"

Marcus growled. No one would stand between him and

Tessa. Not even his alpha.

*"She called* you *alpha."*

Now was not the time to give fuel to his dweller. Even if it was right.

"Do you understand?" Dexter bit out each word, right in Marcus's face.

"Yes."

Instead of letting up on him, Dexter pushed harder with his elbow, cutting off Marcus's air. The normally placid expression on Dexter's face was twisted into the closest thing to rage Marcus had ever seen. Dexter must really think that Marcus was out to start his own pack.

*"Or he wants to claim her for himself."*

Marcus was glad for the lack of air. It helped stifle his growl.

Dexter gave one last shove with his elbow. Marcus heard the bone in his neck snap as pain seared through him, his trachea collapsing. If he'd been human, Dexter would have just killed him. But Marcus wasn't human. And if Dexter really wanted him dead, all he would have had to do was stab him with that sword.

"We're warning you, Marcus. Stay away from Tessa."

Dexter shoved Marcus to the ground, stepping over him as he coughed and retched, clawing at the floor while his body repaired itself.

# Chapter Eleven

Tessa stayed alert as Porter led them down the pristine white hallway. She was pretty sure she'd just heard somebody get slammed against the wall of the garage. Since she didn't hear screaming as someone was torn to pieces, Marcus was probably having what passed for a 'friendly conversation' among werewolves—letting the boss know exactly what Marcus thought of the stunt Dexter had pulled back on their bikes.

*Hoverbikes.*

She focused on her environment, looking for more of the Blades' super-advanced technology. The walls and ceilings were almost completely smooth, except for a few vents near lights built into the surfaces. Only the floor showed signs of use, with a few scuff marks here and there. She could see the outlines of a couple of doors, but might have missed them if it wasn't for the keypads and scanners next to them.

When she'd been piling it on Marcus at the junkyard about Blades being divorced from reality, she'd had no idea how right she was. Between the hoverbikes and this, she felt like she was on some sort of spaceship. Knowing what she did about dwellers, the thought was unnerving.

Footsteps were approaching from behind. She looked over her shoulder to see Porter's twin smiling at her. Dexter. He looked pretty happy for a guy who'd just faced down a werewolf.

Where was Marcus?

The twins were so creepy. The only difference she'd been able to detect was that Porter seemed to radiate a bit less malice than Dexter. Both men looked like they could rip her apart with smiles on their faces. Identical smiles that never reached their eyes. Worse, they both looked exactly like Brock—only older. She would even say they sounded like him, except for how they always used 'we.' They must take the whole team aspect of the Blades pretty seriously.

The resemblance had to be why it was so hard to look at them, why she felt a stabbing flash of grief every time they spoke or said her name. Especially when they used 'Rhodes.'

*How did they find out my name so fast?*

As far as she was concerned, Tessa Rhodes died along with her family over a decade ago. She was just Tessa now.

The uncertainty of it all was getting to her. She couldn't see Marcus, and that made her *more afraid*. She should be relieved to be away from him. Instead, she wished he was at her side.

She slowed down when he appeared at the end of the hallway. He was walking with his head bent. At first, she thought he was in pain. The hunched shoulders, fists clenched at his sides…

No, he was angry. Killing-angry.

"Marcus?" she said.

His gaze snapped to hers. The light reflecting off his glasses couldn't hide their glow.

Shit, he looked like he was about to rip Dexter's head off. So why did she find herself walking back down the hallway toward him?

She told herself she didn't want to be in the middle of something with these guys. They were both deadly. But she had a feeling she stood a better chance of survival with Marcus, especially after fighting back-to-back at the junkyard—and what they'd *almost* done after.

Dexter shifted so he was more than half-blocking the hallway. He was even creepier up close. So like Brock, but… wrong.

"Excuse me." She tried to brush past him on her way to Marcus.

"Where do you think you're going?" Dexter reached toward her arm, but she spun away and glared at him.

"When you're at a strange party, it's best to stay with your ride." She took Marcus's hand. Took a goddammed werewolf's hand. Voluntarily. While it was still attached to his arm.

Her heart was thundering in her chest.

She was just maximizing her chances of survival. That was all. It didn't matter how warm his hand felt, or that he gently interlaced their fingers.

She kept glaring at Dexter as they passed him. Vaughn and Porter had already disappeared through an open doorway. Tessa focused on following and not the soft footfalls of the guy walking behind them. The warmth and... menace Marcus was putting off next to her was actually reassuring.

*And I didn't think my life could get any weirder.*

The room they entered was a sparsely furnished... office maybe? The Blades apparently didn't squander resources on cushy furniture. At least, not in the 'sublevels.' There was a plain metal table in the middle of the wall opposite the door with a huge array of monitors above it. A few mesh chairs formed a semi-circle around the table. Vaughn was sitting at one, her back stiff and lips pulled in a deep frown.

"Thanks for joining us," Porter said.

If he was surprised to see Marcus and Tessa holding hands, he didn't let on. Vaughn was another matter. She glared at them briefly, then spun around and started tapping hard on the table.

"We were able to gather some great footage from today's patrol," Vaughn said.

The monitor lit up as her fingers danced over the table

in front of her. Tessa stepped closer to get a better view. She could see etchings on the surface. The keyboard was built into it? There was even a square section that seemed to be a trackpad. Up this close, Tessa noticed that Vaughn was wearing a watch with a large blank face that she was pretty sure hadn't come off a factory line.

"Slick," Tessa said.

Porter sat in one of the chairs next to Vaughn. "It would be even more impressive if Vaughn had managed to record the audio as well as the video."

Vaughn shrugged. "Nobody's perfect."

Tessa looked back up at the monitors. Her face filled one of the screens, the footage taken from an oddly close angle. She was standing in the alley where she'd first met Marcus. How the hell had they taken that picture? It was almost as if—

"You have a camera in your glasses?" She felt her cheeks heat. He had seen… They had done…

She pulled her hand from his.

"I *had* a camera in my glasses," Marcus said. "It… um. Broke."

Vaughn snorted. "At the same time your earpiece went out."

"Which was right after we killed the queen," Marcus said. "Before we… went to the van."

Dammit. She'd almost hoped that he'd recorded their make-out session. It would prove that he was an unfeeling monster—or at least an asshole. Instead, his weirdly self-conscious and apologetic behavior was making him more sympathetic.

He was an alpha werewolf, for crying out loud. Why did he care about her feelings?

*How dare he be considerate.* She shook her head and laughed inwardly at her thought.

"Sorry about all the technical difficulties tonight," Marcus said.

Vaughn shrugged. "Forget it. I can make another set."

Marcus finally took off his glasses, setting them on the table. He turned to Tessa and her breath hitched.

His eyes had looked pretty before—what she could make out through the constant glare on the lenses. But seeing them uncovered—bright gold next to his thick, inky black lashes—they were absolutely gorgeous. Their color seemed to intensify as their gazes held, glittering lights sparking to life in their depths.

"If you guys can quit with the meaningful gazes for a minute, I have some questions," Vaughn said.

Tessa snapped herself out of it, shifting her focus to Vaughn gladly. Not reluctantly. Not at all.

"I thought you Blades had all the answers," Tessa said.

"Tonight has shown us our true ignorance." Porter gestured to one of the mesh chairs. "Please."

Marcus walked around behind the chair and held the back as he pushed it slightly toward her. The gesture was oddly gallant. She wished it was a straight-backed chair so that she could sit in it backwards and show them all that she wasn't some wilting flower. Instead, she glared at them and sat on the table, only realizing afterwards that she might be hitting some sort of controls. She half-twisted around, looking at the table space nearest her. No etchings. That didn't mean sitting on the table was a good idea, but she was trying to prove a point and didn't want to move.

"Is it okay if I sit here?" Tessa asked.

Vaughn's bright blue eyes darted to her briefly. "Sure."

Tessa smiled at her, which was easy to do. Of all the Blades she'd met, Vaughn seemed the least abnormal. Plus, it had been a very long time since Tessa had been able to spend time with another woman. Not since it was just Tessa and her mom…

Her eyes burned as the darkest memory of her life rose to the surface—even worse than when Tessa had been 'colonized.' She forced herself to focus. Her mother often warned, '*Distraction will get you killed quicker than anything.*' She wasn't wrong.

Tessa cleared her throat and said, "What questions do you have?"

"First on my list, could you see Marcus's eyes clearly through his glasses?" Vaughn asked. "Especially their color."

That surprised Tessa. "Not well. I kind of thought they looked gold, but wasn't sure."

"I'll up the reflective index to obscure them better."

"You made them that way on purpose?"

"Everything I do is on purpose," Vaughn said.

Marcus let out a cough that sounded suspiciously like a laugh.

Vaughn glared at him. "It just doesn't always turn out the way I plan."

"We were able to extrapolate the Redcaps' physiology better based on what the glasses picked up and what Vaughn overheard." Porter pointed to a different monitor.

A freeze-frame of the corpse-riding Redcaps in the alley filled the screen. As Tessa watched, Vaughn's computer drew a series of red gridlines over one of them. The rest of the image disappeared, leaving just the one Redcap and its ride filling the left side of the screen.

Another image appeared on the right. A Redcap without a host. The same gridlines appeared over its body, only blue, making its form more discernible. Tessa wished it had stayed vague. Its tendrils were much longer and thicker than she expected. It looked kind of like a jellyfish, with the spider-crab body at the top. She suppressed a shiver.

The computer shrank the un-obscured image of the Redcap on the right and superimposed it over the one on the left—the one disguised as a human. She could see the Redcap's tendrils snaking through the corpse's limbs and torso, the dweller clearly defined sitting on its neck. The eyestalks and pincered arms were pulled back into the Redcap's body, making it look... not really human at all.

"Add a bandana and sunglasses, and you've got a human you wouldn't *want* to stare at," Vaughn said. "They try to look intimidating so that people don't make eye contact. If you don't study their faces too much, you don't realize what you're looking at."

"It's remarkable," Porter said. He was staring at the monitor with an almost rapt smile on his face.

"Porter is our resident Doctor," Vaughn said. "If dwellers didn't vaporize when they died, we'd probably have a morgue filled with dissected specimens. I'm working on a stasis field for him, but we haven't been able to get many test subjects back to the ranch."

"We content ourselves with logging everything we can in the Blades' dweller database." Porter turned to her and smiled. "Redcaps have shown an amazing ability to adapt to their environment."

"You might want to hold off on starting a fan club," Tessa said.

Porter's smile didn't flicker. "There's nothing wrong with respecting your adversary."

"So, you admit that they're your adversary?" she said.

"Of course." Porter leaned back in his chair. "Redcaps can't be reasoned with. They're one of the few types of dweller that have a kill order among the Blades."

"Unlike—" She stopped herself from saying,

'werewolves.' As if they didn't already know what Marcus was. Then again, maybe they didn't.

She couldn't believe that the tiny possibility that it would endanger Marcus had stopped her from mentioning it. Why the hell was she protecting him? She was still considering killing him herself. Wasn't she?

Dexter picked up on what she'd been about to say anyway. "Werewolves don't have an instant kill order. We monitor their behavior, hopefully getting to them before they commit a capital offense. So far, Marcus is the only one we've been able to spare."

She wasn't surprised. Werewolves were incredibly violent. Strong, territorial—when they settled in one place —and fiercely protective when it came to their pack. And they were carnivores. Like most dwellers.

"Since the earpiece and glasses didn't work as well as we'd hoped, how about you take us through it the old-fashioned way." Porter picked up what looked like a chrome clipboard and a stylus and crossed his legs, using his thigh as a flat surface to support his writing.

"That's old-fashioned?" She was sure the 'clipboard' was actually some kind of computer.

Porter just smiled. "Walk us through it. You tagged one of the Redcaps and followed it to its nest in the junkyard."

She didn't see the harm in teaching them about Redcaps —especially if it meant the Blades would become more effective at taking them out. Fewer bugs for her to stomp.

"Right," she said. "The nest is where the queen lives. The main tunnel usually leads straight down to the queen's cavern."

Vaughn tapped on the table again, and an image of the cavern Tessa and Marcus had just cleared came into view. More gridlines appeared, with numbers scrolling on one side of the screen. She recognized a few dimensions and angles, but most of it didn't make sense to her.

The picture of the cavern blinked a few times, then an image of the queen appeared. The same analysis repeated, but this one had biometrics as well. It also had some pretty gnarly freeze-frames of the queen with her mouth fully extended.

"Well, I'm going to have nightmares tonight," Vaughn said.

Tessa agreed. "I'm glad I'm usually too busy killing them to look at them."

Marcus was standing behind Vaughn's chair. He reached out and rested his hand on Vaughn's shoulder. The sweet gesture was out of place from someone on the road to becoming a vicious killer, but not quite so out of place as the brief surge of jealousy that welled up within Tessa.

*What the fuck is wrong with me?*

"What's the standard procedure for killing them?" Dexter talked about killing monsters as if he was writing a technical manual. For all she knew, the Blades had one.

The thought was appealing. She wondered if she could

get a peek. If nothing else, it would be entertaining.

"I use bug repellers to paralyze the little ones, then head into the nest with my flamethrower."

"Hold on a minute," Vaughn said. "Bug repellers? "

"Yeah, the sonic ones. I don't know how well they work on bugs, but something about them freezes Redcaps." Tessa stopped herself from adding, '*Just make sure you use ones with fresh batteries, even if you think you'll be in and out of the nest in no time.*' It was such a rookie mistake.

Porter turned to Marcus and said, "Now that we know Redcaps are actually quite small, the next time you encounter one, we want you to bring it back here for study."

"Bringing a dweller into your home is—" Tessa stopped herself as all four Blades turned to look at her. "Okay, bringing a *dangerous* dweller into your home is insane. I don't know how you domesticated Marcus."

His eyes flashed gold and his lips pulled back from his teeth. It looked like he was stifling a snarl. He took a deep breath and let it out slowly, glaring at her the whole time.

"Marcus isn't an animal," Vaughn said. "He can control himself."

"For the moment." Tessa still hadn't figured out what was going on with him.

With all those scars, he had to be an alpha. That made it a little more believable that he could control himself better than most werewolves. It did *not* cover why he let Dexter and Porter order him around or why he was so tender with Vaughn. Marcus had been nothing but gentle with Tessa as well.

It seemed like a fairytale that he could actually control himself. Then again, her life often felt like it was taken right out of a storybook. One of the dark ones, where people were eaten when they ventured too far into the forest.

Leaving town immediately wasn't an option anymore. She had no transportation, no weapons. Even the clothes she wore were borrowed. If she hung around the Blades, she could watch Marcus, then decide whether to kill him before she left. Her brain felt better having made that decision. Still, she only had two days.

"Let's get back to the debriefing, shall we?" Porter said. "What happens after you get into the lair and have incapacitated the Redcaps?"

Tessa shrugged. "Once I locate the queen, I hose it down with fire till it's nice and melty, add a few grenades, and run like hell."

"Calling it a queen implies a female gender, yet you insist on calling her an 'it,'" Porter said.

"What, you can be picky with your pronouns, but I can't?" She glared at him.

Porter kept smirking and went on as if she hadn't spoken. "How do you know for certain that the queen is dead?"

Tessa snorted and decided to let him off the hook. For the moment.

"If I'm too far away to see the glow, I can tell by its brood on the surface. They all die when I take it out."

"Vaughn said you killed the queen, but you were neck deep in Redcaps when we showed up," Dexter said.

Tessa shook her head. "I haven't figured that out yet. Marcus killed the queen. All its brood died around us."

"Maybe the ones who attacked us afterwards were tied to the king and they didn't die with him," Marcus said.

Porter swiveled toward Marcus. "King?"

"Yeah," Marcus said. "An even bigger dweller attacked us after we killed the queen. Its markings were different, but it was structurally similar. We figured it was probably a king."

"How did you deal with it?" Dexter asked.

"It got its head stuck in my van." Tessa glared at Marcus, willing him to gloss over the details. "Which was rigged with explosives. We set them off after getting far enough away."

She wasn't ready for the Blades to know about her infection. The look on Porter's face when he was talking about bringing a Redcap to their base... She almost felt sorry for the thing. He'd probably vivisect it or something.

Maybe she *should* just blow out of town and leave Marcus for the Blades to deal with.

She kept them on the topic of Redcaps, hoping to keep the scrutiny off of herself. "Everything about this hunt was different. I've never encountered a mobile queen outside of its nest. The king was new, too."

"It sounds like you interrupted their spawning practice," Porter said.

Tessa shivered. "That's a really disturbing thought."

"If it was some sort of Redcap mating ritual, there could be more than one queen involved." Vaughn shrugged when all eyes turned to her. "It's the simplest explanation. Many species have multiple females to one male."

"I hope you're wrong," Tessa said.

Vaughn turned to her. "Why?"

"Because, based on how many Redcaps attacked us, I think there's more than one queen left. And they're probably really pissed."

# Chapter Twelve

Marcus could feel Dexter's gaze boring into his back. After working together to protect humans—and dwellers —for almost a decade, there was still little trust between them. What did that say for the hope that dwellers and humans could live and work alongside each other peacefully?

Marcus would never turn Tessa—or anyone. He wasn't out to increase his pack, no matter what she said about dwellers wanting to reproduce. Yes, he felt the urge, but he refused to give in to it.

Based on the exchange in the garage, Dexter had to have the same concerns. Why else would he be so worked up over Tessa already?

Then again, the same could be asked of Marcus. No one had ever affected him the way she did. One moment, she'd be connecting with him on a level he didn't think was possible. The next, she'd shut him out, painfully. It seemed like she'd crack a joke, then threaten to kill him in the space of a breath. Trying to figure out the mixed signals she was sending could get him killed.

*"It's worth the risk."*

Marcus found himself agreeing with the voice in his head once again. That was happening more and more often, which disturbed him.

"We need time to analyze the information you've brought us," Porter said. "We're sure Marcus would love to show Tessa around the ranch."

*Absolutely.*

He was surprised Porter made the suggestion, though. Dexter would probably want to come along as a chaperone. Marcus could deal with that, as long as he could stay close to her. The bosses' attention on her was making him want to growl, even without his dweller's influence.

Marcus took a step toward her and she slid off the table —angling away from him—and headed for the door. Dexter was leaning against the wall next to it, arms crossed and knowing smirk on his face. Marcus wanted to rip it off.

Tessa turned back to Porter and did a small, strange wave. It took Vaughn snickering for Marcus to realize she was imitating a royal gesture, playing on the twins' weird use of pronouns. He mashed his lips together to stifle a laugh.

As they neared the door, Dexter said, "Vaughn, why don't you go with them?"

"Me?" Vaughn looked back and forth between Dexter and Porter.

Porter smiled. "It'll be good for you to stretch your legs."

"Sure." Vaughn let out a sigh, then stood, keying in some commands with her watch. She strode to the door and rested her palm on the scanner. When the door opened, she looked pointedly at Marcus and gestured to the door. Under her breath, Marcus heard her say, "Leaders first."

Marcus hesitated for a moment. If Dexter heard Vaughn talking like that, Marcus wouldn't be the only one on the chopping block. Dexter didn't want Marcus having *any* kind of pack, even if some members were human. Maybe it was a way of trying to help Marcus hold on to his humanity and not connect as strongly with his dweller nature. But denying his nature wasn't always a good idea. Until recently, thinking of Dexter as the alpha helped Marcus stay calm. Following orders chafed, but didn't send Marcus spiraling out of control if he told himself that Dexter was in charge.

Dexter had killed *all* the werewolves in what would have become Marcus's pack. While Marcus was trying to fight them off, the werewolves had talked about violence being used to establish dominance. If that was how rank was determined, Dexter was absolutely the alpha.

But Vaughn knew that sometimes when she left a room first, it set Marcus off. Marcus had never explained why, and from that comment, she had it all wrong. Marcus would explain as soon as he could—to let her know it wasn't about dominance. Not entirely, anyway.

Having Dexter leave a room first wasn't about showing deference for their leader—it was about knowing how skilled Dexter was in combat. If something was lying in wait on the other side of the door, it would get its ass handed to it as soon as it attacked. Dexter was not someone to mess with.

With Vaughn—and now Tessa—Marcus wanted to go first. He wanted to make sure that the hallway was safe, even though he knew his concern was ridiculous. They were in the sublevels of the ranch. There wasn't a safer place in Providence, maybe even on the whole planet. The overwhelming urge to protect his pack—no, his *friends*—was one of the few aspects of being a werewolf that Marcus didn't mind.

Marcus waited outside the door and followed as Vaughn led the way to the elevator at the far end of the hall. When the doors opened, Marcus stepped in between them so he could see both spaces at once until everyone was safely inside.

The elevator felt smaller than usual. Tessa started to hum some music as they rose toward the ranch. Vaughn snorted, but then joined in, adding a nice harmony, while Marcus shook his head. A false door made to look like part of the bookshelf in the library swung forward as the elevator opened.

Marcus infinitely preferred the ranch to the stark walls

and too-bright surfaces of the sublevels. Up here, even the presence of his dweller seemed lessened—as if it thought nothing interesting enough to hold its attention could happen in Marcus's home. He hoped that would always be true.

Simple dark burgundy curtains hung open on the windows. There were no sunny spots on his favorite chair, though. Raindrops pelted the glass.

Tessa's stomach growled, reminding him that she'd thrown up her breakfast—which hadn't been much in the first place.

"Let's start in the kitchen," Marcus said.

"Always thinking with your stomach." Vaughn laughed, then turned to Tessa and gestured to the other room. "This way."

The kitchen was Marcus's favorite room at the ranch. It reminded him of home and family in the best possible way. Of course, his family's house hadn't sported the sleek chrome appliances, the rich bamboo flooring, or the tools that Vaughn had 'upgraded.'

"Vaughn is amazing in the kitchen," Marcus said.

"Excuse me, I'm amazing *everywhere*." Vaughn briefly touched her chest as she turned and walked backwards, leading them into the kitchen. She spread her arms wide after crossing the threshold. "Behold my other kingdom."

She ran her fingertips over the black surface of the island in the center of the space. Four stools were tucked under the bar portion of it. They would need to get another for Tessa. A huge cutting board dominated the workspace on the island, with Vaughn's favorite knife resting on it.

The cutting board wasn't made of wood. Marcus had no idea what it was crafted from. He did know that it was unbreakable, unburnable, and unscratchable. Vaughn had insisted Marcus help test it out—in his other form. It had been a fun afternoon. Regular knives were dulled almost immediately by it, but of course Vaughn had tweaked the knives as well.

"What are you in the mood for today, Marcus?" she asked. "Bacon, eggs, and bacon? Steak and bacon and eggs? Steak and steak and bacon? Or just steak?"

"Whatever Tessa wants." Marcus was still hurting from seeing how she'd been living. He wanted to show her that he could provide anything she needed.

Tessa crossed her arms and glared at them. "I'm vegan."

Vaughn sighed. "Of course you are. I can work with that. You do know that Marcus, being what he is, pretty much only eats meat, right? Any time he eats something that used to have leaves, I'm afraid I'm going to find it hacked up on the carpet."

Tessa busted out laughing. Vaughn cleared her throat as Marcus glared at her.

"Luckily, some of us need to eat a healthy, well-rounded diet," Vaughn said. "We have fruit, cereal, salad…"

"I can make my own food." Tessa walked over to the nearest cabinet and opened it. There were only plates inside.

"Um, the kitchen is my domain," Vaughn said.

"I think I can pour my own cereal." Tessa turned around and glared at the other woman.

Vaughn sighed, then picked up her knife. "What's this?"

"A knife." Tessa glanced over at Marcus and spread her hands in an 'Is she serious?' gesture.

"Look closer." Vaughn held the knife up for Tessa to inspect.

Tessa leaned in, and said, "Okay, it's an electric knife."

"You think you can slice up some fruit with this bad boy?" Vaughn said.

Tessa shrugged. "Yeah."

Vaughn put an apple on the cutting board, then switched the knife on. It hummed and snapped as it powered up. The serrated blade blurred to the point that the edge looked perfectly smooth. Blue light glittered across the metal.

Tessa's eyes widened and she took a step forward. "What is that?"

"Just one of my kitchen doodads." Vaughn batted her eyelashes with a smile, then touched the knife to the apple. Where the knife touched the fruit, it melted into what smelled like applesauce. Only the edges farthest from the blade were left intact.

"That is so cool," Tessa said.

Vaughn clicked off the knife and smiled at Marcus. If Tessa wanted to win Vaughn over, praising her tech was the best way to do it.

Tessa reached for one of the remaining bits of apple that had skin on it, and brought it to her nose. Her smile vanished, and she dropped it back on the pile, wiping her right hand on her pant leg.

"What's wrong?" Vaughn asked.

"It has blood on it."

"What?" Vaughn looked at the knife. "How can you tell?"

"I can fee—" Tessa abruptly cut off what she was about to say. "I can smell it."

Vaughn glanced over at Marcus, eyebrows hitched up. Marcus shook his head briefly, out of Tessa's line of sight.

"I must have forgotten to run the self-cleaner after making Marcus dinner last night," Vaughn said. She pressed her thumb against the handle and more blue light flickered up along the blade. "There. All clean and set for *apple*."

"I'll just go for a whole one." Tessa picked up a large apple from the bowl, sniffed it, then started to eat.

Vaughn looked crestfallen. "I'll be sure to get more next time I order groceries."

"What, you can't be bothered to buy your own groceries?" Tessa asked.

"I do buy our groceries, I just have them delivered." Vaughn crossed her arms over her chest. "It's called being efficient."

"Vaughn doesn't like to leave the house," Marcus said.

Tessa snorted. "If I had a place like this, I wouldn't want to leave, either."

Her statement seemed to placate Vaughn a bit. Marcus rested his hand on Vaughn's shoulder briefly, and said, "Steak sounds good. Do you mind?"

"Sure." Vaughn's face brightened as she adjusted the setting again. "You'll love this. Unless the whole vegan thing is because you can't stand the thought of eating animals. In which case, you should probably go back to the library."

"She's not going anywhere." Marcus opened the pantry doors and stepped into the closet-sized space. He pulled out some cereal boxes and took them to Tessa. One apple was not enough. When he set the boxes next to her, she bit into her apple and held it in her mouth, picking up the boxes and reading the ingredients.

"I'll get you a bowl," Marcus said.

Tessa grunted as she bit through the apple. Around the huge bite, she said, "No need."

She sat on one of the barstools, then opened a cereal box and reached in, popping the flakes into her mouth like popcorn. Vaughn's eyebrows were spiked up her forehead again. Her mouth was even hanging open a bit.

"You've got yourself a real keeper there," she said.

Tessa snorted again at the same time Marcus let out a growl. She glared at him.

"Nobody *keeps* me," she said.

"Okay, then." Vaughn looked back and forth between them for a moment, then went to the fridge.

She returned with a large hunk of steak. There was more in the freezer built into the back of the pantry. A whole cow's worth. Vaughn picked up her knife and switched it on, then started on Marcus's breakfast.

"On this setting, my knife can cut slices of steak tartare thin enough to see through." She held up one of the slices proudly before setting it aside. "It cuts through flesh and bone like they're butter that's been sitting out in the sun. It *even*... cuts through awkward moments."

"Very useful." Tessa grinned.

"We have spoons, too, you know," Vaughn said.

"What do they do?"

Vaughn shrugged in an exaggerated manner. "Lift food to your mouth."

Tessa laughed again. "I think I can manage on my own." She stuffed another handful of cereal into her mouth.

"We are going to have to teach you some table manners," Vaughn said. "And you made a crack about us domesticating Marcus."

"One I didn't like." Marcus stepped next to Vaughn and picked up a slice of meat. Feeling oddly self-conscious, he turned his back to them before eating it.

"Now you're doing it, too," Vaughn said. "Get a plate."

Marcus grinned before obliging. He passed the plate to Vaughn, who heaped the sliced meat onto it. As Marcus sat next to Tessa, Vaughn picked up the remains of the first apple and tossed them in the trash. She pressed a button on the cutting board—causing more crackling light to spread over its surface, cleaning it—then did the same to her knife. With Tessa's attention diverted, Marcus ate as quickly as he could.

"Marcus, you know I don't like it when you wolf down your food," Vaughn said, making her voice as patronizing as she could for comic effect. "It furthers the stereotype."

"I must have finally gone insane." Tessa laughed and shook her head.

Vaughn turned from the sink where she was washing her hands. "Come on. Your manners aren't *that* bad. Although, I am wondering about you a little since you turned down my cooking."

"All I've seen you make is sliced raw meat and applesauce."

Vaughn looked offended. "I can cook."

"She really can," Marcus said.

Praising Vaughn's tech was a great way to appeal to her.

Insulting her cooking would start a war. Marcus had to maintain the peace between her and Tessa. He *needed* them to get along.

"Porter talks about it all the time, as well as other Blades who have visited," Marcus said. "And it smells so good, I'm sometimes tempted to try it, even with my... special needs."

"I believe you." Tessa laughed again.

Special needs... He wondered if Tessa's vegan diet was somehow tied to her dweller. If Marcus ate anything other than raw meat, it didn't upset his stomach, but it did upset his mood. He became volatile and it was harder to maintain control. He made a note to ask about her dweller as soon as they were alone. She obviously didn't want the others to know about it. With everything she was dealing with, he couldn't blame her.

"Anyway, what's insane about this?" Marcus said.

"Everything. I'm sitting in a Blades of Janus base, laughing while having breakfast with a werewolf and his personal chef—"

"Excuse me," Vaughn said. "I'm the IT guy. Gal."

"That's not making it any less weird," Tessa said.

"Marcus is a Blade, like any other." Vaughn stepped back to the counter. "Just sometimes a little hairier. Although, that new guy they just recruited in Atlanta..."

Marcus snorted.

"You have a base in Atlanta, too?" Tessa asked.

"We have bases all over the world," Marcus said. "Dwellers don't care about human territories."

"But they're also nomadic," Tessa said. "How do you handle that?"

"Marcus isn't handling anything until he washes his hands." Vaughn cocked her head toward the sink.

Marcus picked up his plate, then headed for the sink. He brushed his shoulder against Vaughn's as he passed, hoping she knew how much it meant that she was trying to get along with Tessa.

Tessa let out another burst of laughter and gestured at Marcus as he started to wash his hands. "And how do you do *that?*"

"Do what?" Vaughn asked.

"Order around a werewolf without getting your head ripped off?"

Vaughn went from looking confused to angry. "Marcus would never hurt anyone who doesn't deserve it. He's a good person."

"He's not a person," Tessa said. "He's a *werewolf.*"

Marcus actually had to grab Vaughn's elbow to hold her back. A fight wouldn't end well for Vaughn. Tessa was a seasoned hunter. She set down her box of cereal and stood, squaring off with them. Marcus felt his skin start to itch. Tessa was challenging him, which he liked. But she was doing it in front of Vaughn. She was bringing disorder to their precarious balance.

"Being evil or good is a choice," Vaughn said.

Tessa snorted. "Dwellers don't have human values like good and evil. They're *aliens*. For them it's hosts and prey. They can't control it. The urge to propagate will win out eventually."

"That's not true." Marcus dug his fingertips into his palms to keep his claws from sprouting. "I'm always in control."

Always in control. No matter how painful it was. No matter how much he wanted to cut loose.

"Like back in the van?" Tessa crossed her arms and glared at him.

"That was different."

"What happened in the van?" Vaughn asked.

Before they could say more, Porter and Dexter walked into the room. Marcus was almost relieved to see them.

Almost.

"Are we interrupting something?" Porter said.

A chill swept over Marcus's skin at the uncanny similarity in their movements as the twins approached. Their feet and arms moved in synch. He wished they would go back to rarely being in the same room at once.

Dexter stopped near the counter on Marcus and Vaughn's side. Porter stood near Tessa.

"We see your tour ended early," Porter said. "If you've eaten enough, perhaps you'd like to see your room." He gestured toward the other exit from the kitchen that led to the rest of the ranch and the front foyer.

"Sounds great." Tessa dusted off her hands. "I can't wait to see the freaking four poster, king sized bed and spa tub that probably comes along with it."

Dexter smirked at her. "If you'd prefer, we can throw a blanket on the couch."

She glared at him, then grabbed her box of cereal.

"Let's go." She looked at Marcus. *Marcus.*

He took a step toward her, but Dexter slid in front of him. "We have more debriefing to do."

Marcus let out a low growl. His hands flexed.

Dexter only smiled at him. "Are we going to have a problem, Marcus?"

An image of Marcus ripping off Dexter's head filled his mind. But Dexter was within reach of Vaughn's knife, and Marcus knew he'd be deadly with it. He wouldn't even need silver to take Marcus down.

Tessa was safe with all the Blades. Marcus was sure of it. The sooner he let her go, the sooner he could deal with Dexter and then check on her.

"No problem," Marcus said.

Tessa actually looked disappointed for a moment. But then she shook her head and said, "Fine. *We* shall leave."

She followed Porter out of the room.

# Chapter Thirteen

How the hell was Tessa wishing that she was still with the werewolf? It had to be part of his dweller nature. Maybe being an alpha made him charismatic or something. He sure had Vaughn wrapped around his finger. Then again, Vaughn was an indoctrinated idiot.

Well, not really an idiot.

Tessa thought back over the tech that Vaughn had apparently designed. She was probably the smartest person Tessa had ever met. But Vaughn was fooling herself if she thought that Marcus wouldn't turn on her—wouldn't *turn* her—eventually.

There was no such thing as a 'good' dweller.

*Now who sounds indoctrinated?*

Her mother was right, though. All the training she had put Tessa through after Edgar killed Brock and her dad… Everything her mom had said had been confirmed when Edgar caught up with them. After he had killed her mother and 'adopted' Tessa as his own.

She couldn't call Edgar cruel or ruthless. He was beyond being sociopathic. He existed outside of human society, *had* no humanity. His sense of morals was completely alien.

She shook her head as memories of her time with him threatened to flood her mind. If she thought about it, she'd break down.

"You okay?" Porter asked.

"No."

"You want to talk about it?"

"No."

He laughed. "No wonder you and Marcus are getting along so well. You're both people of few words."

"We fought together and almost died together. It creates an artificial sense of camaraderie."

Technically, *she* was the one who had almost died. Marcus could have run away whenever he wanted. Easily. But he had stayed to protect her. He had saved her life. Repeatedly. What did he want from her in return?

"That's possible," Porter said. "We've never seen him so taken with someone before, though."

Again with the royal 'we.' What was with these guys? Porter stopped in front of a door and put his hand on the doorknob. Before Tessa could ask about his weird grammar quirk, he paused and leaned toward her.

"He didn't hurt you, did he?"

Something about his intensity made her pause before making a flippant remark. Maybe the Blades would take care of her werewolf problem after all. Porter seemed to be searching for a reason to take Marcus out, and she doubted

Dexter would think twice about it. All she had to do was lie.

"He didn't hurt me at all," she said. "He saved me. Twice. Three times if you count carrying me through those Redcaps that showed up at the end."

Redcaps that meant there were more queens lurking around, waiting to make more spider-headed zombies. Providence was in for more missing persons cases. More death and grief. More broken families.

Porter smiled as if they weren't having a conversation that might have resulted in him putting down a member of his own team. The coldness in his eyes made her shiver.

"Good." He opened the door and gestured for her to enter first.

Marcus would have gone in before her and checked the room. She noticed how he scoped out the hallway and elevator before letting Vaughn or Tessa enter the spaces.

It was just as well. She didn't need a bodyguard. She sure as hell shouldn't get used to having one. Or people watching her back. Or food. Or a bed.

*Holy shit.*

She hadn't been wrong about her room being tricked out. The bed didn't have a canopy or anything, but it was king-sized. There was a desk and chair along the wall on her left, a set of bookshelves on her right, and a freaking big-screen TV flush against the wall. Two doors led from the room. Bathroom and… closet, maybe?

There was a small table near the door. She set her cereal box on it as she walked inside. Her feet sank into the soft, plush carpet. Feet that were spared from cuts because Marcus had carried her out of the junkyard.

She needed to stop thinking about him. Especially in warm and fuzzy ways.

"Nice place," she said. "I still won't be staying long."

"Give it a few days. You might change your mind."

If she stayed that long, a lot more than her mind would change.

"I don't like to stay put. Dwellers are nomadic. So am I."

"Not all dwellers move around," Porter said. "Providence has a rather high population of stationary dwellers. They seem to be drawn here."

*Drawn?* Shit. She'd be leaving sooner than she thought.

"Must be you Blades and your magnetic personalities." She spoke without giving it much thought, too occupied with running through what she would need to steal from them as soon as possible.

Clothing, food, weapons. A fucking car. Maybe she could manage one of the fancy vans in the garage, if she could work her way past whatever security system Vaughn had no doubt developed.

Tessa also needed time. Time to plan, rest up, maybe get a night—or day—of sleep when she wasn't clutching a weapon and keeping one eye open. For all their weirdness, she felt like she could trust the Blades to keep her safe.

"We're pretty certain it's the alien spacecraft buried beneath the ranch that's attracting them," Porter said.

"Wait... What?" Her mind was suddenly spinning in neutral, trying to process his words.

His smile broadened. "The alien spacecraft. The one that brought dwellers to this planet. It crashed a few millennia ago. Right here."

"I... don't know how to respond to that."

"The life forms aboard spread out into Earth's ecosystem, finding ways to survive by attaching themselves to whatever species they were most compatible with, hybridizing until they found viable forms. Humans built up stories around them, treating them as legend and myth—trying to make sense of things that are literally alien to them."

Tessa's forehead started to cramp from how high her eyebrows were arching. Her mouth hung open.

She knew dwellers were aliens, but had always been too concerned with how to get rid of them to give much thought to how they arrived. Edgar had dropped hints, but she deliberately shut him down to keep him from sharing the 'legacy' that she was going to become part of. Now, she kind of wished she'd listened to his side of the dwellers' origin story.

"How did you find the ship?" she said.

"Over time, it was buried, but Vaughn's family

discovered it when they settled here. They kept it hidden for generations. They had to wait until human technology advanced enough to take advantage of it. Her father started harvesting the ship for parts to found his tech company. Now that her father has passed, Vaughn keeps the company going, but uses the tech she pulls out to help us in our mission."

"That's… a lot."

"Give it some time to sink in. And while you do, there's one more thing we'd like you to think about."

What the hell could he follow with after that?

"From what we've seen, you'd make a great Blade," Porter said.

*Right. That.*

Here it came. The ultimate temptation.

"We'd like you to join us," he said. "Train as a Blade. Maybe settle here in Providence. We understand if you need to think about it."

"What I need is a shower and about five hours of uninterrupted sleep to process all of this."

"By all means." He walked to one of the doors and opened it, then stepped aside so she could see what was within.

Black clothing hung neatly from hangars. More was stacked on shelves, along with several sets of boots. Better yet, there were weapons hanging on the walls. Axes, swords, even a mace.

"Oh, you Blades do know how to tempt a hunter." She ran her fingers along the hilt of an axe. "Any of these have fancy settings like Vaughn's cutlery?"

"We keep the advanced weaponry in the sublevels. You'll need training on them before you can use them."

"Training."

She looked at the clothing again. Everything was smaller than she expected. The T-shirts, pants, boots—all were her size. Porter and Dexter weren't as huge as Marcus, but they were big enough that she'd be able to tell if these were their spares.

"How'd you have clothing in my size on hand?"

"We have a variety of Blades in our employ. We keep all bases stocked with supplies for everyone, just in case we have to do some shuffling."

Shuffling... If she didn't have to stay in one place, maybe she *could* become a Blade.

She shook the thought from her mind immediately.

He selected an outfit for her, going so far as to open a drawer she hadn't noticed and pulling out a sports bra and pair of boy briefs. He handed her the pile, then pointed toward the other door.

"Take that shower and get some sleep," he said. "We're heading back to the junkyard tonight. If, after that, you feel like we don't have anything to offer you... Well, no hard feelings. We'll replace what you lost—with upgrades —and send you on your way."

"Seriously?" She shook her head. "There has to be a catch."

"If it seems too good to be true, then let us add this. We're making this generous offer because we're that confident we can convince you to stay."

"That's a little creepy. And seriously, what is with the 'us' and 'we?'"

His smile broadened. "You'll get used to it."

She wasn't sure if he was referring to their general creepiness or the way they talked. She actually stammered a bit, trying to formulate a response. She couldn't think of any. Instead, she said, "Thanks for setting me up. You can go now."

"That's not happening." He walked to the desk and sat in the chair next to it.

"What?"

"You've been through a lot. It's our job to keep you safe."

"Can't you do that from outside?"

"Marcus has arrived and is standing in the hall currently."

"How do you know that?"

Porter interlaced his fingers over his chest and leaned back. "If you want a five hour nap, you'd better get on that shower."

He obviously wasn't going to budge and there was nothing lascivious in his gaze. She headed for the bathroom, pretending it didn't bother her that he'd be waiting for her when she was done—telling herself it was better that Porter was watching over her than Marcus.

*At least I know how to lie to myself.*

Of all the crazy things that had happened since she arrived in Providence, realizing that she felt safer with a werewolf than a human was about the strangest. But it was true.

She pulled off her clothes and hopped under the hot water. Absolute bliss. She couldn't remember the last time she'd had a real shower. There was soap, shampoo, and even conditioner.

She hurried through cleaning herself, not wanting to get used to it. Leaving was already going to be harder than it should be. She didn't want anything else tying her to this place—these people.

Still, as her hands drifted over her body, she remembered Marcus's touch. The heat of him, his weight on top of her, the passion in his kiss.

The way he had stopped her from ripping his clothes off and having sex. Because he knew she wouldn't want to have sex with a werewolf.

Not just any werewolf, anyway.

Her mother would disown her if she could hear Tessa's thoughts.

*"Dwellers may look human, but they aren't. The minute you forget that, you're dead. Just like your father."*

Her mom had never mentioned Brock. She refused to talk about him—ever. Tessa figured it was just too painful. Knowing how much *she* hurt… Yeah, that was probably it. But not talking about him made Tessa miss Brock more. Especially now, after meeting Dexter and Porter. They reminded her so much of Brock. How could they all three be so similar?

There couldn't be a connection. Not unless Brock had been one of a set of triplets separated at birth.

She knew that Brock was adopted. His dark eyes were a genetic impossibility with their parents' paler color. Brock had called them out on the matter in high school, and her parents had called the family together to explain.

Mom and Dad said they knew Brock's parents and were there when he was born. His biological mother had died in childbirth, and they'd decided to take Brock in and raise him as their own. It would have been a huge oversight to not mention that he'd been one of a set of triplets.

For a moment—only a moment—Tessa let herself wonder if it was possible.

Her parents would have told her, though. *Brock* would have told her—if he'd known.

Between the twins' eerie similarities to her brother, Vaughn's disarming personality, and Marcus's… being Marcus, this place felt weirdly like home. How could that happen in a matter of hours?

They would go from laughing to being at each other's

throats and back again in moments. It felt like her family before Edgar. Her real family. Her human family.

Brock had teased her all the time. They would laugh and fight and their dad would come in and mediate and get them to make up. Dad would always say that nothing was more important than family. She believed him.

It made it hurt even worse when they were all taken away.

She wished she could kill Edgar, but he was too powerful. It would be one thing if his physiology was the same as the comparatively simple creatures his dwellers transformed humans into. But Edgar... He was something much more complicated. And some day, she would be, too.

She checked her wristband again. It was waterproof, and she'd been careful when cleaning the skin around it. She hadn't noticed any suspicious lumps on her body. Hadn't felt them chewing away at any part of her but her wrist.

When Marcus was eating his breakfast, they had stirred. It had taken all of her willpower to act like nothing was wrong. Edgar's creations needed to eat meat to survive. Dead meat was their favorite, which made them not as bad as many of the other dwellers she'd encountered.

Werewolves, for instance. They liked their meat to run and scream.

So did Edgar.

So would she.

Her stomach twisted. She covered her mouth to keep her breakfast down.

Marcus was so different from the werewolves she'd met. It was hard to believe he was the same type of dweller.

A crazy idea hit her. Maybe he *wasn't*.

The Blades were ignorant about dwellers. They could be wrong about what Marcus was. There were other dwellers who had golden eyes. She knew of a few rare ones. The chupacabra, for instance. They were only dangerous to goats and other livestock. They didn't attack humans unless the human attacked them—which was a very bad idea. The hunter who'd lectured her mother and Tessa about them had been missing several body parts.

Chupacabra looked a lot like werewolves. Except for the wings... But maybe Marcus was some sort of mutant offshoot that didn't have any. It seemed a lot more believable than an alpha werewolf taking orders from a bunch of humans and being a decent guy.

She dried off and dressed quickly, then grabbed the stingray out of her other pants. They were going to fight together that night. She would keep an eye on Marcus and look for signs that the Blades were wrong about the type of dweller infecting him. But first, she needed some rest.

Porter was still sitting in the chair by the desk when she exited the bathroom. He had closed the curtains at some point, blocking out what dim light the storm wasn't stifling.

"Did you have a nice shower?"

"Yeah, thanks." She crossed to the closet and opened the doors.

One of the knives had caught her eye earlier. It was about as long as her forearm, had a sensible sheath, and was pretty flat. She could easily sleep with it under her pillow.

The stingray was… Well, it was awesome. But she didn't think it was a good idea to use it as her go-to weapon when sleeping in a strange place for the first time.

She grabbed the knife, then walked to the bed and pulled down the covers. "Are you really going to sit there and watch me sleep?"

"I sure am."

"Wait a minute. 'I?'"

He smiled again. "Go to sleep."

There was something different about his smile. It actually reached his eyes this time. Maybe he and Dexter just put on that hardcore façade to keep their crew in check and Porter was feeling more personable with it being just the two of them. It could also be a recruiting tactic. If so, it was kind of working.

*Weird.*

She couldn't stay, though. The dwellers in her arm were like a beacon for Edgar. He was always only a few days behind her. Eventually, he would catch up. She didn't know if she could convince the Blades to 'shuffle' her to other sites that quickly. Especially if they wanted to train her in their protocols.

Facing Edgar with the Blades of Janus backing her up would be better than dealing with him on her own. Except it wouldn't be *her* and the Blades. Edgar would gain more control over the dwellers in her arm as he drew near. He could activate them fully—order them to spread through Tessa's body, despite her best efforts to keep them dormant. He would take her over and the Blades would have *two* Hive beings to deal with.

She had to face the hard truth. The Blades couldn't save her. She was already infected. Already compromised.

The knife in her hand was heavy. She was sure its edge would be razor sharp. Vaughn might have even tweaked it, like her kitchen knife. It might not take much force at all to get rid of Tessa's problem permanently. Lop off her dominant arm just below the elbow and all her dweller problems went away.

Porter seemed to be some kind of scientist or doctor. He could probably keep her from bleeding out. She wouldn't have a better opportunity to be free. She wouldn't be as effective as a hunter—or a Blade—but maybe Vaughn could make her a cybernetic arm or something. It wouldn't be a death sentence. Tessa wouldn't be alone.

What the hell was wrong with her? As far as morbid fantasies went, this one was pretty messed up.

Tessa needed to sleep. Her mind was going to weird places. She couldn't remember the last good night's sleep she'd had.

And there Porter sat next to her bed, that half-smug, half-affectionate smile on his face that made her want to cry and scream and hug him.

She wished he would stop. He reminded her of Brock even more when he looked at her that way. Then again, holding on to that thought might help her sleep next to him.

She drew her new knife and felt its weight, slashing at nothing. It was balanced perfectly. She tossed it in the air and caught it a few times, then put it back in its sheath and slid it under her pillow.

"Feel better?" he asked.

"Yeah."

She took the stingray out of her pocket and set it on the bedside table, then crawled into bed and turned so her back was to him. She'd rather give him her back than open her eyes and see him sitting there, watching her.

"No one will hurt you while you're here," Porter said. "I promise you."

"I hear that a lot from you Blades. Marcus said the same thing."

Porter chuckled. "If he said it, he meant it. And as a hunter, you should know how safe it makes you when a werewolf offers their protection."

"Lucky me."

The lights clicked off. Porter was silent for a few moments, then he spoke in a gentle voice.

"Tessa…"

"Yeah?"

"I'm glad we found you."

*So weird.*

She did her best to turn it into a joke. Her eyes were burning.

"Me, too. This bed sure as hell beats my van."

Porter laughed softly and shifted in his chair. Listening to his steady breath—knowing Marcus was right outside her door—she managed a minor miracle. She fell asleep.

# Chapter Fourteen

Two hours of sleep was barely enough to keep Vaughn on her feet, but there was data to parse, algorithms to tweak, and enhancements to add to the vehicles. Thanks to Tessa's information about Redcaps, and after thoroughly studying her bug repellers, everything housed in the garage could now emit a sound that would paralyze Redcaps.

Vaughn had added a sound on top of the noise they would broadcast that was within the range of human hearing. Even though she didn't make it into the field... well, ever... she imagined what it must be like quite often. Being able to hear the emitter would sure as hell reassure her if she was walking into a Redcap nest.

She could have slept more, but Tessa had wounded her pride when she talked about Vaughn's cooking. The table was set with a vegan feast that would show Tessa what Vaughn was made of in the kitchen. She was glad Tessa had at least been impressed by her knife.

She was more impressed with Marcus.

*That way lies madness.*

But it was impossible not to think about.

Vaughn and Marcus had been partners for years. Friends. And even though nothing romantic had ever developed between them, Vaughn had always wondered if it might. Marcus had never shown interest in anyone—or anything—before. Until Tessa.

Whatever was building between them was fast and intense. And probably not safe. Vaughn was afraid for both of them. For everyone, really. There was no telling how forming a bond like this would affect Marcus's control, especially given the challenges he was already dealing with.

Vaughn was the only person Marcus had confided in. For the moment, anyway. He'd probably tell Tessa all about it.

"Ugh. Stop." Vaughn dragged out the last word, a huge yawn stretching her face.

She turned the corner on the way to Tessa's room and saw Marcus pacing in front of her door. He was wearing the same clothes as yesterday. The pants still had dirt from the Redcaps' nest on their cuffs.

"Have you been out here all day?" Vaughn said.

Marcus glared at her. "Yes."

"You should have slept."

"I don't need to sleep."

"You don't need *as much* sleep. There's a difference." Vaughn let out a sigh. "You don't want your reflexes to be slow for the big fight tonight."

"My reflexes are fine."

Before she could stop herself, Vaughn said, "What is it about this hunter that has you so worked up?"

Marcus shook his head. "I don't know."

"Yeah, well, she'll be a great partner for you in the field." Vaughn turned to leave, but Marcus grabbed her elbow.

"You're still my partner."

"Until Tessa signs up—and she'd be crazy not to. Then you'll be doing your super-awesome team thing, while I'm stuck here crunching numbers and making gadgets."

"Vaughn—"

"Not that I want to be in the field, but at least working with you I felt like I was having a real-time impact."

"You do. Your tech—"

"Records your amazing feats of bravery and fighting... ness." Vaughn shook her head. "I didn't get much sleep. I shouldn't be talking right now."

"Tessa and I working together... It isn't the same."

Vaughn snorted. "Yeah. She's an upgrade. I get it."

She started to leave again, but Marcus pulled her back, wheeling Vaughn around and pinning her shoulders to the wall. Marcus stepped in close, eyes glowing bright gold. This level of proximity was new. And not nearly as pleasant as Vaughn had imagined it would be.

"She isn't an upgrade," Marcus said. "No matter what happens, she isn't replacing you. You're more than my partner. You're—"

"Don't. Don't say it." Vaughn had to be half-asleep or half-crazy, challenging Marcus when he was already so worked up. "I don't want to hear that I'm your best friend or 'like a sister.'"

"That isn't what I was going to say."

Vaughn knew their relationship would be different after this, no matter what Marcus said. They had always been close. Since the moment they met, they'd bonded. Now that Vaughn thought about it, it had been about as quick as Marcus seemed to be bonding with Tessa.

Communicating with people had never been one of Vaughn's strengths. Marcus was her first real friend. Vaughn needed that as much as Marcus did.

"What, then?" Vaughn asked.

"You're more than friend. More than family." Marcus leaned in closer and dropped his voice, his breath warming Vaughn's neck. "You're *pack*."

Vaughn felt like her stomach dropped through the floor. If Dexter heard Marcus talking like that, he would kill him. Which only made it mean more that Marcus had dared to say it.

The door opened at that moment and one of the bosses walked out. Porter, maybe? He smiled at them instead of attacking.

Probably Porter.

"We're not interrupting anything, are we?" he said.

Tessa followed him, in full Blade attire. She was even armed. Her hair was pulled up in a tight bun on the back of her head.

She arched an eyebrow at them. "You guys sure do spend a lot of time pinning each other to walls."

Marcus growled at her and she raised her hands as if in surrender.

"I don't judge," she said.

Vaughn laughed and shook her head. She liked Tessa. She wished she didn't, but she did.

"If you're done here, it's time to get to work," Porter said. "Debriefing is in the dining room. We'll plan while we eat. Vaughn has outdone herself yet again."

Dexter must have told Porter about the spread through their earpieces. Vaughn couldn't remember hearing Dexter say anything while they were talking in the dining room earlier, though. She was too tired to try to puzzle it out.

Marcus stepped back and Vaughn straightened her T-shirt.

"I have," Vaughn said. "And it'll taste better warm, so let's go."

# Chapter Fifteen

Marcus led the way into the dining room. Tessa fell in step right behind him, almost like she was as eager to be close as he was.

That was probably his imagination.

Waiting outside her door had been humiliating. He wasn't some dog to exile into the back yard when company was over. He wouldn't hurt her.

Dexter and Porter... That was starting to feel like another matter.

If Marcus had demanded to stay in the room with her, there would have been a fight. He was pretty sure he wouldn't have come out on top. Depending on Dexter's mood, Marcus might not even have been around afterwards to protect Tessa. Dexter seemed pretty set on keeping them apart.

So Marcus had stayed outside her door, listening to the rising and falling beat of her heart. Trying to ignore the steadier pace of Porter's so close to her.

At least Marcus knew his bosses weren't attracted to her. Intrigued, yeah. More than Marcus could explain. But there was nothing more to it that he could detect.

Dexter was already sitting at the far end of the large, rectangular table when they arrived. He locked his gaze with Marcus's the moment their group entered the room.

"Good evening." He gestured to the chair next to him. "Have a seat, Tessa."

"Why not?" She headed for Dexter, but didn't sit. Instead, she pulled out the chair that would be on her left side—the side away from Dexter. "Marcus?"

Dexter shifted forward in his seat. "Actually—"

"I need a werewolf nose to make sure there are absolutely no animal products in the food." Tessa stared Dexter down with a smile. "I'm very serious about my lifestyle choices."

He leaned back in his chair, a matching smirk on his face. "We assure you, Vaughn took that into account while making dinner."

"Vaughn is also standing right here," Vaughn said. "And doesn't like being talked about in the third person while she's present."

Marcus smiled at his beta—best—friend. His *best* friend. Damn, he had to stop thinking like that, defining people by pack hierarchy. It was only getting worse since Tessa had arrived.

"Let's all just sit down," Porter said.

Marcus strode to Tessa's side, hoping to pull out her chair for her. The baleful glare she cast at him made him think twice. He pulled out his own chair and sat, gratified when she shifted her chair closer as she joined him. Vaughn sat across from him and Porter took the end of the table opposite Dexter.

"Is that hummus?" Tessa leaned forward, her eyes growing wide as she took in the array of food on the table.

Vaughn grinned. "Not just hummus. Homemade hummus. Along with fresh baked pita bread and spaghetti squash pasta with a basil pesto made from Marcus's garden out back."

"You have a garden?" Tessa arched an eyebrow at Marcus.

"I can have layers," Marcus said.

Tessa snorted, but the smile she cast at him seemed genuine and not mocking. She turned her attention back to the table.

"If this is the way you react any time someone insults your food, I'm going to have to think of more bad things to say about it." Tessa closed her eyes and inhaled deeply. "Like, 'I've never smelled anything more disgusting than this in my life.'"

She picked up the closest dish and started shoveling food onto her plate. Vaughn's smile widened. Dexter passed Tessa another dish, and she repeated the process. Over and over, till her plate was piled high and everything mixed together. She picked up a wedge of pita bread and grabbed a handful of hummus and pasta with it, but paused right before shoving it into her mouth.

"Shit, I almost forgot." She dropped the bite back on her mountain of food, then picked up her plate and held it under Marcus's nose. "Smell this."

Vaughn busted out laughing. She didn't stop, even when Marcus glared at her.

"Sorry." Vaughn shook her head.

"Tessa doesn't stand much on manners," Porter said.

Everyone turned to look at him. Even Dexter.

Porter cleared his throat. "Or so I've noticed. There's still a half-eaten box of cereal in her room."

*'I've' noticed?*

That was unusual. Tessa's teasing had renewed Marcus's awareness of the weird way Porter and Dexter talked about themselves. Marcus held Porter's gaze for a few more moments before turning back to Tessa's plate and sniffing it. There wasn't a trace of animal in it. No meat, blood, or even milk products. Usually, Vaughn cooked with butter and meats. Those components at least caught Marcus's attention. But this… It turned his stomach a bit.

"It's clean." Marcus angled away from the plate.

"Thanks," Tessa said. The edge that normally laced her voice was muted. "I forgot smelling the wrong kind of food can be unpleasant for dwellers."

"Do you have extensive experience with werewolves?" Dexter had already filled a plate and started eating, along with the others.

"More than I'd like," she said. "Present company excluded."

For some reason, it felt like she was making some kind of inside joke. Marcus was distracted from her words when her knee brushed against his leg. His breath hitched. He coughed to try to cover it, which was equally weird for him. He didn't get sick or have allergies.

Tessa smirked, then picked up the drenched bite of pita and popped it into her mouth. Her eyes rolled shut and she let out a moan. "Holy shit, Vaughn. This is amazing."

The food might not smell good to Marcus, but Tessa…

"I'm glad you're… enjoying it." Vaughn's eyebrows climbed her forehead as she watched Tessa eat.

Marcus closed his eyes and covered his face briefly with his hands. If she kept *enjoying it* this much, he was going to have some issues.

Her thigh was still pressed against his.

She knew he was a werewolf now, but she wasn't giving him crap about it anymore. He wondered what would happen if he kissed her. Then again, if he let himself—and she responded in kind—he probably wouldn't want to stop there. And Dexter would definitely kill Marcus.

"Maybe we should go over tonight's mission," Vaughn said.

She slowly turned to the large monitor that hung on the wall opposite them, as if it was hard to look away from the spectacle of Tessa eating. Vaughn tapped her watch briefly and the screen flickered to life.

"The police are done at the site," Vaughn said. "Aside from the remains of Tessa's van, they didn't find anything that set them off."

Tessa mumbled something around a mouthful of food. The mess on her plate was already smaller.

"I'm sorry, what was that?" Vaughn said.

"She said Redcaps don't leave meat behind." Porter paused with his fork halfway to his mouth, taking in the stares of everyone around the table. Even Tessa had stopped shoveling food into her mouth.

"That's some impressive translating, boss," Vaughn said.

Porter cleared his throat and pointed at the screen. "Get back to the briefing."

Something was off about him. Marcus took a deep breath as discretely as he could. There was a subtle shift in Porter's scent, the musty notes growing more pronounced. Porter's mannerisms had changed, too. And he kept staring at Tessa and smiling. If his expression had been keen, Marcus might have... ripped off his face. Instead, there was a tenderness to it. For whatever reason, Porter cared about Tessa. That would go a long way toward keeping her safe. The twins were amazing in battle.

Marcus tensed as the voice in his head spoke to him. *"So are you. It isn't their place."*

The hair on his arms stood on end and his shoulders bunched. He took a deep breath and let it out slowly. The more people who were determined to protect her, the safer Tessa would be. Dexter and Porter weren't threats or competitors. They were allies. They were pack.

His dweller snarled. *"What kind of alpha are you?"*

*"The kind that doesn't judge people by their classification in the Blades' dweller database. I don't care that my pack is filled with humans."*

Vaughn was still talking. Marcus pulled his attention outward to listen.

"Luckily, blowing up the van set off the grenades Marcus dropped." Vaughn glanced over at Tessa, her expression reverting to its earlier shocked fascination. Vaughn continued, but her words came out slower than usual. "We'd be skirting more intense scrutiny if the police had found those."

Tessa pushed her plate away and leaned back in her chair. She let out a contented sigh. Marcus stifled a rumbling growl of approval. She stretched her legs under the table, leaving one ankle resting on his shin.

"Dexter, Marcus, and Tessa will head back to the junkyard tonight." Porter nodded toward Tessa. "Tessa will ride with Dexter."

"I know how to drive a motorcycle," Tessa said.

Vaughn laughed. "You'd need a pilot's license for our bikes."

"Then I'll ride with Marcus." Tessa shrugged.

"You'll ride with Dexter." Porter was insistent. More so than Marcus had ever seen before. Dexter was usually the one giving orders.

"I thought I made it clear earlier." Tessa leaned forward and glared at Porter. "*Marcus* is my ride."

She rested her hand on Marcus's thigh under the table. High up on his thigh. Really close to…

His knee bounced up from the contact like he'd touched a live wire. He hit the bottom of the table hard enough that everyone's plates and utensils rattled. Tessa arched an eyebrow at Marcus, tightening her grip on his leg.

"You okay there?" Vaughn said.

Marcus grabbed Tessa's hand with as much subtlety as he could, interlacing their fingers. Dexter and Porter both glared at him.

Marcus didn't care.

That had never happened before. He'd always fought for their approval—even while fighting off visions of killing them. Suddenly the only opinions that really mattered to him were Tessa's and Vaughn's.

Vaughn cleared her throat. "Okay, then. Back to the mission. I've upgraded all the vehicles so they'll broadcast the same frequency as Tessa's bug repellers. I added an overlay sound so that we mere humans know it's working."

"Sweet." Tessa squeezed Marcus's hand.

His heart pounded in his chest. Marcus hadn't expected her to let him hold her hand. The only reason he'd tried was to get her hand off his thigh. A couple of inches higher, and she'd have been holding a lot more than his leg. Dexter and Porter were already pissed enough. If they saw how worked up Marcus was from her touch… That was a situation he wanted to avoid. On many levels.

Tessa leaned forward to make better eye contact with Vaughn. "What's the range?"

"A hundred yards."

"You're freaking kidding me." She beamed at Vaughn. "That's fantastic."

Vaughn shrugged, smiling back at her. "Well—"

Before she could go on, Dexter interrupted. "That'll take care of the Redcaps, but not the remaining queens. Tessa, do you have any recommendations for taking them out?"

"Do you guys have any missile launchers?"

"Those would be too loud," Vaughn said "We're trying to keep this low-key."

Tessa stared at her. "Seriously? You guys have missile launchers?"

"Well, prototypes…" Vaughn looked back and forth between Dexter and Porter, as if looking for help.

"Fire is best for Redcap queens," Tessa said. "Their bodies are too big to make most other weapons effective. You can waste a lot of time and ammo trying to find their vital organs."

"Flamethrowers it is." Dexter was smiling.

She shook her head. "We're going to need a lot of fuel for this barbeque."

"I think Vaughn's tanks are up to the task." Dexter stood.

Vaughn let out a brief chuckle. When everyone looked at her, she coughed, then said, "My tanks... Nevermind."

"Must be nice having that alien technology to build on right underneath your feet," Tessa said.

The room went still. Porter glanced away as even Dexter glared at him.

Vaughn was the one to break the silence. "You told her about my ship?"

Porter hesitated a moment. "Yes."

"He was asking me to be a Blade," Tessa said. "I thought it was part of the recruitment package. 'Join the team. We have a spaceship.'"

"None of the other Blades know." Marcus kept his voice calm, though he could practically feel the rage rolling off of Vaughn.

"Seriously?" Tessa cast a look at Porter and shook her head.

"You had no right." Vaughn's hands clenched into fists on the table.

"Vaughn—" Porter said.

"You had *no right*." This time, Vaughn shouted the

words.

Tessa's voice was a gentle counterpoint. "Hey, there's no way I'm going to tell anybody about it. Even if I thought people might believe me, I wouldn't do that to you."

"That's so reassuring from the woman I've known for less than a day." Vaughn snorted. "What is it about you, anyway? Why is everybody making such a big deal out of you?"

Tessa let out a similar sound. "I wish I knew. I don't *want* to be a big deal. I wanted to live a quiet, normal life. I was in the fucking chess club when I was a kid. I had boy band posters on my walls."

"My heart bleeds for you," Vaughn said.

"I don't know what happened to any of it." The light glinted off Tessa's eyes. "We had to leave in the middle of the night. We couldn't even go back for the cat. I've been fighting dwellers on the run since I was twelve years old. I *wish* no one had noticed me. I *wish* they had just…" She clenched her eyes shut tight for a few seconds, shaking her head. When she spoke again, her voice was calmer. It was low and level. "I don't give a fuck about your ship or your tech or your stupid Blade protocols. I just want to kill dwellers."

Despite her words, she kept a tight hold on Marcus's hand.

"Let's get back to it, then," Dexter said.

"We'll need to lure them into the open." Tessa's attention was fixed on the monitor. "There's that big open space with nothing but packed earth. The stacks of cars will obscure the view from the road. All we need is a choice piece of bait."

"I can do it," Marcus said.

Tessa shook her head. "No, you can't."

He sucked in a breath and turned to her, ready to argue. He was more than capable in a fight.

"Don't get your alpha-britches in a bunch." She headed off his argument, giving his hand a squeeze.

It was so different from what he expected after their 'heart-to-heart' in the junkyard. Even their exchange in the kitchen. What had changed her mind?

"Dwellers don't usually go after each other," she said. "They'll ignore you. Which leaves me and your fearless leaders here."

Dexter smirked as she nodded toward him. "Vaughn, you'll need to fit Tessa for a flamethrower and teach her how to work the controls you've designed. She and I will wait in the clearing for the queens."

Now Dexter was doing it, too. Using 'I' instead of 'we.' Marcus took a deep breath, trying to notice if anything else was off about them. Aside from the usual musty scent being a bit stronger, he didn't notice anything.

The challenge in Dexter's dark gaze was unmistakable. "If we keep our backs to each other, we should be able to roast anything that gets too close. Right, Marcus?"

There was a definite threat there, and Marcus was well aware of how flammable he was. He was also aware of the silver worked into Dexter's swords, and how deadly the man was with them.

He was also sure of something else.

*"He's not your alpha,"* the voice of his dweller said.

*"I know."*

Marcus couldn't believe he was making that admission, even to himself. Thinking of Dexter as the alpha had helped Marcus hold himself together over and over again. Now, he had something else to hold him together. He looked back to Tessa and then to Vaughn.

"Sounds like a good plan," Marcus said.

"Then let's get moving." Tessa gave his hand one more squeeze before letting it go and pushing herself away from the table. "The queens will be more vulnerable while the sun's out. We have about two hours of daylight left." She stood and grabbed her dishes.

"Leave those for me," Vaughn said.

"Actually, I'll take care of cleaning up." Porter nodded at Tessa. "Take Tessa to the armory. I want her fully prepared for the fight."

"Sure." Vaughn stood and headed for the door. When Tessa joined her, Vaughn said, "You coming, Marcus?"

"I'll catch up." Marcus and Dexter had locked gazes again. Marcus wasn't about to look away.

"Let's go." Vaughn could clearly see that trouble was brewing. She hurried Tessa from the room.

Flat black eyes. Why had Marcus ever had trouble meeting them before? He felt his own eyes start to tingle, a surge of adrenaline flowing over his skin not unlike a change. Just without the fur.

Dexter let out a chuckle. "I wondered when this moment would come. I thought it would be sooner."

"You can't keep me from her."

"I noticed." For the first time, Dexter broke eye contact first. He shifted his gaze to Porter.

Another rush flooded Marcus's system. It didn't matter that there was nothing submissive in Dexter's expression or body language. There was also nothing *dominant* about it.

"You're not my alpha," Marcus said.

"Of course not." Dexter actually laughed. "That was your assumption."

Marcus was reeling. His dweller wasn't so much talking to him as feeding images of Marcus ripping Dexter's head off and doing unsavory things to it.

"Why would you let me think that?"

"Because you needed to," Dexter said. "You needed someone to tell you what to do. You needed to be able to tell yourself that you weren't alone, that you had someone to help you fight the urges that plagued you after being turned."

The world felt like it was shifting on its axis, the room tilting around Marcus as he tried to get his bearings in this new reality. He thought back over his time with the Blades and knew Dexter was right. His influence had been critical in those first few months. Years even. But not anymore. Marcus could control himself.

Dexter stood and crossed the room to stand behind his twin. "It doesn't matter that you don't have an alpha. You still have a boss. And if you want to remain a Blade, you'll follow my orders."

"You mean, if I want to keep my head."

Dexter's eyes became colder. Marcus didn't know they could. An eerie feeling crept down his spine as they held each other's gaze, sizing each other up anew.

Dexter wasn't afraid of Marcus. Not a single bit. Marcus knew how ruthless and skilled Dexter was in battle and had a healthy respect for his 'boss.' And yeah, Marcus was a little bit afraid of Dexter. He was self-aware enough to admit it.

But Dexter had also seen Marcus in action. He knew what Marcus was capable of.

Why wasn't Dexter scared?

The werewolves he'd taken out were cocky and arrogant. They weren't expecting an attack. And even after seeing Dexter wielding his swords, they hadn't taken him seriously until it was too late.

Marcus knew not to make that mistake. Which meant

that Dexter didn't have the advantage of surprise. Every time he turned his back on Marcus—hell, every time Dexter went to sleep—he had to be thinking that there was a seriously pissed off werewolf close enough to strike.

But Dexter had never put off the faintest hint of unease in Marcus's presence. Or ever, really.

The only shift Marcus had ever detected in Dexter's scent was that weird musty smell getting stronger around Tessa, just like Porter's did. There was something going on between all three of them—and that didn't sit well with Marcus.

As if reading his thoughts, Porter said, "Tessa can be headstrong and stubborn. It's obvious she's taken an interest in you—an interest that you will discourage."

"No, I won't. Tessa is..." Marcus stopped himself, conditioning taking hold where fear no longer existed. He shook his head.

Just because Dexter wasn't the alpha of Marcus's pack, that didn't mean there wasn't one. *Marcus* was the alpha. It was time to start acting like it.

He stood, and said, "Tessa is pack."

"She's *family*." Porter slammed his fist on the table.

*What the hell?*

*"More and more interesting,"* his dweller thought.

Dexter put his hand on Porter's shoulder. Porter closed his eyes and took a few deep breaths. Dexter held Marcus's gaze, challenging him openly. Their scent intensified again—old earth and stale leaves. The energy in the room crackled with the threat of violence.

The problem was, if a fight started, Marcus wasn't sure who or even *what* he'd be dealing with. Not his alpha. Not his boss. In that moment, he wasn't even sure… He wasn't sure they were human.

He thought about what Tessa had said about her family. About how she'd mistaken Porter for her brother, Brock.

*"What* is *he?"* The voice in Marcus's head almost sounded frustrated.

Marcus wasn't as concerned with the 'what' as the 'who.' And how that might impact Tessa.

"We're all a family," Dexter said. "All the Blades. And Tessa is one of us now, whether she's ready to admit it or not."

Marcus snorted. "Yeah. That's what Porter meant."

"The world is full of mysteries," Porter said. "And monsters. Some of which need to be taken care of. Are you going to follow orders, or will Dexter and Tessa be heading to the junkyard on their own?"

"I'll handle your orders in the field," Marcus said. "But outside of that… That's between Tessa and me. It's none of your business."

Porter grimaced, but didn't say anything. Skin prickling, Marcus turned his back on the pair, even though he wasn't entirely sure they wouldn't use the opportunity to launch an attack. His muscles rippled with the urge to change.

At the door, Dexter called out to him. "One more thing, Marcus."

Marcus paused and looked back over his shoulder.

With the same casual smirk on his face, Dexter said, "If you hurt Tessa in any way, I won't just kill you. I'll *peel* you. Understood?"

He wasn't trying to order Marcus away from her anymore. That was progress. And it was as close as Marcus was going to get to having their blessing.

He nodded. "Understood."

# Chapter Sixteen

Not much had changed at the junkyard. Tire tracks furrowed the dirt heading into the place, little puddles forming in them from the bit of rain that had managed to fall during the day. Heavy gray clouds hung low and menacing over their heads. Tessa wondered how their flamethrowers would hold up in a thunderstorm. She hoped they wouldn't have to find out.

She slid off the back of Marcus's bike and walked to the thickest cluster of tracks. "Looks like they sent in a lot of emergency response vehicles. Those people have no idea how lucky they are. Walking into a space with so many Redcaps…" She shook her head.

"Hey, resident Redcap expert. Maybe you can answer a question that's been bothering me."

Tessa jumped as Vaughn's voice spoke directly into her ear. It was unusual enough having partners in a hunt. Having backup right in her ear was just plain weird.

She looked at Marcus and he nodded. Feeling a little self-conscious, she spoke as if Vaughn was there, thinking how strange it would seem from outside that she was talking to herself. Then again, everyone who *was* there was on the same frequency and could hear everything being said. She'd have to watch out for that.

"Go ahead," Tessa said.

"Why don't the Redcaps attack police?" Vaughn asked. "Or EMTs, for that matter. In all my reports, I've never heard of an emergency responder going missing."

"If something shows up with lights and sirens, they know to run and hide. They're not completely stupid."

"Hmm."

Tessa could hear Vaughn typing on the keyboard built into her desk in the ops center and envisioned her staring at the screens, taking in all the data she could. After being trained on the slick flamethrower she'd invented herself, Tessa's estimation of the Blades' 'IT gal' was pretty much through the roof.

A small tank was strapped to Tessa's back. It conformed to her body well enough that it wouldn't interfere with her movement, even with the harness attached to it. She barely felt its extra weight. Vaughn had told her its burn time quadrupled what her old one could do. The hose for it was built into Tessa's jacket—completely undetectable from the outside. If Tessa needed to use the flamethrower, she could twist her hand a certain way and the nozzle would spring out from the jacket's cuff. The controls were on the nozzle itself.

She'd been skeptical about how safe the whole thing was until Vaughn had taken her through a practice run in one of their training rooms. Its accuracy was incredible, as was its range. The fire came out more like a stream than a cloud. Efficient and easier to control.

The whole time, all Tessa could think was, *"Damn, Blades have it easy."*

And, *"I could get used to this."*

If she let herself. Which she would not. Probably.

She heard a low, sustained note behind her. Marcus's bike emitting its Redcap repeller.

Marcus walked up next to her. "Are you sure you're okay with this?"

"What, walking into the middle of Redcap territory that's home to multiple queens and hoping they're in the mood for a snack?" She grinned at him. *"Pfft.* Piece of cake."

Dexter joined them after parking his bike a few yards away and starting up its repelling note. "Remember the parameters. We need to keep as low a profile as we can. The stacks of cars should obscure line of sight for anyone driving by, which might be unlikely in this section of town this time of day, but we still need to be careful. Vaughn is monitoring police bands and will let us know if anyone gets curious."

"I'm still not sure these flamethrowers will be enough to take down a queen," Tessa said. There was a lot of flesh they'd need to roast to take them out.

"Who said we're only using flamethrowers?" Dexter

drew one of the short swords strapped to his back.

She shook her head. "You are absolutely insane."

Dexter smirked. "Welcome to the family."

He probably meant it as a joke, but with the way he reminded her of Brock, it just pissed her off.

"One thing before we go in," she said. "If I'm taken out, burn me. Don't leave anything behind."

"Tessa—"

She cut off Marcus before he could give away anything about her 'unfortunate situation.'

"I'm serious," she said. "I won't be a meat puppet."

"It won't be an issue." Dexter spoke with such conviction. So damn cocky—all of these guys.

Tessa snorted. "Is this the part where you tell me you're not going to let anything happen to me?"

"No. It's the part where we remind you that *Marcus* won't let anything happen to you. But yeah, same here."

There was that weird 'we' again. Porter had been right, though. She was getting used to it.

Dexter nodded at Marcus. "Suit up."

She looked at Marcus, wondering what Dexter was talking about. Marcus was the only one without a flamethrower. Now that she thought about it, he didn't have any weapons she could see. There was probably a stun gun somewhere in his duster. The thought of searching him for it was a pleasant—if dangerous—distraction. Until she looked at his face.

"You can't be serious." He'd actually gone pale, his gold eyes wide.

Dexter cocked his head. "What's the matter, Marcus? Afraid to show Tessa your real moves?"

"Wait…" Tessa's mind was balking from the obvious meaning of their conversation. "You're not talking about Marcus changing, are you?"

"He'll be deadlier in his other form," Dexter said.

"Yeah. To *all* of us." She couldn't believe Dexter was even suggesting it. It would be easier for Marcus to control himself in his human form. No matter what he was—chupacabra or werewolf—activating his dweller nature right before a fight seemed like a really bad idea. "Now I *know* you're nuts."

"It's okay, Tessa." Marcus's voice was quiet.

"No, it isn't. Transforming would basically amount to you giving your body over to your dweller. The control you've shown so far has been remarkable, but no one could handle that."

"I can." He spoke with utter confidence.

All of her mother's lessons, everything Tessa herself had witnessed, demonstrated that werewolves were violent monsters. Their dwellers turned them into killing machines who lived to inflict pain and suffering. They were almost as bad as the thing she would turn into if she wasn't careful—or if Edgar caught up with her. There was no way Marcus could be a werewolf. Werewolves needed the support structure of their pack to remain even mildly sane and functional.

Marcus was stable. Protective. Kind, even. The Blades had to have it wrong. Didn't they?

An edge crept into his voice. "Not all werewolves are mindless killers."

"You don't know what you're talking about," Tessa said.

"As a matter of fact, I do." He stared at her, gold eyes igniting.

He let his duster slide down his arms, then tossed it toward his bike. Once again, she was struck by his amazing physique—the lean muscles of his forearms, his narrow waist and broad chest.

Dexter took a few steps back. "You might want to give him some space."

Tessa stayed put. She wasn't sure if she was trying to show Marcus that she refused to be intimidated or maybe... that she was starting to believe him.

He took out his earpiece and tossed it to Dexter, then pulled his black T-shirt over his head and threw it on top of his duster.

So many scars.

Now this—*this*—she could believe was the work of a werewolf. Of a pack.

Bite marks. Claws. She had seen similar patterns on corpses. Never on someone who had survived. She had watched a pack play with their victims at one of Edgar's revolting 'dinner parties.' Tessa had been powerless to do anything about it then. All she could do was vow that she would never turn into a creature capable of such cruelty.

But if Marcus was a werewolf, and he was this in control…

She looked past the scars, to the lines of muscle, the rows of abs beneath his olive skin. The strong arms that he had wrapped around her, offering comfort, keeping her from doing something he knew she would regret later. He hadn't hurt her. She'd never been afraid of him or even *near* him. He made her feel as close to safe as she'd felt since her family was torn apart, before she knew that monsters were real and she was in their crosshairs.

It didn't seem possible, but in the short time she'd known him, he'd started to feel like home.

He kicked off his shoes, his bare toes curling on the ground. He began to unfasten his pants, but paused.

"Do you mind?" he said.

She smirked at him. "Are you kidding? This is the best part."

If they'd had sex before she knew about him—about what he was—she would have regretted it. But now…

"I need you to stop looking at me like that." His nostrils flared and he closed his eyes for a moment. "And I really need you to stop smelling like that."

"Like what?"

"I think you know." He lowered his voice. "I'd rather not have my boss see me with a raging hard-on."

"Seconded," Dexter said. "Quit flirting and get to work."

Tessa crossed her arms and stared at Marcus, no longer afraid to hold his gaze. "Maybe you should think about baseball or something then."

He sighed, but quickly undid his pants and slipped out of them, tossing them on the pile.

Marcus—naked—was absolutely glorious. His legs were corded with muscle, toned and not bulky. A light dusting of dark hair covered his thighs. According to the Blades, that would be turning to fur soon. The thought of it helped squelch her libido. His dick, on the other hand... That was another matter entirely.

There was so much they could do together. But first, they had to deal with these Redcaps. She pulled her gaze away from his groin and stared at him expectantly.

"One last thing," he said.

Before she could ask what he wanted, he stepped forward and gripped her by the hips, pulling her against his chest. Her hands went to his shoulders more to keep her balance than anything else.

Until she felt the heat of him. Until his lips came crashing down on hers, his tongue thrusting into her mouth.

He brought one hand up to grab the back of her head,

holding her where he wanted her. She grabbed his hair in a grip that wasn't nearly as gentle. She needed him to know she could match his passion, if not his strength. She used her other arm to pull herself up higher, pressing more of their bodies together.

She bit at his tongue, tangled hers with his, raked her nails along the side of his neck. He wrapped his free arm around the small of her back, lifting her up off her feet. She was just about to wrap her legs around his waist when Dexter cleared his throat behind them.

"Stop messing around," Dexter said. "We have a job to do."

Marcus let out a low growl as they released each other and Tessa slid down his body. His eyes glowed so brightly, they cast shadows on his features, emphasizing his cheekbones and the line of his jaw.

Tessa laughed, trying to ease the tension between them. "If you were trying to avoid a hard-on, that was a very confusing choice."

Marcus was radiating tightly controlled fury. She was kind of pissed herself. That had been a hell of a kiss.

"I wasn't sure you'd let me kiss you again after this," Marcus said.

"I have a lot more than kissing planned when this is done."

Dexter exhaled through his nose. "Come on."

Marcus ignored him. "What changed your mind?"

"You did. But my mind isn't completely made up yet." She took a deep breath, dropping her hands to her sides, not knowing what she wanted, what she *needed* from him. Before she could think better of it, she spoke. As honestly as she ever had. "Show me. Give me hope."

Her eyes blurred. She blinked quickly to clear them, but knew he had seen. She willed him to understand what she was asking for.

It wasn't just hope for a home, hope for a relationship. If Marcus was a werewolf—even she realized that the chupacabra theory was a stretch—and he could control his dweller, then maybe she could control herself when her own change inevitably came. Because she knew it wasn't a matter of *if* her dwellers escaped. It was a matter of *when*.

Marcus nodded. Then he stepped back, keeping eye contact as he started to change.

Ripples of pale blue light spread over his skin, pulsing and quickening. His chest rose and fell faster as the light intensified. His skin darkened, muscles flexing and bones popping. His lips twitched right before his nose and mouth distended into a muzzle. He shook his head as his ears lengthened and his shoulders bunched.

Fur sprouted everywhere. His... manly parts... pulled back into his torso as his chest extended. His ankles elongated till he was standing on the balls of his feet. His arms lengthened, too, but not as much as his nails—his claws. They curved in sharp crescents three inches at least from the tip of each finger, tapering into deadly points.

The light faded and she was left standing two feet away from a towering, fully-active dweller, who was absolutely, positively, without doubt, a werewolf.

*Shit.*

She was within range. Easily. He looked down at her, eyes blazing gold, and let out a low, rumbling growl. His breath was warm on her face. Behind her, she heard Dexter draw his other sword. He'd told her they were infused with silver. Silver worked against any number of dwellers. She didn't know why it was such a common allergy for alien species. Now she was sure he carried those swords specifically to deal with Marcus.

"Marcus." Dexter's low voice was a warning.

Marcus narrowed his eyes—the growl deepening—and Tessa did the unthinkable. She stepped forward and put her hand on Marcus's chest.

# Chapter Seventeen

Tessa was touching him. Her cool fingers splayed across Marcus's chest, firm enough to touch his skin through the thick pelt of fur that protected him in this form. Not only that, but she was standing between Marcus and Dexter. She was protecting him, like a packmate should.

Like a... *mate.*

Marcus lowered his head to hers, gently brushing their cheeks together. She let out a shaky sigh and burrowed her fingers deeper into his fur.

"Get to the top of that stack of cars," Dexter said.

Marcus growled at the interruption. Tessa pressed against his chest more firmly, stepping closer.

*God, her touch...*

"Marcus," Dexter snapped.

Marcus felt his lips twitch back from his teeth. Tessa curled her fingers, gently raking her nails across his skin. She kept a brave air, but he could feel her trembling. She was still afraid of him. But she was even more afraid *for* him. She was pushing through her fear to help him, opening herself up—again.

He couldn't believe that she had asked him for help, for reassurance about her own change. He needed to show her that he could protect her and keep her safe—and that being a dweller wasn't the end of the world. He needed her to not give up.

"That surveillance point." Dexter nodded toward a tall tower of crushed vehicles. "Now."

Marcus would be able to see the entire clearing from there. More than that, he would be able to leap to just about any spot in it, instantly being on top of anything that dared come near Tessa.

"Go," she said. "I'll be okay."

He growled again. He'd never tried to speak in this form before, but couldn't leave without reassuring her.

"I know," he said. His voice echoed, deep and resonant. Her eyes widened and she let out a gasp.

Marcus looked over at Dexter. Even he looked surprised—his eyebrows were hitched up and his lips slightly parted instead of being in a stern line or condescending smirk.

"Protect her," Marcus said. "Or your swords will not protect you from me."

Dexter's cheek twitched. The stern line returned briefly as his expression transformed into a glower that let Marcus know Dexter still wasn't afraid of any dweller—not even a werewolf.

Marcus was well aware that Dexter had good reason for

his confidence. He'd seen firsthand what Dexter was capable of. But there was something more intimidating than the memory of Dexter single-handedly taking out the entire pack that had killed Marcus's family. Something Marcus couldn't believe he'd never realized before, but now felt with absolute certainty.

One man versus a pack of werewolves wouldn't stand a chance. One *human* man.

Marcus stared at his leader hard, took a deep breath through his nose. Dirt and rust formed the baseline of what he smelled in the area. Then there was Tessa, her scent still sweet from her recent arousal, spiked through with the stronger notes of her fear. And underlying that, the thickness of leaf rot that centered strongly on her right arm. Her dweller.

And from Dexter… Nothing. Not sweat. Not fear or anger or the adrenaline of heading into battle. Only that weird musty smell, like the pages of an old book.

"We don't need your threats to make us protect her," Dexter said.

"Oh, for fuck's sake," Tessa said. "I don't need either of you to protect me. I can protect myself." Tessa pushed against Marcus's chest. When he didn't budge, she stepped back herself. "You guys need to get out more."

She made the flamethrower's nozzle release into her hand and gripped it tight. Pointing it away from them, she activated it for long enough to let out a steady stream of fire. A borderline maniacal grin split her face.

"But I have to tell you, at this moment in time, Vaughn is my favorite." She paused for a moment, then let out a laugh. "Vaughn says to leave her out of it, in case you're wondering."

*"Your pack is bonding,"* his dweller thought.

Marcus made a sound that was half-chuckle, half-growl.

"The running commentary is awesome," she said. "And here I thought you just kept Vaughn around for the gadgets." Tessa's smile broadened. She's giving me grief for that. And reminding me that we have about twenty minutes of daylight left. Damn, with Vaughn as your copilot, no wonder you're not afraid."

Marcus wished he could keep his earpiece in place when he changed. Normally, when it was necessary to change, Marcus was with Dexter or on his own. Not having Vaughn in his ear had always made Marcus feel… alone. He glanced from Dexter back to Tessa, who was still smiling and looking a little distracted—probably from something Vaughn was saying. Marcus hadn't felt less alone since… Well, it had been a long time.

"Keep each other safe," Marcus said.

Tessa smiled at him. "That's better."

He turned and leapt to the nearest car, scaling the stack as quietly as he could, then making his way to the top of the sturdiest-looking tower. Once he was in position, he knelt down to watch his team enter the expanse of packed dirt at the center of the ring of cars.

When the junkyard had been operational, the open area would have been where people parked before going to the small office tucked beside the crane that Marcus had used to kill the first queen. There was police tape over the door to the run-down building. Someone had retracted the crane's hook. He hoped they wouldn't need it, but it was still good to know it was ready to be dropped again.

Tessa and Dexter walked to the center of the space, then stood back-to-back, gazing out at their surroundings. Waiting.

The Redcaps would be paralyzed by Vaughn's emitters. Marcus was certain it was working. He doubted they would have been able to have their little chat uninterrupted otherwise. Plus, he couldn't hear anything scurrying beneath the earth.

Tessa glanced up at him and winked. He let out a snort. Things changed so quickly.

She had plans for him. After seeing how she'd eyed his body right before he changed, he had a very good idea what those plans were. He could hardly wait to take care of these queens and get Tessa back home to the ranch. To start working on making it feel like her home as well.

Minutes passed, the sun sliding further toward the horizon. He didn't want to face the queens after dark. Marcus would be able to see even better, but Tessa wouldn't. He wasn't sure about Dexter.

"These things aren't that fast," Tessa said. "Let's get a little distance between us. They may not like the idea of taking on two targets at once."

Dexter nodded and moved a few steps away. Marcus didn't like it. His growl turned back into an uneasy sound. They shouldn't be separating. It would make them easier targets. Then again, they hadn't seen any sign of the queens at all. Maybe they had moved on now that the king was gone and their spawning session had been interrupted.

The cars beneath him vibrated ever so slightly. Marcus looked around, trying to find the source of the movement, but he couldn't see or hear anything. The queens had been huge. If they were approaching, it would be easy to see them, to feel them. There were no visible entrances to their tunnels…

*Shit, their tunnels…*

"Tessa!"

She looked up at Marcus as he shouted, then took a step toward him. The earth collapsed beneath her feet. Her fuel tank caught on the lip of what looked like a pit trap from Marcus's vantage point.

As Marcus leapt to the ground, Dexter dropped his swords and threw himself onto his stomach, grabbing Tessa beneath her arms before she could slide all the way into the trap. The bright scent of her blood filled Marcus's nose.

Marcus reached for her, but she shook her head. Lines formed at the edges of her eyes and she grunted in pain.

"Something has my legs," she yelled. "You'll pull me in half if you try."

"Tessa…" Dexter said.

From this close, Marcus could barely hear Vaughn saying something in Tessa's earpiece, but couldn't make out the words. Her eyes filled with tears.

She grunted again. "Let me go and run. I'll blow the tank underground and take them with me."

"No," Marcus roared.

He grabbed the bottom of her tank, holding her in place, then punched through the edge of the hole with his free arm, making it big enough for him to reach into.

A queen was there, staring up at him with dozens of glittering black eyes. Its tendrils were wrapped around Tessa's legs, the pincers embedded in her flesh. Marcus roared again, shoving his torso through the small opening he'd made. He grabbed the queen's tendrils with both hands and started to pull. The smaller ones tore and the creature let out a horrible shriek that thrilled Marcus. It had attacked his mate. Made her bleed.

*"Make it pay a thousandfold,"* his dweller thought.

*"I will."*

He crushed its mouth in his grip. Beside him, he felt Tessa shift as the tendrils holding onto her let go. Dexter dragged her to safety. That was all Marcus needed.

With a last burst of energy, he sank his weight into his legs and pulled as hard as he could. The queen slid out of the earth, still shrieking. Marcus kept his grip on the tendrils and pincers coming out of the queen's face with one clawed hand. He wrapped his other arm around the closest thing to a neck the creature had and squeezed. Gray ichor poured out of its mouth.

It was a start.

He squeezed the queen's neck harder, twisting his body at the same time. With a last horrible shriek and a loud pop, its head came off.

Breathing hard, Marcus looked down at Tessa and Dexter. They were both still on the ground, arms around each other and eyes wide as they stared at Marcus. He held up the queen's head for Tessa to see. He couldn't force words from his mouth. Too much energy surged through his body, testing the limits of his control. But he willed her to understand.

*I did this for you. I can protect you. I* will *protect you.*

His skin tingled almost like he was changing again. Bright blue light covered the queen's head and body, devouring its flesh and leaving nothing behind. Even the blood and gore in Marcus's fur was vanishing, making his skin prickle.

He threw back his head and howled.

# Chapter Eighteen

What the fuck had just happened? Had Marcus really pulled off a Redcap queen's head? Killed it with his bare hands?

Tessa couldn't even say he'd used his claws. He hadn't needed them.

"Holy shit," she said.

"What's going on?" Vaughn's panicked voice cut in. "Too much happened underground. I couldn't see, even with my borrowed satellite. Is everyone okay?"

"We're okay, Vaughn." Mostly, anyway.

Pain was starting to register. Some of the cuts on Tessa's legs were deep. Her dwellers secreted something that made her heal quickly, but until her wounds were closed, she didn't feel much like moving. Dexter still had his arms around her shoulders and they were both on the ground. She was trembling so bad, it felt like the earth was shaking.

*Wait a minute...*

"Look out!"

Her warning came too late, as not one but *two* Redcap queens burst out of the ground, flanking Marcus. They each grabbed one of his arms, wrapping their strong tendrils around him, snapping at him with their pincers. Marcus snarled and flexed his arms, trying to pull himself free. The queens slid a little closer at first, then were able to stop.

As Tessa watched in horror, they started undulating backwards, away from Marcus. He couldn't get leverage to fight, couldn't claw at them with his arms held tight. The queens were going to tear him in half right in front of her.

"Shit, shit, shit." Vaughn's words echoed Tessa's thoughts. "Somebody, do something!"

Tessa shoved away from Dexter and scrambled for one of his swords, then rose to her feet. Part of her realized that this was the best chance she would ever have to kill Marcus. He was helpless. She was armed with silver.

Marcus met her gaze, and she knew he could see the doubt in her eyes. He knew what she was thinking. Her heart seemed to freeze, seeing the mix of pain and resignation etched in his features. The disbelief and despair.

Her mother would tell her to end him. One less werewolf. He was sure to lose control eventually and innocents would die. He would spread his infection. Make more of his kind. Tessa was duty-bound to destroy any dweller she could. Even herself, when the time came.

She ground her teeth together, tightened her grip on the

sword.

*Fuck that.*

She ran at Marcus, sword raised—and brought it down on the tendrils holding onto his left arm. The sword was sharper than she'd thought. The queen shrieked as the tendrils holding onto him fell to the ground, twitching and writhing before the blue glow claimed them.

She shifted the sword to her left hand, then grabbed onto the nozzle of her flamethrower and pointed it right at the face of the queen she'd attacked. "He's *mine.*"

Then she pressed the button to activate it and held on.

Flames poured out at the queen. It shrieked more, undulating backwards, trying to get away from the fire, but Tessa followed, her pace steady, keeping it aimed at the queen's head. It backed up as far as it could—cars caging it in—and started shuddering. With a final shriek, its head exploded, spraying Tessa with boiling gray ichor. Whatever material her jacket was made of, it couldn't protect her enough. The ichor melted through the thick material.

Tessa screamed and stumbled backwards, letting off the flamethrower and dropping her sword. She ripped the harness off and peeled her jacket from her arms so she could scrape the stuff off of her body.

More hands were suddenly on her. Human hands. Dexter—helping her to wipe the burning stuff off of her until it finally glowed blue and vaporized. Her body was sending her so many signals, she couldn't sort them out. Stinging, burning, and worst of all, the writhing beneath her wristband.

She swatted Dexter away, grabbing her right arm and looking at her skin, searching for signs that her dwellers had escaped. Splotches of red, crinkled skin covered her arm in a few places, but the burned spots seemed to have missed her wristband.

She let out a shaky breath. That had been way too close.

Dexter wrapped his arm around Tessa with surprising gentleness. He steered her around so that he was standing between her and the clearing.

Very calmly, he said, "Tessa, Porter is on the way. But right now, we need you to run. Just run."

She wanted to give him crap about the pronoun thing again, but he was so damn serious. Deadly serious.

She followed his gaze across the clearing, where Marcus was still ripping apart the other queen, even though it was obviously dead. He was covered in gore. Slowly, he turned toward them, head low, lips curled away from his teeth.

"You need to run," Dexter said. "We're not sure if we can take him. We've never seen him like this before."

She shook her head. "He won't hurt me."

In her earpiece, Vaughn said, "He might not think of it as hurting you. You're injured. He may try to infect you to help you heal."

Tessa let out a bitter laugh before she could stop herself. "It's too late for that."

"What do you mean?" Dexter said.

"I'm already infected."

Dexter turned toward her—his expression filled with pain and worry—and in that moment, he looked so much like Brock that she felt as if her heart was breaking.

She lurched away from him, heading for Marcus. Her legs ached and her skin burned as her body healed.

Vaughn was right about the risk. She wasn't sure Marcus was in control enough to remember that if he tried to infect her, it wouldn't take. Not while she was already occupied. She kept her right arm between them, lifting it to his face as she neared, making sure he could catch her scent.

"You can't infect me," she said. "It's too late for that. But I'm starting to believe... Maybe it isn't too late for *me*. You were going to give me hope, Marcus. Remember? Please, give me hope that I'll be able to control myself when I change. That I won't infect people or hurt them. I need you to help me believe."

Behind him, the body of the other queen flashed a bright blue, an outline of its form lingering for a few seconds before vanishing completely. The remains worked into Marcus's fur, his claws, his... teeth... started to glow as well, vaporizing. But it didn't stop there.

He dropped to his knees in front of her, head bowed.

The light covering him intensified, consuming the fur, working into his muscles as his body shifted back, his face returning to normal.

No, not quite normal.

His features were distorted with pain, even though he didn't seem to be injured. He dropped forward onto his hands, panting. The light faded and he sat back on his heels, looking up at her.

For the second time, she grabbed his head and pressed it against her stomach, holding him close. An alpha werewolf. A prime target for a hunter. Enemy to humanity. *Her* sworn enemy.

At least, that's what she'd been taught.

There were some lessons she needed to unlearn. If she only had more time—if she didn't have to keep running.

Marcus wrapped his arms around her waist. Warm, real, present. At least, for now.

*Until I have to run again.*

Light poured out of the holes where the queens had emerged. Enough that Tessa was certain all of their brood had died.

*Four* Redcap queens.

"Is that it?" Vaughn asked, her voice shaky. "Is it over?"

"It's never over," Tessa murmured.

Dexter headed toward the bikes. She heard the Redcap repellers shut down. And waited.

Nothing stirred. Nothing attacked them.

In the quiet that followed, she held on to Marcus, to that moment of calm. It was probably all she was going to get.

Unless...

Unless she was willing to risk everything. Willing to put her faith in the Blades and all their promises.

*Kyle made promises.*

But that was different. These people were different.

Porter was a doctor and he knew about dwellers. She sometimes gave herself shit about cutting off her arm, but knew it was bravado. She'd never have the guts to do it. But Porter could actually remove it safely. Surgically.

And Vaughn—with all her amazing inventions—could probably build Tessa a new one. Hell, Vaughn could load the thing up with useful tools. Weapons, lasers... bottle openers.

Tessa let out a little snorting laugh, running her fingers through Marcus's dark hair. It was so much softer than his pelt. His breathing had slowed and he seemed absolutely content to stay there, kneeling in the dirt—totally naked—while they embraced. It didn't make sense, and she didn't give a damn.

She could have a home. Safety. Friends. A family. She could have Marcus.

If she was brave enough.

Dexter returned, carrying Marcus's clothes. He didn't

toss them on the ground, as she sort of expected. Instead, he held them out to Marcus.

"We made enough noise that we shouldn't stick around," Dexter said.

Tessa finally let go of Marcus, though he seemed about as reluctant to end their embrace as she was. He stood and took the clothes, putting his earpiece back in place first thing. Marcus started to dress as Dexter dove into the dreaded topic.

"How long have you been infected?"

"It's going on seven years," she said.

Had it really been that long?

Seven years of running—of constantly looking over her shoulder. Seven years of nightmares and granola bars when all she wanted was a steak. She almost laughed, but knew the sound would come out a little crazed.

"And I'm not really a dweller," she said. "Not exactly."

"Then what *exactly* is going on?" He glanced at her arms. "Your wounds are already healing."

"Yeah. That's one of the perks of being occupied."

"Occupied?" he said. "How is that different than being a dweller?"

"They haven't fully integrated with my body yet. The infection is contained." She held up her wristband.

"Multiple dwellers," Dexter said. "What kind?"

Tears filled her eyes. Goddammit, she shouldn't let Edgar have that much power over her. But then, that was what her life was all about now. Running from him. Running from what he'd done.

She had to clear her throat before she could speak. "Ghoul."

Marcus pushed his feet into his boots. He actually smiled as he straightened his shirt.

"Ghouls aren't so bad," he said.

"Apex. Apex ghoul." Her voice had grown so small.

"Is that like being an alpha werewolf?" He actually looked happy about it.

She hated to disillusion him, but had to. "When the dwellers in my arm are fully activated, they'll spread through my entire body, devouring it and remaking it in their image. They'll multiply. I'll become a Hive Mother."

"Werewolves are similar," Marcus said. "The dwellers spread through our bodies, infecting every cell and changing our DNA on a fundamental level."

She had to swallow before she could force out more words. "This is different."

"You'll still be you." Marcus was ever the optimist.

"I'm hoping I never have to find out." Tessa could hear Vaughn typing again, probably skimming through her database or taking notes.

"What are the characteristics?" Vaughn said.

"Hive Mothers and Fathers are where ghouls come from," Tessa said. "They—we—have little maggot-things inside us. If one of those gets into a human host, they become a ghoul."

"Ghouls are necrophages." The distinctive thumping of Vaughn's fingers on her custom keyboard continued along with her narration. "They only eat the dead and are pretty benign as far as dwellers go."

"Apex ghouls aren't." Tessa let out a sharp sound that was more a release of pent-up terror than laughter. "He called it… green meat. When I change… What I'll need to eat…"

The tears finally spilled over her cheeks. How could she have ever thought she could control this? Knowing what she knew, seeing what she had seen?

Marcus grabbed her and crushed her to his chest, wrapping his arms around her and smoothing down her hair. She couldn't remember when it had come out of its bun.

"We'll find a way to stop it," he said. "You've kept them at bay for seven years already, and that was on your own. Vaughn and Porter will find a way."

"I've never heard of a dweller taking that long to activate." There was a breathy quality to Dexter's voice, as if he was having trouble forming words. And he'd dropped the 'we' again.

It didn't seem important anymore.

"I do things to keep them dormant, like not eating meat," she said. "Anything that comes from an animal riles them up. Makes them want to get to my stomach to share in the snack."

"That sounds gruesome," Vaughn said. "And painful."

"That's why I've been avoiding it. I managed to escape right after the Hive Father infected me. He told me the dwellers he put in me needed time to study my DNA before he activated them fully." She shivered as memories surfaced that she wanted to keep buried. "I've managed to stay far enough ahead of him to avoid that."

"He's still chasing you?" Dexter said.

"Yeah. I've managed to escape him so far, but my luck is bound to run out. He's been getting closer every time I slow down. At first, it took him a few months to catch up. Then a few weeks. Now he catches up to me in a matter of days. It's why I never stay anyplace longer than three days. Somehow, he always finds me."

Marcus started to growl. "Why doesn't he just pick another person to infect? If he's so intent on making another of his kind…"

Tessa shook her head. "It's personal. He told me my mom killed his wife and child. She probably did—she was a hunter before settling down and starting a family. He says that's why he killed my family and took me. It's his way of 'balancing the scales.' A child for a child. When I didn't play along with his warped version of family life…"

She bit the inside of her cheek hard enough to draw blood. She had to get through this. They needed to know what Edgar had done to her—what she was facing. It was the only way they'd understand when she asked for the extreme help she needed.

"He and his ghouls caught up with my mom and I when I was fourteen. She couldn't… There were just too many of them." Tessa forced the words around the lump in her throat. Her stomach roiled. "He took me with him. Told me he was my foster father. I was with him for years. *Years*. The things I saw…"

She shook her head harder, as if that could rid her of the memories. "When I turned seventeen, he came into my room and said that since I didn't want to be his daughter, I could fill the other role. I could become his mate. Then he bit me."

Marcus gripped the back of her head, holding her even closer against his chest. She could feel the steady growl he was putting off.

Why couldn't she have been attacked by a werewolf? She couldn't believe she was jealous of another person's dweller. But Marcus could get by eating raw steak. Her dwellers would force her to eat creatures that were still alive. She could only hope they didn't have to be human.

She didn't think Edgar had even bothered to try other animals. He didn't seem to mind his dietary needs at all.

She clenched her eyes tight and buried her face against Marcus's chest, wrapping her arms around him. She tried to let herself feel safe, knowing he'd do anything to protect her. The problem was, she was probably too late to save. She wasn't sure her crazy idea would work, even if she could convince them to help her.

"Who infected you?" Dexter said. "What was his name?"

"He calls himself Edgar Eaton."

She expected Dexter to respond. When he didn't, she looked over at him, blinking to clear her eyes.

His knuckles had gone white on the hilt of his sword. Muscles were straining on both sides of his jaw. She might have just signed her death warrant. At least if he knew how dangerous she would eventually become, he would be sure to burn her body.

It was a small comfort.

"Guys..." Vaughn's voice was tense in her earpiece. "Porter just freaked out."

"Freaked out how?" Marcus shifted slightly, putting more of himself between Dexter and Tessa.

"I'm monitoring him remotely in his lab. I didn't think he was paying much attention to the mission, but he just picked up a chair and threw it across the room. He's smashing his monitors now and... There went the camera. I lost the feed."

"Lock down the ops center." Marcus turned so that he was completely blocking Dexter's view of Tessa.

"I'm guessing you know the guy?" Tessa said.

Dexter ignored her question. Instead, he asked his own. "Is there anything else I should know?"

They were probably trying to figure out ways to destroy or contain her. She couldn't blame them—especially if they'd encountered Edgar before.

Everybody had a reason for entering this kind of life. Even the creepy twins. She hoped Edgar wasn't the one who had pushed them into joining the Blades.

"I'm sorry I didn't tell you sooner, but I didn't think I'd be around long enough for it to be an issue." She still wasn't sure.

"And now?" Dexter said.

"Now, I have a plan."

"I can't wait to hear it." Dexter spoke in a rough, cold voice.

She shook her head. "Later. Right now, I need…"

Shit, what did she need? A new life. Her family back. Her body hers and hers alone. She didn't even need all of it.

She just wanted to be free.

"I need to talk to Marcus," she said. "Dweller to… 'dweller-to-be.'"

"That's not a good idea," Dexter said.

"I didn't ask you." Tessa grabbed Marcus's hand and started walking toward the bikes.

Marcus pulled out his earpiece and tossed it to Dexter, who easily caught it. Tessa did the same.

"We'll use the communications on the bike if we need it," Marcus said. "Don't contact us. Don't come after us.

Don't even track us. We'll be back when we're ready."

Spoken like a true alpha. It didn't even bother her anymore. How had her perspective shifted so radically in such a short amount of time?

She was on the cusp of an even bigger change. She could feel it. Her world had been altered irrevocably the moment Marcus walked into her life. She wasn't sure she'd ever be able to walk out of his.

# Chapter Nineteen

Marcus drove his bike in silence down unlit country roads. At Tessa's request, he'd taken them out of the city. Away from people and the complications they represented.

He was still having trouble reconciling everything she had told them and wasn't sure how she expected him to help, but he'd do whatever she needed. The first thing he wanted to do was give her a chance to decompress.

Even his dweller seemed to want to help. Marcus could feel it backing away, his mind filled with thoughts that were only his own.

Using his werewolf vision, he could keep the lights off. The motorcycle made almost no noise. He hoped she found the ride as peaceful as he did.

Since her jacket had been destroyed, she was wearing his duster. She'd tucked it in under her bottom, even though Vaughn's design made it impossible for things to get caught in the wheels of the bike. Tessa was also wearing the helmet, with the night-vision turned on so that she wasn't floating through total darkness.

She squeezed his waist and then pointed to a tree-lined road that was barely more than a dirt trail. They weren't too far into the woods when she squeezed his waist again. He slowed down and pulled his bike over on a somewhat level area and then killed the engine.

She swung her leg over the back of the bike and walked around, peering at the trees. When she returned to his side, she took off the helmet and set it on the bike's seat.

"Come on." She grabbed his hand and led him toward the forest.

"Where are we going?"

"Away from the bike. I don't want anyone listening in."

"Then maybe I should lead." He wasn't sure how much her dweller helped her see in the dark and didn't want to ask.

He took them deeper into the trees, far enough that the microphones on the bike and helmet wouldn't be able to pick up their conversation.

"This should be far enough," he said. "What did you want to talk about?"

The earth was damp from the recent rain. More was sure to come. She took off his duster and laid it on the ground, probably wanting a comfortable place to sit. Except then she took off her shirt as well.

He curled his hands into fists to keep from reaching for her. There was no light to catch her skin. The thick clouds overhead blocked out everything. He could still make out the outline of her waist, the curve of her breasts.

"Tessa—"

"No," she said. "No talking. No thinking. No planning."

She kicked off her shoes, then shimmied out of her cargo pants and pulled off her socks. When she was totally naked, she held out her hand to him.

"Please, Marcus. Just for a little while. Help me to not think."

Because if she thought about it, having sex with a werewolf would probably seem like a bad idea. He didn't know if he could handle the fallout when she realized she'd made a mistake.

"This isn't a good idea," he said. "I don't want you to have any regrets."

"My life is filled with regrets. No matter what happens next, if I don't share this with you, I know I'll have another one."

Shit. He couldn't think of a counter to that.

*"She's yours. Claim her."*

He let out a sigh. Of all the times for his dweller to chime in, this was about the least welcome.

*"Stay out of this,"* he thought.

Surprisingly, the presence receded again.

"I know what I want," she said. "I want you."

He wanted her, too.

He didn't respond with words. Instead, he pulled off his shirt and stepped out of his boots. Their design enabled him to do so easily, and he never wore socks with them.

He had to be able to strip fast when a change came on unexpectedly. Heading toward Tessa, he probably broke all his records. He was naked by the time he was close enough to take her hand. She pulled him to the ground with her, leaving him enough space that he wouldn't have to sit on the damp ground.

"I'm really sorry about what happened between us earlier," she said. "I didn't know... a lot of things then."

"I should have told you before we even kissed."

She let out a laugh. "As I recall, I was the main one who kept starting things. I didn't give you much of a chance to speak. Besides, we were both keeping secrets then."

"Maybe we should stop."

"Maybe we should stop talking." She leaned in and kissed him, her lips soft against his.

Talking was overrated. He burrowed his fingers through her hair, holding the back of her head as he deepened the kiss. Her hands found his chest, tracing his muscles, running along his sides. They dropped lower.

He grunted when her fingertips wrapped around his shaft, squeezing and stroking it in languid movements. Compared to the blaze of passion they'd shared earlier, this was... almost baffling.

Heat spread through his body, like his bones were warming up, relaxing the muscles and tendons attached to them. He imagined sinking into her, the soft wetness, her warmth. After everything they'd been through together— knowing what he knew about her, what he'd learned about himself—he didn't feel like he had to hold himself back anymore.

She pulled away from his kiss. He let go of his hold on her to give her the space she wanted. Her hand kept moving on his dick, though. He wanted to lean back and close his eyes. He also wanted to watch everything she did —to not miss a moment.

"You've never been with anyone before?" she said.

"Just you."

"Have you ever gotten yourself off?"

"I thought we weren't talking."

"This is important."

He sighed. "No. I didn't feel safe letting myself get that worked up."

"Then maybe we should try something a little safer before we go for the main event."

"I don't understand."

"We need to be sure you can control yourself when you come."

"I would never hurt you."

"Not on purpose. But things can get… extreme during sex."

He spoke each word crisply, as he repeated, "I would *never* hurt you."

"Lay back."

He went ahead and did as she asked, though he wasn't sure how it was supposed to help her feel better. If it kept her hands on him, he was all for it, even though he wanted to feel more. He wanted their skin to touch, their bodies to press together—

"Put your hands behind your head and keep them there."

Again he did as she said. Somehow, following her instructions didn't chafe the way orders from others sometimes did. Especially while she was doing this.

"You sure do know how to sweet-talk a guy."

She smiled at him, then used her free hand to run her nails down his chest. He sucked in a breath, the stimulation sending lightning arcs of pleasure through him. He wanted to touch her, to pull her on top of him so he could—

"Hands behind your head," she said.

He hadn't realized they weren't. But he was reaching for her. Maybe he wasn't as in control as he thought.

He put his hands back in place, interlacing his fingers behind his head, and gave more of his attention to keeping them that way—which was no easy feat, with how much he wanted to keep his attention on *her* hands.

She leaned over him, biting and then kissing the side of his neck. He sucked in a quick breath, and let it out as a rumbling growl. Her mouth moved over his chest with the same combination of teeth, tongue, and lips. She kept stroking him the whole time.

His hips pressed up against her, wanting more. His need for her was so strong, he could hardly bear it. And that was precisely why he needed to. He needed to show them both that they could be together like this safely.

She kissed his navel, her cheek brushing against the tip of his dick.

"Tessa…"

He could roll her over and bury himself in her. Fuck her senseless, make her scream in pleasure and forget about everything else.

She ran her tongue down the length of his shaft.

His back arced off the ground. The lightning bolts of pleasure coalesced into live plasma, sizzling through him, growing brighter.

He wasn't afraid to let go with her anymore. He wanted —needed—her to feel the same way. If this is what it took, he sure as hell wasn't going to argue.

She wrapped her lips around his dick, pressing her tongue against it, wetting it more, and taking the tip as deep into her mouth as she could. Nothing had *ever* felt so good.

Her tongue kept working, lapping at him, giving long strokes to his shaft as she moved him in and out of her mouth. Her hand tightened, pumping him hard.

The ball of liquid energy boiling in him collapsed on itself for a brief instant, before exploding through his body, electrifying every cell with pleasure so intense he felt his consciousness grow dark around the edges. It felt like a change and reverting all rolled into one moment. The power of his other form merged with the senses of his human body.

He spilled himself into her and she took everything he had to give, hand still squeezing, mouth working his tip. His hips bucked against her—he couldn't stop himself. But he kept his hands behind his head. He never reached for her, no matter how much he wanted to.

The arcs of light on the backs of his eyelids dimmed, as well as the pleasure thrumming through him. He relaxed against the ground as she slowed her pace, then finally released him.

Panting, he opened his eyes to gaze at her. "Did I pass your test?"

She licked her lips with a smile. "And then some."

"Thank God. Now it's my turn."

He didn't wait for her to argue. He rose to his knees, then threaded his arms behind her back and drew her to the ground. She was putting off so much heat. He covered her with his body, his dick resting on her stomach. It couldn't get hard again fast enough. Even soft as it was, he loved the feel of her skin against it, against him.

He rocked his hips against hers, letting her core wet him. She wiggled her hips, shifting against him and letting out a moan.

"Show me what you want," he said.

# Chapter Twenty

How could anyone resist a command like that? After taking Marcus to the edge and happily pushing him over it, Tessa was certain they could have sex safely. She wasn't sure where to start.

She hadn't branched off into that much of the more entertaining aspects of sex. It had always been about getting off as quickly as possible and moving on to the next hunt. She had never taken the time to figure out what she really enjoyed.

"I hear *quid pro quo* is nice," she said.

His brow furrowed for a moment, but then a smile crept across his face. He lifted her arms above her head and held them there. She hadn't realized how large his hands were, but he could easily pin both her wrists to the ground.

"Careful with the wristband."

"I know." Marcus nuzzled her neck again. "I plan to be careful with all of you."

The tender sentiment, mixed with the way he pressed his body against hers, gently running the fingertips of his free hand across her cheek… It was intense.

He shifted his weight, lifting his hips from her and

using his knee to spread her legs farther apart. Arcing his back, he was able to press a slow, lingering kiss against her left breast.

He was taking his time, and she didn't mind at all. Especially when he sucked one of her nipples into his mouth, circling it with his tongue. She groaned and tried to wrap her leg around him. She wanted to pull him back on top of her, but he had her pinned.

She couldn't believe she was trusting a werewolf with her body. Until she corrected herself. She was trusting *Marcus*.

Without releasing her breast, he flattened his palm against her stomach and ran it all the way down to the apex of her legs. She hitched in a breath as he encountered her wetness, her heat.

His fingers curled, raking against her soft flesh a little less than gently. She felt him take a few deep breaths, then he slid his fingers across her core.

His explorations were incredible. He wet his finger, sliding it in deep, then pulled it out, trailing across her clit until she gasped. He kissed her neck, lying against her side. She could feel his dick, rock hard again, as he ground his hips against her.

"I can hear your heartbeat," he said. "Even more than your breath—telling me what you like. What you want."

He slid a finger deep into her core, swirling it around. She arced her back against him, but he pressed her to the ground with his body and nipped at her neck. He let out a low growl.

What she wanted was for him to bury himself inside of her. And she wanted it now.

"I want more," she said.

"I know."

He slid another finger in deep, thrusting them in and out. His thumb worked her clit, bringing her closer to the edge. She could feel the fireworks starting, her body lighting up everywhere they touched.

"Marcus, I want—"

He cut her off with a kiss, his lips devouring hers, his tongue demanding entry. At the same time, he added a third finger, his hand working magic on her body. She writhed beneath him, wanting him in her so badly, trying to shift herself under him, but he held her firm.

The fireworks erupted into a full nuclear blast. He paused for the briefest of moments, then started pumping his fingers into her. Her body clenched around him, not wanting to let go, wanting more of him, all of him, even while he was giving her this miraculous pleasure. Her heart pounded in her chest as she finally started to come back down.

He slowed his hand as he broke off the kiss. Smiling, he said, "You want?"

She slid her thigh up his leg. "More."

He let out a rumbling sound, half-chuckle, half-growl,

then let go of her wrists. Instead of rolling on top of her, he slid down her stomach. She propped herself up on her elbows to watch what he was doing.

"I think I'm getting the idea of this," he said.

"You do seem to be taking to it."

He knelt between her legs, running his hands over her thighs possessively. In the near-dark, she could barely see the outline of his erection jutting out at her, begging for attention. She started to shift so that she could take him in her mouth again, but he grabbed her legs by the backs of her knees and pulled her closer. She fell back with a laugh.

If he was going for the main event, she wouldn't argue. She was far past ready. She let herself relax, waiting for the feel of his warm body pressed against hers.

He looped his arms beneath her knees. An ambitious position, but she was game if he was. She felt his warmth as he moved between her legs, expecting to feel his dick. She felt his breath on her instead as he bent down to her.

She wanted to say, "Seriously?" but he didn't give her a chance. The words were swallowed in a gasp as he pressed his tongue to her. He wrapped his arms around her legs, keeping her feet on his back to give him full access. His tongue delved into her, swirling and thrusting.

After the first amazing orgasm, she didn't think she could get to the edge so fast, but when he reached around and started flicking his thumb over her clit, heat built to an inferno in seconds. Sparks arced across the backs of her clenched eyelids. He wasn't just giving her pleasure—he was demanding it. Her body wasn't about to disobey.

She wanted *him*, though. Wanted to feel him inside her, filling her.

"Marcus…" Her voice had become a breathy gasp she barely recognized. She ran her fingers through his hair. Feeling the movement of his head as he worked her set off even more sparks through her body. "Please. I need more."

She squirmed beneath him again. Her knees rose, but he kept on his relentless assault on her pleasure centers. Her legs clenched together against his head as his tongue kept on, his fingers still stimulating her.

"Please. Please!" The last word was a screech as her back arced off the ground.

His strong hands gripped her knees, pulling them apart. She was panting so heavily, she thought she might pass out. Marcus's silhouette was barely visible above her as he pulled her closer again, this time partly up onto his lap. He lined up her core and drove himself into her in one fluid movement.

Her body pulsed around him, faint echoes from the first orgasm. And then he was pounding into her, his hips crashing against hers as his dick filled her over and over again. Only her shoulders and the back of her head were touching the ground as he rose on his knees, gripping her legs tightly.

She locked her ankles behind his waist and he let out a

gasp, falling forward with his arms on the ground. With the new leverage, his thrusts became stronger, deeper. She felt her back pressing into the soft earth. Her body was coiling and waiting for the release she knew he could give her.

He kept their chests pressing together, wrapping his arms around her back, his hands on her shoulders to keep her where he wanted her. His hips never stopped their relentless pumping.

"Tessa…" He raked his teeth across her neck, almost hard enough to hurt. When he said her name again, it came out as more of a scream.

His body pulsed inside of her, setting off the chain reaction she knew would come. Her entire body was fire. Muscles, blood, bones. She let out a shriek as blinding pleasure flooded her senses, consuming her. Marcus never slowed as he spilled himself in her. He just finally stopped, his dick buried deep in her, pinning her to the earth.

Sweat pooled between her breasts. More dripped from his brow. She could barely catch her breath.

Finally, she managed to open her eyes. Marcus had his head bowed and was breathing almost as heavy as she was.

"That was amazing," she panted.

He looked up at her with eyes glowing bright gold, and smiled. "That was just the beginning."

A laugh bubbled up through her before she could stop

it. The absurdity of her life was hitting her hard. She was as close to happy as she could remember being in a very long time—because of a werewolf. Because of Marcus.

He slid from her body, but kept holding her close, nuzzling her neck and pressing kisses haphazardly over her skin. After a particularly long inhale, he let out a sigh and rolled to his side, propping himself up on his elbow to look toward the sky.

"What is it?" Tessa could only make out vague shapes of trees that were slightly darker than the cloud cover overhead.

"It's going to start raining again. I don't want you out in it."

"I'm not afraid of a little rain."

He let out a small laugh. "I don't doubt it. From what I've seen, you're not afraid of anything. Like Porter and Dexter."

"No. Not like them." She shook her head. "I seem fearless because I'm constantly terrified. But if I let the fear stop me, people will die. I'd never do anything again. I'd just sit in a corner and chew on my hair—and trust me, plenty of days that sounds really appealing. If I ever gave in to fear, I'm afraid I'd never claw my way out of that hole."

"I get it."

"Seriously?" She laughed. "The big bad werewolf understands fear?"

"I'm always scared, too. That I'll lose control. Hurt someone. Turn them."

She felt him start to move away, but sat up and put her hand on his shoulder. "You won't."

"How can you be sure?"

"Because I've met other werewolves. Talked to them outside of hunting or being hunted."

She shivered at the memory. Edgar had insisted that she learn to entertain other dwellers. He had called them her new family.

"You're nothing like them," she said.

"I've never met another werewolf. All I know is my own experience. And even that's been changing since I met you."

"How?"

"I just feel… more in control. Like I'm finally getting comfortable in my own skin." He chuckled. "Both of them."

"I'm glad to be such a good influence."

A drop of rain hit her shoulder, colder than she expected. She pressed herself into the warmth of his chest.

"Come on," he said. "We can talk more back at the ranch. Figure out what to do next."

She burrowed her fingers through his hair, pulling his head toward her for a brief, passionate kiss. "The only thing I'm interested in figuring out back there is how soundproofed the walls of your room are."

Even in the dark, she could see him grin.

# Chapter Twenty-One

They hadn't left their little clearing immediately after that kiss, but still managed to make it back to the ranch just before the rain started in earnest. Remembering everything they'd done in the woods as they approached the barn, Marcus wasn't sure they would make it to his room. The living room couch could be very comfortable…

He needed her in his bed as quickly as possible. Pulling his bike into the stark garage beneath the barn, he realized that wouldn't be an option.

Dexter was leaning against the van, arms crossed over his chest.

"Glad to see you made it back okay," he said.

Marcus killed the engine and set the kickstand as Tessa slid off the back of the bike. She stretched, lingering nearby as he finished parking.

Dexter's presence implied that he was worried about Tessa. As if Marcus would ever let anything happen to her.

*"Rip. Off. His. Head."*

Marcus didn't want to get into it with his dweller. He just thought back, *"Fuck. You."*

"Nice of you to wait up," Tessa said.

Marcus's voice was a low growl. "And completely unnecessary."

"We disagree," Dexter said. "Porter needs to examine Tessa immediately. She's harboring an un-catalogued dweller, and that needs to be checked out." Dexter pushed away from the van and approached them, keeping his gaze locked on Tessa. "We like to keep track of possible threats. Right, Marcus?"

Marcus growled and started forward. If Dexter wanted a threat, Marcus would give him one.

"Easy." Tessa stepped between them, pushing against Marcus's chest. "It's a legitimate concern. Besides, I need to talk to Porter anyway."

She wrapped her arm around Marcus's waist, tucking herself in close. Marcus rested his arm on her shoulders.

"Lead on," she said.

Dexter smiled, but the tightness around his eyes conveyed his disapproval better than any words could. Tessa had issued her own challenge.

If Dexter insisted that they go first, he'd be demonstrating that he thought of them as a threat—that he wasn't willing to give them his back. Marcus knew he was always being supervised, but walking in front of Dexter now would almost feel like they were prisoners.

After pausing for a few moments, Dexter crossed the room to the door. He didn't hesitate when it opened, leading them down the blank hallway. Marcus exhaled as

Tessa pulled him along with her.

Porter and Vaughn were waiting in one of the secondary labs. Vaughn was shifting her weight from one foot to another, holding one of her shiny chrome clipboard computers. She called them PAWN units. She tapped on it as they entered, and the monitor over her shoulder flickered on.

"Okay, I get that you're a genius designer, but how do you *make* those fancy gadgets?" Tessa said. "I mean, everything is custom."

Vaughn smiled. "I own a tech company and spread the contract work for components over multiple factories. Then I assemble everything myself either in the garage or my main lab down in…"

Her voice diminished, along with her smile. She glared at Porter.

"Vaughn, I swear to you, I will never tell anyone about your spaceship," Tessa said. "I've been working with hunters for years and never let it slip that dwellers are aliens."

Vaughn half-shrugged and gave Tessa a weak smile. "I suppose that's something. How did you know about the origin of dwellers in the first place?"

"Some of *them* know." She squeezed Marcus's waist tighter. "Edgar knew."

"How could he?" Dexter leaned against the wall, arms crossed.

"I think he was one of the original occupants of the ship." She was trembling.

Marcus pulled her closer to his side, bending down to kiss the top of her head. He wished he could shield her from this conversation, but she'd made it clear that it was important to her to get through it.

Porter cut into their moment, his voice sharp. "It seems unlikely a specimen could live for that long."

Tessa shrugged. "He regenerates."

"So do any number of dwellers," Porter said. "But most seem to age at a normal human rate. The longest lived beings we've encountered were only a few hundred years old, if that."

Tessa shook her head. "Edgar is a hive creature, constantly replacing scouts as they're lost to age or the elements or to... infecting others."

"Like he infected you?" Porter's voice gentled a bit.

"No. Not like what he did to me."

"Right," Dexter said. "Because what *you* are is more dangerous."

Marcus started to growl. Tessa wasn't the most dangerous person in that room. Dexter needed to remember that.

She blew out a shaky breath. "I know I should have told you sooner. I wasn't planning on sticking around long enough for it to be an issue. But you don't have to worry about me being a threat. My dwellers are contained."

"Through your wristband," Porter said.

"Yeah. The things aren't strong. They can't push past the elastic. And they won't actively try to spread unless they're triggered."

Porter took a step toward Tessa. "Would you mind letting us take a closer look?"

Marcus expected her to balk, but instead she stepped forward. He willed himself to let her go. She held up her arm and Porter gently grasped her hand and elbow, peering intently at her skin.

"Do you know how many are in there?" Porter asked.

"A dozen or so at least."

Vaughn let out a gasp. "A dozen? The ghouls we've encountered so far only have one dweller."

"Those weren't apex ghouls," Tessa said. "Apex ghouls are the ones who make others."

"Most of what we know about ghouls, we learned from subject G-405," Porter said. "A female ghoul who transitioned in her early thirties an undetermined amount of time ago."

Vaughn tapped on her PAWN and the monitor displayed a picture of the ghoul Marcus had captured the previous year. G-405 had been skeletal-thin. Her clothes were tattered and dirty, her skin so gray it was impossible to tell what her complexion originally looked like, and her cheeks and eyes were sunken. She looked like a walking corpse. She'd been a ghoul so long, she couldn't even remember what her human name had been.

Marcus didn't know how long werewolves could live. He knew that he seemed to be aging at the same rate as a normal human. He was spared the diseases and other unpleasant side-effects of not having an alien immune system constantly defending his body. But ghouls...

The alien parasites changed their hosts. Made them into something... else. G-405 could have been over a hundred, for all they knew.

Marcus remembered how easily she'd been captured— almost like she was tired of her existence. He couldn't entirely blame her. He had caught her in one of the local cemeteries, feeding off of a dead body she'd dug up. What he didn't understand was why Porter had been obsessed with her.

For several weeks, the ghoul had lived at the ranch. Porter had fed her, cared for her, and asked her endless questions—all the while, running test after test. Vaughn had been involved, developing new technology to get the data Porter needed.

Eventually, Vaughn had brought Marcus in and warned him that Porter was about to cross a line. He wanted to extract G-405's dweller, even though they knew it would kill her. Painfully.

Marcus had overheard Porter arguing with Eli, the head of the Blades' medical division, through Vaughn's comm system. From the sound of it, another Blade's life was on the line—someone important. Marcus thought the ghoul's life was important, too. Apparently, *she* didn't agree.

When Porter asked G-405 about the procedure and told her it could save lives, she'd happily accepted. She said she could remember enough of what it had been like to be human to be disgusted by what she had to do to survive. She was done. If she could help people on the way out, so much the better.

Would Tessa ever reach that point? Was she already there?

"For ghouls, the dweller lives inside the host's brain," Porter said. "Transition includes the body's tissues becoming extremely dehydrated, giving them a gaunt and emaciated appearance. That plus the change in skin color and texture makes them obvious dwellers."

"It takes years for them to reach that point," Tessa said.

Porter finally stopped examining her arm. His gaze snapped to hers. "It's not part of their initial transition?"

"No. Becoming a ghoul isn't as quick or dramatic as becoming a werewolf." She shifted her weight and glanced over at Marcus again.

*"Infect her. Let our nature fill her body and push out these invaders. Make her one of us."*

*Shit.*

That was tempting. What if his werewolf nature could keep Tessa from suffering the same fate—or worse—as G-405? But Marcus had no idea what trying to turn Tessa would actually do to her.

He was even more frightened by the fact that he wasn't dismissing the idea outright.

"You should tell Porter everything." Marcus took a step closer. "The more he knows, the better he'll be able to help you."

And if Porter and the Blades couldn't, Marcus would. Somehow. Somehow *not* related to changing her.

"Apex ghouls usually create drones by spitting one of the dwellers in their body into their target's ear." Tessa pulled her arm away from Porter, cradling it against her middle. "If they can't get a hold of their victim, they can drop it onto their hair or clothes. The closer to the ears the better, though. The dweller makes its way into the brain and starts secreting chemicals that transform the body. But it takes time."

"How much time?" Porter asked.

Tessa shrugged. "It varies from person to person. But the change takes place gradually. The first chemicals the dweller secretes make the human susceptible to suggestion from the apex ghoul. They become thralls. Edgar used to target rich people and get them to sign over their money to him. If they ran out of resources and couldn't pass for human anymore, he would ditch them."

"Nice guy," Vaughn said.

"How long can the dwellers live outside of a human host?" Porter seemed determined to keep the conversation on track.

"If it's a scout that's never integrated with a host, indefinitely."

"Indefinitely…" Porter shook his head. "The one we extracted only lived for a few seconds."

"Extracted?" Tessa said. Her eyes widened in horror, her scent gaining a sharp edge of fear. "Oh my God. You took a dweller out of a ghoul?"

"We needed to study it." Porter remained impassive.

"That's vivisection." Tessa took a few steps away from him, but then realized she was heading closer to Dexter and stopped. Marcus stepped toward her, but she leapt away, keeping all of them at a distance.

"Your concern is surprising," Dexter said. "Only yesterday you were saying all dwellers should die."

"A quick death," she said. "As clean as possible."

"No one is dying." Marcus stalked up to Tessa, following when she retreated. He gripped her arms firmly. "No one here will hurt you. I won't let them." More quietly, he added, "I'll protect you with my life."

She let out a shuddering breath, but didn't lean against him as he'd hoped. Instead, she pushed him aside, standing next to him to face the others. Which… felt even better than him protecting her. Tessa at his side, standing strong. It was as the universe intended things.

"G-405 volunteered for the procedure." Vaughn's voice was so low, it was a wonder anyone could hear it. She cleared her throat before continuing. "We were able to render her unconscious with an electrical charge just below the kill range, then froze her body while the extraction was performed. We monitored her brainwaves carefully the entire time to ensure she didn't wake up… while it was happening."

"But she must have known she would die," Tessa said.

"Look at her, Tessa." Vaughn pointed at the screen. "She'd been a ghoul for so long. Alone. She hadn't been able to pass for human in decades, probably. No dwellers wanted her around, either, from what she told us. The loneliness was killing her more slowly—and cruelly—than Porter's procedure."

"I assumed the ghouls who left Edgar banded together." Tessa looked stunned. "He was always surrounded by other dwellers."

"That probably had resources and could be of use to him, from what you've said." Vaughn let out a deep sigh. "I know the type—and it's not limited to dwellers."

The conversation was stirring up personal demons for everyone in the room, it seemed. From what Vaughn had shared with Marcus, Edgar sounded a lot like her dad. Using people and then discarding them when they couldn't —or wouldn't—serve him anymore. As soon as Marcus had a chance, he would check in with Vaughn and make sure she was okay—make sure she understood that everyone in the pack was important.

"Ghouls are specialized necrophages," Dexter said. "They eat human corpses to sustain themselves. G-405 said her dietary needs were driving her insane."

"Lots of dwellers have to subsist on meat," Tessa said. "But it doesn't always have to be human. Couldn't anything else work?"

Porter broke in. "We tried. Nothing else could sustain her form."

*"Ghouls eat humans,"* Marcus's dweller said. *"It's the only way they can maintain the integrity of their host's cellular structure."*

Holy shit. His dweller had just given him some useful information. Horrible information, but still… How did it even know?

*"I've always been here to help you, Marcus."*

Marcus stifled a chill. His dweller seldom used his name. When it did, it made the voice in his head creepier —made Marcus wonder what was really riding around with him.

"Great." Tessa let out a sound that was half-sob, half-laugh. "Something to look forward to. Except I won't be able to eat the dead. I'll have to eat…" She was trembling again, her heart pounding fast.

*"Apex ghouls can only eat the living."* His dweller was silent for a moment, then added, *"And* you *are the one condemning her to this fate."*

Marcus shoved his dweller's thought away. He took

Tessa's hand and interlaced their fingers. "We'll find another way."

She shook her head sharply. "I already have one. Porter, you probably stitch up your Blades all the time, right?"

"All Blade doctors do."

"Have you ever performed surgery?"

Porter opened his mouth, then closed it again. "We don't like where this is going."

"Neither do I." Marcus tightened his grip on her hand— her left hand—and pulled her closer.

"This is the direction I've been heading in ever since Edgar infected me," Tessa said. "But I finally feel like I have a chance—a real chance—at getting my life back. If all it costs me is an arm, that's a fair trade."

"You can't be serious." And yet, Marcus knew she was.

It wasn't just the way she was staring at him, the set line of her jaw. It was everything he'd learned about her in their brief time together. Her determination, her drive.

He still felt half-sick. There had to be some way they could cure her without having to remove her arm.

*"Without infecting her myself."* He thought the words as strongly as he could, making sure his dweller knew where he stood.

Porter's expression had gone cold again. Calculating. He would probably love the chance to study Tessa's dwellers.

*"He's just as bad as Dexter."*

Marcus started to growl. His skin prickled and tingled, his hair standing on end.

"Stop." Tessa shifted closer to him and ran the fingertips of her free hand over his jaw—the hand she was contemplating losing.

Marcus grabbed her wrist above her wristband and pressed her palm against his cheek. He had to be able to protect her better than this. He had to keep her whole.

"My dad—my human dad—was a doctor," Tessa said. "We talked about situations like this sometimes. Sacrifices that had to be made to save people. Removing disease so that the person could flourish."

Marcus shook his head, pulling her hand away from his face. "Tessa…"

"Humans have been dealing with this kind of choice forever," she said. "Think of sailors who had to have amputations at sea. I'll have a clean OR, an extraordinarily qualified surgeon—given Porter's knowledge of dwellers —and probably some kind of freaking laser-cutter-scalpel thanks to Vaughn."

"Actually—" Vaughn had perked up, but her expression fell under the weight of Marcus's glare. After a moment, Vaughn returned it and shook her head. "You know what? No. Not this time. It's too important." Vaughn stepped right in front of Marcus, PAWN at her side. Normally, she held it up like a shield. "People deal with all kinds of necessary modifications to their bodies nowadays, Marcus.

Is it a big deal? Yeah. But it becomes a bigger deal if you just ignore it and hope it'll go away. If removing her arm will spare Tessa from having to eat people—*living people*—I say we go for it."

*"Your beta has a spine after all."*

Marcus growled, willing his dweller to shut the fuck up. His voice was harsher than he intended when he spoke. "There has to be another way."

"I watched cancer kill my mom," Vaughn said. "I watched it eat her up from the inside over years. *Years*, Marcus. If there was anything that could have been done to save her—*anything*—I would have made sure it happened. Whatever it took, whatever it cost me—*or her,* if that was her choice. You shouldn't be fighting Tessa on this. You should be supporting her."

*Shit.*

"Thanks, Vaughn," Tessa said.

Vaughn was right. They were both right.

Tessa squeezed Marcus's hand and let out a tiny laugh. "As much as I know you'd love to pin Vaughn to the wall, this is my decision. And I choose to stay human."

*To stay human.*

Even if Marcus was willing to infect her, she wouldn't be willing to let him try.

"I've seen…" Tessa took a deep, shaky breath, then let it out slow. "I've seen Edgar feed. I won't let that happen. I won't become that. It's this or the incinerator."

Marcus pulled her against his chest, burrowing his head in the nape of her neck. What the hell kind of alpha was he if he couldn't protect his pack? And what would happen between them if Tessa became fully human again? What if it made it harder for him to control himself? Or he slipped up and turned her?

He wanted to tell himself it wouldn't be that bad if she became a Hive Mother. But after everything he'd learned, he couldn't fool himself. And he knew he was being selfish.

Just because he couldn't protect her from things that had happened in her past didn't mean he couldn't protect her in the present—or the future. He would control himself, even if she didn't have the buffer of her dweller keeping him in check. He would watch over Porter to be sure Tessa was treated right. And he would take care of her while she healed.

The thought of it, though. It was almost too much. His skin was crawling. He wanted to howl.

Tessa wrapped her arms around his neck, stroking his hair. No matter how brave a face she was putting on, he could feel her trembling. He could smell her fear.

He could also smell her dwellers. The scent was growing stronger.

Porter's voice sounded behind them. "Vaughn, prep the stasis chamber."

"What… now?" Vaughn said. "Shouldn't we, I don't

know, wait till tomorrow morning? Give her some time to psych herself up?"

Tessa pulled away from Marcus. This time, he didn't fight it. He didn't let himself. He followed her instead.

"Porter's right," she said. "We need to do this as soon as possible."

"If Edgar is on her trail, there's no telling how quickly he'll show up." Porter was already opening drawers that were built into the walls, pulling out tools and lining them up inside the glovebox in the lab. "We need these dwellers incapacitated before that happens, especially if he's able to awaken them from their dormancy."

"Wait, 'incapacitated' or 'fried?'" Tessa said.

"We can't let go of this opportunity to study them," Porter said. "There's too much at stake."

"Like the Blade you were trying to save with G-450?" Tessa challenged.

"That's G-405." Porter gave her another placid smile. "If the stasis field doesn't work, the chamber can be flooded with fire, cold, or electricity."

"Cold will just slow them down," Tessa said. "And fire will only work if you can completely incinerate my arm instantly. Like even turning the bone to ash. Otherwise, they'll spread."

"Electricity it is, then." Porter turned back to the chamber. "We already know it works for both stunning and destruction from our experience with G-405. Vaughn, if you could assist."

"Yeah." Vaughn had gone pale. She glanced at Tessa, then bowed her head and joined Porter.

The room changed as they worked. A stinging antiseptic smell tainted the air. Even the spectrum of the lights shifted, adding a pale blue glow to the walls.

Tessa leaned into Marcus. He wrapped his arms around her shoulders and hugged her tight.

"Are you sure you want to do this?" he said.

She laughed. "I'm sure I *don't* want to do this. But I have to."

He kissed the top of her head, wishing there was another way. Knowing there wasn't.

"I'll take care of you afterwards," he said. "While you heal."

"I know. That's why I think I can go through with this." She pulled back enough that she could look up into his eyes. "I'm done running, Marcus."

Before he could think better of it, he leaned down and kissed her. Slow, deep, possessive.

*She was done running.* And if this was how she was taking her stand, he would be right at her side.

# Chapter Twenty-Two

The way her stomach was flopping around, Tessa wondered if it thought *it* was on the chopping block instead of her arm. Her mouth was dry and the fingers of both hands had a pins-and-needles sensation from the adrenaline in her system.

She needed to calm down. Getting worked up would set off her dwellers. Huddling closer to Marcus's chest helped. His arms were warm and strong around her.

Holy shit, her life had changed dramatically in twenty-four hours.

Marcus seemed even more upset about the procedure than she was. But then, he didn't know what was really at stake. He'd never sat through one of Edgar's meals.

She shook her head and wrapped her arms around Marcus, squeezing him tighter. He probably thought she was nervous about losing her arm. She was more worried about *not* losing it.

"We're ready," Porter said.

He was standing next to what looked like a modified glovebox. Vaughn was a few feet away, holding her shiny clipboard-computer-thing in clenched hands. Marcus put his arm around Tessa's shoulders as they walked toward the box.

"What do I do?" she said.

"Push your arm through there." Porter nodded toward a circular access panel in the side of the box that was sealed with what looked like flexible plastic.

She did as he said and gave a nervous laugh. "My dad used to let me go to work with him sometimes when I was a little girl. I always thought these things were so cool."

"I guarantee you've never seen one as cool as this," Vaughn said.

Her smile was so forced, it hurt to look at her. Tessa tried to smile back. Pretending that everything was okay.

Her hand was shaking.

Porter slid his arms into the gloves built into the side of the box. He surprised her by grasping her hand in one of his and giving it a reassuring squeeze.

"Marcus, if you could stand behind Tessa and help hold her still if needed," he said.

"Hey." She mustered as much bravado as she could. "I'm still a hunter. I can handle this."

Dexter had been hanging back, but he stepped into her periphery. "You're not a hunter anymore. You're a Blade."

Somehow, hearing him say that made her eyes flood with tears. She forced them back, letting out a half-strangled laugh. Marcus's grip on her shoulders increased and he moved closer, his chest pressed against her back.

"I guess once you go through losing an appendage together, it forms a lifelong bond," she said.

"Tessa, I…" Porter looked at her with sudden warmth. He squeezed her hand tighter. He opened his mouth as if to say something, but then winced and snapped it shut. The warmth fled, and he turned back to look at her arm with a dispassionate stare.

"You sure you're up for this?" she asked.

He chuckled briefly. "We're sure."

*So weird.*

He let go of her hand and started prepping her arm for the surgery, messing with the tools he'd put in the glovebox. The first thing he did was apply a tourniquet a few inches above her wristband. It was much tighter than she was used to, which was reassuring. The temperature inside the box dropped. Vaughn was tapping more commands into her clipboard.

"What is that thing, anyway?" Tessa shivered as the skin on her arm raised in goosebumps.

"It's a PAWN," Vaugh said. "P-A-W-N. Like a portable computer, only cooler."

"Of course." Tessa laughed, grateful for the distraction. "What do the letters stand for?"

"Portable Access to the Wireless Network." Vaughn glanced over and gave her another half-smile. "It sounded better in my head. Nobody's ever asked before."

"You all really need to talk more," Tessa said.

"At the moment, Vaughn needs to focus." Porter was staring intently at Tessa's arm. "Drop the temperature by another ten degrees, please."

Vaughn tapped on the PAWN and the temperature in the box immediately lowered.

"That's a neat trick," Tessa said. "I guess you weren't kidding about being able to flood the box with electricity or fire."

"I promise I will do my best not to incinerate or electrocute you." Vaughn cast a strained grin at her. "Unless you want me to."

"I'll let you know." Tessa leaned against Marcus's chest, grateful for his support. "Wait, if you electrocute me, is there a chance you'll catch Marcus as well?"

"Don't worry about it," Marcus said. "Even if something goes south and they hit me, too, electricity doesn't stun or kill werewolves. It just hurts like hell."

"And fills the room with the smell of burnt dog hair." Vaughn laughed. "Hey, finally, something we know that the hunter doesn't."

Tessa snorted. "If this goes well enough, we'll have plenty of time to compare notes."

Porter picked up something that looked like a scalpel, but with a larger handle. Tessa tried not to look at the other tools, but it was hard to avoid them.

Scalpels, tweezers, swabs, something that looked like a high-tech bone saw...

She wanted to look up at the ceiling, but forced herself to keep watching what he was doing. If even one of her dwellers escaped, they would all be in danger. Turning into a ghoul was only moderately better than becoming a Hive Mother. She took a deep breath and blew it out, focusing on Marcus's warmth behind her.

"The cold will slow them down," Porter said. He lifted her arm and slid a metal trough underneath, then set her arm on top of it.

"What's that?" she said.

"Stasis chamber." Vaughn tapped on her PAWN some more.

Tessa shook her head. "Okay, we really need to talk about this. You're not trying to capture some of these, are you?"

"You said they're subcutaneous—living just beneath your skin," Porter said.

"Yeah, but that doesn't mean you can safely pick a few out and keep them around as pets."

"If we thought we could remove all of your dwellers safely, we'd be working on an extraction instead of an amputation," he said.

"Then why the stasis chamber?"

"We need to see how they react to a threat. If we can capture one in the process, so much the better."

"But—"

Porter cut her off. "This procedure will take time. If

your dwellers decide to burrow into your muscle tissue or bone to spread through your body before we're done, there will be no stopping them."

Shit. That was a terrifying thought.

"They've never done anything like that before," Tessa said. That didn't mean it wasn't possible.

Porter was peering at a screen built into the top of the glovebox that magnified her arm. She could see it as well. The fine hairs sprouting from her skin looked as big as trees.

"You've probably never done anything like this before," he said.

Her stomach clenched. "Actually, I have."

Everyone looked at her. She thought she could even feel Marcus's stare from over her shoulder. There was no point in waiting for follow-up questions, so she dove in.

"A year after I was infected, I hooked up with this guy named Kyle. He had a degree in biology and was working through med school. He'd stumbled across dwellers, and I helped him not get himself killed." At least, not by the Redcap he was stupidly trying to capture.

"Did he try to remove your dwellers?" Porter asked.

"Just one. To study." She shook her head, biting the inside of her cheek to try to push back the guilt and grief that always surged through her when she thought about Kyle. They'd already run so many tests by then. They thought it would be safe to remove one. To see if they could cure her.

After a few moments of silence, Vaughn was the one who asked, "What happened?"

"Kyle was able to remove one," Tessa said. "But the rest in my arm went nuts. He was so focused on tightening the tourniquets he had put on my wrist and arm and making sure they didn't spread that... he lost track of the one he'd removed."

She closed her eyes and shook her head, trying not to remember the fear in his eyes, how he'd screamed when the thing made it to his ear without them knowing.

How he'd begged her—*begged her*—not to kill him afterwards.

*"Please, Tess. I don't feel any different. It's still me."*

Marcus tightened his grip on her again. She felt him lean his forehead on the top of her head. Killing someone was bad enough. Infecting them...

Marcus knew that fear. She was sure of it. He had to feel the urge to spread his infection, to make more of his kind. He was fighting it—and winning. She would fight, too.

"Kyle tried to cure me," Tessa said. "He wound up becoming infected. I won't let anyone here risk that. So take off my arm and burn it."

If her warning scared Porter at all, he didn't show it. He just kept staring at her with that stupid little smile. He turned to Vaughn, who tapped furiously on her PAWN.

The air in the chamber became colder. Tessa's fingertips were turning blue.

Porter looked back at his screen. "We are a bit more experienced, here. But the tourniquet at the wrist is a good idea."

He added the other tourniquet as if it was no big deal. What did it take to rattle these guys?

Finally, the moment she was dreading even more than the first cut happened. Porter hooked one gloved finger under her wristband and pulled it down her arm.

Tessa didn't get a chance to look at the area often. She forced herself to keep looking now.

The skin was completely white. It glistened in the light, a waxy cast to it. The scar from the Hive Father's teeth formed a circle on the side of her forearm. Seeing it again prompted a fresh wave of hatred for Edgar to wash through her body.

She had to survive. To survive and kill the bastard who had done this to her. Who had killed her family and so many others.

"They're larger than we anticipated." Porter brought his scalpel near one of the inch-long lumps just under her skin. It shifted away from the blade. He kept talking, as if he was carrying on a conversation with someone who wasn't in the room. "They're remarkably aware of their surroundings. How must their senses work…"

Marcus let out a low growl behind her. "Tessa, are you

okay?"

"Yeah." She nodded. "The cold is making my arm numb. And they aren't as... wriggly... as usual."

"I think I'm going to be sick." Vaughn started to move away, but Dexter grabbed her shoulder and held her in place.

"Hold it together for a little longer," Dexter said. "That goes for you, too, Marcus."

Tessa didn't know what was going on behind her, but Marcus had been growling pretty steadily since Porter peeled off her wristband. She lifted her head toward Marcus, trying to reassure him.

"How bad is it?" His voice was a deep, guttural sound.

Porter didn't seem to notice. He was too busy studying the dwellers lurking beneath her skin. "There's only one way to be sure. Vaughn, initiate the chamber."

After a few taps, the metal trough—*stasis chamber*— buzzed. Ripples of energy spread over her forearm up to her elbow, bringing an odd tingling sensation with them.

"Whoa, what the hell is that?" Tessa said.

Vaughn managed a slight smile. "It's a suspension field that—"

"Later, Vaughn." Porter turned Tessa's arm slightly, then brought his scalpel closer.

"You can't cut her without anesthetic," Marcus yelled.

Porter didn't flinch. "The cold is more than enough to manage her pain. And we have no idea how these dwellers would react to the chemicals needed to numb her."

*Shit.*

Tessa felt another surge of pity for G-405. At least they had stunned the ghoul into unconsciousness before operating.

With a deftness that surprised Tessa, Porter cut along one of the lumps in her arm, squeezing her flesh so that the dweller dropped toward the stasis chamber. It twisted back and forth on itself for a fraction of a second, like a beached fish, but as soon as it fell past the top of the chamber, it went limp.

And the others woke up.

She couldn't feel them. She was so glad she couldn't feel them. But she could see them.

They were all writhing beneath her skin. Wriggling and churning. Heading toward her body. The lumps were growing smaller, as if… As if they were burrowing deeper.

"Porter…" Tessa said.

"We see them." He grabbed a metal cuff and wrapped it around her forearm. "Vaughn, now."

"Shit." Vaughn tapped something on her PAWN. "I'm sorry."

*Sorry for wh—*

Tessa's thought cut off as arcs of lightning shot up her arm and into her body. Her fingers twitched involuntarily, her arm spasming. Marcus held onto her, keeping her upright. He grabbed her forehead, hugging it to his chest as she thrashed. The room blacked out several times before settling into a blurry gray.

The ceiling tiles moved—or maybe she was the one moving. She felt something flat beneath her, her body supported. Muffled voices bounced around in her head as she floated to a stop.

Faces appeared above her. Marcus. Brock. No, one of the twins.

"What the fuck was that?" Marcus. He was angry. That was bad.

If he became too angry, he would change. Dexter would attack, and Tessa wouldn't be able to keep them from fighting.

A calm, cold voice floated into her awareness. Porter. "We had to stun them to keep them from spreading."

"I'm so sorry, Marcus." Vaughn.

"You electrocuted her!"

"We did what was necessary." Threat. Dexter. "Now stand down."

Tessa had to stop them. But she couldn't move. Her tongue felt thick—too big for her mouth. Her head was pounding and her vision was still dark around the edges.

She heard Marcus growl.

"Stop." A new voice. Weak. Muffled. Hers?

"Stop," she said again, stronger this time.

"Tessa." Marcus's face drew closer. She knew it was him because his eyes were bright, bright gold. So bright, it made her head hurt worse to look at them.

She reached out to cover them, but ended up sort of squishing his nose to the side. Her wristband was back on, tourniquets still in place.

Vaughn let out a sharp laugh. "Sorry. It's the tension. Plus, that was pretty funny."

Tessa laughed, too, her eyes rolling shut briefly. "Vaughn…"

There was a pause, then the rustling sound of fabric as Vaughn approached. Her face joined Marcus's above her, blue eyes bright as always.

"Yeah, Tessa?" Vaughn said, her voice soft and earnest.

Tessa licked her lips, trying to force out words. "You suck."

A broad smile spread across Vaughn's face and she bowed her head, her shoulders shaking. Tessa didn't know if it was laughter or something else. Vaughn's eyes glistened when she looked at Tessa again.

Sniffing, Vaughn said, "Yeah. Sorry about that. I know we said we'd wait to electrocute you until you asked, but there was a time factor."

"I get it." It was truer than Vaughn knew. Tessa's thoughts were clearing, but her mind was still filled with darkness. "I'm guessing this means surgery isn't an option?"

"Unfortunately, no," Porter said.

"What about just lopping it off?" Tessa said. "You have

to have some kind of weapon you can use. A guillotine, maybe."

Porter's voice was still calm, wherever he was standing. "Let's save that for a worst case scenario."

Tessa was *living* a worst case scenario.

She didn't bother looking for Porter's face. It probably had another of those cold smiles on it. She closed her eyes instead, visualizing her future.

The Blades wouldn't let her walk into an incinerator. She was sure of it. They also probably wouldn't want her to leave. But she had to. They had no idea what Edgar was capable of.

Tessa needed more time, but had already been in Providence for over a day. Porter would probably want to study her to figure out a safe way to remove her arm—or her dwellers. It wouldn't be long before Edgar arrived—and she would not lead him to the Blades.

Her eyes filled with tears as the only option for keeping the people she cared about safe presented itself.

Apparently, she wasn't done running after all.

# Chapter Twenty-Three

Two sleepless nights in a row. Vaughn had dealt with worse, but the emotional and mental toll was making the physical drain much more brutal than she was used to. The other bases were starting to check in more often, wondering when Vaughn would take them out of lockdown, feeling her absence as she focused on the Providence base—which needed all of her attention at the moment..

Porter and Dexter were acting weird. With them, that was saying something. Marcus was more intense and focused than ever. And Tessa—the source of all the upheaval in Vaughn's life—was growing on her.

And sitting at the kitchen counter. Alone.

Vaughn balked at the entrance to the room. She hadn't expected to run into Tessa solo with the way she and Marcus had glommed on to each other. She was leaning over a bowl of cereal, the open box and a carton of rice milk at her elbow.

She looked as tired and wrung out as Vaughn felt. Plus, Tessa was so lost in thought, she didn't notice Vaughn approach. Or she noticed and didn't deem her enough of a threat to react to her presence. Vaughn took a deep breath before stepping into the room.

"Look what the werewolf dragged in," she said.

Tessa started guiltily, her mouth popping open, then snapping shut into a thin line. She stared at Vaughn for a moment before letting out a scoffing laugh and nodding.

Vaughn had seen that look too many times not to recognize it—in her own mirror when she was a kid, before her dad had shipped her off to boarding school. The guilty, 'nothing-to-see-here' smile. A mask to pretend that nothing was wrong, when she felt like her world was falling apart.

Tessa was going to run.

*Goddammit.*

"Actually, I dragged myself in." Tessa threw a fake smile at Vaughn. "Marcus was still sleeping, and I was hungry."

So she dressed herself for the field, complete with weapons from the looks of it. Yeah. Vaughn wasn't buying it.

"He usually conks out after a full transformation," Vaughn said.

The cap wasn't on the rice milk. She stalked over and sealed it before putting it back in the fridge.

"Sorry about that," Tessa said. "I'm not used to having a fridge. Or... you know. Perishable food."

"For such a sucky existence, you sure seem in a hurry

to get back to it." Vaughn set her hands on the counter and leaned forward, glaring at Tessa.

"What are you talking about?"

"You're planning to leave."

"How do you…" Tessa shook her head and glared at Vaughn. "Forget it. I don't care how you know. Just don't tell Marcus."

"Why? So you don't have to deal with the fallout?"

Tessa's icy veneer cracked. "I'll come back. As soon as I've dealt with this, I'll come back." She held up her right hand.

The black wristband made the waxy cast to her skin that much more evident. It might be Vaughn's imagination, but Tessa's hand actually looked worse since the failed procedure Porter had attempted last night.

"And how long will that take?" Vaughn said.

Tessa let out a hollow laugh, stretching her arm out and resting her palm on the counter, as if she was trying to keep it as far away from her body as possible.

"How long will it take for me to find someone willing to chop the damn thing off?" Tessa said. "I'd ask another hunter to do it, but by the time I explained, they'd just kill me and be done with it."

"Porter will find a way. He's still working on it."

"He doesn't have time. Edgar will be here soon. Maybe in less than a day. I need to be gone when that happens. For all our sakes."

"So, you run."

Tessa's glare returned in full force. "You don't get what it's like in the field. You sit here behind your computers and your weird technology—"

"Um, *weird?*" Vaughn actually sputtered.

Tessa plowed on. "Has your life ever been on the line? Really, urgently threatened?"

"Yeah, as a matter of fact, it has."

That earned Vaughn a skeptical stare. She wasn't about to satisfy Tessa's curiosity, or let Tessa get away with dismissing her.

"I know that everyone in this house could kill me without breaking a sweat," Vaughn said. "I also know that everyone would be dead if it wasn't for me. Several times over."

"Present company excluded, unless you're counting when you electrocuted me."

"Who do you think talked Marcus through the controls for the crane he used to crush the first Redcap queen in the junkyard? Who activated the hoverbike and had it waiting out of reach above all the Redcaps that almost killed you afterwards?"

Tessa's look of surprise wasn't enough for Vaughn. Tessa was about to hurt Marcus, and it was up to Vaughn to stop it from happening.

"I don't go into the field because I'm not cut out for it," Vaughn said. "But backing you all up isn't a cakewalk. It's fucking terrifying. Do you know how many times Dexter and Marcus and all the other Blades have put their lives in my hands? How many times it's come down to the weapons and defenses that I've designed to keep them safe? Just because I'm not risking my own life every day, that doesn't mean what I do is easy. That it doesn't hurt me to see them hurt."

"I don't want to hurt Marcus," Tessa said.

"What do you think leaving will do?"

She was quiet for a moment, then said, "You realize that out of everyone here, you're probably in the most danger if I stay, right?"

"Fine. Then let me make the decision. Don't leave."

"It's not that simple," Tessa said. "You don't know what you're risking."

"And you don't know what you're throwing away."

Tessa started to pull back. Vaughn reached across the counter and grabbed her right hand—grabbed it and held on, even though her heart started pounding and her stomach roiled. She had seen the things in Tessa's arm up close. Vaughn and Porter had stayed up studying the one in the stasis field. Even without what they'd learned so far, from everything Tessa had told them, Vaughn found her dwellers absolutely terrifying. But she swallowed her fear.

"I know what it's like to be alone," Vaughn said. "And I know how hard it can be to ask for help. You need to think long and hard about what you do next, Tessa. Because if you leave, you're *choosing* to be alone. That's you turning your back on yourself. And trust me, that feels a hell of a lot worse than when others turn their backs on you."

She held Tessa's gaze for several long moments. Tessa turned her hand over in Vaughn's and squeezed it. Her eyes glistened. Vaughn's vision blurred as tears came to her eyes as well.

Dammit, she already cared. One more person to keep safe. One more opportunity for loss and pain.

Images started popping into Vaughn's head for a robotic arm she could build for Tessa. And—more macabre—ideas for devices to remove Tessa's arm quickly and safely. Everything would take time. She only hoped Tessa would give it to them.

"Am I interrupting something?"

Vaughn jumped at Marcus's voice. Tessa let go of Vaughn's hand quickly and sat back on her barstool, wiping at her eyes.

"We were just talking," Tessa said.

"I can see that." Marcus walked over to them, yawning. "I feel like I walked in on an intense moment."

"We're just bonding," Vaughn said. "I'm trying to get your girlfriend to officially sign up for the Blades."

"Then *I'm* making *you* breakfast this morning." Marcus bumped against Vaughn's shoulder as he walked to the fridge.

Tessa smiled. "I can't believe I'm saying this, but that

was so cute."

Marcus paused and stared at Tessa. Vaughn had never seen Marcus look so relaxed. Or sleepy.

"Well, I guess he is rocking the bed-head look," Vaughn said.

"No, the little werewolf bump there." Tessa wagged her finger at them. "That shoulder-bump. Werewolves do that with packmates to show affection."

Vaughn hissed in a breath. "We don't use the p-word here."

"What, 'pack?'" Tessa looked genuinely surprised.

"Yes. That one." Vaughn shook her head. "Dexter doesn't want Marcus getting any ideas."

"It's okay, Vaughn." Marcus squeezed Vaughn's shoulder briefly before giving up on the fridge and walking around the counter to sit next to Tessa. "Dexter and I have come to an understanding."

"Oh." Vaughn thought for a moment. "When did that happen?"

"I don't know." Marcus put his head on Tessa's shoulder, his eyes closed. "Yesterday sometime?"

Tessa reached up and ran her fingers through his hair. "An alpha, a pre-apex ghoul, and…"

When she looked up at Vaughn, she said, "An IT gal."

Tessa let out a huge laugh. "It sounds like the start of a really bad joke. This is the weirdest pack I've ever heard of."

"The awesomest, you mean." Vaughn put on a confused air. "Wait, is that right? 'Most awesome…'"

Tessa laughed again, and mouthed, "Thank you."

Vaughn bowed her head as her eyes filled with tears again. Relief flooded through her.

"Forget about signing up for the Blades," Marcus said. "You just called yourself part of my pack."

Tessa shrugged. "I can think of worse things. Like really worse—"

Marcus cut her off with a kiss that raised the temperature of the room several degrees.

"Oh, come on," Vaughn said, pretending to shield her eyes. "Go to your room. Take it out of my kitchen."

Tessa slid off her stool and took Marcus's hand, leading him away. She smiled at Vaughn one more time before they headed out of sight.

Once again, Vaughn had kept Marcus from harm. And if Tessa was what Marcus needed to be happy… Vaughn would support him—support them both. However she could.

# Chapter Twenty-Four

Marcus gunned the engine and bounced the front end of his bike off the ground, skidding down the drive on the back wheel. He wore his helmet more to hide his smile than anything else. Well, that and to talk to Vaughn—his beta. He had forgotten his earpiece, but didn't feel like going back for it. The sooner he finished his patrol, the sooner he could get back to Tessa. He didn't even mind the steady rain pinging off of his visor and shoulders. He was glad that his duster was waterproof, though.

"Okay, settle down," Vaughn said. "Tessa's not around to watch you show off."

"I'm not showing off." Marcus laughed. "I'm just happy."

Happier than he could ever remember being. After spending the night and most of the morning in bed with Tessa, Marcus was feeling... at home in his skin. For a werewolf who was also a Blade, that was saying something. He would have spent the entire day sleeping and... not sleeping... with her, but Vaughn had picked up a weird police report that Marcus needed to check out.

The gates to the main road opened and Marcus sped

through, spinning the bike in an arc and using his leg to keep himself upright. Werewolf strength and agility definitely had their perks.

Vaughn picked up in his ear again. "I'm glad to hear that, but you're going to draw too much attention to yourself if you pull stunts like that in town."

"I have no intention of—"

He swore as a figure stepped onto the road right in front of him. Marcus jerked the handlebars of his bike too hard, twisting it to the side in an attempt to lay it down and skid away from the guy. Inertia took over, and his bike toppled over.

He leaned into the bike, trying to roll with it. His right leg hit the wet pavement first, his ankle snapping from the impact. The bike crushed the rest of his leg before bouncing over him. He felt his shoulder pop out of its socket as he landed. The bike's weight smashed into his chest briefly. More bones cracked. He couldn't breathe.

Marcus did his best to relax his grip and let the bike go on without him. It crashed into his left arm and thigh before rolling a few more times and then skittering to a stop several feet away.

"Fuck! Marcus? Marcus, are you okay?" Vaughn was screaming through the helmet's comm system.

Marcus's mouth filled with warm liquid. He coughed, and blood spattered the inside of his visor.

"Jesus, Marcus," Vaughn said, her voice shaking. "I'm

sending Dexter. Just hang on."

Hanging on wasn't going to be easy. His skin prickled as Marcus felt a change coming on. Changing would heal him faster. But whoever had walked out in front of him would become dinner. Marcus wasn't sure he could control himself when he was this hurt. He couldn't take that chance.

He thought about Tessa. About Vaughn. Keeping them safe was more important than healing. Marcus had endured more for his loved ones—when he was first colonized. This was *nothing* compared to that.

His bones were already mending, the blood pooling in his mouth lessening. What he had splattered on the visor had already glowed blue and vaporized. Everything on his skin would be reabsorbed, he knew. He took a deep breath, and didn't feel like he was drowning in his own body.

"Ouch. That looks painful." A strange voice spoke right above him. Strong and deep. "Let me help you."

Someone gripped Marcus's helmet and jiggled it till it came off. If Marcus had been human, that could easily have severed his spinal cord. Luckily, he wasn't.

"Better get that shoulder back in place." The man grabbed Marcus's right arm. "On 'three.' One…"

He yanked on Marcus's arm, popping his shoulder back into its socket. Marcus grunted, the pain of it barely registering in the chaos his senses were throwing at him.

"I find these things go easier when unexpected." The

man pulled Marcus to a sitting position, then wrapped his arms around Marcus's middle and helped him stand. "Come on. Walk it off."

The man supported Marcus's weight as they took a few steps together. Marcus felt his pain recede—gravity and his dweller nature aligning his leg and anklebones and knitting them back together. His mind cleared enough to think.

*Why doesn't this guy feel like prey?*

The man turned in Marcus's grasp so that they stood face-to-face, holding onto each other's shoulders as Marcus swayed on his feet. The voice in his head was silent as Marcus tried to figure out who this person was.

Dark gray hair with streaks of silver, tan skin, a nice suit—somehow untouched by the rain—and flat black eyes. The fading light that fought its way through the cloud cover didn't cast any reflection in them.

"There you are, brother." He cast a warm smile at Marcus. "Good as new."

Marcus coughed again and shook his head. He swallowed down what little blood remained in his mouth, then took a deep breath through his nose.

The scent of leaf rot filled his lungs. The scent of Tessa's dwellers. Which meant…

"I'm Edgar," the man said. The guileless smile remained on his face. "I'm here for my wife, Tessa."

Marcus roared. He grabbed Edgar by the sides of his

head—briefly registering the confused expression on Edgar's face—then twisted and pulled. Edgar's head popped off in Marcus's hands.

"That was extremely rude," Edgar said.

The shock of it was enough that Marcus let the head drop to the ground. He staggered back a step.

Edgar's body hadn't fallen and didn't look put out in any way by what Marcus had done. It bent down and picked up Edgar's head. As the body held the head on top of its neck stump, the tissues of Edgar's neck reformed, pulling his head back in place. Edgar worked his jaw a few times, turned his head side to side, then straightened his tie.

And smiled.

"Did that help you feel better?" Edgar said.

Marcus couldn't bring himself to speak. He stood in place, ready to fight or... run? He had torn Edgar's head off, and it hadn't made the man bat an eye.

"I've heard of you," Edgar said. "The werewolf who fights for the Blades."

Where the hell was Dexter?

Edgar chuckled. "You need to be careful about that. It isn't natural for us to oppose each other. We should be helping one another. Which brings me back to my business here. Tessa."

"You can't have her," Marcus growled.

"Is that so?"

"She's joined my pack. She's mine."

"I see." Edgar laughed and shook his head. "She's wrapped you around her finger, hasn't she."

Marcus growled again.

"My friend, Tessa is a hunter. She would never join a werewolf's pack, unless she was trying to take them down from within. She's also a master manipulator, who is very adept at using men to get what she wants. Human or dweller."

"It isn't like that," Marcus said.

"Isn't it?"

No. She wasn't using him. The connection they had—the feelings growing between them—were real. Even if they'd happened in only a couple of days...

Edgar shook his head. "Well, then, I suppose you'll want to turn her. It doesn't make sense to have a ghoul living in a pack of werewolves. I'll just retrieve my dwellers and be on my way."

"You can do that?" The words escaped before Marcus could stop them, filled with a desperation he knew he shouldn't reveal. And worse—triggering a longing he didn't want to recognize.

Once her dwellers were removed, Tessa would be free of Edgar. Free and whole. And human.

*"You could turn her. Make her one of us."*

Marcus shook his head, as if that could dislodge the thought—the thought he wasn't entirely certain came from his dweller.

Edgar smiled. "I wouldn't lie to you."

It didn't matter if Tessa could become a werewolf. She wouldn't want to. And Marcus would never turn her against her will.

He growled louder and took a step toward Edgar.

Edgar held up his hands and stepped back. "I don't want to fight you, brother. I honor our customs and will leave you in peace. But I must retrieve what I came for."

Gravel crunched behind them as one of the vans approached. Finally, some backup.

"You took your sweet time," Marcus said.

He kept his gaze on Edgar. After that trick with the head, Marcus didn't want to let Edgar out of his sight.

In his periphery, Marcus saw a stingray held in violently shaking hands. Shaking hands attached to thin, pale arms that looked unaccustomed to outdoors or natural sunlight. Feminine arms.

"Vaughn?" Marcus said. "What are you doing here?"

"Freaking the fuck out." Vaughn pointed the stingray at Edgar aggressively. In a shrill voice unlike anything Marcus had ever heard from her, she said, "Don't try anything. We've studied your physiology and know enough electricity will kill you. This weapon is maxed out."

Edgar held up his hands.

"Where's Dexter?" Marcus said.

"Prepping the pit." Vaughn sounded as if she was about to hyperventilate. Her face was even paler than usual, her lips bloodless. "Porter wants this guy brought in."

"Why aren't you the one prepping the pit?"

"I don't know," Vaughn yelled. "I only work here!"

The pit was the highest security holding cell they had. Marcus wasn't sure it would be enough. But if Edgar really could cure Tessa... They had to take the chance. Marcus would make sure that Edgar never got close to Tessa. Whatever he had in mind to remove his dwellers from her, Porter would vet the procedure, and Marcus would be there every step of the way.

He could save her. He could keep her whole. But first he had to get Vaughn back inside. Being out like this had to be torture with her agoraphobia.

He stalked past Edgar and pushed his motorcycle upright. The wheels wouldn't turn anymore, so Marcus lifted it over his head and carried it to the van. He leapt to the roof, then set the wreckage down with a grunt. He jumped back to the ground and picked up his helmet.

"You just have to love werewolf strength," Edgar said, his smile never fading.

Marcus held out his hand to Vaughn. "Give me the stingray."

"What?" she said.

"Brute force doesn't work on this guy. I need you to drive us in."

"This is such a bad idea." Vaughn handed over the weapon reluctantly and took Marcus's helmet, then backed up several more paces. She tapped some commands into her watch and the back doors of the van opened. Her face was ashen white and her heart was pounding. Marcus could hear it. If they didn't get back inside soon, Vaughn might pass out.

Marcus pointed the stingray at Edgar. "Get in the van."

"Just… don't let him spit anything on me, okay?" Vaughn said.

"Spit on you?" Edgar looked genuinely confused. "Why would I do that?"

"To turn me into one of your ghoul lackeys." Vaughn sounded a bit uncertain.

Edgar just laughed. "You certainly have some colorful ideas. But don't worry, I'll play nice." As Edgar passed Marcus, he said, "Your human pet is cute."

"Hey, I heard that." Vaughn craned her neck to look at them around the van, then ran to the driver's seat.

"Get in." Marcus waited for Edgar to jump into the back of the van before following. They sat across from each other on the bench seats.

The back doors closed automatically, and the faint buzzing from the front let Marcus know that Vaughn had turned on an electrical field meant to keep her safe. Marcus hoped it would work. When they started to move, Marcus brought his full attention back to Edgar, watching him for any sign of aggression. Edgar kept his hands folded in his lap, giving Marcus that unnervingly placid smile.

Strangely, the expression reminded him of Porter. Marcus tried to shake the thought away, but something was nagging at the back of his mind.

"Nice ride," Edgar said. "I'm glad to see that Tessa will be well taken care of."

Marcus growled. "How will you remove the dwellers? I'm not going to let you touch her."

"That won't be necessary," Edgar said. "If I'm close enough, I can call them back. The process won't be completely painless, however."

"Wait, this guy can take out Tessa's dwellers?" Vaughn said.

Marcus nodded. "That's what he says."

"I still think this is a bad idea, but I get why we're doing it now." Vaughn pulled the van into the garage beneath the barn, then looked back at them over her shoulder. "We've made it this far. Dexter says the pit is ready. He wants us to help our guest settle in."

The back doors swung open. Marcus stood—crouched over—and leapt to the floor. He kept the stingray trained on Edgar as the Hive Father followed.

"Very nice." Edgar straightened the lapels of his jacket as he looked around.

Vaughn opened the access door to the sublevel of the

ranch. As the ramp to the barn garage above lifted shut, she let out a huge breath, visibly relaxing. "This way."

"Of course," Edgar said.

He was being too cooperative. It was grating on Marcus's nerves. But then, if they fought, someone would have to kill Edgar... somehow. And any hope for curing Tessa without removing her arm would be gone.

They all entered the elevator. Marcus stood between Vaughn and Edgar.

"This technology is... interesting." For the first time, Edgar's smile seemed a bit forced. He looked around at the elevator, then to the stingray Marcus held. The doors whooshed open again. Edgar hesitated before stepping out.

"Go on," Marcus said.

Edgar did as instructed, stepping into the slate-gray hallway of the pit. Cells lined the hall, made of a transparent material that wasn't glass or clear plastic, but something stronger. Something Vaughn had 'dreamed up' and that had taken her company several years to develop in her factories.

"Who designed this place?" Edgar said.

"Actually—"

Marcus cut her off with a sharp shake of his head.

"Actually, that's none of your business," she said. "Keep walking."

Edgar's interest in the site was setting Marcus off. If that interest turned to Vaughn, it would be that much worse.

*Protect the pack.*

Marcus could tell it was his own thought. Not his dweller's. The voice in his head was still being quiet, but he could feel its steady presence in the back of his mind, watching.

Marcus stopped at the end of the hallway in front of the door to the only cell that was lit. "This is it."

The cells at least looked more like the levels above. Everything inside was white and chrome. The walls were completely smooth, with no places for anyone—or anything—to grip and tear. And even if something managed to smash through them, they would find another layer of Vaughn's... unbreakable... not-glass. Then cinderblock. Then bedrock.

The ceilings were smooth as well, with lights built into the material. Some cells had a small opening for passing food into the room, but not this one. All it had was a vent made of pin-sized holes high up in the wall above the bench seat opposite the door.

Edgar wasn't going anywhere.

He walked into the cell and turned in a slow circle. That damned smile returned. Vaughn keyed in a command sequence using her watch and the door slid shut. Marcus could hear the room pressurizing.

"I hope you like the place," she said. "Because you're going to be here for a while."

"Like it?" Edgar stared at Vaughn with the same intense scrutiny he'd been scanning the area with. "Why, it feels just like home."

Marcus growled and stepped forward. Vaughn put a hand on his chest, holding him back.

"Hey. Come on," she said. "This guy isn't going anywhere. Let's get back upstairs. We can monitor him remotely."

They headed down the hall to the elevator. Edgar stood calmly in the center of his cell, hands in his pockets, as the doors to the elevator closed.

# Chapter Twenty-Five

Sleeping in Marcus's bed was a hell of a lot more comfortable than Tessa's old van. She rolled over and stretched, reaching for him. All she found were cold sheets.

"Marcus?" She propped herself up on her elbows and looked around. There was no sign of him.

Yawning, she rose and sat on the edge of the bed. Maybe he was getting ready to go on patrol. If so, she wanted to tag along. She grabbed her clothes and pulled them on, checking her pocket to make sure the stingray was in place. As soon as she could, she'd ask Dexter about getting an upgrade. Now seemed like a pretty good time. She headed to the ops room, thinking Vaughn would be there. She would be able to tell Tessa where everybody was—including Marcus.

Tessa hummed some corny music as the elevator's doors whooshed shut. Halfway through her song, her arm started to itch under her wristband. Her dwellers were probably still riled up from the surgery. She hummed louder, trying to ignore it.

By the time the elevator stopped and the doors opened,

the itching had turned to stinging. She needed Porter, but wasn't sure where he was and didn't have time to search for him. She ran to the ops room for help.

Vaughn was tapping away on her desk next to Marcus, who was leaning against the table's surface. His arms were crossed over his chest, showcasing his muscles. It was almost enough to distract Tessa from the wriggling under her skin.

Almost.

He took one look at her and stood, hands curling into fists at his sides. "What's wrong?"

She hurried over to them, at least letting herself be reassured by Marcus's closeness.

"Do you know where Porter…" Her voice trailed off as she glanced at the monitors. One showed a man sitting in a plain cell on a smooth bench, hands folded in his lap, familiar smile on his face.

The view was new. The subject wasn't.

*Edgar…*

"What the fuck is that?" Tessa yelled, pointing at the monitor.

Vaughn glanced up at it and started stammering. "Oh, that… Um… That's…"

Tessa grabbed Vaughn's arm and yanked her out of her chair. "We have to get out of here. Come on."

"Tessa, relax," Vaughn said. "We've been watching him the whole time he's been in there. All twenty minutes of it."

"You have no idea how dangerous he is," Tessa said. "Or what you're dealing with."

"There's no way for him to get out." Vaughn shrugged off Tessa's grip and sat back at her desk, typing in commands. One of the monitors flickered, then showed a rotating line drawing of Edgar's cell. "The door is the only way in or out of the room. When we close it, it's hermetically sealed."

"So it's airtight?" she said.

"The door is." Vaughn tapped a few more times on the desk, and a band that ran along the back wall of the cell was highlighted—the wall above where Edgar was sitting. "There's a row of tiny holes for ventilation, but you couldn't fit a needle through them. Even if he sent out a scout, Edgar's dwellers are too big to fit through them."

"No one can escape from that cell," Marcus said.

Tessa's heart was pounding so hard she couldn't swallow. She had to push her words out to speak. Edgar had surprised her too many times before. Not even she knew the limits of what he could do.

"Edgar Eaton isn't just anyone." Or any*thing*. Tessa turned and started to run toward the door.

Marcus followed, grabbing her arm. "He's contained."

She shook him off. "You're delusional."

The door whooshed open as she turned, fully prepared to run as fast as she could in any direction that took her away from the ranch. She made it one step before bouncing into a broad, black-clad chest. Strong hands clasped her arms.

Dexter stepped into the room, pushing her back in with him. He looked down at her, something close to concern etching a line between his dark brows.

"What's going on?" he said.

"What the fuck is Edgar doing here?" Tessa's voice was high and thin, cracking with the energy of her fear.

She shoved Dexter away, backing into a corner, glancing all around the room, wondering how tight the seals in the light fixtures were. The vents suddenly looked huge.

"I captured him," Marcus said.

Tessa froze, her stomach clenching. "You? You brought him here?"

Marcus was supposed to be keeping her safe. Not letting her personal nemesis into the house she had hoped would become her home.

"This is what happens when I let my guard down. This is what happens when…" Tessa shook her head sharply. "Forget it. You're all insane or too cocky or just plain stupid. I'm out."

She tried to walk around Dexter, but he stepped in front of the door, blocking her path. Rage swelled up in her. The stinging of her dwellers had turned to a steady burn. The hair on both of her arms stood on end. She prayed it was just from the adrenaline.

"You did *not* just do that," she said.

Dexter's voice was calm. "Tessa, we can keep you safe."

"Step. Aside."

Dexter didn't move. Not even when she pulled the stingray out of her pocket and pointed it at him.

Marcus stepped between them. "Tessa, what are you doing?"

Her hand was shaking. Because her dwellers were activating—not because pointing a weapon at Marcus was breaking her heart.

"Step aside, Marcus. I don't want to shoot you, but I will."

"Go ahead," Dexter said. "It won't kill him."

Vaughn stood up, gently easing a little closer. "But it will piss him off."

Marcus let out a low growl, glaring at Vaughn for a moment. She froze in place, frowning deeply.

"If you need to leave to feel safe, that's fine," Marcus said. "But you're not going alone."

"Take one of the vans," Vaughn said. "I can keep you posted on what's happening here."

"Vaughn, you can't stay." Tessa let out a breath that was half-sob, half exasperated sigh. "None of you can stay. It isn't safe."

"There's more at stake here than you realize," Dexter

said. "We can't walk away from this."

"Fine," Tessa said. "It's your funeral. Just let me go."

Dexter snorted and stepped into her line of sight. She pointed the stingray at him instead of Marcus. It made her feel a tiny bit better.

"If you run now, you'll always be running," Dexter said.

*Shit.*

Maybe they were stupid, cocky, and crazy. Maybe she was, too. Because she knew in her heart he was right. And she also knew she couldn't leave them with no idea of how much danger they were in. They needed to understand.

"We all need to go," she said. "Right now. Please. We can regroup and come back…"

"You have a chance to stop this," Dexter said. "To stop him and save yourself. And me."

"What are you talking about?" Her arms felt heavy. Tessa lowered the weapon a fraction of an inch.

Dexter smiled, the normal cold passiveness of his face vanishing. He shook his head and half-shrugged. "Come on, Chicken. Haven't you figured it out yet?"

The room blurred as her eyes filled with tears. Dammit, she couldn't afford the lapse in her senses. Especially since she was pretty sure she had just hopped on the crazy train with the rest of the Blades. She wiped her eyes clear quickly with the back of her left hand.

"You can't be." She shook her head again, her panic

causing the motion to make her dizzy. "He's dead. My family... Everyone is dead."

Vaughn leaned closer to Marcus. "What is she talking about?"

"Tessa's brother," Marcus said.

Vaughn looked confused. "Dexter is Tessa's brother?"

"No, Brock is." Tessa pointed at Dexter emphatically with the stingray. "Not you."

"Chicken..." he said.

"Don't call me that!" Her hands were shaking so badly, she was afraid she'd fire by accident. She let her arms drop to her sides.

"You can't be him." Her voice caught on a sob.

But she knew. Staring at him, she wondered how she could have ever doubted it. His features, his voice...

It was Brock. But not Brock.

"You're a dweller," she said.

Vaughn laughed. "Don't be ridiculous."

"She's right," Dexter... *Brock* said.

"Wait, seriously?" Vaughn took a step closer to Marcus.

"What killed you?" Tessa's voice was so low, she wasn't sure Brock would hear. She should have known better. He was a dweller, after all.

"Nothing," Brock said. "I've always been this. Even when we were growing up."

"No..."

"Come on, Chicken. You knew I was adopted. Mom

and dad just didn't tell us the whole story until... Until I manifested."

"No. This isn't—" Her heart pounded, her throat constricting around words she couldn't force out.

"It happened when I turned eighteen. Dad was driving me home from school. He knew if mom found out my dweller nature had finally emerged, that I had somehow created copies of myself—replicants—that she would..." Brock's mouth pulled into a thin line.

*"Every dweller is a threat."* Their mom must have told Tessa that a thousand times. It took on a whole new meaning now that Tessa knew about Brock.

"We thought you were both dead," Tessa said, her tone demanding answers. "Mom told me that he'd found us. That Edgar found where we lived and killed you both."

Brock shook his head. "I'm so sorry. We had to run—after dad explained everything to me. Told me about the deal he made with Mom."

"What deal?" Tessa's voice was shrill. The level of what she could take had already been maxed out. Her sanity was red-lining.

"My biological mother was a human woman," Brock said. "Edgar married her and... He wanted to know what would happen if an apex ghoul and a human had a child. I'm the result."

Tessa let out a half-sob, half-groan, clutching her middle as if she'd been struck. Marcus came to stand behind her. She let herself lean on him. It was that or fall to the floor.

"My birth mother found Mom and asked for help," Brock continued. "Mom was still a hunter back then. She and Dad were sort of involved, but not serious yet. Mom went to Dad for help delivering me. He was a medical examiner and they'd been investigating cases involving dwellers together."

Tessa couldn't believe it. Her mother had explained about being a hunter before settling down with their dad and starting a family. But she hadn't told Tessa any of this.

"After I was born, my birth mother... changed," Brock said. "She attacked them. Mom killed her and wanted to kill me, too, but Dad stopped her. I seemed human, so he was able to convince Mom to spare me—unless I manifested. They got married and raised me as their own to keep an eye on me. Then they had you. They tried to give us a normal life for as long as they could. They didn't know when or if I would manifest a dweller nature."

Tessa shook her head, the motion setting tears running down her face. "What are you?"

Brock shrugged. "I don't know. I'm the only one of my kind."

"Excuse me," Vaughn said. "Two of your kind. Because, you know... Porter."

Brock laughed harshly. "You're right. Except that there are more than two of us."

"How many more?" Vaughn asked.

"Counting my original body, there are nine of us, total."

Vaughn's eyebrows hitched up her forehead. "Nine?"

"Mom did kill Edgar's wife," Brock said. "But not his child. Tessa, it's me. Edgar Eaton is my father."

"This is too much." Tessa's right arm had gone numb. She managed to pass her stingray to her left hand, and slid it into one of the pockets of her cargo pants. She was shaking too bad to use it safely.

"This is so messed up." Vaughn sank back into her chair.

Tessa wished she could sink through the floor. She wanted to scream or laugh or hit something. But she was frozen in place, her mind reeling. And then, Brock sent her further over the edge.

"Dad's alive," he said.

"What?" The word came out as a gasp.

"He took me away when I manifested," Brock said. "He knew that Mom would kill me if she found out I was more dweller than human. Edgar had nothing to do with us leaving. We didn't think you'd go on the run."

Tessa shook her head. She wished she could say he was wrong, but she knew better. After Brock and Dad had died —*left*—her mother had changed. She'd told Tessa everything about dwellers and hunters, and how it was time to learn about the 'real world.' Tessa had always thought her mother was putting on a brave face while training Tessa to be a hunter—that their real life was the one with soccer games and nail polish and family board game night. But her mother had never seemed more at ease than when she was training Tessa. Their normal life had been the lie.

How much more could Tessa take before her sanity snapped once and for all? Her family—at least part of it—was alive. And nothing like what she'd thought.

"We still need to run," Tessa said. "Edgar is more dangerous than you could possibly imagine."

"I know he's dangerous," Brock said. "But we need to study him."

"Are you even listening to me?"

"Tessa, I'm dying. We're all dying." Brock shook his head. "Edgar might hold the key to saving me. To saving all of my replicants—saving the Blades. We started this organization to try to find a way for dwellers and humans to live in peace together. To prove that it could be done. If I die—if we all die—I don't know what will happen. All our progress could be lost."

"If Edgar gets to us, it won't matter," Tessa said. "We'll all be dwellers, and I promise you, Edgar doesn't give a shit about peaceful coexistence."

"We've been watching him the whole time he's been here." Vaughn tapped on her desktop and zoomed in on Edgar sitting in his cell, eyes closed. He was in the exact same position as when Tessa had first seen him. Even his expression seemed frozen on his face. "He hasn't moved an inch since he sat down."

Tessa's panic reached a new level. "I've seen that look before. He's husked."

"What does that mean?" Vaughn leaned closer to the monitor.

"Turn up the vents," Tessa said. "Direct the air at him if you can."

Vaughn typed in a few commands. Edgar's hair stirred in a gentle breeze that grew stronger. His face collapsed on itself, his body turning to dust that sparkled before vanishing in a blue haze.

"Oh," Vaughn said. "That's not good."

"Edgar is not a distinct life form," Tessa said. "He's a Hive Father. *Hive*. His dwellers exist as a sort of collective consciousness. He can control them over hundreds of feet."

"But they're still too big to fit through the vents." Vaughn didn't sound very confident. "Right?"

A soft *thunk* sounded on the table. Tessa's skin began to crawl—literally, under her wristband.

"Edgar..." She turned toward the sound, knowing what she'd see. A small maggot-like creature, wriggling on the table near Vaughn.

"Look out!" Marcus leapt at Vaughn, pulling her from her chair.

"Shit! How did it get in here?" Vaughn said.

Everyone looked at the ceiling, where long string-like filaments were filtering through the vents. As they fell, they shortened and plumped into the same kind of wriggling creature that was crawling on the table.

"We need to leave," Marcus said. "Now."

Brock nodded. "Agreed."

"Final-fucking-ly." Tessa ran to the door.

Vaughn let out a shriek. Tessa turned back to her, heart in her throat. Vaughn was shaking her head oddly, then started beating at her hair.

"One's on me!" She screamed, shaking her head harder.

Marcus grabbed her cheeks and turned her head side-to-side, looking for the dweller. But Tessa knew that if Vaughn could feel it, it was already too late. Tessa fought back the tears that tried to fill her eyes, the despair and nausea that threatened to dull her focus.

"We have to move," Tessa yelled. "Carry her if you have to."

Vaughn would change. There was no getting around that. But Tessa wouldn't give up on her. If they could keep Vaughn away from Edgar, maybe some semblance of her personality could be saved.

Marcus tried to pull Vaughn's arm over his shoulders, but she swatted him away. It seemed too soon for Edgar's influence to be asserting itself. With a grunt, she typed something into her watch.

"The vents are sealed." She wrapped an arm around

Marcus as they staggered toward the door.

Porter was waiting for them in the hall. His eyes were wide. "The garage isn't an option. It looks like Edgar's dwellers dropped down from the ceiling onto the vehicles. There are hundreds of them."

"He can spread himself out, but is stronger as a collected entity," Tessa said. "We need to escape through the house if the elevator is clear."

Vaughn groaned as she stretched her arm to type on her watch again. She was rubbing her left ear against her shoulder. A muffled *whoosh* came from the elevator. Its doors opened, belching a ball of fire into the hallway. The fire dispersed quickly, leaving scorch marks on the walls.

"It is now," she said.

By the time they reached the elevator, Vaughn was practically hyperventilating. Her face had broken out with red spots and her ear was bleeding. Tessa had never seen someone have a reaction like that before, and she'd seen Edgar infect plenty of humans.

"Tessa…" Brock's voice was faint.

She tore her gaze from Vaughn and looked down the hallway.

Edgar was walking toward them, a smug smile on his face. He straightened his tie, the light gleaming off of his teeth.

"Hello, darling," he said.

They crowded into the elevator. Tessa's heart was

pounding hard against her ribs. She was close to hyperventilating herself. The doors closed. She felt infinitesimally better as the elevator started to climb. She tried not to show her fear, to put on a brave face, but she knew the truth.

None of them were getting out of this alive. Not unchanged.

# Chapter Twenty-Six

"How do we kill Edgar?"

Marcus forced his voice to sound human, even though all he wanted to do was throw his head back and howl. He could smell Vaughn's scent changing, the mustiness of the dweller integrating with her body.

If Marcus lost it and changed, he wouldn't be able to help anyone. He would go on a rampage.

Tessa was staring at Vaughn, eyes wide. Tessa's chest heaved with each breath, her panic obvious.

"Tessa, how do we kill Edgar?" Marcus said again.

She shook her head. "We don't. Even a flamethrower won't work on him when he's separated. All it takes is one of his dwellers to survive—and they can last outside of his body a lot longer than a dweller that's already integrated into a human. It can find a new host and take over its consciousness. Slowly change its physiology to match his. Make more of itself."

"I thought when it was only one dweller it just turned humans into…" Brock didn't finish his sentence. He glanced at Vaughn, then looked away.

"Only if the Hive consciousness is intact," she said.

"He explained it to me while trying to convince me it wasn't a bad thing to be infected. He said he was offering me immortality."

"Not what it's cracked up to be," Vaughn grunted out each word. She was trembling violently, but still trying to make a goddammed joke.

"I've never seen someone react to one of Edgar's dwellers this way," Tessa said.

"Could it be an allergic reaction?" Porter said.

He and Brock were keeping their distance from Vaughn. Tessa should be as well, but either she wasn't worried or she cared about Vaughn more than she feared for herself. Marcus was betting on the latter.

"I've never heard of human physiology rejecting a dweller," Tessa said.

"Maybe it's... rejecting me," Vaughn said.

The elevator doors opened on the ground level. Marcus blew out a quick breath—not really feeling relief, but just trying to keep himself human. Or as close to human as he could manage. They poured out of the elevator, heading for the front door. Rain pelted the window across the library from them, darkening the sky to an unnatural gray.

"I don't want to become a ghoul," Vaughn said.

Marcus tightened his grip on Vaughn's waist. "We'll figure something out."

"No," she said. "Marcus, I don't want to change into that. Please—"

"Forget it." Marcus knew where this was heading. There was no way he was killing Vaughn. They *would* find a way to save her. "No matter what you are, you're part of my pack. I'm not letting you go so easily."

Vaughn actually laughed, but it was a joyless sound. "Glad to know you still care."

She let out a pained grunt as her legs gave out. Marcus tried to hold her up, but Vaughn started writhing against him. He lowered them both to the tiled floor of the kitchen. Tessa knelt beside them.

"This isn't right," Vaughn said. "This isn't…"

She started to scream, then rolled onto her back, clutching her head. Her body shook violently all over, like she was having a seizure. Marcus held onto her, trying to keep her from hurting herself as she thrashed on the floor.

"What the hell is happening?" Brock said.

"I don't know," Tessa yelled.

The red splotches on Vaughn's skin were growing, white lines forming between them in a large scale-like pattern. Her skin suddenly turned ashen gray, then the center of each sectioned area turned pink. The white lines faded as Vaughn's normal skin tone spread over her face, neck, and arms—everything that Marcus could see. She arched her back, taking in a huge, gasping breath, then collapsed.

"What the fuck?" Tessa said.

Blood was pooling beneath Vaughn's head, trickling out

from her left ear. Marcus heard a splat as the dweller wriggled out, its body blackened. It thrashed around a few more times, then curled up and stopped moving. Within seconds, it glowed with a soft blue light and vanished.

"What does that mean?" Porter asked.

"I don't know." Tessa was shaking her head, her eyes wide with shock. She kept repeating, "I don't know."

"Is she infected or not?" he snapped.

Marcus growled at Porter before saying, "Watch your tone."

"I don't think she is," Tessa said. "I can't explain it."

Vaughn stirred, slowly opening her eyes. She looked around at the people hovering over her. "Um… Hi?"

Tessa and Marcus helped Vaughn to her feet. She was still unsteady, so Marcus draped her arm across his shoulders again.

"What happened?" Vaughn said.

"We can figure that out later," Tessa said. "Right now, we need to get as far from Edgar as possible. If we run through the woods, he won't be able to follow us with one of the cars and maybe we can—"

"Oh, sweetie, it's much too late for that." Edgar was standing in the archway that led to the dining room, blocking the way to the front door.

Tessa let out a little yelp and backed away from him. Her scent grew thick with terror. Vaughn let go of Marcus's shoulders, giving him the space he needed to fight, and stumbled toward the counter, leaning on it to stay upright. Marcus stepped forward.

"You can't have them," he said. "They're mine."

Edgar just smiled. "Is that so?"

Tessa bolted for the other door. If Marcus could hold off Edgar, she could escape. All of them could.

"Everyone, run," Marcus said.

He let the change flow over him, tearing his clothes from his body with hands that already ended in claws. He dropped the tattered fabric on the ground as he stepped right in front of Edgar and roared a challenge.

"Brute force? You think you can beat us in a fight?" Edgar laughed, then took a step *closer* to Marcus. "Brother, you don't even know the battlefield you're standing on."

*Us?*

Edgar looked over Marcus's shoulder as Vaughn muttered an expletive. Tessa's scent strengthened in the room. Why had she come back?

When she whimpered, Marcus wheeled around. A man was holding her in the doorway—one arm tight around her waist and her neck pinched in his other hand. A man who looked exactly like Edgar, even down to the suit.

The new Edgar smiled in a mirror expression to the first. He nuzzled the side of Tessa's head. "We've been waiting for this moment for a long time. Did you really think we'd leave anything to chance?"

Marcus turned, slashing at the first Edgar, claws raking over the Hive Father's face. Dozens of his white maggoty dwellers fell to the ground, then crawled back to his shoes and merged into his body. The claw marks sealed as Marcus watched. He hadn't even managed to wipe the smile off the bastard's face.

"Try that again, and we'll break her neck." The first Edgar nodded at the second.

"I thought you wanted her," Porter said.

The first Edgar gave a half-shrug and his smile deepened. "We want a lot of things right now. And we never said we needed her alive."

Many dwellers transformed corpses. Marcus's skin felt electrified from the adrenaline in his system, his fur standing on end. He didn't know how to protect Tessa—or anyone.

"Marcus, stand down." Dexter was back. Who the hell knew where Brock had gone.

Marcus would always be able to tell them apart now, though. And he didn't need the fucking pronouns to know when Brock was somehow occupying one of his replicants' bodies. Just like he'd be able to know if Edgar was in more than one place by how the Hive Father spoke.

"We said stand down," Dexter repeated.

Marcus growled and stepped back, positioning himself closer to Tessa.

"Well done," The second Edgar said. "Commanding an

alpha werewolf."

"But then, we'd expect nothing less from you." The first Edgar actually sounded moved as he finished his statement. "Our son."

Dexter's perpetual smirk had turned into a snarl. His lip was twitching, as if he wanted to kill Edgar as much as Marcus did. Maybe more.

"We have a father," Dexter said. "His name is Eli."

Tessa let out a sound like a strangled moan.

*Eli* was her father? The head of the Blades' medical division? Marcus had met Eli before. He was a good man. They had to get through this. Marcus had to get them to safety—to reunite Tessa's family.

"Still clinging to the humans who raised you?" The second Edgar's smile turned to a hard, cold line. "They weren't a father and mother. They were a kidnapper and a murderer."

Disgust clouded Dexter's features. "You might have seduced our biological mother into marrying you, but if she'd known what you were—"

"Those humans you're so fond of didn't give her a chance," the first Edgar snapped. "If she hadn't run, we could have been a family. Instead, your 'parents' killed her and took you from us. And now you've made this perverse organization."

"Coming from you, that's rich," Dexter said.

"Dwellers don't fight amongst ourselves," the first

Edgar said. "We help each other or ignore each other. We don't turn on each other."

Maybe that was why Marcus's dweller was being so quiet around Edgar. Dexter had no problem speaking up, though.

"The Blades don't exist to kill dwellers," Dexter said. "We're working toward peace."

"Peace with this primitive species?" The first Edgar snorted. "Humans haven't even forged peace among their own kind."

The second Edgar stepped closer to Dexter, bringing Tessa along. "There are thousands of dweller species on this planet, all coexisting in harmony. Until you."

"*Thousands* of species?" Porter's face lit with curiosity.

Marcus didn't like it. He *did* like how everyone's attention was diverted, allowing him to inch closer to Tessa.

"If we had been able to raise you, we would have taught you your true origins," the second Edgar said. "We could have shown you what you are."

"And what's that?"

"A hydra." The first Edgar smiled. His voice became a little breathless as he went on. "We had no idea what would happen when we mingled our genes with your human mother. This is better than anything we'd imagined."

"A hydra? Like in Greek mythology?" Porter stepped

closer.

The first Edgar nodded. "They're very rare. We've never met one in person. Human legends about dwellers always have some basis in truth. They say that when you chop off one of a hydra's many heads, two more sprout up in its place. How does that manifest with you?"

Porter let out a tiny huff of breath. "Unpleasantly."

The first Edgar's smile grew.

"We always wondered where hydra came from," the second Edgar said. "Now that we know, we'll be sure to make more. After we take care of business here."

Marcus growled, his hands curling as he waited for an opening. He would grab the second Edgar's arms and crush them into maggots, letting Tessa escape. He just needed a chance… But the second Edgar wasn't looking at Tessa. She seemed almost forgotten in his grip. He was looking at Vaughn instead.

"You really have gathered an odd assortment of beings around you, son," the second Edgar said. "An alpha werewolf without a pack, a proto-Hive Mother managing to keep her infection at bay, and most interestingly…"

The first Edgar took a step closer to Vaughn. Dexter drew his sword and brought it to Edgar's neck in a graceful move that took a fraction of a second.

"It might not kill you, but it'll slow you down," Dexter said.

The first Edgar laughed. "You have no idea, do you?

The danger lurking in your midst."

Marcus had always considered himself the hidden danger among the Blades. The one werewolf operating as a Guard. But both Edgars were still looking at Vaughn.

"What… me?" Vaughn said. "I'm just the IT guy. Gal."

"Hmm." The first Edgar nodded. "You designed the prison? And all the technology we've seen so far?"

"I have a knack for engineering. So what?" Vaughn shrugged, backing toward the fridge as the second Edgar took a step forward, Tessa held tight in his grip.

"Not a knack," the second Edgar said. "We tasted it in your genes. The purest sample we've come across in centuries. You're a curator."

*"Shit."*

Marcus was stunned at his dweller's response—and at the visceral fear that shot through his body. For the first time, it fed him images of killing *Vaughn*. A quick snap of the neck. A clean ending, not like the ones it constantly fed Marcus about Dexter.

*"Kill her,"* it thought. *"Kill her now, or your planet is doomed."*

*"We are done."* Marcus yelled the words in his mind. There was no way—no *fucking* way—he was going to hurt Vaughn. And he wasn't about to let the Edgars near his beta.

"What's a curator?" Porter said.

"Something much more dangerous than any dweller

you've encountered," the second Edgar said. "Killing her is more important than anything else. Not just for dwellers, but for all life on this planet. If you want to protect everyone, as you say, you'll kill her immediately."

"I'm just the IT guy…" Vaughn said again.

"You aren't *just* anything." The first Edgar's smile turned to a grimace, all of his teeth showing as his lips peeled back further than any human's could. He pressed against Dexter's sword, the metal easily parting the Hive Father's flesh—which sealed itself on the other side.

The second Edgar took another step forward, pushing Tessa along with him, then finally did what Marcus was waiting for. He relaxed his grip on Tessa's throat.

# Chapter Twenty-Seven

The instant the version of Edgar holding her lightened his chokehold, Marcus was on him. Tessa knew it would happen and had been readying herself. She *didn't* know Marcus was going to grab that Edgar's arm and... rip it off.

Lines of white-hot pain streaked across her neck as the Hive Father's nails dug through her flesh. She would survive—as long as she kept it together. And as long as the Edgar holding on to her did as well.

Edgar maintaining a semblance of human form meant she had something to gain leverage against. Tessa rammed her elbow hard into the Edgar's gut, twisting out of his grip.

The arm in Marcus's hand exploded into a shower of tiny maggot-things. At the same time, the rest of that Edgar's body dropped its form, dwellers raining down on the floor around where he had stood.

"Don't let any of them touch you." Tessa's throat felt raw as she shouted her warning.

She grabbed Vaughn's arm and pushed her behind the kitchen island, picking up the closest weapon—Vaughn's carving knife. Vaughn grabbed a fire extinguisher, and started spraying down the dwellers writhing on the floor. The cold seemed to be slowing them down.

*Genius.*

The first Edgar swiveled around with Dexter's sword still buried in his throat. He smacked Dexter's arm hard enough to make him lose his grip. Dexter leapt back out of reach.

The maggots on the ground were slowly crawling toward Edgar, merging with his into one body. If they could break him down into those tiny pieces, they still couldn't crush every single dweller. She didn't think they could even keep track of them all. But if he stayed together, maybe they had a chance... To escape, at least.

"Children." Edgar pulled the sword from his neck and let it clatter to the ground. "We're going to be a family, one way or another. Tessa's even picked out a pet."

Marcus let out a low growl, then stomped his foot down in the mass of dwellers on the floor. Edgar just laughed, teeth still bared in a skeleton's grin.

"How petty. And futile. But by all means, continue if it makes you feel better." Edgar took a deep breath through his nose, then pointed at the fridge. "There's plenty of biomatter in there to create more of me."

Tessa wished he would revert to his human appearance. He normally only wore his grimace when he was about to feed.

She stepped in front of Vaughn, pointing the knife at Edgar. "Put away your teeth. Vaughn isn't on the menu."

Edgar hissed in a breath. "Eat a curator? Disgusting. I just want to kill her."

"Over my dead body," Tessa said.

"Darling, your death has been on the agenda since before you were born." Edgar laughed. "Your mother saw to that. Once you die, my dwellers can spread without any resistance."

"You lied to me," she said. "You told me you killed my family."

"No, I said your family was dead." He shrugged. "I figured they probably were. I was only trying to protect you."

She let out an incredulous breath. "From what?"

"Hope. The absolute worst human emotion. The most dangerous. It makes humans do stupid things. Dangerous things. Like hope making you think you can protect Vaughn from me. You can't."

"You'll have to go through all of us to get to her." Dexter pulled out a larger version of Vaughn's stingray.

"So dramatic." Edgar shook his head. "But I don't have to get past you. I'm already right where I want to be."

He stared at Tessa, and suddenly her right arm started to spasm. Pain radiated up from her forearm.

Her dwellers were awake.

The knife clattered onto the kitchen island as she

staggered forward, grabbing onto her arm and squeezing, trying to keep the dwellers from spreading. She could see lumps forming under her wristband as they wriggled around, could feel sharp spikes of agony as they ate her flesh.

"Porter!" Marcus slashed his claws across Edgar's chest, spilling out more dwellers, and forcing the Hive Father back a few paces.

Porter ran to Tessa's side. "He's activated them. We can't make them go dormant again."

"Don't touch me," Tessa ground out. "They'll try to infect you, too."

"You seem to think you have a choice about how this will go." The wounds on Edgar's body were already healing. His voice had lost even a façade of warmth. "You don't."

"Says you." Tessa picked up Vaughn's knife with her left hand and flicked it to the highest setting. She brought it down on her right arm just below her elbow.

"Tessa!" Vaughn grabbed her shoulders and pulled her away from the counter.

Her arm stayed where it was.

Blood poured from the stump. Plain, human blood. No wriggling dwellers.

She was free.

She started to laugh, but then the pain hit her again— worse than the dwellers eating her alive. Screaming wasn't an option. She was starting to hyperventilate.

Porter grabbed a towel and wrapped it around the wound, holding her arm tight. "We have to get her out of here."

"Marcus," Dexter yelled. "Use a bigger shoe."

Marcus let out a devastating roar, then grabbed the kitchen island and tore it from its moorings. He picked it up and crushed Edgar with it.

"Help Vaughn," Marcus yelled. He grabbed Tessa and pulled her against his chest, then ran.

Shapes and colors blurred together. One moment, they were in the house. Then there was a crash of glass and the world turned gray and green. Drops of cold water pattered on her face. She was shivering and couldn't stop. The pain in her arm had become a dull throbbing beat that kept time with her heart.

It was slowing down.

Nothing felt as urgent as it should. Marcus was saying things, but he seemed far away.

A wave of dizziness hit her as he set her on the ground, hovering over her. Faces swam in and out of view above her. She felt someone jiggling her arm, pressure pinching her right bicep. She struggled to understand the shouting around her. Everyone's voices were strangely muffled.

"She's bleeding out," one of the twins said.

"Don't get too close." The other twin this time. "Some of the Hive Father's dwellers might have made it into her body."

"Fuck you! That's my sister."

Brock was there? Tessa felt another set of hands on her, smoothing her hair away from her face. Tears filled her eyes. She didn't want him to have to watch her die. It wasn't right.

Edgar was right about hope. She'd been ready to die until she met the Blades. Until she met Marcus. She had started hoping for another life. Dying now… It hurt so much more.

And Brock must be feeling the same thing. Her father, too. God, her father was going to lose his daughter all over again.

She felt tears roll down her cheeks—only slightly warmer than the rain hitting her face.

"I'm sorry." Speaking exhausted her. She just wanted to rest.

Someone pulled her face to his neck. No fur. Must be Brock. She could still feel the warmth of Marcus's pelt. He was holding her against his chest.

"Tessa," Brock said.

Marcus started to growl. Someone pulled Brock away.

"He's about to lose it. Edgar is probably en route. We have to get you out of here."

"I'm your goddamned *progenitor*. You do as I say and I say we stay."

She hadn't heard anything from Vaughn. Not a quip,

not a laugh, nothing. Panic surged through her strong enough to make her feel again, to think with a little bit of clarity.

"Vaughn?"

"Yeah, I'm here, Tessa."

Tessa heard a splash as Vaughn knelt next to her, felt Vaughn's hand on her shoulder, and forced herself to focus on her friend. Vaughn was a wreck. Her eyes were red and her nose was running. She was rocking back and forth. The rain had plastered her hair to her pale face. There was still blood soaking her neck and shoulder. She looked like she was about to pass out.

"Thanks for convincing me not to run," Tessa said.

"You should have run." Vaughn's voice shook. "I'm so sorry."

"No. This was inevitable." Tessa's eyes drifted shut again. She was too tired to stop it. "I'm glad I got to be part of something first. A family."

Marcus growled louder. "Vaughn, can you hold yourself together?"

"Are you kidding? Being outside isn't nearly as scary as what's in our house right now."

Marcus leaned forward, his warmth vanishing as Vaughn slid behind Tessa to hold her up.

"Look at me, Tessa," Marcus said.

She forced her eyes open again, wanting to see Marcus one more time—human or not.

Definitely not.

His gray fur had darkened from the rain. His eyes glowed so brightly, she could barely stand to look into them.

"You told me you were done running," he said.

"I guess I am."

He let out another low growl. "Are you done fighting?"

She was so tired. Why wouldn't he just let her go? There was nothing left to do. She was out of options.

"Tessa, are you done fighting?" Marcus was holding onto her shoulders so hard. It probably would have hurt if she could still feel.

Of course she was done. It would take a miracle to save her. A miracle…

Her heart seemed to stutter as she realized what he was saying, what he was asking.

She didn't need a miracle to live. She just needed Marcus.

She reached out with her left hand and grabbed the side of his face, burying her fingers in the thick pelt. In a stronger voice than she thought she could manage, she said, "I'm not."

# Chapter Twenty-Eight

Every cell in his body was thrumming. Marcus was going to turn someone. Someone who was willing to change. He was turning *Tessa*.

The only possible obstacles stood a few feet away. Dexter was still holding onto Brock. They were both staring at Marcus.

"Don't interfere," Marcus said.

"Do it," Brock said. "Now, before it's too late."

Marcus turned back to Tessa, letting his instincts guide him. The voice in his head hadn't said anything since its outburst in the kitchen. He wasn't sure he'd ever hear it again. He *was* sure he didn't need it now.

Right shoulder, above the injury, but close enough that his dweller nature could help her heal. Stop the bleeding.

During their night together, she'd explained how a werewolf's alpha status was based on how hard they fought to survive, to protect those they loved. Marcus had fought as hard as he could. Tessa had cut off her own arm. She would only have one scar from her turning, but she would still be an alpha as far as he was concerned.

His mate.

With a snarl, he lashed out, quickly latching onto her shoulder and sinking his teeth into her flesh. She sucked in a breath and held it. Marcus shook his head. He couldn't stop himself. He needed more access. More connection. Her blood splashed onto his tongue, warm and fresh. Human.

He'd never tasted human blood before. It was so much better than the meat he normally ate.

"Keep it together, Marcus." Vaughn's voice brought him back to himself. Kept him grounded.

The clouds hung low in the sky and the trees wove a tight ceiling above them, but they were still outside—and Vaughn was holding it together. If she could, surely Marcus could as well.

Tessa finally let out her breath. It escaped in quick, choppy jerks. Her body started to shake.

"Jesus, what the hell is that?" Vaughn said.

Marcus couldn't see what was going on. He just knew he couldn't let go of Tessa. Not yet.

"Take off the tourniquet," Dexter said. "Quickly."

"I think I'm going to be sick." Vaughn made a stifled gagging sound.

"The wound is closing off," Brock said. "It's a good thing."

The turning was healing her. Just as Marcus had hoped. A surge of excitement flooded his system again and his jaws tightened reflexively. She let out a grunt, then grabbed his throat with her left hand. Her grip was strong. Inhumanly so.

His muscles were singing, his senses focused on her. The erratic pounding of her heart was stabilizing into a steady pulse. Her breath became more regular. She warmed in his arms. He pulled her away from Vaughn and stood, teeth still buried in her shoulder. Marcus held her close against his chest, not sure if she could support herself yet. She tightened her grip on his neck—hard enough *to hurt*. Tessa snarled, then shoved him away.

Marcus staggered back, his teeth dripping. Her shoulder was wet with her own blood. She was holding her right arm close to her chest, the stump covered in smooth skin. Red stained her neck and cheek. She ran her left hand across her mouth—smearing it crimson—and stared at him. Stared at him with glowing gold eyes. He roared a laugh, then threw his head back and howled. Tessa let out a low, warning growl.

"Isn't this a happy ending. Everyone gets what they wanted."

His hackles rose at the now-familiar voice. Edgar.

Marcus turned around, pulling up to his full height. "She. Is. Mine."

"I am no one's," Tessa growled.

Marcus grinned, letting Edgar see his teeth.

"Aren't you?" Edgar said.

Stepping to the side, Edgar revealed a woman who'd

been standing behind him out of sight. She was wearing a fitted black suit with a short skirt. Her hair was pulled up in a tight bun. Her eyes were a dull, flat black, just like Edgar's. She hooked her arm through his elbow, smiling at the group.

"What am I seeing?" Vaughn said.

Marcus's brain was having trouble processing it as well. The woman… It was Tessa. Marcus looked back at his mate, then to the woman on Edgar's arm. Beneath the blood and disheveled hair—*his* Tessa's blood and disheveled hair—they were identical.

"How…" His Tessa shook her head.

"I didn't need all of you," Edgar said. "Leaving me your arm provided plenty of genetic material to form a viable mate. That plus your generously stocked kitchen." He let out a genial laugh. "Like I said. Plenty of biomatter."

The Hive Mother smiled at them. "I've been waiting for a long time to awaken."

She leaned into Edgar and he shifted his arm to wrap it around her waist. He bent to her lips and kissed her.

"Okay, this is even worse than watching Tessa's arm grow new skin," Vaughn said.

Marcus felt another adrenaline surge. This one wasn't coming from his own body. Tessa's remaining  hand was curled into a claw-like fist at her side. Her chest heaved with each quick breath and her eyes were glowing even more brightly.

*"Rip off their faces and shove them down their throats…"*

Bloody images accompanied the words. The voice in his head was *Tessa's.*

*"Calm yourself,"* he thought at her.

She growled low, slowly craning her neck to look at him. Suddenly, those bloody thoughts were directed at him. He could take it.

He remembered how it had felt right after he'd been turned. The weeks he'd spent in a cell while Dexter talked him down from changes Marcus couldn't control. The urge to hurt everyone and everything around him.

*"You aren't my alpha,"* she thought.

*"No. But I am your mate."*

Her eyes widened and her mouth opened as she sucked in a quick breath. Warmth flooded through him as he felt a mirror of his own feelings for her reflected back at him. The bond they had already somehow been forging strengthened as they accepted each other as pack.

"It's nice, isn't it? Having someone else in your mind." Edgar turned to them with a smile. "Don't worry—we can't hear your thoughts. But we know the look. Werewolves are just another type of hive. Somewhat more individuated, but a hive nonetheless."

"An infinity preferable one," Tessa said.

The other Tessa shrugged. "To each their own. I have

no complaints." She rested her right hand on Edgar's stomach.

Tessa stared at it. Marcus could feel her fury building.

"Now we can be a family." The Hive Mother turned her smile on Brock and Dexter. "I don't have Tessa's memories, but I look forward to making new ones with you."

"Not interested," Brock said.

Vaughn laughed. She cleared her throat when everyone looked at her.

"Sorry. It's just your step-mom is also your foster-sister." Vaughn shook her head, then held her arms out briefly as if the movement had made her dizzy. "And I thought my family was messed up."

"Speaking of your family," Edgar said. "We're going to need a list of names and addresses of all your blood relatives. To get DNA as pure as yours, they must have recessive strains of curator DNA. It's best to be thorough when stamping that out."

"Well, let's see," Vaughn said. "You can find them all at the corner of *Are You Kidding Me* Avenue and *Go Fuck Yourself* Lane."

"Always making things difficult." Edgar shook his head. "It's one of the things curators and humans have in common. We'll just have to torture it out of you."

Vaughn swallowed hard. "Or, you know, use the Internet?"

"Let's not give the bad guys any ideas," Brock said.

"Sorry." Vaughn turned back to Edgar. "Before either you kill us or we kill you, could you at least tell me what a curator is?"

"It's driving you a little crazy, isn't it?" Edgar laughed. "Keeping that to myself seems like a great way to start tormenting you."

"Wow, you really are an asshole." Vaughn waved at Edgar. "Marcus, could you please kill him now?"

"No one is killing anyone," Dexter said.

Tessa growled at him. Marcus grabbed her shoulder and held her in place.

"We need him," Dexter said. "Brock is dying, remember? Edgar may have the key to saving him."

Marcus could feel Tessa's frustration—and also her fear. She knew better than any of them what Edgar was capable of. How dangerous he was. They should have listened to her warnings from the start.

*"How do we kill them?"* Marcus thought. *"You lived with him for years. Surely you know of a weakness."*

*"We have to get all of their dwellers at the same time."*

Marcus had noticed both Hive beings were referring to themselves as 'I.'

*"From the way they're talking, all of their hive components are here. But there are* two *of them now."*

*"We'd need a flamethrower or something to kill them all,"* Tessa thought. *"And with this rain, that might not*

*even work."*

He felt an idea begin to form in her mind.

*"I still have my stingray,"* she thought.

Marcus remembered the procedure in Porter's lab when they had removed a dweller from her arm. Cold would slow Edgar and his mate down. Fire would kill them—and so would electricity.

But electricity wouldn't kill a werewolf.

Conveniently, there were ample puddles around. They just had to maneuver their prey into position.

*"Are you thinking what I'm thinking?"* He felt her approval as a wave of tingling warmth down his spine.

The only question that remained was—could she control herself once she changed?

# Chapter Twenty-Nine

"My son is dying?" Edgar cocked his head to the side.

Tessa wanted to rip it off his neck, but not if he could help Brock. She had to control herself until she was sure.

It wasn't easy.

Her teeth felt sharper than normal. The hairs on her skin kept standing on end as frissons of sensation swept over her body. She felt exhilarated, energized.

Hungry.

Brock, Dexter, and Vaughn had meat. Blood and meat that she could claw through with ease—once she let the waves of her transformation sink bone-deep. She kept her focus on the two dwellers in front of her, pushing the human…ish beings out of her awareness.

Dust and leaf rot. That's what the apex ghouls smelled like. Unpalatable.

"I guess that explains why hydra are so rare," Edgar said. "If they can't survive on their own, they aren't a viable hybridization."

"Don't worry," the Hive Mother said. "You can always make more as we need them. And the next ones, we'll raise together."

Tessa's stomach heaved. Seeing herself reflected in that warped mirror—the future that could so easily have been hers... She shook her head, hard, wishing her ears were longer, her fingers sharp.

*"It wouldn't make a difference. I can barely slow them down, even in this form."*

She heard Marcus's voice in her mind. A voice of reason and comfort. Her heart pounded harder at the warmth that flooded through her body knowing he was close. He was *hers*.

No wonder they had bonded so quickly. If this is what he'd been feeling toward her all along...

Visions of slashing Edgar filtered into her consciousness, Marcus sharing his memories of their fight. Brute force might not be enough to kill an apex ghoul, but it could help maneuver them into a situation that was fatal.

"You won't help Brock." She didn't bother making her words a question.

"Natural selection at work," Edgar said.

Tessa snorted. "There's nothing natural about any of us."

"You need to expand your thinking." Edgar's smile broadened. At least he wasn't grimacing anymore.

"I have something else in mind." She drew her stingray out of her pocket, glad that it was already on her left side.

Her stomach lurched as she remembered why that was a good thing. Her arm...

She pulled her thoughts sharply back to task. She didn't have time to freak out. Not yet.

"I don't need your toys anymore." Tessa tossed the weapon to Vaughn.

Vaughn scrambled to catch it, her hands still shaking. She cleared her throat and said, "That's actually hurtful."

"Get over it." Tessa glared at her, eyes narrowed, hoping Vaughn would catch on that they had a plan.

Vaughn's brow furrowed. Tessa locked her eyes on the nearest puddle pointedly, then looked back to the weapon. Reaching out for Marcus in her mind, she could feel that he was ready.

Finally, she let go.

The gooseflesh that had been rippling over her skin intensified, a pleasure so intense it almost hurt. It soaked into her muscles, vibrated in her bones, reached into her marrow, and then exploded outward.

She ripped off her shirt as her chest changed dimensions. Marcus was at her side, tearing at her cargo pants with his claws. Her feet elongated to the point that she could simply step out of her boots. She shook off her socks.

The world was changed. Halos surrounded everyone around her—Brock's and Dexter's a soft orange, Vaughn's more gold-tinged. Tessa could feel their warmth, hear the blood rushing through their veins. It took effort not to lick her lips.

*"Not prey,"* Marcus thought to her.

She repeated it like a mantra. *"Not prey."*

She felt his warmth most of all. Affection blossoming into something stronger. A bond that connected them on a level that went deeper than the physical, energy flowing between them somehow.

And his scent…

Cool wind after a summer storm. Warm earth that was just overturned. A hint of cinnamon mixed into his fur.

Edgar and the other Tessa were surrounded in a dark, somber blue. The only thing Tessa heard from them was the soft squicking sound of their dwellers crawling around within their humanlike carapaces.

"Are we going to do this or what?" the Hive Mother said.

Tessa took a deep breath through her long muzzle, taking in the symphony of scents in the air—rainwater, traces of her human blood on the ground—and focusing on the ones she was about to end.

With a roar, she leapt forward.

She sensed Marcus's attack more than she saw it. A blur of gray in her periphery, clawing at Edgar. Tessa focused on her target—on the thing that had stolen her form.

Slashing wouldn't work. It would only spread their dwellers around. Plus, with only one hand, she couldn't do as much damage as she'd like. At least the wound had healed over. Her arm would be an effective bludgeoning weapon.

Tessa swung at the Hive Mother. The creature only grinned, letting the blow connect. Her cheek collapsed on itself, but then reformed around Tessa's fur-covered arm and held it fast. She felt the dwellers in the thing's body wriggling around what was left of her forearm—the *outside* of her arm. They would never get under her skin again.

The Hive Mother smiled. "There's no way you can win. We shouldn't be fighting in the first place. We should be working together."

Tessa didn't bother trying to pull her arm free. With her left hand, she grabbed the Hive Mother by her neck and lifted her from the ground, crushing what would have been her windpipe if she was human. It didn't seem to make any difference at all—and why would it? She was a bag of maggots. Too bad Tessa didn't have any bug spray.

But she had Vaughn.

Tessa heard the distinctive sound of the stingray powering up. A high-pitched whine she hoped only she and Marcus could detect.

"Give us the curator," the Hive Mother said. "You have to feel that she needs to die. You're one of us now."

"And Vaughn is one of my pack." Tessa tightened her grip, crushing the Hive Mother's neck further.

*"Tessa. Here."*

A loud splash coupled with Marcus's words in her mind

helped Tessa maneuver to the puddle they would be using to ensure the apex ghouls' destruction. She slammed her prey to the ground. With her stump still buried in the thing's face, it was easy to push the Hive Mother under the water.

"Fool," the Hive Mother said. "Fighting against us. Not using your claws or teeth. You're thinking like a human."

Tessa didn't understand how the Hive Mother was still talking. The voice was coming from her chest.

Looking down, Tessa saw another face pressing up just past the thing's collarbones. She felt the dwellers morphing, changing to escape Tessa's grasp. Shapeless tendrils of gray flesh wrapped around her arms and started to squeeze.

The face in the Hive Mother's chest grinned, showing all of her teeth as her mouth stretched closer to Tessa's neck. From the corner of her eye, she could see that Marcus was in a similar situation.

"You can't drown us," the Hive Mother said.

"We're not trying to drown you."

The Hive Mother narrowed her eyes in confusion. If she figured out the plan, she would have a chance to try to escape. They were out of time.

"Vaughn, now!" Tessa said.

"This is going to hurt," Vaughn shouted.

Tessa heard the high buzz of the stingray grow closer, then a splash as it landed in the puddle. Her vision turned to molten white. Pain arced through her body, dancing through each nerve-ending. Marcus roared, his pain adding to hers. She could feel the Hive Mother convulsing beneath her. The tendrils wrapped around Tessa's arms hardened and then snapped off. The pain receded.

An etched outline of the thing beneath her became visible, its outer shell bubbling and morphing, until finally melting into the puddle. Thousands of the little maggoty dwellers floated to the surface. Tessa looked over at Marcus. He was panting, staring with wide eyes at the water they were crouching in. She heard his voice in her mind again.

*"Did it work?"*

Soft blue light illuminated his chest, catching in the drops of water falling from his pelt. She turned back to the puddle. The one Marcus had chosen for their trap was huge, and glowing so brightly it hurt her eyes to watch. Still, she wouldn't let herself look away. She didn't dare to blink. After all these years, she had to see Edgar's end— and the destruction of the thing he had created from Tessa. The water level dropped as the light started to dim.

Vaughn was the first one to speak. "Is it over?"

Tessa's heart pounded in her chest. She still had a heart in this form. And yes, she had—was?—a dweller now, but she was still Tessa. She was still herself.

She started to laugh. "Yeah. I think so."

Marcus rose up on his knees, clawed hands curled and

dripping water. He threw his head back and howled. The surge of emotion that flooded her was beyond anything she had ever felt.

*"Victory."* She didn't know if the thought was his or her own, and she didn't care.

They had defeated the enemy. Protected *their* pack.

Tessa's laugh turned into a deep roar, then she threw her head back and let her voice join Marcus's in a howl that seemed to carry out all the fear and pain Edgar had brought into her life.

Behind her, she heard Vaughn say, "What the hell," then she added her shaky voice to their song.

Marcus broke off the howl first, laughing as he stood. Tessa joined him as he turned to stare at Vaughn.

"When in Rome, do what the werewolves do." Vaughn shrugged, then crinkled up her nose. "Ugh. You guys smell like burnt wet dog."

Tessa laughed.

*"Are you all right?"* Marcus looked at her. She could sense tension and anxiety in him.

*"I'm fine."*

*"Tessa—"*

She cut him off before he could start on a line of inquiry that would most likely push her over the edge. The adrenaline rush was distorting everything, making it easier not to think about her arm. She wanted—needed—to delay processing that loss. First, she needed to process what she'd become.

*"I'm. Fine. Are you?"*

*"Yes."* He kept staring at her.

Without thinking about it, she leaned forward and butted her head against his shoulder. *"You don't feel fine."*

*"I had trouble controlling myself when I first changed."*

*"You were alone. I have you."*

She felt a wave of… something stronger than affection. Something she wasn't ready to name, but that echoed back to him. He reached for her waist, pulling her close. Together, they let go of the energy holding them in their other forms. It felt like a long exhale, her body growing lighter, smaller. The world glowed blue around her, then faded back to the dim greens and grays she was accustomed to. She had never felt more alive.

When the adrenaline faded and the reality sank in—of changing, losing her arm, of finally not having to look over her shoulder constantly—she had no doubt that she would well and truly freak out. But for the moment, all that she could think about was what she had gained from her sacrifice. Freedom. A family.

"We did it," she said. "It's over."

"Don't jinx it," Vaughn said. She stared at the puddle. "That's usually when the bad guy jumps up behind the heroes and—"

"This isn't that kind of story." Tessa shook her head and laughed again. "I'm not living in a horror movie anymore."

Brock approached them, still staring at the puddle. "Well, technically, you're a werewolf who polices alien monsters, so…"

Tessa kicked him in the shin.

"Ow! Geeze, werewolf powers." He bent down and rubbed the spot.

"Sorry," she said. "I thought I was going easy on you."

He grinned at her, then pulled her into a hug. She was hugging her brother—*her brother.*

Of all the things that had happened, this seemed the most impossible. The most miraculous. Her brother was alive. And they would figure out how to keep him that way.

Marcus rested his hand on her back. Tessa felt Vaughn approach and reached for her, drawing her into the hug with Brock. Marcus wrapped his arms around the group. Dexter hovered a few feet away.

Tessa cocked her head back enough to look at him. "You want in on this?"

He smirked and shook his head. "No thanks. I'm good."

"Don't be a dick," Marcus said. "We're family."

Dexter chuckled. "Funny, I would've thought you would say *pack*."

"There isn't a difference." Marcus held out his hand.

Dexter stared at it for a moment, then shook his head again and walked to the group. Marcus put his arm around

Dexter.

"Bring it in," Vaughn said. "Group hug."

# Chapter Thirty

His pack was whole. Marcus wrapped his arms around them all—even Dexter. This was his family now.

"This would be a lot less awkward if Tessa and Marcus weren't naked," Vaughn said.

Marcus laughed. "You have a point."

The group spread apart. Vaughn picked up Tessa's soaked T-shirt and shredded pants. "You werewolves sure do go through outfits. This is why Marcus always wears a duster, by the way."

Tessa nodded. "That finally makes sense. I guess we'll need to get one for me, too."

She smiled at Marcus and his heart seemed to skip a beat. He had never seen her look so purely happy.

And he could *feel* it. Everything she felt flowed into him, deepening his emotions, strengthening them—and him. He was calmer than he'd ever felt, more in control and balanced. The voice in his head had been silent for so long. Marcus couldn't even sense its presence.

"If it's really over, can we *please* go back inside now?" Vaughn said.

"It's really over." Tessa pulled Marcus along after the

others. The moment they were inside, she headed for the kitchen. "I hope they didn't eat everything. I'm starving."

The apex ghouls must have been as well. Marcus couldn't catch a trace of Tessa's human blood anywhere. He tried not to think about that too hard.

Tessa didn't seem to have picked up on his unease, or she wasn't talking about it. He was glad to know they could control the telepathy and wouldn't share everything that passed through their minds. Still, he could sense the underlying turmoil of everything they'd been through, the trauma she hadn't started to process yet. He would give her the time she needed. And he would be there for her when she was ready.

"I'll get you guys some clothes." Vaughn was leaning against one of the walls. Her heartbeat was finally slowing.

"Dexter, go with her." Brock picked up one of the barstools, then slumped onto it.

"Only after you stop borrowing Porter," Dexter said. "It depletes your energy."

Brock scowled at him.

A spike of fear drove through Marcus. Not from him— from Tessa.

"Are you really dying?" she said.

Brock's scowl softened into a smile. "We can talk about that later, Chicken."

"Don't call me that." She growled for good measure,

but Marcus could sense her anxiety. He shared it even without their bond.

Brock blinked a few times, then sat up straighter. *Porter* let out a sigh.

"This could get tedious," he said. "Brock gets us in trouble, then leaves before he has to deal with the repercussions."

"Welcome back, Porter," Marcus said. "You missed the excitement."

"Oh, we were there for it. We just had a different perspective."

"Back to using the royal 'we,'" Tessa said.

Vaughn laughed. "You are *really* going to have to explain how that works. For the database, if nothing else. Or have you already entered yourself… Selves?"

"We haven't taken that step yet, but after today, we may have to," Porter said. "Things will be changing among the Blades."

"Oh shit." Vaughn's eyes were wide as saucers. "One of the other bases mentioned 'the twins' when we were talking about our bosses. I assumed they meant you guys. Were they talking about another pair of replicants?"

"Later," Dexter said. "Come on."

Vaughn was still asking questions as they headed down the hallway that led to the bedrooms.

"This place is a mess," Porter said. "Would you two mind?"

Tessa looked around at the demolished kitchen. "What do you expect us to do?"

All traces of the dwellers had vaporized, but the kitchen island was still on the other side of the room. Wires stuck up from the floor, and broken tiles mixed with white froth from the fire extinguisher.

Marcus picked up the kitchen island, then set it back in place. "We can do more thorough repairs later."

"That is so cool." Tessa walked over to the island and picked it up and set it down a few times, pressing both forearms tight against it for grip.

Marcus was amazed at how well she was managing… everything.

"Werewolf strength is good for many things," Porter said.

Her stomach growled.

"You'd better eat," Marcus said. "A hungry werewolf is no one's friend."

"What's safe?" She opened the refrigerator and started rooting around inside.

"Anything." Marcus picked up two more barstools and set them near the island. "But meat will be your favorite. Too much raw vegetable matter will make you cranky."

She laughed. Her excitement and happiness was so strong, it was palpable. He wasn't even sure it was their connection making him sense it. Porter was smiling as he watched her.

Vaughn and Dexter returned with clothes.

"We come bearing…" Vaughn's voice trailed off as Tessa popped her head out from behind the fridge door. She was holding half a brick of cheese in her mouth.

"Seriously?" Vaughn said. "I didn't think your table manners could get any worse."

Tessa bit off the cheese and chewed a few quick times, then mumbled, "I'm not at a table."

"Things will certainly be even more animated around here now," Porter said.

Vaughn shook her head as she handed Marcus a stack of clothing, then headed for Tessa as Marcus dressed. Tessa bit down on the rest of the cheese, holding it with her teeth as she grabbed the top item of clothing and pulled it on awkwardly. Vaughn stood there with one eyebrow cocked. She had the good sense to not try to help. As soon as Tessa had taken the last piece of clothing Vaughn held, she lifted her hands and walked away.

"Tessa might be a lost cause when it comes to etiquette," Vaughn said.

Tessa took the wedge of cheese from her mouth and pointed it at Vaughn. "Cut me a break. I haven't *had* a table in years."

"Okay, that's fair." Vaughn nodded and sat on one of the barstools.

Tessa piled the kitchen island high with food, tossing things onto its countertop straight from the fridge, then she started working her way through it. Marcus brought over another barstool for her to sit on, and stood next to her. He wanted to support her however he could. He still couldn't believe what she had done—what she had sacrificed to survive. The smooth skin covering the end of her forearm was a harsh reminder.

"What do you suppose Edgar meant about me being the most dangerous of us?" Vaughn's voice was still shaky. There was no joking lilt to her tone or playful smile to cover her nervousness.

"You're the one who designs all our weapons," Dexter said. "The Blades wouldn't be nearly as effective without you."

"Well, thanks for the first ever compliment." Vaughn shook her head. "But that's not what he was talking about. He tried to infect me and it didn't take. And what's a curator? Am I… not human?"

"We didn't find anything unusual in your genetic screening when you came to work for us," Porter said. "But we can run more tests."

"Goodie." Vaughn scowled. Her attention was drawn back to Tessa as she picked up a hunk of meat and started tearing into it. "And… gross."

Tessa wiped her mouth with the back of her hand. "Sorry. I'm just really hungry."

"Nobody wants to deal with a hungry werewolf," Marcus said.

*"The more I eat, the less I want to—"* Tessa broke off her thought, staring guiltily at Vaughn.

Marcus knew what she was feeling without sharing it through their bond. He blocked himself from that emotion, not wanting to fuel it in her. Her dweller nature was telling her that Vaughn was prey. Whatever a curator was, Vaughn was the most human being in the room. Marcus knew it wouldn't be long before Tessa fully adjusted and bonded with Vaughn as pack.

*"I was the same when I first turned,"* he thought to her. *"You'll feel it whenever you encounter humans for a while. But it gets easier to block those thoughts."*

*"That's a relief."*

*"Just make sure you never let yourself get really hungry."*

*"That's less of a relief."*

He gave her shoulder a squeeze and smiled at her.

Vaughn broke into their conversation. "We're well aware of how cranky hungry werewolves are. Just be sure to wash your hands when you're done. And your face. Not all of us have your immune system."

"Okay." Tessa glanced at Marcus briefly.

Marcus opened one of the cabinets and pulled out the packages of jerky he kept around for when he needed to load up on protein quickly. Tessa tore into the bag using her teeth.

"Does anyone else think this feels a little

anticlimactic?" Vaughn said. "I mean, we just defeated two seriously bad baddies, Tessa's a werewolf now, our bosses are…" She stared at Porter for a moment, then shook her head. "And we're sitting around watching Tessa eat cheese and jerky."

"Hey." Tessa shook her jerky at Vaughn, talking around another huge mouthful. "If you hadn't had any meat or cheese in seven years, you would realize the importance of this moment."

Vaughn laughed.

"I think we could all use a little peace and quiet to get our bearings," Marcus said. "Tessa needs to learn about her dweller nature, and we all need to… settle in with each other again."

He stared at Dexter. Things between them had changed permanently. Marcus wanted to be sure Dexter understood that.

"We're going to have to take care of that on the job," Porter said. "Dwellers don't take vacations just because we're changing up our ranks. We need you out on the street again as soon as possible."

Dexter nodded. "And we need to overhaul our systems to make sure we don't have a breach like this one again. We have some VIPs coming, and this place needs to be airtight before that happens. Unless Tessa isn't interested in seeing Brock and Dad in person again."

Tessa stopped mid-chew, pressing her hand to the

countertop. It took her a moment to swallow. Marcus could feel her excitement, her nervousness.

*"Will they accept me?"*

Marcus nuzzled the side of her head. *"Of course they will."*

"They're coming here?" she said. "Both of them?"

"If we can make the ranch secure enough." Dexter turned to Vaughn. "Which means you have a lot of work ahead of you."

Vaughn shrugged. "I *am* the tech guy. Gal. I have some ideas for screens we can place over the vents. Maybe an energetic filtration system that zaps—"

"We're glad to hear it," Dexter cut in. "But we need to make one more thing clear."

Porter stood and walked to Dexter's side. The closer they became, the more synchronized their movements. Marcus was surprised he'd never noticed it before. Their breathing, the angle of their bodies, even their heartbeats were in synch.

"You're all still Blades," Porter said.

"And we're still the boss." Dexter glared at Marcus, daring him to object.

Marcus didn't care. Dexter and Porter could be in charge of the Blades. That didn't make them his alpha. And when it came to his pack, Marcus knew that he—and Tessa—would be making the final calls.

Marcus nodded, then turned to Tessa. "How about it?

Do you still want to join?"

"Do I get a hoverbike?"

Porter's smirk deepened. "Once you learn how to pilot one, sure."

"Can Vaughn make me a robot hand? Maybe one that stays on when I change?" She held up her right arm briefly, then tucked it protectively against her chest. "It'll make me more useful in the field."

"A cyborg werewolf on a hoverbike." Vaughn looked stunned for a moment, then spun around in her chair to face Porter. "Please, tell me I can make her a robot hand. I'm not above begging."

Porter let out a sigh. "We can discuss it."

"In that case…" Tessa slid off her barstool, wiping her left hand on the back of her pants. She stared at Dexter and Porter for a moment.

With a smile, she straightened and said, "Reporting for duty."

—

Thank you so much for reading *Pack*, the first novel in *The Blades of Janus* series! I love all these characters so much, and spend quite a bit of my time in Providence (at least, in my head). These characters and their world are dear to my heart and feel almost real to me. I hope you love them as well!

Tessa may be free of Edgar, but his shadow is still falling over her foster-brother, Brock. With time ticking down, will the Blades be able to work together to save their leader? Read on for a sneak peek at the second *Blades of Janus* novel, *Progenitor*.

# Progenitor

## The Blades of Janus
## Book Two

*"Please don't kill me…"*

## Chapter One

*"This is a dead end. Let's head back to the bike."* Brock projected his thoughts into Dexter's mind—which wasn't hard, since they were sharing the same brain at the

moment.

*"If you're bored, you can always visit one of your other replicants,"* Dexter thought back. *"Zach is tracking a kelpie in Europa."*

*"No thanks. I'm sure you'll find a dweller to deal with eventually. Providence is crawling with them. Present company included."*

*"Thanks for the reminder."*

Dexter's thoughts retreated. If Brock didn't know better, he'd think Dexter was sulking. At least the distance meant he'd stop bugging Brock about going back to his own body for a while. Probably.

Brock wanted to stay near town mentally as well as physically. His family was finally whole again, now that he and his dad had found Tessa. With everyone living at the ranch along with the other Blades of Janus who were assigned to Providence, it felt like home.

He was still a little tempted to hop over to Zach's body. Watching Zach fight a kelpie would be a lot more interesting than hanging out with Dexter while he patrolled some defunct Redcap tunnels they'd discovered in Greenbriar Park.

The most interesting thing Dexter had done all night was temporarily activate his bike's flight protocols to avoid running over a possum. Tearing down the road on the alien-tech infused motorcycle was a hell of a lot better than this nighttime stroll.

*"Tessa said other dwellers often move into Redcap tunnels,"* Brock thought. *"But I'm not noticing anything."*

*"You shouldn't be trying to,"* Dexter projected. *"Eli says you need rest."*

*"Rest isn't going to help me and you know it."*

Brock's birthday was less than a week away. There was no way he'd survive it. He'd be damned if he was going to spend his last few days on Earth confined to bed in a body that barely functioned, no matter what his dad said. Especially when Brock had eight perfectly healthy replicant bodies whose minds he could piggyback on.

All part of the perks of being not-exactly-human himself.

*"You've given up already,"* Dexter thought.

*"Don't be naïve. We know what's going to happen. It's the end of another three-year cycle. The last one."*

*"You can't be sure."*

*"Come on, Dexter. I was in a coma for a week last time. Dad barely managed to keep me alive, and you were all basically dead."*

*"We weren't dead."*

*"You didn't have any life signs,"* Brock thought. *"The only reason Dad knew you were still alive is that none of you vaporized. If he hadn't called in the other replicant pairs so he could monitor everyone, the Blades at your bases probably would have buried you."*

Brock wondered if his body would disappear in the

glowing blue light that consumed dwellers who had died—or been killed by his Blades. After he was gone, they'd finally know once and for all just how much of a dweller he was.

His dad said every test showed that Brock was one-hundred percent human. The tests were wrong. And Brock's non-human nature was about to kill him.

*"The others should be here,"* Dexter thought.

*"Don't want them to miss the party?"*

*"The increase in dweller activity at our other bases is too much of a coincidence,"* Dexter projected. *"We should all be at the ranch to protect you."*

*"You should be at your own bases helping your teams for as long as possible. I'm not worried about my safety."*

*"You should be. If Vaughn can finish building the stasis chambers, it'll give Eli more time to—"*

*"To do what?"* Brock shot back. *"Dad can't fix this. It's who I am. Who we are. The sooner you can accept that, the sooner we can all have a little fun before—"*

*"Shh."*

None of Brock's replicants ever shushed him. Dexter paused, cocking his head to the side as he turned in a slow circle. He stopped, staring back at the bridge they had just crossed.

*"We need to gather our resources,"* Dexter thought.

Every time a replicant used their weird plural pronoun when talking about themselves, Brock felt a shiver in his mind, like a tuning fork had been struck and then pointed at his soul. He knew that each pair of replicants was a single entity that shared two bodies, like the one that inhabited both Dexter and Porter.

After all these years, it was still surreal to experience their existence along with them—and to know his own body had created them. Eight exact copies of Brock as he'd looked on the birthday when they... emerged. He suppressed a shudder, shielding Dexter from the revulsion Brock always felt when he remembered the process.

The replicants might not process emotions the same way humans did, but that didn't mean they didn't feel. Knowing how dedicated his replicants were to him, Brock didn't want to put that on Dexter, even if his very first copy could be kind of an ass.

Brock pushed closer to Dexter's senses, feeling a weird pressure as Dexter drew mental power from his other body, Porter, and focused his entire consciousness on this one. Back at the ranch, Brock felt Porter going dormant, frozen over his microscope and not seeing with that set of eyes anymore.

All of their brains' processing power channeled toward Dexter along the connections Brock could sense between all of them—every single replicant. Brock had to admit, it was an incredible rush.

*"Getting kind of crowded in here, DP."* Brock tried to project some humor along with his thought, using the

combined name for the consciousness that controlled this pair of replicants—DP. Of course, DP didn't react.

Brock wasn't picking up on anything, but the Dexter replicant could detect things Brock couldn't, especially when he was using both his brains to parse through the data this body's senses fed him. Now, if Brock decided to take over Dexter's body, it would be a different matter.

Shortly after arriving at the ranch, Vaughn tried to explain her theory that Brock's mind was a hub that his replicants communicated through and used to share 'mental processing power.' Something about quantum computing. If Brock hadn't been so exhausted, it probably would have been fascinating. He had fallen asleep a few minutes into the lecture.

*"Something is under the bridge."* Dexter reached over his shoulders to draw both of the swords strapped to his back.

The ground on either side of the paved path had been disturbed in several places. It didn't seem out of the ordinary to Brock.

*"Looks like groundhogs,"* Brock thought.

*"We're linking with Bradley."*

Shit. Not groundhogs, then.

The pressure against Brock's mind vanished in a rush of spectacular mental energy. Dexter's thoughts surged around Brock's consciousness, faster than he could track. His vision fractured for a moment into five hexagonal sections, like he imagined a wasp might see.

The Brad replicant was sitting on a veranda going over data on one of the paper-thin tablet PCs Vaughn had designed, sipping coffee as the sun rose over the ocean on the East coast. Lee was in the weapon's room at the Caiman Beach base, putting away a wicked looking double-headed axe. Both bodies froze in what they were doing, as if someone had hit the pause button on Brock's view.

Then there were the more familiar views. Brock could see the tiny organisms Porter's eyes were staring at through his microscope as well as Dexter's view of the bridge and park.

The fifth view—the one in the middle that bridged them all—was black. Brock's eyes were closed as his true body lay in bed, a crushing weight no one could explain trapping him there.

He could hear his dad moving around the room and the soft hum of the instruments and machines that Vaughn had coaxed back to life in the ship where Brock was staying. In the *crashed alien spaceship* buried deep beneath the ranch.

Brock's life was beyond bizarre.

His vision collapsed into a single view of the park. He felt, saw, and heard so much more than before. He could calculate the temperature by listening to the crickets, see the edges of each leaf with a crispness his own eyes could never perceive—or, rather, his own brain couldn't process.

Everything around them slowed, as if time itself was no match for their combined mental acuity.

*I will never get used to this.* Brock kept that thought to himself, which was probably why Bradley opened with snark.

*"Hey, pretty boy,"* Bradley projected. *"Need some help keeping that pristine body intact?"*

Sometimes, Brock really wanted to punch Bradley in the face. In both his faces.

Yeah, the Dexter and Porter pair were the only replicants who weren't covered in scars. But that was only because they hadn't lost a body fighting dwellers. Yet.

Having experienced every single 'death' along with the replicant who lost a body, as well as the hell that came afterwards when they re-grew a new one... Brock wouldn't wish that on anyone, not even the beings that had somehow spawned from him, breaking his own body in the process. He also wouldn't let his replicants wish that on each other.

They all had cold streaks. Brock did his best to watch out for those thoughts and shut them down.

*"Have you ever heard* me *complain about DP's appearance?"* Brock projected the thought fiercely. They could never forget that Brock didn't just endure their deaths with them—he also carried the scars of the wounds responsible. Death marks. His body was covered in them. His face...

He couldn't think about that. No matter how good he was at shielding and filtering his thoughts, he never wanted to risk the more recently created replicants sensing just how repulsed he was by his own appearance. By *their* appearances, too.

They had to know how he felt. They were too smart not to have figured that out. But they sure as hell didn't have to share his emotions on top of that.

*"Apologies, progenitor,"* Bradley projected. *"We didn't know you were visiting DP."*

*"That shouldn't make a difference."* Brock didn't mind them feeling his displeasure over their comment.

Aside from the small scar that ran along their left cheekbone, the Brad and Lee replicants could easily conceal the rest of their death marks with their clothing. Brock had gained that scar when Lee was killed getting it —before Zachary had emerged, so Zach and Carey had it, too.

Those two sets had split off from Brock's body before the shit really hit the fan. They all had more scars. So many more.

Malcolm's first death had left the pair so disfigured, they couldn't be assigned a base. No amount of makeup could hide their scars, and it would be impossible to explain how the marks on their faces were identical.

Having a set of replicants freed up to travel wherever they were needed was helpful. They'd been all over the world, but Brock almost never visited them. It hurt too much to see how people reacted to them—and knowing he would have to deal with the same gasps and staring eyes if he was capable of travel.

Brock felt the hair on his own body's arms lift back at the ranch, remembering the last time he'd been brave enough to look at himself in the mirror. Even if his replicants would let him, Brock had given up on walking among humans long ago.

*"You okay, Brock?"* DP must be picking up on Brock's emotions. The replicants almost never used Brock's name.

*"Yeah,"* Brock thought.

*"Good, because we all need to focus."* Dexter stepped off the paved trail.

Brock calmed himself, taking in the surroundings along with all the other consciousnesses linked to the Dexter body in that moment. Wind whispering through the trees, water trickling under the bridge, something moving in the earth. Something… big.

Spindly arms burst through the topsoil and reached for Dexter's legs. Dexter leapt into the air, swinging his swords as he reached the apex of his flip—upside-down. The blades flashed, reflecting the light from the lampposts along the path. A thick fluid sprayed the ground as he severed the creatures' arms at their elbows.

Even through the ground, Brock could hear the screeches of the dwellers Dexter had maimed. The loss of a couple of limbs probably wouldn't stop them. Sure enough, the ground rippled as the things pushed their way closer to the surface.

Dexter spun his swords in graceful arcs as he finished his flip, the tips of both weapons pointing at the ground. He stabbed them through the earth as he landed in a crouch.

A normal person could never have pulled off that maneuver. Dexter was far from normal.

Brock could feel Dexter drawing on all of their bodies —using the mental power of five brains, the muscle memory of five bodies. These dwellers didn't stand a chance.

More screeches came from below. Thick brown-green blood welled up around the blades as Dexter twisted their hilts. He pulled the swords with him as he stood, flicking them to the side to cut off more arms reaching for him from the ground.

Brock was about to pull back and leave Dexter to his gruesome work when a different type of scream hit his ears. Human.

*"Dexter—"* Brock thought.

*"We know."* Dexter ran toward the sound, hacking at limbs as he did, leaping over forms emerging from the earth. Time slowed again, letting Brock get a good look at the creatures.

Filthy clothes hung from their impossibly thin bodies.

Their skin was coated in fine silver fur. As far as dwellers went, that wasn't so bad. It was their faces that Brock was sure he'd be having nightmares about.

The gray skin that mostly covered their eyes was wrinkled and puckered. It looked like someone had taken two clods of mud and rubbed them into their otherwise empty eye sockets. Their noses were tiny slits and oversized teeth that were jagged triangles filled their mouths, shark-like. Two tiny flaps of skin stuck out from the sides of their heads roughly where their ears should be.

*"Trolls,"* Bradley projected.

Brock almost wished he had kept his distance from Dexter's consciousness so these things would be out of focus. He'd studied the entry on trolls in Vaughn's Dweller's Database, and knew they were ugly. Seeing them up close and clearly was much worse than the digitized files. No wonder Vaughn called them mole-people.

*"Tessa warned us that other dwellers tend to move into Redcap tunnels after an infestation has been cleared,"* DP thought. *"Trolls were at the top of her watchlist."*

*"Great,"* Brock projected.

Dexter leapt over a troll and hit the ground in a roll. Brock felt him calculating his inertia against his heightened strength and speed. At the end of the roll, Dexter launched off the ground, practically flying at the mass of trolls surrounding their prey. They had her on the ground and were hunched over her, punching and kicking. The woman's screams had subsided to low sobs.

*"Be careful you don't hurt her,"* Brock thought to Dexter.

*"We* have *done this before,"* Dexter replied.

Brock couldn't keep himself from worrying. The writhing mass of dwellers would make it difficult for Dexter to see where his swords were landing.

A few feet from the group, Dexter skidded to a stop. He shouted, "Hey," using his voice instead of his mind.

The sound startled Brock. Dexter was one of the least chatty of the replicants. What was he doing?

Brock pushed closer to Dexter's awareness, feeling the strength in Dexter's limbs as he held both swords ready at his sides. Half a dozen of the trolls turned, sniffing the air. They stepped away from the woman, collapsing their torsos into short, squat forms rather than the long, thin creatures they'd originally appeared to be.

Dexter launched himself at them. He'd decapitated four before the others even realized what was going on. The other two who had noticed Dexter sprang at him, their bodies distending like macabre accordions.

Dexter shifted his weight to the right, then stabbed up with the sword in his left hand, skewering the troll on that side. He pivoted, pulling the weapon free and using his other blade to slash the throat of the last attacking troll in a move that was as graceful as it was brutal.

The dead dwellers started to glow with a soft blue light. It consumed them, like flame devouring paper. Even without eyes, the other trolls seemed to register it. They all turned, leaving the woman they'd been beating curled in a ball on the ground. As one, they charged at Dexter.

Looking through Dexter's eyes nearly made Brock seasick. Turns, twirls, leaps, like a violent form of ballet. It hadn't been too many years ago when Brock could perform those maneuvers himself. He remembered the rush of drawing on all of his replicants at once during battle—before they'd decided it was too dangerous for him to be in the field.

Within seconds, Dexter had killed or incapacitated every single troll. He looked around at the still forms lying on the ground, taking note of which ones weren't disintegrating yet and finishing them off.

Brock felt a snap in his mind as Bradley's consciousness disconnected. It took him a moment to adjust to Dexter's senses being muted—or at least seeming so. This was actually closer to his usual levels of perception. Brock felt Porter begin moving about his lab, working on his latest research project.

*"Dexter,"* Brock prompted.

*"Yes?"*

*"The woman."*

*"She's fine."*

*"Check on her, please."* Brock sent the thought with a

little force behind it.

Dexter headed toward her. She was huddled in a ball, arms held defensively in the air. The denim jacket she wore looked ancient and barely fit her. There were stains and tears all over it. Most looked older than this encounter. She was compact and stick-thin. Her dark hair was pulled into a tight bun. Brock caught glimpses of a shining metal collar around her neck.

"Please don't kill me," she said, her voice low and raspy.

Dexter cocked his head to the side, saying nothing. He stepped warily around the woman, studying her as if she was a threat.

*"Dexter, you need to reassure her,"* Brock thought. *"She was just attacked."*

*"Something isn't right."*

The only thing Brock could see that was wrong was how Dexter was treating this woman. It was inhumane not to comfort her. Sometimes, he had to remind his replicants of how to at least pretend to be human.

*"Talk to her,"* Brock projected.

"Who are you?" Dexter spoke in a harsh, commanding voice.

If Brock had been fully occupying a body at that moment, he would have covered his face with his hands. He didn't bother trying to hide the frustration flooding through him.

"Meg," the woman said. "I'm Meg. I won't try to hurt you, I promise. Please don't kill me."

Brock's frustration turned to confusion.

*"Why is she promising not to hurt you?"* Brock sent.

Brock ignored the ripple of smugness that flowed from Dexter as he pointed the tip of one sword at the woman and stepped back, giving himself more room to react.

There was a reason that DP was the only replicant set that had never experienced a death. He was the most paranoid.

"Stand," Dexter said.

Meg rose on shaking legs. Her eyes were clenched shut and her hands clasped in front of her as she was begging for her life.

"Please don't kill me," she said. "I've never hurt anyone. I swear it."

*"She's a dweller,"* Brock sent.

*"Why were the trolls attacking her then?"*

Different types of dwellers seldom interacted with each other at all. The trolls had given this woman a beating. There were bruises marring her face. Blood trickled from her nose and her lip was split.

Except, as Brock observed through Dexter's eyes, the cut sealed itself. Her bruises faded and her skin absorbed the blood.

"Open your eyes," Dexter said. His voice wasn't as dispassionate as usual. He was agitated. That wasn't good.

*"She said she won't hurt us,"* Brock sent. *"The trolls might have been attacking her because she doesn't prey on humans. We've seen it happen before."*

Meg let out a whimper. "I won't hurt you. Please…"

"Open them."

*"Dexter, give her a—"*

Brock's thought cut off as she opened her eyes. Light spilled out of them. They were gleaming bright gold.

Dexter raised his left sword—the one infused with silver—his arm aligned to slash her throat.

—

Check out my website to see where you can get *Progenitor* now! I'd love to keep in touch. Join my newsletter to get sneak peeks and behind-the-scenes insight into my many worlds, and check out other ways to join my community on my website at cassandra-chandler.com/community. I really want to know what *you* think. If you enjoyed this book, please consider leaving a review at your favorite book review site. I'd really appreciate it—reviews help readers and authors alike!

Thank you for reading *Pack!*

Cassandra Chandler

## About the Author

USA Today Bestselling author Cassandra Chandler uses her vivid imagination to make the world more interesting, spawning the ideas she turns into her captivating Science Fiction Romances and enthralling Paranormal and Urban Fantasy Romances. Fast-paced and funny, lighthearted or filled with suspense, her stories will introduce you to characters you'll fall in love with and worlds you long to explore.